Michael Wood is a freelan[...] [...]
in Sheffield. As a journalis[...] [...]
throughout Sheffield, gaining first-hand knowledge of police
proced[...] [...] reviews books for CrimeSqua[...]
dedicated to crime fiction.

twitter.com/MichaelHWood
facebook.com/MichaelWoodBooks

Also by Michael Wood

THE LOST CHILDREN

MICHAEL WOOD

One More Chapter
a division of HarperCollins*Publishers*
1 London Bridge Street
London SE1 9GF
www.harpercollins.co.uk

HarperCollins*Publishers*
1st Floor, Watermarque Building, Ringsend Road
Dublin 4, Ireland

This paperback edition 2022

1

First published in Great Britain in ebook format
by HarperCollins*Publishers* 2022

A catalogue record of this book
is available from the British Library

ISBN: 978-0-00-853557-5

Printed and bound in the UK using 100% Renewable Electricity
by CPI Group (UK) Ltd

To 'Mr Tidd'
For his expert knowledge and always answering my persistent
questions.

Content Notice

The Lost Children explores many themes, the main one being child abuse and historical sexual abuse.

While all of this is fictional and takes places in a fictional world, these things occur in reality and many people reading this book may find this difficult to read in places. It is not my intention to ever make a reader feel uncomfortable and I hope you can enjoy this book for what it is, a crime fiction novel and a form of entertainment.

However, if you are affected by anything in this book, please seek advice from professionals. Talking is important and there are people out there waiting to listen.

Michael Wood
April 2022

Prologue

Thursday 23rd January 1997 – South Yorkshire Police
Headquarters, Sheffield

'I'm here to see the Chief Constable. He's expecting me,' the Reverend Peter Ogilvy said in his most confident and forceful tone.

He was told to take a seat while a call was made. Peter chose the middle seat in a row of five, sitting with his back straight, his head high and his legs crossed. His expression was stern. He was tired of being fobbed off. Something had to be done.

Peter's appointment was for ten o'clock and he'd arrived in plenty of time. He despised tardiness. At ten past ten, he was still waiting. By twenty past, he felt an ache in his lower back from maintaining his erect position. He started to slouch. At half past ten, he returned to the counter.

'My appointment was for half an hour ago,' Peter said, making a point of adjusting his dog collar to show he was a man of the cloth, and not a random member of the public who could be played mind games with.

'The Chief Constable knows you're here,' the uniformed constable said, looking up briefly from the pad he was doodling on.

It was five minutes to eleven before Peter Ogilvy was called, and no apology was given.

Chief Constable Tony Bates sat behind his huge desk on the top floor of the building with a sprawling view of Sheffield behind him. It was a cold day and heavy clouds covered the city.

Tony looked harassed. It was still early morning, yet his loose collar, his crooked tie and his unbuttoned jacket gave the impression of a man who'd already done a full day's work.

'Father Ogilvy, it's lovely to see you. Please, take a seat. Can I get you a tea or coffee?' he asked with an exaggerated smile.

'No, thank you,' Peter replied, irked by being kept waiting for almost an hour. The less time he spent in this smoke-hued room, the better. He stifled a cough.

'What can I do for you?' Tony asked, sitting down and leaning on his desk, his huge hands folded in front of him.

'Chief Constable, I know you're a busy man and are doing a very difficult job. However, I've reported a crime on three separate occasions, and nothing has been done about it.'

'I'm sorry to hear that. What was the crime?'

'Murder.' He purposely refused to elaborate until pressed, to allow the enormity of the single word to sink in.

'You're aware of a murder?'

'That's correct.'

'Do you know the name of the victim?' Tony asked, picking up a silver-plated Parker.

'Sean Evans. He was seven years old, and he was killed on

Saturday the fourth of January this year. I've given all the details three times to three different members of your staff.'

'Right. Where was Sean murdered?'

'At Magnolia House Children's Home.'

'And where is the body now?'

'I don't know,' he said, looking down, crestfallen.

'You don't know?'

'No.'

'Right,' Tony said, making another note.

Peter fished into his inside pocket and took out an envelope. He looked at it. This was the point of no return. Reluctantly, he handed it over.

'This is my statement telling you who is involved in Sean Evans's death and everything else that has been going on at Magnolia House.'

Tony, a deep frown on his face, took the envelope from him and held it by the corners as if there was something corrosive on it, burning his fingertips. He ran a steel letter opener under the flap, took out the folded sheets of paper inside and sat back as he cast his eye over the neatly written four-page statement.

He looked up. 'You're not serious.'

'I am deadly serious.'

'Do you have any idea what damage this could do if it was released to the wider public?'

'I'm aware,' Peter Ogilvy said, his voice quivering with fear. 'Look, Chief Constable, I know what I've said is an explosive allegation, but it's all true. Every single word of that statement is gospel. I implore you, please, for the sake of Sean Evans, and everyone living at Magnolia House, you need to take this seriously and launch a full investigation.'

Tony thought for a moment. A sheen of sweat appeared on

his forehead which he wiped away with the back of his left hand. He fingered his collar despite it already being loose.

'Leave it with me.'

Peter Ogilvy gave up the house he was allocated by the Church of England when he moved to his parish in Sheffield as soon as Magnolia House Children's Home was up and running. He decided it would be better for the boys if he lived on site, so he had two of the rooms on the ground floor converted into a bedroom and personal bathroom. It was small, but it was cosy, and he was on hand if any of the boys needed him, which they often did.

Lying on his back in the dark, staring up at the ceiling, he had no idea if he could trust the Chief Constable to look into his allegations. He'd met him on two occasions and wasn't impressed with his appearance. He didn't have the air of a man who could be responsible for an entire county. He'd give him a week, and if he hadn't heard anything from him, he'd go above him. But who was higher than a Chief Constable? He couldn't go to his local MP. Who was in charge at the Home Office these days?

There was a noise outside his room. It sounded like creaking on the stairs. It was probably one of the boys sneaking down to get a biscuit. Peter smiled to himself. He didn't mind a bit of pilfering and purposely left an open packet of chocolate digestives in a cupboard, so they'd easily be found. The boys got pleasure out of stealing a snack and if it made them smile for five minutes, who was he to take that joy away from them?

The knob on his door started to rattle. He sat up. He opened his mouth and was about to call out 'Hello?' when the door burst open. It all happened so fast, he didn't have time to take in what was going on. Two, three, or was it four, huge figures dressed in black, with balaclavas covering their faces, charged into the room. One of them slammed him back down on the bed, pinning him to the mattress with a beefy arm across his chest. Something cold and wet was placed over his face. It smelled medicinal. He blacked out.

Reverend Peter Ogilvy opened his eyes. He was tied to a wooden chair in what he soon recognised as the shed in the grounds of Magnolia House. He was still wearing his blue-and-white-striped pyjamas. He was barefoot and freezing cold. He looked around him in the dark but couldn't make out who was in there with him.

Outside, wind was howling, and rain was hammering down on the roof. His pyjamas were wet. He wasn't sure what was rain and what was sweat. Peter could feel every inch of himself physically shaking with fear. He had never known terror like this before in his life.

'He's awake,' a voice whispered.

'You visited the police station this morning, Peter,' a voice from the shadows said.

'I did,' Peter said, defiantly.

'Your fourth visit in a month. You're persistent.'

'A boy has died,' he said. There was no strength to his words, and he almost had to force them out.

'So?'

'Is that all you can say?' He found a modicum of anger from somewhere. His protection over the boys in his care was greater than his own need to survive. 'A boy. A seven-year-old boy was murdered. It needs to be investigated. Someone needs to answer—'

'You need to shut your mouth,' the voice interrupted.

It sounded mean and threatening – and it worked, shutting Peter up.

'Who are you?'

'Like I'm going to tell you.'

'What do you want?'

'I want you to keep your mouth shut. Sean Evans is dead. Leave it.'

Peter swallowed hard. 'I can't do that.'

There was a sigh. 'Do you think your dog collar gives you protection?'

'Yes. I do. It means I'll be listened to when I go to my MP, the newspapers, the BBC, and tell anyone who'll put a microphone in front of me that a boy, an orphan, was murdered and people tried to shut me up.'

A figure stepped forward. He had a dirty white cloth in his hand, no bigger than a handkerchief, that he wrapped around Peter's mouth, tying it tightly at the back of his head. Peter choked and struggled, but he was no match against his restraints. He could taste dirt and oil. The cloth was putrid.

A second figure stepped forward. He held up a heavy petrol can and slowly unscrewed the cap. He waved it under Peter's nose so he could smell what was inside. Peter turned away. The figure tipped the contents over Peter's head, soaking him, drenching him in the fuel. The liquid was cold. The shock of his plunging body temperature made him to want to scream out, but it was hopeless. He squeezed his eyes tightly shut and struggled against the ropes that held him to the chair. He tried to scream but the gag was too tight, his cries were muffled. He choked on the smell and taste of the rancid petrol.

Once the can was empty and the jeers had died down, he dared to open his eyes. All he saw in front of him was blackness.

A third figure by the door flicked a lighter. The face was lit up, but behind the balaclava, all Peter could make out were two wide brown eyes.

'This is a warning, Peter. Your first and your last. One more word to the police, and we'll tie you to a chair again. Only next time, it won't be you we pour petrol over, it will be every single boy living here in Magnolia House. We'll line them up, douse them in petrol and set them alight right in front of you.'

The figure who'd poured the petrol over him squatted down in front of Peter. 'Keep your fucking mouth shut,' he said, slapping him hard across the face with every word.

One by one, the masked men left the shed, leaving Peter tied to the chair, soaked to the skin, chilled to the bone and frightened for his life and the lives of every single boy in his charge.

Chapter One

Detective Chief Inspector Matilda Darke was given clearance to enter the crime scene. She'd been told it was, in the words of DS Scott Andrews, 'a fucking horror film up there', and to prepare herself. She wasn't prepared.

Turn around. Go back home.

She stood in the vast hallway of the grand detached property and squeezed herself into the white paper forensic suit. She looked up. A team of crime-scene investigators was going through the house, looking for clues on how the killer gained entry, dusting for prints, bagging and tagging anything that might give some kind of a hint as to the identity of the killer.

In the kitchen, Matilda could hear the sound of wailing from the cleaner who had walked in on her employer and found him dead. It had been more than an hour since she made the initial 999 call, and she was still sobbing hard. There was talk of calling for a doctor.

Matilda pulled up the hood and covered her short, dark hair. She put a mask over her mouth and nose, placed her feet into overshoes and headed for the staircase. The only visible part of her was her eyes, and they were what she wished she could cover up the most. Her eyes gave her away. They showed her fear. She swallowed hard and could taste this morning's breakfast repeating on her. At the bottom of the stairs, she stopped, and looked up, taking a deep breath to compose herself. She stuck to the left and took care not to touch the banister, even though she was wearing latex gloves. With every step, her heart beat louder in her chest. She wondered who else would be able to hear it.

On her way up, she glanced at the framed photographs on the walls. The occupier of the house – easy to spot, being six foot three and weighing close to twenty stone, shaking hands with the great and the good, the powerful and the influential. She stood at the top of the stairs and looked closely at a photograph that made her smile but brought a lump of emotion to her throat. There were four men and two women in the picture. Her eyes were drawn to the man on the far right – back straight, head high, designer stubble, twinkling ice-blue eyes, looking almost edible in his Ted Baker suit. Matilda's late husband, James Darke. He looked happy and seemed to be enjoying himself, but she knew how much he hated dressing up for formal functions and would have been itching to get out of that suit. She tried to recall the event and if she'd been with him on that night. She probably had been. James would never have gone alone.

The sound of vomiting brought Matilda out of her reverie. She turned and saw the master bedroom straight ahead.

A man came out, hand over his mouth, bent double. He paused in the doorway, retched a few times, then vomited again, his regurgitated breakfast oozing out between his fingers.

Go home, Matilda. Let someone else deal with this. Delegate.

'Good morning, Finn,' Matilda said.

DC Finn Cotton wiped his mouth with the back of his hand. He took a few deep breaths. 'I'm so sorry.'

'I've been told it's bad,' she said, almost deadpan.

'I've never—' he didn't finish. He ran straight into the bathroom next door and retched again.

Matilda closed her eyes and inhaled. Even through the mask she could smell the vomit. She bypassed the pool of sick and entered the bedroom. Straight away, she understood why Finn had thrown up.

The room was large and in the middle was a king-size bed with what seemed to be a bespoke oak bed-frame with ornate carvings on the headboard. The duvet had been pulled off and two scene-of-crime officers were struggling to put it into a large evidence bag. The duvet was saturated in blood.

In the centre of the blood-soaked mattress, a man lay flat. He was tall and he was large, running to obese.

'Richard Ashton,' Matilda said, softly.

'That's right,' DS Andrews confirmed. 'He was found by his cleaning lady, Leslie Hicks. That's her pool of vomit over there by the window.'

Matilda glanced to the window in the far corner of the room. 'Why did she go all the way over there to be sick?'

'She came in and it was dark. She went over to the window to pull open the curtains, turned back, saw … well, saw what we can see, and obviously doesn't have a strong stomach like we have.'

'Is she any relation to Finn?' Matilda asked, a nervous smile in her voice. 'Morning, Adele,' she said to the Home Office Pathologist who was squatting down next to the body.

'You always think you've seen everything there is to see, then you come across something like this,' she said.

Matilda studied the body. Richard Ashton, stark naked, was covered in blood from the waist down. His huge, solid stomach, hairy and blotchy, did not show any signs of a stab wound or gunshot wound. His face was bloated, his jowls unshaven, broken capillaries on his nose and beneath his sunken eyes. There were old acne scars and blackheads on his cheeks. Covering his mouth was a large strip of duct tape.

'Was he found in this exact position?' Matilda asked.

'Yes,' Scott answered.

'He wasn't on his side, holding himself, just … lying back as if asleep?'

'Yes.'

'Strange,' she frowned.'What killed him?' she asked Adele.

'What killed him was what made your DC vomit. Donal?' She instructed her anatomical assistant to help her. Together, they leaned forward, placed their hands on Richard's stomach and lifted the huge weight up. 'Take a look.'

Reluctantly, Matilda moved to the bottom end of the bed and looked at what was hiding beneath his stomach – or rather, what wasn't beneath his stomach. All she could see was a gaping hole.

'He's been castrated,' Adele said. 'A single clean cut to remove his penis and testicles. He simply bled out.'

'Oh, my God!' Matilda exclaimed. She looked down, hid her eyes from her team so they couldn't see the fear, the horror, the nerves, the pain.

Breathe. Take slow, deep breaths.

'I said something similar,' Scott said. 'But with a few more f-words.'

Matilda looked up. 'Is there no evidence of him struggling or writhing about?'

'No.'

'Could his wrists and ankles have been tied?'

'No evidence of glue from tape or burns from a rope,' Adele said.

'Was he drugged?'

'I can't find any trace of a needle mark, but I'll let you know when I get him back to the lab. I'll do a full tox screening, too.'

'Why the tape around his mouth?' Matilda asked, moving back to the body.

'To stop him screaming, presumably,' Scott said.

'But this house is far back from the road. They wouldn't have heard him, anyway.'

'Perhaps the killer didn't want to take any risk.'

Matilda moved away from the body. The metallic smell of blood was making her feel faint. 'Why do you castrate someone?' she pondered.

'Maybe he's a rapist,' Scott shrugged.

'Maybe. I met him once. It was years ago at a function; something to do with the unveiling of a new housing development he was building. He's actually got a photo of him with my James on the landing. I can't say I know much about him.' Matilda looked back to the body. She frowned.There was something the scene wasn't telling her, and she couldn't marshal her thoughts into any semblance of order. All she could take in was the horror of a man bleeding out, lying back and having to watch his life drain away. She had a dark feeling this was not going to be an open-and-shut case. This was going to haunt her. She could feel it already.

'I've called Sian to run a check on him, but she didn't answer,' Scott said. 'I'm guessing she's still in with the ACC. It's D-Day, after all.'

'Ah, yes, I'd forgotten about that.'

'I was trying to forget.'

'Have we found his penis yet?' Matilda asked, getting back to topic, trying to keep her mind focused.

'SOCOs are looking through the house,' Scott said, wrinkling his face up. 'I hope we haven't got one of those killers on our hands who collects body parts as trophies.' He shuddered. 'Is anyone else thinking of the film Seven, here?'

'I'm guessing he'd be gluttony,' Donal Youngblood said. His Irish accent was soft and smooth.

Scott turned to look at him and smiled. All he could see were his brown eyes; the mask, hood and forensic suit covered up everything else. They maintained a lengthy eye contact before Scott turned away.

Matilda's frown deepened. 'Castrating someone is a very personal crime. I think it's safe to say whoever did this is showing a great deal of anger towards this man. The killer will most likely have destroyed them, maybe put them in the waste disposal or fed them to a dog.'

Finn Cotton walked back into the room. He'd changed into a clean set of forensic overalls.

'I'm sorry about that. I feel better now.'

'We're all done here, Matilda. If you've seen enough, we're ready to move him,' Adele said. 'PM won't be until tomorrow morning, though. We've got them stacked up at the moment.'

'I've more than seen enough,' Scott said.

'I don't know,' Matilda mused, folding her arms across her chest. She couldn't tear her gaze away from his face. She was getting into her stride now. She'd calmed down. Her mind had got used to the horror in front of her and her nerves were settling. Her thinking was clearing. 'There's something about that tape that's bothering me.'

'What?'

'I'm not sure. Adele, can you remove it?'

'Sure. Donal, pass me the tweezers.'

'What are you thinking?' Scott asked.

'He didn't thrash about. There's no evidence of him being tied up, so it's more than likely he was drugged. If that's the case, he's not going to have screamed when he was castrated, so why tape his mouth shut unless it's symbolic.'

'Oh, my God, you don't think he's removed his tongue as well, do you?' Finn asked, one hand on his stomach, the other hovering in front of his mouth.

Matilda hesitated to reply. 'That was my first thought.'

Matilda stepped back while Adele set about removing the tape carefully from the victim's mouth. Donal held out an evidence bag for her to place the tape in. She looked at the underside of the tape and showed it to Matilda.

'Blood,' she said.

'I don't like the look of this.'

'Pass me a torch,' Adele asked.

She turned on the small pen torch and prised open the jaw.

'Well, I think it's safe to say I wasn't expecting that,' she said.

'Oh, my God, I don't think I can look,' Finn said, half-turning.

'You can call off the search for his penis and testicles. They've been rammed down his throat.'

Finn ran back out onto the landing, his hand clasped over his mouth again.

Chapter Two

Matilda and Scott were sitting in the study on the ground floor of the six-bedroom house. The room had a leatherysmell emanating from the chairs they were sitting on, and there was also the odour of newly applied inlay in the oak desk. The walls were adorned with shelves which held trophies, awards and framed photographs featuring Richard Ashton and the important people he'd met over the years.

'This doesn't feel like a home, does it?' Matilda asked. She'd been in the bathroom on the ground floor, washed her hands, splashed her face, looked at her pale face in the mirror, and had a harsh word with her reflection. She felt better. 'Where are the photos of holidays and parties? They're all of Richard meeting figures of industry. Surely, you'd have pictures like this in the office to impress clients.'

'Maybe he liked to impress his guests.'

'Maybe. So, go on, then, tell me about Richard Ashton,' she said, leaning back in the high-backed chair, enjoying the luxury.

'Richard Ashton, OBE, aged sixty-one—'

'Huh. He looked older,' Matilda interrupted.

'… Sheffield born and bred. A working-class lad made good. He owns Ashton Developments, which—'

'I know who Ashton Developments are. My husband was an architect, remember?'

'Did he know Richard Ashton?'

'I don't think so. We used to go to some swanky parties, development unveilings, that kind of thing. We didn't go to many, as James hated having to dress smart.' She smiled at the memory. 'Everyone commented, saying how sexy he looked in his fitted suits, but to him, they were restrictive. He was much happier in dirty jeans and a torn jumper. I remember meeting Richard. His handshake was like a vice. I didn't like him.'

'Why not?'

'Have you ever been to a party where one person has stood out for being so loud and obnoxious? You're in a room crammed full of people, everyone talking, music blaring, yet you can still hear that one person? That was him.'

'I can't stand people like that.'

'Me neither.'

'Anything on the computer?' Scott nodded at the desk.

'No. It's password protected. We'll need to get Forensics in.'

'Strange Bob,' Scott said with a smile.

'He's not strange. He's … unique.'

'That's one word for it. It might be worth trying to hack our way into it ourselves. They're as short-staffed as we are.'

'Not my problem.'

'They also found an iPad under his bed.'

'Why would it be under his bed?' Matilda frowned.

'I keep mine under my bed when I'm out, just in case the flat gets burgled.'

'I'd think of a new hiding place, if I were you. It seems to be an obvious choice.' She opened the drawers in the desk and had a rifle around. 'There's no old-fashioned diary in here. I'm guessing it's all on there,' she nodded to the computer. 'How did the killer get in? Any sign of forced entry?'

'No. The cleaner came in through the back door in the kitchen. When uniform arrived, they came through the same way, then opened up the front door.'

'Hmm,' Matilda thought. 'So, he knew his killer.'

'It looks like he knew a lot of people.'

Scott stood up and went over to the shelves. He picked up a framed photograph of Richard Ashton shaking hands with James Dyson, grinning maniacally to the camera. None of the pictures were personal. They were all taken at functions and events. It wasn't difficult to spot Richard; he was a heavy man, an imposing figure who filled three-quarters of the frame.

'Is that Boris Johnson?' Scott asked, pointing to a picture.

'Yes. That would be our venereal leader.'

'Don't you mean venerable?'

'I know what I mean,' she said with a smirk. 'I doubt this is connected to his business. If he's done some kind of dodgy dealing, then surely they'll shoot him or stab him,' Matilda said. 'Cutting off his balls and stuffing them down his throat is more personal.'

'Unless the killer is being clever and wants us to think it's personal when in fact it's all about money.'

'You've been spending too long with Finn.'

'Speak of the devil,' Scott said as Finn entered the study.

'I'm really sorry for throwing up,' he said, looking pale and peaky.

'Twice,' Scott added.

'I'm normally fine at the crime scene. I don't know what came over me.'

'You haven't got this Coronavirus that's going around, have you?' Scott asked.

'No. I was fine when I woke up this morning. It was just seeing … well, you know.'

'His balls—'

'That'll do, Scott,' Matilda warned. 'Finn, you've no need to apologise. It's perfectly understandable. Now, I want you to pop along to Ashton Developments. They've got an office down Attercliffe way, I think. Talk to his secretary and business partners, have a look at his diary and find out who his rivals are. When was the last time he popped into the office, last known sightings, anything troubling him, the usual.'

'Will do.'

'Perhaps pop home and have a quick shower first, though.'

Finn looked down at his vomit-splattered shirt. 'Right.'

'What do you want me to do?' Scott asked.

'Have a word with the cleaner. We need to establish when he was last seen and his last known whereabouts. Find out how the door-to-door is going. I know the houses aren't exactly on top of each other around here, but someone might have seen something strange lately, and I'm guessing you're going to scream a bit if someone takes a pair of secateurs to your privates.'

'Do you want me to give you a lift back to the station?'

'No. I'll cadge a lift from one of the uniforms,' she looked at her watch. 'Is Christian here?'

'I haven't seen him. Maybe he stayed at the station. He said last night that he was going to have a final chat with Sian.'

Matilda sank into the chair. 'I hope she's not going to do something she's going to regret.'

'Do you think she will?'

'She's only thinking in the present. She's not looking at

what's going to happen a month, a year, five years down the line.'

Finn popped his head around the door frame. 'Scott, are you going to be talking to the cleaner?'

'Yes. Why?'

'Forensics have asked me to find out if Richard Ashton had a dog. There's no sign of one but they've found dog hairs in the bedroom.'

'I'll ask her.'

'Thanks.'

Matilda frowned. 'I've never known a killer bring a dog with them to commit murder.'

'Maybe he couldn't find someone to sit with it. It could have been worse; he could have brought his old gran with him.'

Matilda laughed. She stood up to leave the room and glanced at more photo frames on the wall. She saw another picture featuring her dead husband, a group shot, everyone grinning to the camera, James on the end, looking awkward, but still so sexy. Her heart felt heavy, and not just because she missed him. She didn't like the thought of a random stranger having a photograph of her husband in their house.

Chapter Three

There had been a case that haunted HMCU – the Homicide and Major Crime Unit – for years: the killing of sex workers in Sheffield. Last September, the killer was identified as Stuart Mills, the husband of Detective Sergeant Sian Mills. She had no knowledge of the secret life her husband had been leading, and through him asking her how her day had been and seeming to be the perfect husband, she had, inadvertently, informed him how to commit his crimes without appearing on the team's radar.

Sian had been placed on leave while an independent enquiry looked into the case and any involvement Sian may have had. After three months, they ruled Sian out as an accomplice and allowed her to return to active duty and assume her role in HMCU. However, she was a changed woman. The self-appointed mother-figure of the group who always nurtured new members and was a shoulder to cry on for everyone in the team, was gone. Sian was more reserved, quieter, and admitted to being ashamed of not knowing sooner what her husband was up to.

Last night, while she was sitting in the living room watching a mind-numbing game show on television, her phone had rung. Gone were the days she was frightened of answering the phone in case it was a journalist wanting an interview. Her husband had long since disappeared from the front pages and the fickle media had moved on to the next "crisis". She'd picked up her phone and swiped to answer. It was the assistant chief constable, asking her to come in early tomorrow for a private consult. She'd been waiting for this. She knew exactly what he was going to say, and she was worried she might end up agreeing with his pleas.

Now, Sian refused his offer of tea and coffee. She shook her head when he offered a small bottle of sparkling water, and she didn't want a mint imperial from the bowl on his desk either. What she did want was for him to bloody get on with it.

ACC Benjamin Ridley cleared his throat several times and adjusted his position on the high-back chair. He looked fresh in his crisp uniform and gave off a heady scent of whatever he had liberally sprayed over himself this morning.

'Sian, as you know, I haven't been here long; I'm still seeing new faces in the canteen,' he said, smiling. 'However, in that time, I've learned of who the dedicated officers are, the ones I know I'll be able to rely on as my predecessor did. There's Matilda, obviously, and there's you, too. You're an exceptional detective, your record speaks for itself. You're a well-respected and highly regarded person within the force.'

Sian didn't smile. She could tell a placatory statement a mile off and if he tried to butter her up anymore, she'd need treatment for high cholesterol. She looked down and played with her fingers.

'It's been three weeks since we had our last little chat. You

promised you'd think it over and today would be the final day
– the point of no return, as it were. Have you changed your
mind?'

Sian looked up. There were tears in her eyes. 'I'm afraid
not,' she eventually said. 'I can't stay working as a detective
when the man I was married to for more than twenty-five
years is in prison for murder. Nobody's said anything, and I
don't expect them to, but I can see it in their eyes. How can I
not have known what he'd been doing for all those years? It's a
question I ask myself on an almost nightly basis. Why didn't I
see it? I'm sorry, sir. I love my job, I love working in HMCU,
but that bastard has ruined it.' She took a deep breath. 'I'd like
you to formally accept my resignation as of today.'

Sian walked slowly down the corridor towards the HMCU
suite of offices. She'd worked in this building for more than
twenty years. It seemed strange that her time here was coming
to an abrupt end. She passed a couple of uniformed officers
and a member of the civilian staff, all of whom gave her a
friendly smile. In the past, Sian would have smiled back, said
hello, engaged them in conversation, but she couldn't even
make eye contact with them anymore. Their lips may have
been smiling, but their eyes weren't. They were looking at her
with pity, some even with suspicion. Despite Matilda and the
team telling her nobody suspected her of knowing her
husband was a killer, she couldn't help, at the back of her
mind, thinking the gossips were castigating her behind her
back.

She pushed open the glass door to the suite and walked in.

The Homicide and Major Crime Unit at South Yorkshire Police Headquarters had moved about in the past year. Following the shooting in January 2019 in which several of their number were killed, the team relocated to less salubrious offices, which were too small and had an unpleasant odour emanating from beneath the carpet. The attack on DC Zofia Nowak last September that had left her confined to a wheelchair meant a more accessible suite was required. So, the team now called home a luxurious open-plan affair on the ground floor that was bright and airy, and made use of new technology, so Zofia would be able to manoeuvre herself with ease through the well-planned desk and seating area when she was ready to return. Sian breathed in the scent of new carpet and went over to her desk, plonking herself down on the ergonomic chair. She had four more weeks left.

To take her mind off her own worries, she picked up the remote and pointed it at the wide-screen TV on the wall. It went straight to the BBC News channel.

'*The death toll from Coronavirus in the UK has passed one hundred and now stands at 104. Prime Minister Boris Johnson will be giving a press conference later, where he is expected to confirm that all schools and colleges will close from this Friday until further notice, to stop the spread of the virus.*'

'They're closing the schools?' DCI Matilda Darke said.

Sian jumped. She hadn't seen her come in.

'It looks like it.'

'But what are the kids going to do?'

Sian muted the TV. 'Well, Gregory's teachers are setting up classes via Zoom. I've had to buy him his own laptop, as he's always used Belinda's for his homework.'

'Doesn't Belinda have exams this summer?'

'They've already been cancelled.'

'How can they cancel exams? What's going to happen? Surely they can't just hold back a whole year?'

Sian shrugged. 'I don't know. I don't think anyone knows what's going to happen. It's worrying, isn't it?'

Matilda studied Sian, pulled a chair over and sat by her desk. 'Are you all right?'

'I'm fine,' she gave a fake smile. 'Tough as old boots, me.'

'Except you're not, are you? Have you been for your appointment with the ACC?'

She nodded.

'And?'

'You've got me for another four weeks. That's it.'

'Sian, don't. You can't leave.'

'I can't stay,' she said, a catch in her throat.

'We can't lose you, Sian. You're far too important to this team. We need you. And you need us.'

She shrugged, not daring to speak in case she started crying.

'I've got four weeks to make you change your mind. I don't quit. You should know that by now.'

Sian stifled a smile.

'Look, I need to make a phone call. Will you do me a favour and try and find everything you can about a bloke called Richard Ashton. He was found dead this morning.'

'Name sounds familiar,' Sian said, pulling her wireless keyboard towards her.

'He owns Ashton Developments. They throw up ugly box houses and apartment blocks all over the county ... Speaking of throwing up, Finn almost ruined the crime scene, twice.'

'That bad?'

'He'd been castrated and force-fed his cock and balls. Blood everywhere.'

'Oh, my God,' Sian put a hand over her mouth. 'I've brought meatballs for my lunch, as well.'

Matilda burst out laughing and headed for her office.

Chapter Four

DCI Matilda Darke, herself a casualty of the shooting fifteen months ago, had a brand-new office in the corner of the suite that was much larger than she was used to. She liked it, and, egotistically, felt at home behind the oak-veneer desk and high-backed chair. She couldn't wait to bark orders at someone and feel like a commander. It wasn't anywhere near as posh and elegant as the study in Richard Ashton's home, but she liked it.

As she entered, she closed the door behind her. Matilda usually maintained an open-door policy, but everyone knew that when the door was closed, she was not to be disturbed. The truth was, she had lied about her state of mind on her return to work. She knew exactly what kind of questions she would be asked at the assessment and answered accordingly. She failed to mention the nightmares, the flashbacks, the post-traumatic stress disorder, and the lack of self-confidence. She assumed she knew her state of mind more than anyone else and hoped surrounding herself with a strong team would help give her the boost she needed. It had. In a way. But there were times, like now, when even she doubted she had made the correct decision in returning to work at all. She let out a heavy sigh. Since the shooting, she was constantly questioning her abilities, despite having evidence to the contrary that she was an exceptional DCI.

She scrolled through her mobile. Her finger hovered over the number, and she released a deep sigh. She knew what she was doing was wrong.

Put the phone away. Get on with your work.

She ignored herself and made the call.

'Good morning, Matilda,' the greeting came.

She softened at the familiar Scottish accent she had grown to like over the months. 'Good morning, Grey, are you well?'

'I am, actually. My youngest son passed his driving test at the first attempt on Monday and last night my youngest daughter came to tell us she's pregnant. Glasses of sparkling fizz all round.'

'That's ... good,' Matilda hesitated. It had been so long since she had heard good news, she had forgotten how to react. She tucked her short hair behind her ears.

'However, I'm guessing you didn't call for a simple chit-chat and a catch-up.'

'No. I'm sorry. I really am pleased things are going well for your family.'

He sighed. 'Matilda, does anyone know you keep calling me?'

It was a while before she answered. 'No.'

'Are you sure you should? I'm not going to be telling you anything different from the last time you called.'

'I know. It's just ... I need to know. For my own state of mind.'

'And how is your state of mind when you end the call?'

'You sound like my therapist.'

'Do you dodge her questions, too?'

'No. She doesn't let me.'

'I'm not going to win this one, am I?'

'Nope.'

'Okay.' The Chief Officer of the Supermax wing at Wakefield Prison sighed. 'Let me give you the lowdown. Steve Harrison is confined to a maximum-security cell twenty-four hours a day. For one of those hours, he gets to leave his cell to have a shower and a bit of fresh air in a small rectangle of a prison yard that is surrounded on all sides by a ten-foot wall topped with razor wire. Since he was moved here in January 2019, he has had no visitors, his mail is read before it's sent out and incoming mail is read before it's given to him. Happy?'

'Maybe not happy. Satisfied,' she admitted.

Steve Harrison was a former PC at South Yorkshire Police who, in 2017, turned serial killer, and blamed Matilda for his lifestyle change. Although he didn't pull the trigger in the shootings in January 2019, he was the mastermind behind the whole rampage. There was no chance he would leave prison alive, but while he was still breathing, for Matilda, there was always the distinct possibility he could concoct another atrocity and this time, she might not survive. And that thought scared her more than anything else.

'Can I give you a word of advice, Matilda?' Grey Saunders asked.

'I'd rather you didn't.'

'Well, I'm going to anyway. Stop calling me. I enjoy chatting with you. I think you're a wonderful woman and I'd happily chat the night away with you over a pint, or whatever your tipple is, but this is not healthy for you. We both know that.'

Matilda chewed hard on her bottom lip to stave off the emotions she could feel rising up inside her. 'I know.'

A silence developed between them.

'So ...?' he asked.

'I'll call you in a few weeks,' she said, ending the call before he could say anything else.

Matilda Darke liked to be in control of her life. Getting shot in the head and the aftermath and recovery was not something she had any say over. She was at the mercy of doctors, physiotherapists, psychotherapists and nurses, and she hated it. Now, physically, she was back to her pre-shooting best. And she intended to stay that way. If only her mental health would hurry up and recover, too.

Someone cleared their throat. Matilda turned around to see DI Christian Brady standing in the doorway. He had a surprised expression on his face.

'How much of that did you hear?' she asked.

'Enough.'

'You should have knocked.'

'You hadn't closed the door properly.'

'Oh. I thought I had,' she said, looking dejected, almost guilty, a child being caught with her hand in her mother's purse.

'You're checking up on Steve Harrison?'

'No,' she said, getting up off her desk and going over to the window. She missed her view of the sprawling steel city from her old office. On the ground floor all she could see was the back of the custody suite and the bins. 'Yes,' she admitted.

'Why? You know he's on the never-never list. The only way he'll be leaving Wakefield Prison is in a wooden box, feet first.'

'I just ... I need to keep reminding myself. I don't ...' She struggled to find the right words. She turned to looked at Christian, who was unmoved. 'Don't judge me.'

'I'm not,' he held his hands up in submission. 'I promise, I'm not. If it helps you, then keep calling. It could be worse; you could be driving out to Wakefield once a month to visit him.'

Matilda gave him a crafty smile. 'It's probably best not to put ideas in my head.'

He laughed. 'Sorry. Anyway, there's something I need to tell you about the murder of Richard Ashton.'

Matilda sat down at her desk and beckoned to Christian to do the same. He closed the door to the office. This did not go unnoticed with Matilda. She suddenly saw the grave look of sadness on her DI's face. She was dreading what he was going to tell her and hoped it was fixable.

'Does the name Richard Ashton ring any bells with you?' Christian asked. He'd sat with his legs firmly together, his hands clasped between them. He looked fragile.

'Sort of, but only because he was in a similar business with James.'

'No. I mean away from the business side of things.'

'I don't think so.'

'Remember last September, when we were investigating the murders of the sex workers, and Paul Chattle killed himself in front of me?'

'I do.'

'Before he pulled the trigger, Paul talked about why he'd turned to drink and drugs. He told me how he'd been abandoned as a child, fostered, abused, abandoned again and ended up in care, where, once again, he was abused. He named his abuser as—'

'Richard Ashton,' Matilda finished his sentence for him. 'I

remember. You wanted to investigate him and I ...' She stopped when the memory fully returned.

Matilda had only recently returned to work following the shooting, and she wasn't fully recovered. Her mental health was still damaged, and she wanted to prove herself capable of the demands the role of DCI gave her. She was determined to uncover the killer who had been targeting sex workers for years and would let nothing get in her way, including an investigation into child abuse. She'd lambasted Christian in front of the whole team, something she'd never done before, and which added weight to the claim that she was in no way fit for work.

Christian cleared his throat. 'I went to Paul's funeral. It was paid for by the council. A pauper's funeral. It was the saddest service I've ever attended. It was so impersonal. Apart from me, there was one other person there. I chatted to him when it was all over, asked how he knew Paul, and he said they'd met when they were kids. I asked if they were in care together, he said yes. When he asked who I was and I told him I was a DI with the police, he did a runner.

'The thing is, I've been trying to investigate Richard Ashton since last September. I've read everything I can find about him online. Apart from a few dodgy dealings in his business, there's nothing remotely personal about him. I spoke to someone who used to work for him. He said Ashton was a heart attack waiting to happen and not just because of his size. The bloke was a workaholic. He had no personal life whatsoever. I hit a brick wall straight away, and I've been banging my head against it ever since.'

Matilda chewed her bottom lip. 'Is it possible Paul could be wrong, or you misheard?'

'I didn't mishear. Paul definitely said, "Richard Ashton,

OBE." And he's the only Richard Ashton I've been able to find with an OBE. And he wasn't wrong. And he wasn't lying,' Christian stated. 'He killed himself, Matilda. He put a gun in his mouth and pulled the trigger in front of me. Why lie when you're going to do that?'

Matilda leaned back in her chair and folded her arms. 'Okay. Well, we've now got access to his mobile phone, home computer and tablets. Fingers crossed, that will provide us with evidence of abuse. If so, we'll go from there.'

'But what if it doesn't? He seems to have played everything so closely to his chest. What if there's nothing on his computer?'

'I don't know.'

'This is a personal murder, Mat. Whoever did it, cut off his balls. That, to me, sounds like one of his victims seeking revenge. The abuse definitely happened.' Christian was obviously taking this case to heart. He was deeply affected by Paul Chattle taking his own life and wanted Ashton to face justice for what he'd put him, and possibly others, through.

Matilda nodded. 'I know. Like I said, let's see what Forensics discover, and we'll go from there. Look, Christian, do you want to go home?'

'No. I'm fine. You're right. Ashton probably thought he'd cleared his hard drive, but they never do, do they? We can always find something.'

'Exactly.'

There was a tap on the glass door. Matilda looked up and saw Sian on the other side. Matilda waved her in.

'Sorry to interrupt, but I thought you'd want to know: Ashton Developments have released a statement about Richard Ashton being found dead,' she said, handing over her iPad.

It is with deepest regret that we announce the sudden death of the founder of Ashton Developments, Richard Ashton, OBE, who was discovered dead at his home earlier this morning. All staff at Ashton Developments are in shock, as Richard was more than an employer, he was a friend, and will be sadly missed. Today, our offices will be closed, but Richard would not have wanted us to mourn his passing for too long, and work will resume tomorrow. Please join us, wherever you are in the world, at six o'clock this evening to raise a glass of your favourite drink in honouring Richard Ashton and the immense impression he has had on our lives. RIP Richard. You'll be forever missed.

'Bloody hell! They're not wasting any time,' Matilda said.

'Probably thinking of their share prices,' Sian said with a smile.

'So cynical.'

'A smokescreen,' Christian said, standing up. 'They're painting him out to be a saint.'

'Finn called just before the statement came out. He's spoken to some of the staff, and they're all gutted about it. They've said he was the perfect employer. He pays well, gives them plenty of holiday entitlement, bonuses at Christmas. It's a shame he wasn't in charge of the police force,' Sian laughed.

'The bloke was a bastard and people are going to be mourning him, saying how wonderful he was. I'm not going to let that happen,' Christian said, standing up and storming out of Matilda's office, almost knocking Sian out of the way.

'What's that all about?'

Matilda frowned. 'I'm not entirely sure. Yet.'

Chapter Five

Teas were made and handed around and Sian's snack drawer had been pilfered; all signs that the morning briefing was about to begin. Matilda left her office and went to make herself a coffee. While the kettle boiled again for Matilda, she stooped down to Sian's drawer and rifled through it.

'Who took the last Topic?'

'I had that yesterday,' Sian said.

'I see the dark-chocolate Bountys have gone, too.'

'Yes. That was me as well.'

Matilda picked up a packet of Maltesers then went over to the kettle to make her drink.

'Scott ...' Sian said, leaning over towards her fellow DS and lowered her voice. 'I've put on a bit of weight recently – comfort eating, for obvious reasons. You're into fitness and exercise. Can you give me some tips on how to lose it?'

'Well, I'd start by not opening that Snickers and giving it to me,' he said with a cheeky grin.

Reluctantly, she handed it to him.

'Thank you.' He smiled. 'What kind of thing do you like doing?'

'What do you mean?'

'Well, if you going to slog at losing weight, you may as well choose something you like doing. Swimming is an excellent form of exercise, but I hate it, so I don't do it.'

'Oh. I see. That makes sense. Well, I used to like jogging when I was younger. That was before I had four kids. Me and …' she baulked at merely mentioning his name. 'We enjoyed going walking, hiking in Derbyshire, that kind of thing.'

'That's good. Why not take that up again?'

'I've nobody to go with,' she said, her voice barely above a whisper. 'If I go on my own, my mind will go into overdrive, and I'll start thinking all sorts of things.'

'Okay. Well, I go out running into Derbyshire. Why not come with me? I can always turn to hiking a couple of times a week.'

'Are you sure?'

'Yes. It'll be fun to have someone to go out with again. It's not been the same since Chris died.'

Sian gave a genuine smile that lit up her face. 'Okay. Thanks, Scott. I appreciate it. I'll go and buy some new walking shoes tonight.'

'Right, then, is everyone ready?' Matilda said. She made her way to the top of the room, mug of tea in one hand and a couple of packets of Maltesers in the other.

'Everyone is here,' Scott said, overstating the word 'everyone'. 'We're packed to the rafters.'

'Yes. I'm aware that we are a small team at the moment. We have funding for two new officers, and I have a number of applications to go through. Interviews will begin in May. Also, DC Nowak will be coming back at some point. In the meantime, we'll just have to band together and take up the slack. Now, what do we know about Richard Ashton?'

Scott tapped on his laptop and the large Victorian property Richard Ashton called home popped up on the electronic whiteboard at the top of the room. 'Richard lived here on his own for the past thirty years, according to one of his neighbours, who has lived in her house since the dawn of time. She said he was the perfect neighbour. He always helped her out, and others, when they needed it. He managed to get the road re-tarmacked when the council ran out of money to do it and, when the council dug up all the trees, he paid for new ones to be planted in the sidings out of his own money.'

'Has he ever been married?' Matilda asked.

'No.'

'Why does he live in a big six-bedroom house on his own?'

'The same reason you live in a five-bedroom house on your own,' Sian said with a smirk.

'Touché,' Matilda replied. 'Although now Adele's living with me, it feels like I've got a full house. Let's have his back story, Scott.'

Scott quickly chewed his mouthful of Snickers and swallowed. 'Leslie Hicks is Richard's cleaner. Oh, by the way, in answer to the dog question, Richard didn't have one, but Leslie does, and he occasionally allowed her to bring it with her when she cleaned. She worked for him three times a week – Monday, Wednesday and Friday – and had done for the past seven years. She says, apart from him being untidy, he was a good employer. He paid well and gave her presents for Christmas and on her birthday. He even visited her in hospital with flowers when she had a hysterectomy a couple of years back. According to her, he'd never been married and had no kids. He didn't have any brothers and sisters and she mentioned that his parents died when he was young. I've had a look online and there's a *Daily Mail*interview with him from 2013, when he was given his OBE, where he states how he got into the property development business. I've downloaded a copy for you all to read if you want to, but basically, it states that he was on holiday with his parents when he was seventeen in France. They both died in a climbing accident. He inherited the family home and his father's life insurance paid off the mortgage. He decided to sell and, rather than spend a couple of months getting pissed and shagging his way around Ayia Napa, like any other seventeen-year-old, he invested the money. He bought a rundown house at auction, made it habitable and sold it for profit. So begins the Ashton Developments empire.'

'Is it an empire?' Matilda asked.

Finn waved his hand to indicate he wanted to answer the question. He had a mouthful of KitKat that he quickly chewed and swallowed. 'I've been on to Ashton's solicitor, and he gave me a ballpark figure, saying Richard's personal fortune was well into seven figures. He's going to dig out all the bumph and give me a call with the details.'

'Never been married, no kids and a huge business empire – that sounds like he was a workaholic to me,' Sian said, dipping a plain Rich Tea biscuit into her tea. 'If he's strong-minded and dedicated, is it possible he's made enemies along the way?'

'I've only skimmed,' Scott continued. 'But he's not been without controversy over the years. He's bought land for knock-down prices. There's been rumours of backhanders to councils and planning committees, and there was even a question-mark over his potential involvement in the Jackson Murphy fire in 2003 which led to Jackson Murphy calling in the receivers when they couldn't build that apartment block in town.'

'I remember that,' Matilda said. 'Didn't one of them go to prison?'

'Leon Jackson served four years for fraud.'

'Was it definitely arson?' Sian asked.

'Absolutely. It wasn't even covered up. It was a twelve-storey block and the first five had been built. The fire was intense, and the structure was rendered unsafe. It had to be demolished and rebuilt. Jackson Murphy couldn't afford to do that once the insurance company refused to pay out.'

'What was the cause of the fire?' Matilda asked.

'Hang on,' Scott scrolled through his laptop. 'Faulty wiring in a fuse box, which just happened to be next to a storage unit containing cladding, which, since Grenfell, has been deemed to be unsafe for use. Fire investigators stated that the wiring was so faulty, a child would have known it should never have been installed.'

'So, where does Richard Ashton's name come into this?' Matilda asked.

'There had been a rivalry of sorts between Ashton Developments and Jackson Murphy. This apartment block was a big deal and we're talking millions of profit. Jackson Murphy pipped Ashton Developments to the post in gaining the contract, and Richard Ashton is on record as saying the apartment block, and this is an official quote, "will be a dangerous eyesore on the Sheffield skyline and won't last twenty years, given their reputation among those in the know."'

'Ouch.'

'Can he say something like that? Isn't it slanderous?' Finn asked.

'It would have been if he hadn't been proven correct by the fire.'

'So, where is Leon Jackson now?'

'He's teaching architecture at the University of Dundee.'

'Check he's still there,' Matilda said.

'I already have done, and he is. He hasn't left the city since Christmas, when he went to visit family in Cockermouth.'

'And where is the Murphy from Jackson Murphy?' Matilda asked.

'Well, he would have gone to prison for fraud along with Jackson, but he hanged himself instead.'

Matilda sat back in her chair and opened a second packet of Maltesers. This was what she liked the most about her job. She was surrounded by her team. Although small, it was filled with people she could trust. The back and forth as a case began, exchanging ideas and theories, and deciding what path to take, was where she could concentrate her energies. And it silenced everything else screaming for attention in her mind.

'While all this is interesting,' Matilda began, 'castrating someone isn't the work of a business feud, is it? It's more of a personal crime. So, he's never been married and has no children, but there's bound to be a couple of failed relationships in the background.'

'I spoke to his secretary, Dolly Caine,' Finn said. 'She was in a bit of a mess, but I managed to get something out of her about him. Dolly's worked for him for close to twenty years, and in all that time she's never seen him with a woman. He's never had a holiday abroad, had a weekend away, talked about going for dinner with a partner, nothing. He lives for his work.'

Christian audibly tutted and shook his head.

'We all work a great deal, but we have down time. We all

have hobbies and things we enjoy outside of work. Anything mentioned there?' Matilda asked.

'Nothing. Dolly said all he spoke about was work. He often asked her if she'd had a good weekend or how her holiday was when she returned to the office, and when she fired the question back and asked him what he'd been up to at the weekend, he simply mentioned work.'

'That's not healthy,' Sian said.

'What about Christmas? Who did he spend his Christmases with?'

'Oh. I'm not sure about that. I didn't ask.'

'There must be someone,' Matilda said, looking up at the whiteboard where a photo of Richard Ashton, printed from the Internet, loomed large. 'I mean, I know he wasn't exactly God's gift, but someone must have found him attractive.'

Sian cleared her throat. 'I'm not being funny or anything, but, like you said, he was no oil painting. I'm guessing the only women he had throwing themselves at him were potential gold diggers after his money.'

'Maybe he had a bad experience,' Scott said. 'Maybe he fell for someone, but, like Sian said, they were only after his money, and it scarred him.'

'Or maybe he wasn't bothered about sex or romance,' Finn said. 'My sister-in-law, Lynne, she's never had a relationship or even a casual partner. She's attractive, funny, outgoing, but she just isn't interested in being with anyone.'

'It's possible,' Matilda mused.

'Look, I'm sorry, but while all this is interesting, we're completely missing the mark here and heading in the wrong direction,' Christian said, exasperation in his voice. 'Richard Ashton was a child abuser.'

'Christian, we have no evidence of that,' Matilda said.

Christian addressed the rest of the room. 'When Paul Chattle shot himself in front of me last September, he told me that he was abused from a young age by Richard Ashton, OBE. Then he put the gun in his mouth and pulled the trigger. That fat bastard,' he said, pointing to Richard's photo, 'sexually abused a young boy, and if he got away with it with Paul, who knows how many other victims are out there?'

'If Richard was a serial child abuser, then we will find something while we're digging around in his life,' Matilda said. 'Until then, there is nothing we can do.'

'What do you mean by "if"?' Christian raised his voice. 'The bloke was castrated and had his balls rammed down his throat. If that's not a sexually motivated crime, I don't know what is.'

'Christian, lower your voice and sit down,' Matilda said.

Christian took a deep breath and flopped down in his seat.

'I admit, this killing bears all the hallmarks of someone seeking revenge of some kind – and you're right, this is sexually motivated, but we have to follow the evidence. Until someone states they were abused by Ashton or until something is found, we cannot investigate, based on the word of a dead man.'

'Then we find the evidence,' Christian said, getting riled up again.

'That's what we are doing! We're talking to his neighbours and colleagues. We're trying to find friends and family members.'

'We're wasting our time looking into his business affairs. A dodgy property developer? Big deal. They're all bloody dodgy,' Christian snapped.

'Christian, stop it, right now!' Matilda shouted. 'I know you're upset about this, but I will not have you kicking off just because the investigation isn't going the way you want it to. We follow the evidence. That's what we've always done.'

He stood up and snatched his coat from the back of his chair.

'Where are you going?' Matilda asked.

'I'm going out for a cigarette.'

'You don't smoke.'

'I feel like starting.' He stormed out of the suite, slamming the door behind him.

The room quickly plunged into an awkward silence.

'I know he took it badly when Paul killed himself last year,' Scott said, 'but he's been seeing a therapist. I thought he was fine.'

Matilda grabbed a chair and sat down with a heavy sigh. 'Christian has been investigating Richard Ashton since last September. He hoped he would have found something in his background, and hasn't. If Ashton was a child abuser, he really covered his tracks.'

'It is a sex crime, though, isn't it?' Finn asked. 'I mean, the killer castrated him. It's sexually motivated. Maybe Christian's right.'

'I think he is, but the evidence just isn't there. We need to find the killer in order to interview him, or her, and uncover the motive. We do that in the usual way – interviewing those who knew the victim and following forensic evidence.'

'We've got his laptop, mobile and tablet, and CID are combing through his house,' Scott said. 'We won't get the results today, though.'

'I know. Christian just needs to be a little patient, that's all. Finn, did you ask his secretary when he was last in the office?'

'Yes. He was in yesterday. He's in every day.' Finn hammered on his laptop and brought up black-and-white footage from a CCTV camera overlooking a car park. 'This is Richard leaving Ashton Developments just after seven o'clock last night. As you can see, the car park is empty. He's the last to leave, which, according to Dolly, was nearly always the case.' The footage showed Richard climbing in behind the wheel of his Bentley and driving away. 'I've got his registration number and I'm going to run it through ANPR.'

'Where's his car now?'

'In his garage.'

'Right. Okay, everyone, carry on. Let's get some statements from neighbours and dig into his private life. I don't care what his secretary said – he must have had one.'

Matilda turned and headed for her office. She glanced back at Christian's empty desk and frowned. She'd never known him fly off the handle like that. There was something going on here she couldn't quite put her finger on.

———

Matilda was staring out of the window of her office.There was a tap on her glass door. She looked up and waved Finn to enter.

'There's someone on the phone who is adamant about speaking to you. I've offered to take his statement, but he says he'll only speak to DCI Darke.'

Matilda's eyes widened.

You're a survivor, aren't you, Matilda? But what's the point of surviving, when everyone around you is dead?

The chilling voice of Jake Harrison, taunting her before opening fire and killing those she loved fifteen months ago, still lived deep in her psyche. Whenever she was confronted with a phone call from an unknown number, or she heard a loud bang that sounded like a gunshot, Jake's deep tones came back to haunt her.

'Who is he?' she asked, trying to keep her voice calm.

'He says his name is Peter Ogilvy. He's a reverend.'

'Oh, God, that's all I need, someone trying to save my soul. Put him through,' she sighed, 'I'll talk to him.'

'Line three,' Finn instructed.

Matilda picked up the phone. 'This is DCI Darke. How may I help you?'

'Good afternoon. Are you leading the investigation into the murder of Richard Ashton?'

The voice was fragile and shaking, as if it belonged to an elderly man.

'The cause of Richard Ashton's death hasn't yet been revealed. What makes you believe he's been murdered?'

'Knowing Richard Ashton, I'm surprised nobody's murdered him sooner.'

Matilda frowned. 'I don't understand.'

'Detective Chief Inspector, I'm not as mobile as I used to be.Would it be possible for you to come and visit me? I have some information that may help in your investigation.'

'Do you know who is responsible for Richard Ashton's death?'

Peter gave a low chuckle. 'I have a list of one hundred and twenty-seven names. Every single one of them has a motive for murdering him.'

Chapter Six

Matilda was sitting in the front passenger seat of her Range Rover while Scott drove. She had her head down, scrolling through her phone. They'd been driving for close to twenty minutes, yet neither of them had said a word. Scott wanted to quiz Matilda about Adele's new anatomical assistant. He'd only seen his dark eyes, as he was covered by his mask and white forensic suit, but there was something in his gaze, his stance, his voice, that made Scott want to know more about him.

Matilda and Scott were more than colleagues. She helped him a great deal when he was struggling to come out at work. When he fell in love with Adele's son, Chris, she allowed them to set up home in the apartment above her garage, and when Chris was killed in the shooting in January 2019, she was there for him, too, when he descended into an uncontrollable self-destructive non-coping mechanism. Now, he wanted her support again to help him understand what he felt towards this Donal bloke, despite only seeing him once and knowing absolutely nothing about him. Why was he having such feelings? Surely it was too soon to think of another man in that way after Chris's murder.

'What are we going to do about Sian leaving?' Scott asked. He needed something to break the silence and stop him from worrying about his own minor problems.

'I'm not sure,' Matilda said. She put her phone away and leaned her elbow on the window and put her head in her hand. She released a heavy sigh.

'Do we start a whip-round for a leaving present, or do we tie her to the chair so she can't leave?'

'I've no idea, Scott. She's leaving for all the wrong reasons. I worry that she'll only realise it when it's too late.'

'Do you want me to talk to her?'

'You can give it a go. I'm not sure what you can say, though.'

'Leave it with me.'

'There's a bottle of champagne in it for you if you can convince her to stay. Turn left here.'

'He couldn't live any further out, this reverend, could he?' Scott said.

They'd left the city behind them long ago and were driving through the stunning views of the Derbyshire countryside. It didn't matter what the season was, whether the landscape was basked in glorious sunshine and the trees teeming with vegetation, or the sun was cold, the trees bare and the wildlife hibernating, there was something magical about the English countryside that was beautiful to look at.

'He's retired,' Matilda said.

'I didn't think members of the Church ever retired.'

'They do when they lose their faith.'

'How do you know he's lost his faith?'

'I've just been reading an interview he gave about fifteen years ago. He mentioned that he was walking around Sheffield City Centre one day, looking at everyone going about their business, and he realised he couldn't help a single one of them. The worse thing about it was, he didn't want to help them, either.'

'Wow. That's deep. Don't priests have someone to go to when they lose their faith in God, to help them reinstate it?'

'Oh, it wasn't his faith in God he lost – he still believes. It was his faith in humanity.'

Scott pulled up at a junction as a slow-moving tractor tried to manoeuvre its way along a narrow country lane. 'What does that mean?'

'It means he realised people are selfish and don't care for each other anymore. There's no such thing as community and society, and everyone is simply looking after number one.'

'I could have told him that,' Scott said, starting the car again.

Matilda looked across at him. 'Do you really believe that?'

'Yes. It's obvious. Nobody cares anymore. Look at this pandemic. People are panic buying. They're emptying the shelves of things, whether they need them or not, simply so someone else can't have them. I was in Sainsbury's the other evening and there were no eggs, no flour, no toilet rolls. I saw one bloke with a trolley piled high with bottled water. Thirty, forty years ago, this wouldn't have happened.'

'So cynical for someone so young.'

'I'm a realist,' Scott stated firmly.

Matilda returned to looking out of the window. She wondered if Scott was correct. She liked to think the threat of a pandemic would bring people together, but there was a niggling sense at the back of her mind that things were going to get a lot worse.

'We're a community,' she said.

'Who are?'

'Us. The police force. Our team in particular. Look at how we've rallied around each other in the past few years; more so since the shooting.'

'Okay. I agree, there are pockets of a community. But things like looking out for your neighbour and street parties, that kind of thing, it's all consigned to the history books. Do I turn right here?'

'Yes. Then pull up just past the phone box.'

Scott pulled up and they both turned to look at the picture-box cottage with a thatched roof and sash windows, a faded white fence in urgent need of painting, a wild but stunning front garden, and a deep-green front door.

'Beautiful house,' Matilda said.

'One hundred and twenty-seven possible suspects? Do we really believe that? According to Ashton's staff, he was practically Father Christmas without the beard.'

'All will be revealed.'

Peter Ogilvy moved to the quaint cottage off Edale Road in the small village of Edale, deep in the Derbyshire countryside, in 2001 when he took early retirement from his duties within the Church of England. He wanted a quiet life away from the hustle and bustle of city life. He wanted to be as far away from people as he could get, while still having the odd one close by as the ravages of age and illness caught up with him.

When he opened the front door to Matilda Darke and Scott

Andrews, he gave them a friendly smile. He held onto the door for stability. He didn't ask them into the house. He directed them around the back of his cottage and into the back garden. In the centre of the perfectly manicured lawn was a wrought-iron table with chairs pulled back. He told them to take a seat.

'On a normal occasion, I would have invited you into the house, popped the kettle on and got out a packet of Mr Kipling's. I don't have visitors that often, but this Coronavirus is a tad scary for us oldies, especially when you have as much wrong with you with as I have.'

Peter was a short, thin, delicate man. He was in his mid-sixties, but looked a great deal older, and had a thin crop of straight grey hair. He walked slowly, with a stick, his back slightly arched. He wore ill-fitting black corduroy trousers, an off-white shirt and a navy cardigan over the top, with something heavy in one of the pockets weighing it down. Walking the fifty paces from his house to the table in the garden seemed to take a great deal of energy from him. He was breathing rapidly, and it took him a while to settle.

'We could have talked over the phone,' Matilda said.

'What I need to tell you is something that needs to be said face to face.'

'You mentioned one hundred and twenty-seven people who could have killed Richard Ashton.'

A hint of a smile spread across Peter's face. 'So, he was murdered then.'

Matilda nodded.

'How?'

'Do you really want to know?'

'Was it that bad?'

'We haven't carried out a post-mortem examination yet, but

Mr Ashton suffered an injury which caused him to bleed to death.'

'He was stabbed?'

'Something like that.'

'You're not going to tell me, are you?'

'Not at the moment.'

'I understand. Maybe if I was still wearing my dog collar, you would have given me the gory details,' he said, smiling.

'Maybe.' Matilda returned the smile.

Peter turned to Scott. 'Young man, would you do an old man a favour, pop into the house and make us all a drink? We can't sit out here on a lovely day without any refreshments.'

Scott smiled. 'Of course.'

'Everything's easy to find. Bring the biscuit barrel with you and just wipe down the handles you touch. No offence, but I don't want to go until I'm ready.'

Peter watched as Scott walked down the garden and into the house. He leaned forward on the table.

'You're DCI Matilda Darke, aren't you?'

'Yes,' she said, a frown on her face.

'Who's your boss?'

'Benjamin Ridley. Assistant Chief Constable.'

'I don't know him. I'm guessing everyone I do know is either retired or dead. Is he a fair man?'

'I think so.'

'Hmm,' he said, sitting back in his chair. He thought for a moment. 'I've read about you. You've worked on some interesting cases over the years. Many a time I picked up the phone to call you, then chickened out. I almost did last year, but then I heard you were shot. How are you now?' he asked, studying her.

'I'm fine,' she lied. 'Why were you going to ring me?' She suddenly felt unsettled. Her life seemed to be all over the Internet, thanks to her work and the intense intrusion from journalists. Complete strangers seemed to know more about her than she did. She longed for privacy.

'I have a story to tell. I've tried to tell it many times in the past but I've been gagged every single time. Literally, on one occasion. All the information is with my solicitor, who will release it upon my death, but I imagine it won't ever see the light of day. Hearing about the death of Richard Ashton on the radio this morning made me decide to give it one last go. I thought, with everything you've been through, you're not going to be easily silenced. Sorry, what do I call you?'

'Matilda's fine.'

'Matilda. Lovely name,' he said, obviously stalling. He took a breath. 'Matilda, what do you know about Magnolia House Children's Home?'

'Not much. It was a children's home which closed down in the early 2000s.'

'2001. *I* closed it down,' he said, tapping himself firmly on the chest. 'I was also the one who opened it ten years earlier.'

Scott came out of the cottage carrying a heavy tray laden with a teapot, three matching cups and saucers and a battered biscuit tin. Carefully, he walked to the table, not taking his eyes off the contents of the tray.

'You have a beautiful kitchen,' Scott said.

'Thank you. All locally sourced when I moved in nearly twenty years ago. The bloke who fitted it said it would live me out. I didn't like the sound of that; a kitchen living longer than me. But, while it's aged very well, I ... well, we don't, do we?' he said, looking down at himself. 'I used to be like you,' he said to Scott. 'I ran the London Marathon three times, climbed

Scarfell Pike goodness knows how many times, and I climbed over two hundred Munros in Scotland. Now look at me – I need a stairlift to get me to bed every night.'

Scott paused mid-pour and looked at Peter with his mouth open. He stuttered as he asked if he wanted milk and sugar.

'Don't look so worried,' he said to Scott. 'This isn't what you look like when you get to be in your sixties. I know I'm not classed as old these days, but I've survived cancer twice, and currently I'm battling my third round,' he said, smiling.

'I'm sorry,' Scott said.

He waved him away. 'Don't be.' He picked up his mug with shaking fingers and leaned back in his seat. 'Now, you'll want to know all about Magnolia House, won't you?'

'Yes,' Matilda said. She hitched her chair closer to the table.

'First of all, let me tell you about myself. I always wanted to help people, from a young age. You see, I was placed in care when I was five years old. My mum died about three weeks after giving birth to me. There were complications with the birth, and she never really recovered. I suppose nowadays they'd have given her a course of penicillin and she'd have been fine, but back then, well, these things happen, don't they? My dad had an industrial accident when I was four and died at work. I went to live with my aunt, his sister, but she suffered with her nerves and couldn't cope with me. So, I was placed in care from the age of five to seven, before I was eventually adopted. A lovely couple took me in and treated me like their own.' He took a noisy sip and placed the cup back in the saucer. 'Perfect cuppa, that, lad,' he said to Scott. 'You'll make someone a fine husband one day.

'As I went through school and college,' he continued, 'I kept thinking back to my time in care. They were the worst two years of my life. Like I said, I wanted to help people, but I didn't know how. I wasn't clever enough to be a doctor and I didn't fancy being a teacher or a social worker. I decided to join the Church of England. I believed in God, and I wanted to do good within the community. When I came to Sheffield in the mid-eighties, I was given a small church, and there was this beautiful old building not five minutes away. I knew it would make a great place for kids to live who'd been abandoned for whatever reason, but I had no idea where to start setting up a children's home.

'The council were useless, as per, so I decided to hit the private sector for donations to help me buy this building. Well, the first person I went to couldn't do enough for me. He loved the idea of what I wanted to achieve.'

'Richard Ashton?' Matilda asked while Peter stopped talking for long enough to have another sip of tea and get his breath back.

'Right. He had a look around the building, saw the potential I saw, and got onto the council. He bought it for pennies. Well, not really, but you know what I mean. I later found out that he used his own money, not from his business. He gutted that place from attic to basement. New roof. Rewired throughout. Walls knocked down. New rooms made. Brand-new kitchen and bathrooms. I visited every day during the renovations and every day it looked completely different. I could see it all taking shape in front of my eyes. It wasn't huge. We'd only be able to take a maximum of a dozen lads at a time, but it was better than nothing in my eyes.'

Peter had brightened up since he began talking. Magnolia House was his dream project, his vision, and his eyes sparkled at the memory of it becoming a reality. Suddenly, his smile dropped.

'I had no idea how hands-on Richard Ashton was going to

be. I thought, once the home was finished and up and running, he'd leave it all to me, but he didn't. He kept turning up at mealtimes, and at the weekends when we had sports events in the grounds. I thought he was protecting his investment, maybe even showing these boys who'd had difficult starts in life that there was something to smile about. He was always playing with them, laughing and joking. It took me years to realise he was grooming them, and I stood back and let it happen.'

'Grooming them?' Matilda asked. 'Are you saying Richard Ashton abused the children at the home?'

'Not children. Boys. His interest was solely in young boys,' Peter said, his voice breaking with emotion. A single tear ran down the wrinkles in his face. 'I'm sorry,' he choked.

'You didn't know,' Matilda said softly.

'But I should have done. I should have seen what he was doing.'

'What was he doing?' Scott asked.

'He was watching the boys, working out who were the most vulnerable, the ones with the least confidence, the ones who wouldn't make a fuss if he tried anything.'

'When did you first get an inkling there was something going on?' Matilda asked.

Peter composed himself. He left a heavy silence before he dared to speak without a torrent of emotions flowing out. 'It was 1995. One of the young lads, Alan Bishop, was in tears. He'd only been with us a couple of months. A shy, timid thing, bless him. I thought he was just scared of being at the home, so I tried to reassure him, encourage him to make friends. Then, one Saturday, we're out in the garden, it was a beautiful day, and Richard drives up in his car. Alan burst into tears and ran indoors. I went after him, asked him what was wrong, and …

he told me. It doesn't matter how many years go by, how many times I tell this story, it doesn't get any easier,' Peter said as he pulled a cotton handkerchief out of his trousers pocket and dabbed at his eyes.

Matilda and Scott exchanged glances. They both looked uneasy with what they were hearing. A cold breeze came from nowhere. Matilda shivered.

'I should have asked you to bring a bottle of whisky out.' Peter smiled to Scott. 'Where was I?'

'Alan Bishop was telling you what happened,' Scott reminded him.

'Oh, yes. Alan told me that the week before, when Richard came over, he took him into one of the empty rooms and sat him on his knee. He talked to him, asked him how he was, if he was settling into Magnolia House, and he hugged him. Alan said that for the first time, he actually felt safe and comforted. His tears didn't match with what he was telling me, but then he went on. Richard ... he ... unzipped his trousers. He told Alan that because he'd made him feel better, he could make Richard feel better, too. He made him ... sorry,' he said, turning away to wipe his eyes.

'Take your time, Peter.'

Peter blew his nose. 'He made him perform a sex act on him. Oral sex. You've seen Richard Ashton; he was always a big bloke. This little lad, Alan, he was only six, bless him. He didn't stand a chance.'

'What did you do?'

'To be honest, I didn't know what to do. I didn't believe it, but what motive did Alan have for making it up? I couldn't match his horror story to the Richard Ashton I knew. It took a while for me to get my head around it. In the end, I had to speak to Richard. I needed to know the truth.'

'What did he say?'

'That's the thing, he could have denied it. He could have said Alan lied, put it down to a damaged boy seeking attention, but he didn't. He admitted it as if it was nothing. He even smiled.' Peter put the handkerchief to his mouth as if he was stopping himself being sick. 'He tried to explain his actions. He sat me down and gave me this lecture about what he called intergenerational relationships.'

'Intergenerational relationships?' Scott echoed.

'Relationships between two people of vast age difference,' Peter said. 'But mostly it's men having sex with children. He mentioned a group he was a part of in the eighties, the Paedophile Liberation Front. "Paedophile" wasn't the strong word it is now, back then. They lobbied the government to have the age of consent abolished.'

'But what he did with Alan Bishop wasn't an intergenerational relationship. He didn't ask Alan's permission. He unzipped and forced him to suck him off,' Scott said, the anger rising in his voice. 'Even if there was no age of consent, he'd still have committed a criminal offence.'

'That's exactly what I said to Richard.' Peter half-smiled.

'And what did he say to that?'

'He said I was too rigid in my thinking; that I needed to open my mind.'

'He was excusing himself for raping young boys!' Scott exclaimed.

'Yes. Let me tell you, I couldn't get out of his house fast enough. I wanted to be sick.'

'What did you do?' Matilda asked.

Peter took a deep breath. 'I sat on it for a few days while I tried to get my head around it. Richard had been so convincing, I actually thought there was a reasoning to his argument. Don't forget, we didn't have the Internet in those days for me to do my own research. However, I soon realised what he was doing wasn't only morally wrong, it was illegal, and he needed to answer for breaking the law. I went straight to South Yorkshire Police HQ.'

'What happened?'

'Nothing.'

'What?' Scott called out.

'I went back a week later. Still nothing. I went back a third time, and that very night Richard Ashton came to visit me in my room. He told me there was no point in going to the police anymore, as nothing would happen. I noticed a change in him then, a smugness. I don't know what was said between Richard and whoever at the police, but there was no way Richard was going to get charged with any kind of criminal activity. He'd got away with it.'

'And it continued?' Matilda asked.

'Oh, yes. You see, unbeknownst to me, Richard Ashton had keys to Magnolia House. He came and went as he pleased, sometimes in the dead of night while I was asleep. He sought out the most vulnerable and used them for his own disturbed pleasure. And there was not a damn thing I could do about it.' Peter broke down, the tears flowed, and they wouldn't stop.

The Coronavirus was momentarily forgotten as Matilda jumped up, went over to Peter and put her arms around him, holding him firmly to her chest.

'I'm sorry,' he said through the tears.

'Don't be silly. You have nothing to apologise for. You reported him. You did everything right.'

Peter lifted himself out of Matilda's embrace and wiped his face on his wrinkled handkerchief.

'It gets worse,' he said. 'It wasn't long before Richard was bringing his mates round to Magnolia House. He didn't even hide it anymore. The abuse was out in the open. He was laughing at me. He knew I couldn't do anything, even when…'

'When what?' Scott asked.

'Even when he killed a boy.'

Chapter Seven

The sky had clouded over, and the sun disappeared. It had been easy to forget it was only March while the sun was shining and the temperatures were high, but there was still a nip in the air when the clouds formed. Peter suggested going into the house, but Matilda said she didn't want to risk his health in case either she or Scott were carrying the Coronavirus.

'You've just hugged me. If you've got it, you've already passed it on,' he said with a devilish smile. 'Besides, I get the feeling you're going to be the person who'll blow this story wide open. I'll be happy to die knowing you're taking up the baton.'

Peter held onto Scott's arm as the DS led the retired reverend into the cottage. Matilda followed a few paces behind with the tea tray. She was seeing a therapist to help her through her struggles and paranoia, but it was a lengthy process, and the nightmares and post-traumatic stress disorder were likely to be with her for many years to come. She could fake her recovery only so far, but when people like Peter Ogilvy put all their faith in her, that's when it hit her. She wasn't the Matilda Darke of old who would move mountains to get to the truth. If only she could go home, lock the front door, and stay there forever, only leaving once a week to put the bins out to be emptied. She was retreating into herself, and she needed to fight against the desire to hide. Finding the strength to do so on a daily basis was not easy.

Peter's cottage was beautifully decorated. The walls in the living room were painted a warm cream, but one feature wall, over the wood burner, was a deep forest green. It was cosy and comfortable with its low ceilings and original beams. There was massive television on the wall in the corner of the room and two Chesterfield sofas, identical to the ones Matilda had in her own living room, though these were much older, and wellworn.

A sideboard was packed with different-sized picture frames. Matilda picked one up. It showed a younger Peter Ogilvy in full reverend costume giving a sermon. Another showed him dressed as a referee, giving what seemed to be a pep talk to a team of young footballers. A third was of Peter and another man, slightly young than him, standing either side of a tall green door, both smiling to the camera. Matilda looked at the pictures as a whole, evidence of a full life lived.

The lounge had originally been two rooms, and in the second part, a large oak desk sat against the far wall, a state-of-the-art laptop open on the top, with files of work scattered about.

Despite the fire not being lit, the room was oppressive in its warmth. Matilda could feel the prickle of sweat in her armpits and smell the heady scent of burnt wood. It reminded her of home, and she felt herself relax, slightly.

'Are you still in touch with any of the boys from Magnolia House?' Matilda asked.

'Only one.' Peter smiled as he lowered himself into the chair at his desk. He was out of breath from the walk from the garden. 'I hated having to close it down, but it was the only way I could get the abuse to stop. There were only five boys at the home at the time and they were all moved on to different care homes. One of the boys, Guy – he was twelve – went to a home close to where I lived. He visited often. He stills does. He helps me out, takes me to hospital for my appointments,' he said, wistfully, almost a hint of sadness in his voice.

'Would he speak to us?'

Peter hesitated before he answered. 'I'm not sure. He's never spoken about any abuse he's suffered, but I know he was one of Richard's victims. The way he's living his life, his demeanour, I know there's pain there. I've tried to get him to open up, but he never has. You can tell him I sent you.' He smiled. 'He looks up to me. He sees me as a surrogate father. I don't mind, but I don't know what he's going to do when I'm gone. He needs closure from his childhood. I hope he gets it.'

Matilda looked to Scott and raised a questioning eyebrow. 'How do we get in touch with him?' she asked.

'He has a fruit-and-veg stall in the Moor Market. Guy Grayston. He's a lovely man, but he's incredibly fragile, despite the thick walls he's built around himself.'

Sounds familiar, thought Matilda.

Peter turned to his laptop. He pressed the space bar and

woke it up. From the top drawer of the desk, he took out a USB memory stick and plugged it in.

'I'm going to entrust you with something,' he said to Matilda. Using the mouse, he clicked on a few files and started to download to the memory stick. He turned in his seat. 'The boys at the home all loved football,' he said with a smile. 'I put on little tournaments for them, put them into teams and even drew up a league table. I thought it was a bit of fun, but they took it very seriously. We ...' He paused; sadness swept over him. 'Richard had kit made for them, the name of his company slapped across the chest. I thought he was being nice,' he shook his head. 'I can't believe I was so trusting, so stupid.'

'You can't beat yourself up, Peter,' Matilda tried to reassure him. 'Richard was a master manipulator. If we start looking for ulterior motives in everyone who does something nice, we'd all be complete basket cases.'

'You're right. I know you're right. But it doesn't help, after everything I witnessed. Anyway, as I was saying, the football matches. I took photographs of all the lads in their kit, posing with their arms folded, like you see the professional footballers do in their team pictures. They're all on here,' he said, pulling out the USB stick. 'And there's a list of all their names, too. I'm not sure where they are now, but I'm guessing you have the capabilities to track them all down. I know it's not possible to prosecute a dead man, but maybe if you speak to some of the men, they'll be able to help you track down the other abusers. And there *were* other abusers.' He handed Matilda the stick with a shaking hand.

Reluctantly, she took it. The magnitude of what was stored on it was not lost on her. The self-doubt was already kicking in.

'I've handed this over before,' he continued. 'More than once, to people who should have been able to help. It was ignored. I always thought one day I'd find someone within the police force who'd have a pair of bollocks big enough to stand up to whoever was silencing them – excuse my language. To me, you look like you've got balls bigger than any man I've ever met. No offence,' Peter added, turning to Scott.

'None taken. You're right. I've never met anyone as strong as Matilda. She took two bullets fifteen months ago and was back at work within nine, chasing down a serial killer and bringing Carl Meagan home.'

'Yes, I read about him,' Peter's eyes lit up. 'Kidnapped and missing for four years, and you brought him home to his parents. I want to shake your hand.' He held out a wizened hand and Matilda shook it lightly. 'How is the young lad doing?'

Matilda blushed slightly at the praise heaped on her. 'He's doing fine. He's quiet, obviously, but he's slowly settling back into some kind of normal routine.'

Peter frowned as he studied Matilda. 'You don't give yourself half as much credit as you should do for your achievements. You keep beating yourself up, don't you?'

'No.'

'Yes, she does,' Scott said.

'I thought so. You remember your failures and allow them to eat away at you and don't consider your successes. A common trait among the British.' He smirked. 'Matilda Darke,' he reached out and took her hands in his. 'You're a good woman in a bizarre world. Stop listening to that little voice in your head telling you what you can't do, because there's evidence around you that one person can make a difference, and that's exactly what you're doing.'

Matilda smiled and nodded, not daring to say anything, in

case a torrent of tears came out. It was a long while before she dared speak.

'Toilet?' she asked.

'Top of the stairs, first on your left.'

She smiled and headed for the door.

'I've embarrassed her,' she heard Peter say quietly.

'No. You've told her exactly what she needed to hear,' Scott replied.

Peter Ogilvy's bathroom was small and cold. A window had been left open and a stiff, chilly breeze was blowing in.

Matilda stood in front of the sink, ran the hot water tap, and splashed herself in the face. She looked up at her reflection in the stained mirror and didn't recognise who was looking back at her.

For the past fifteen months, she had doubted who she was, and what she was capable of, but hearing Peter, a complete stranger, heap her with praise, based only on what he had read about her achievements in the media, struck home. He was right. While her failures were huge, the positive outcomes more than outweighed the cases where she hadn't received the correct result. When she arrested Steve Harrison, nobody could have foreseen that he would plot an atrocity on the scale of the shooting back in January 2019. She couldn't be blamed for the loss of life on that day, yet she felt each and every death as if she'd personally pulled the trigger herself. Her therapist was right, she was suffering with survivor's guilt, but she needed to get over it in order to function as a detective chief inspector, and as a woman.

She splashed her face again, then turned on the cold tap and drank from it, using her cupped right hand as a vessel.

'Come on, Matilda. Think of James. Think of how proud he'd be if you smashed a paedophile ring. Think of all those kids, now grown up, who'd get some kind of closure from knowing their abusers were in prison.'

She took a deep breath and another few mouthfuls of water.

All Matilda needed to do was to keep her focus and not allow her demons to interfere while this case was ongoing.

It sounded so easy in her head.

She pulled her phone out of her trousers pocket and composed a text to Christian:

I've found your proof. Go to Moor Market and find a bloke called Guy Grayston who runs a fruit-and-veg stall. He was at a children's home called Magnolia House. Ashton provided the funds for it, and he abused the boys living there.

Matilda was at the top of the stairs, about to descend, when she felt her phone vibrate. She looked at the screen. A reply from Christian:

Thank you. I'm so sorry for kicking off like I did earlier.

She smiled to herself. She could feel the warmth and the confidence growing inside. Yes, this was a difficult task, but she had the right people around her to help solve it.

The printer next to the laptop came to life and a photo was printed. Peter picked it up with gnarled fingers and handed it to Scott.

'They are your witnesses,' he said. 'They might also be your suspects.'

Scott looked at the picture. It was of two rows of boys wearing red-and-white-striped football shirts. Three at the back and two at the front. They all stood straight and proud, their arms folded across their chests, staring into the camera with beaming smiles on their young faces.

'Do you play football?'

'No.'

'Oh. I thought you might have done,' he said, looking him up and down. 'I like looking at these pictures. The boys were at their happiest when playing football. Even after the games, they'd spend hours talking about them, analysing them. Only, I see Richard Ashton's name on their chests, and I can't help thinking … When I think back to everything he did for the boys at Magnolia House, it was all for his own sick, perverted pleasure. And I thought he was being charitable.'

'There was nothing you could do, Peter. You tried your best.'

'It wasn't enough. I could have done more. I could have shouted louder, made more of a nuisance of myself at the police station. I thought I was getting somewhere at Social Services until …' he sighed.

'Go on,' Scott prompted.

Matilda came back into the living room and sat on one of the sofas.

'There was a woman who worked at Sheffield City Council in the nineties. Barbara Usher. Lovely woman. She was something to do with childcare. She came out to Magnolia

House a few times to do an inspection. We got on very well. I told her once about suspecting Richard Ashton of abuse. I did it in a roundabout way so she'd launch her own enquiry. She did. She came to me a few times about how she'd spoken to police officers and other council officers, and the rumours about Richard and what he was like.'

'What happened?' Matilda asked.

'Barbara was a committed and dedicated woman. She put the children first. She'd stop at nothing to protect them. She'd be trouble. I thought she'd get the abuse to stop.' Peter looked down. When he looked back up, his eyes were full of tears. 'In 1997, she was mugged coming out of the Odeon. She hit her head on the pavement and never regained consciousness. Police put it down to a random incident. I think she was murdered.'

'Do you have proof?'

'No. Her flat was burgled two days later, though. You see, this is what it's been like for decades, Matilda. Whenever I or anyone else has tried to say anything, we've been silenced, or the evidence has been taken away and destroyed. You can't allow that to happen again.' He pleaded with her.

'Aren't you worried about people discovering you've got all this information?' Scott asked, handing the photograph back to him.

'They know,' he nodded. 'They also know that there are several copies with several different solicitors' firms around the country. If I die, they're instructed to pass it on to whoever they know who'll do something with it. I'm not stupid,' he said, tapping the side of his head.

'Peter, were there any other staff at Magnolia House we could talk to?' Matilda asked.

He smiled. 'There wasn't a staff as such. There was me, and

Linda Foreman was the cook who also cleaned and acted as a mother-figure for the boys.'

'Would she speak to us?'

He shook his head. 'She died two years ago. Breast cancer, I think. You could try and track down Nigel Tate. He used to come and tend to the grounds. He was there for a few years, on and off.'

'You mentioned about one of the boys dying.'

Peter looked down and composed himself. When he looked back up at Matilda, his eyes were glassy. 'Sean Evans. He was seven years old. He died at Magnolia House. I don't know the exact cause of death. I'm sorry to say that when I heard of his death, I sort of fell apart. I allowed myself to be manipulated. By the time I pulled myself together the body had gone, and Richard was ordering me to forget it ever happened.'

'Richard killed him?'

'I don't know. Richard was present, as were a few other men.' He reached into the pocket of his cardigan and pulled out a small, black, leatherbound bible that had seen better days. He opened the front cover and took out a photograph. He handed it to Matilda. 'Sean Evans. He was involved in a car crash when he was three. His parents were both killed. He was trapped in the back seat while firefighters had to cut him free. You see the way he has his hair, floppy and over his left eye? He had a scar from the crash he didn't like to be reminded of.'

'Didn't he have any family to take him in?' Matilda asked, looking down at the picture of the young boy sitting on a wall, a football on his lap, grinning to the camera.

'No. He was adopted, but his adoptive parents split up, and Sean was then brought to Magnolia House while another place was being found for him. Then Richard Ashton got his talons on him. I keep that photo with me everywhere I go. I mention

Sean in my prayers every night. He's not at peace, I know he isn't. Until he's found, he won't be either.'

Matilda looked up from the photo. Her gaze met Peter's hopeful eyes.

'The other men who were in the room with Richard when Sean died, who are they?'

'I don't know. I never knew their names. They always hung back in the shadows or turned away whenever I was there. I did recognise one man, as he was our local MP at the time: Lionel Barlow. He wasn't there on the night of Sean's murder, but he was a regular visitor to the home.'

'Lionel Barlow?' Matilda echoed.

'Yes. He's dead now and left behind a legacy of a good life serving his community. There's even a Lionel Barlow Road in North Derbyshire where he was born.' He shook his head in disgust. 'I'm aware I have no evidence, that it's my word against theirs. However, on that memory stick are the names of all one hundred and twenty-seven boys who stayed at Magnolia House in the ten years it was open. Some were adopted, thankfully, and I'm guessing they'll be easily traced. You might want to talk to Duncan Shivers. He replaced Barbara Usher after she died. But talk to the boys. You'll see the pain in their eyes and know the truth.'

Matilda chewed her bottom lip as she thought.'Why did you close down Magnolia House?' she asked.

'It was the only way I could stop the abuse. I lost … my faith,' he said, quietly.

Matilda looked at the cross on the wall. Peter's eyes followed her gaze.

'I didn't lose my faith in God. He's still there, louder than ever. I lost my faith in humanity. How could so many people turn a blind eye to what was so obvious? People always ask how God can allow so much vitriol and horror in the world, but he doesn't. It's us, people, who let it happen. A parent kills their child, and we see stories about how the Social Services knew about abuse taking place and how lessons will be learnt, but they never are. Why? Because human beings are selfish people and only interested in their own gratification. I've seen it first-hand, over and over again.' He sighed and sagged in his seat. 'The first time I realised that, I wept for days. God could say anything he wanted to me, and he did, but I stopped believing in people. That makes me sound incredibly bitter, doesn't it?'

'After everything you've witnessed, I think you're allowed to feel like that,' Matilda said.

'Please, don't let me down, Matilda. I'm not expecting you to restore my faith in humanity, but please, let me have a glimmer of hope in my final days.'

'I'll do my best,' she said, firmly.

'That's all I ask.'

***

'Wow,' Scott said, once they were back in the car. 'That was … intense.'

'Poor man,' Matilda said, looking down at the memory stick in her hand.

'What are we going to do?'

'We're going to identify every single child who went to Magnolia House and talk to them. We'll get names of all the abusers, and we'll make them pay for what they put them through.'

'But what about Barbara Usher? What if she was killed

because she was making a noise? That could happen to us,' Scott said, a heavy frown on his forehead.

'They won't kill us because we're going to shout so loud, everyone in the country will hear us. People like Richard Ashton think they're untouchable – they're not. Their day is over. I don't care who the abusers are, or their position in society. I will find them, and fucking annihilate them,' she spat. 'Or die trying.'

_____

Chapter Eight

The relief Christian felt upon receiving Matilda's text, telling him she'd possibly found proof of Ashton's sexual assaults, was palpable. Since last September he'd scoured the Internet, read everything about Richard, chatted to former staff, had long-winded conversations with neighbours, and not discovered anything. There was nothing about him being a financier of a children's home. If he was doing something so charitable, wouldn't he have shouted about it, especially when he received an OBE in 2013? Surely his donations and charity involvements would have been listed. Nothing. Which only fuelled the rumour that he wanted it kept beneath the radar to stop his nefarious activities from being made public. It was just a shame he'd had to die in order for all this to come to light.

Christian didn't visit Moor Market very often. He wasn't a fan of the city centre and preferred to do his shopping locally where he lived. On the odd occasion he entered the wooden-framed building, he was shrouded by noise, the hustle and bustle of a busy marketplace. Stall-holders shouting their wares, animated conversations between customers, people pushing past each other. Today, it was almost deserted. A few hardy shoppers paced the aisles, but several stalls were already closed, with the threat of a national lockdown looming, and people were staying away in their droves.

It didn't take long for Christian to find the fruit-and-veg stall. The green sign with GRAYSTON'S painted on it in big red letters told him he'd found the right place. There were two men behind the rows of fresh produce. One was a young man with light-brown hair, heavy eyelids and patchy stubble. He kept yawning and obviously wanted to be anywhere else in the world other than here. He was too young to have lived at Magnolia House. The other man was older, early thirties, possibly. He wore a grey hooded sweatshirt. His black hair was neatly styled, and his eyes sparkled as he smiled and spoke to his customers.

'I've popped a few extra apples in your bag, love,' Guy said as he came around from behind the counter with a heavy bag of goods. An elderly customer opened her trolley and he placed it carefully inside. 'We're closing on Friday to stop this virus spreading, but I'm going to be working mobile. Are you on Facebook?'

'I am. I've got grandkids in America I chat to. They got me into it.' She smiled.

Christian frowned. There was something familiar about Guy.

'Here's my card with all my details.' He handed her a crumpled business card from his back pocket. 'Look me up and tell me what you want, and I'll bring it to your house.'

'They were saying on the news that it'll be a good result if we only lose twenty thousand lives, but that's a lot of lives to lose, isn't it?'

Christian could detect the fear in her voice. He'd heard that, too. It scared his kids.

'It is, but as long as we follow the advice, we should be fine,' Guy said with a reassuring smile. 'I tell you what, Rose, you ring me any time if you need anything. I don't want you going out unnecessarily, all right?'

'Thank you, Guy, you're a good lad.' She touched him on the arm and walked away, pulling her heavy trolley behind her.

Christian realised where he'd seen Guy before. He was the other person who attended Paul Chattle's funeral and ran away when he identified himself as a detective.

'You're a mug, mate,' Guy's colleague said. 'You're going to have all the old ones ringing you up, having you running around for a jar of beetroot.'

'These old ones, as you call them, are our customers. And what else am I supposed to do during a lockdown? I'm not like you, playing *World of Warcraft* twenty-four hours a day and drinking Stella until you pass out from exhaustion.'

'Roll on Friday,' he said, rubbing his hands together.

'Guy Grayston?' Christian asked.

'Yes, sir. What can I get you? All prices are lowered, as I don't want anything going off before the end of the week when we close.' He smiled.

Christian showed his warrant card. 'DI Brady. South Yorkshire Police. Would it be possible to have a word?'

'Really? Now? I'm busy.'

'It is rather important.'

'What's he done?' his colleague asked, excitement on his face.

'Keep your mouth shut, Darren. I can give you five minutes,' Guy said.

'That's fine.'

'Frank,' Guy shouted across to the stall opposite. 'Can you keep an eye on this toss-pot for five minutes? I need to step out for a bit.'

'Sure.'

'That's called bullying in the workplace. Are you going to do anything about it, detective?' Darren said.

'Do you have evidence that what he said isn't true?' Christian asked.

Darren paused and Guy laughed.

'He's got you there.'

Christian and Guy headed for the exit.

'I only employ him because his mother practically begged me to give him a chance. He's a lazy sod and been fired from every job he's had after a few weeks. He's actually looking forward to a lockdown, can you believe that?' he said. 'So, what did you want to talk to me about?' He leaned against the wall of the market and pulled an e-cigarette out of his back pocket.

'I want to ask you a few questions about your time at Magnolia House.'

Guy's eyes widened. The twinkle died and his mouth opened slightly.

'I was waiting for this. I heard on the news about Richard Ashton being found dead. He was never mentioned about having anything to do with the home, though. I'm surprised you cottoned on so quick.'

'We didn't. We received a phone call from Peter Ogilvy. He told us about you.'

His face softened. 'Peter, bless him. Magnolia House was his baby. He was gutted when he closed it down. It almost destroyed him when he found out what that bastard was doing there.'

'Guy, I don't know if you remember me, but I saw you last year at Paul Chattle's funeral.'

'I thought you looked familiar. I just assumed you'd bought from my stall. I'm not bad at remembering faces, it's names that trouble me. Look, if you're going to ask some really dark questions, you can buy me a latte.' He nodded towards the Nero kiosk up ahead.

'Sure.'

Coffees bought, they sat on a bench in the middle of the Moor shopping area. Neither of them said anything at first.They sat in silence, sipping their drinks and absorbing what was happening around them.

'Footfall's dropped off dramatically in the last week alone,' Guy said. 'Bloody virus.'

'I heard you talking to that customer about the market closing on Friday.'

'Yes. I don't get it. How can you lockdown an entire country? I know people's lives are more important than money, but the economy is going to go through the floor. Prices of everything will increase, taxes will go up. This is a huge game changer in our lives, isn't it?' he asked, looking across to Christian for an answer.

'I think it probably is, yes. Guy, going back to Magnolia House, what can you tell me about what went on there?'

Guy raised his eyebrows. 'How long have you got? It wasn't just Magnolia House, either, and it wasn't only Richard

Ashton. He used to bring his mates round, and when the home closed, he held Friday-night parties.'

'Can you identify any of Richard's mates?'

'No. I'd recognise them if I saw them. It's strange, but I've often wondered what I'd do if I looked up and saw one of them come to the stall to buy some apples or something. I tell myself I'd want to rip his head off and spit down his throat, but I know I haven't got it in me to do something like that.'

'Are you in touch with anyone from Magnolia House?'

'No,' he answered quickly.

'What about Paul Chattle?'

'I saw his name in the paper when he died. I felt like I needed to say goodbye. I wish I hadn't, though,' he said, draining the last of his latte and picking at the cup.

'Why?'

'I haven't been to many funerals, but his was by far the saddest, simply because there was only you and me there. He doesn't even have a gravestone or anything. He didn't deserve to be treated like that.'

'You know how he died?' Christian asked.

'He shot himself, yes.'

'I was there when he did it.'

Guy turned to Christian for the first time since he'd sat down. 'Did you try to stop him?'

'Of course I did. His girlfriend was a sex worker. She was one of the victims of a serial killer. He couldn't cope with losing her. He told me that Richard had abused him as a child, and that's why he'd turned to drink and drugs. I wanted to investigate, but there was no evidence. Guy,' Christian said, turning and facing him. 'We can't prosecute a dead man, but if there were others involved, we can bring them to justice, but we need firm evidence. We need you to give us a statement.'

Guy shook his head. 'I don't know about that. Besides, there is no evidence. It's my word against theirs, isn't it?'

'But you can help us,' Christian said, hopefully. 'You can help to identify the other kids from Magnolia House. They'll give statements. The more we have, the harder it will be for the abusers to make it go away. But there's nothing we can do without an official statement.'

'No. I'm sorry. I can't go through all this again,' Guy said, standing up and tossing his empty cup into a bin. 'I'm trying to move on, put it all behind me, and I have done, sort of. I can't go back to reliving it all. It'll finish me off,' he looked pained as he spoke.

'Guy, I'm going to tell you something that hasn't been made public,' Christian said. He moved towards him and lowered his voice. 'Ashton was murdered. Someone cut his balls off and he bled to death. To us, that's a sexually motivated crime. We think someone he abused killed him.'

'Good. I hope he fucking suffered,' Guy spat.

'He did. The thing is, whoever did it will get caught and put away for murder. Yet they're a victim. They shouldn't be imprisoned for this. If you give us a statement, if you identify others, and they make statements, it will help whoever killed Ashton to escape prison and be given the help they need.' Guy turned to walk away. Christian grabbed him by the shoulders. 'You're getting on with your life. You may not think it, but you're functioning. You're able to get up in a morning and come to work. I don't think the killer is. Paul couldn't. Others won't either. Their suffering won't be relieved until their abusers are in prison.'

Guy let out a deep sigh. His brow was heavy as he thought, his eyes darting rapidly left to right.

'I can't,' he said quietly. 'I'm sorry, but I can't.' There were tears in his eyes. He walked away, back to the market.

'Guy, I saw Paul kill himself. He put the gun in his mouth and pulled the trigger in front of me. I swore, then and there, that I'd get justice for him. That's what I've been trying to do since last September,' he said, following him, taking huge strides to keep up with him. 'But Richard Ashton was a sneaky bastard who covered his tracks, and there is nothing linking him to any of this. I need you to help me,' he pleaded.

Guy, his hand on the door handle of the tradesmen's entrance to the market, stopped and looked back at Christian. Tears had left track marks down his face.

'I really can't,' he said, pulling open the door and disappearing inside.

'*Fuck!*' Christian screamed.

Chapter Nine

Matilda stood in front of the murder board and looked up at the glaring, grinning face of Richard Ashton, OBE. When she first saw this photograph of him standing outside Buckingham Palace in his grey top hat and tails, holding up his award, a proud smile for the cameras, she thought he looked elated, but after learning of his secret past from Peter Ogilvy, she didn't see pride, she saw smugness. He was getting away with abuse on a massive scale and an OBE was testament to how untouchable he really was. Why?

If Richard Ashton was a senior politician, someone high up in the Metropolitan Police, an A-list celebrity, she could understand why he was being protected, but he wasn't. He was a property developer from Sheffield. He built housing developments, apartment blocks and retail parks throughout Yorkshire. Him being exposed as a prolific child abuser, while still horrific, would not bring down a government or result in a public enquiry. So, who else was involved in the abuse? Who benefited from Richard Ashton being protected?

'According to the files, Barbara Usher's case is closed,' Finn said.

Matilda jumped and turned around. She'd been so absorbed in staring at Ashton's sweaty face, she'd almost forgotten where she was. She was doing her level best to focus on the case and not on her ability to run it.

Positive thinking, Matilda.

'Sorry?'

'Barbara Usher. You asked me to look into her death.'

'Oh, yes, sorry, Finn. I was miles away. Go on.'

'It's exactly as Peter Ogilvy explained it to you. She was coming out of the Odeon in town with a friend after watching *Titanic*when she was knocked to the ground as her bag was snatched. She hit her head hard on the pavement and never woke up. Her parents turned off the life-support machine less than a week later.'

'What about her flat being burgled?'

'Police put it down to an opportunistic burglar. Barbara's mugging was widely reported in the local press and the burglar obviously knew where she lived and took advantage of an empty flat.'

'Did they get anyone for the mugging?'

'No.'

'How soon was the case shelved?'

'Within a few weeks. Her friend gave a statement but couldn't give a description of the mugger, saying it all happened too quickly. There was an appeal for witnesses, but nobody came forward.'

'I'm guessing there were dozens of people coming out of the Odeon at that particular time. Why was she singled out?'

Finn shrugged.

Sian ended the call she was on. 'The mystery deepens.'

'Does anyone want a cuppa?' Finn asked, standing up.

Matilda and Sian both nodded and Finn headed to the drinks station.

'I've just spent the best part of an hour going through various people at the council,' Sian said, running her fingers through her red hair. 'And I finally found someone who was working there in the mid-nineties. Apparently, when Barbara Usher died, she was replaced by a woman called Tracey Fisher.'

Matilda frowned. 'Peter said Duncan Shivers.'

'I know. I asked about Duncan Shivers and this woman told me he never worked for them. She got someone from the central records to take a look while we were chatting and Sheffield City Council have never, in their whole history, or at least as far back as records go, employed a man called Duncan Shivers.'

'But,' Matilda grabbed her laptop. The memory stick Peter had given her was plugged in. 'There's a list of twelve boys who were adopted from Magnolia House. Duncan Shivers arranged it all. He collected the boys from the home.'

'Not for Sheffield Council, he didn't.'

'There wouldn't have been another adoption agency involved, would there?'

'No. It would have all been through Social Services run by the council. I asked,' Sian said, taking the proffered mug of tea from Finn. She opened her bottom drawer, saw the colourful wrappers of snacks and quickly closed it without taking anything.

'So, who is Duncan Shivers, then?' Matilda asked.

'I've no idea. Also, I've run a search on Nigel Tate, the

gardener who worked at Magnolia House, and you'll win a mini Mars if you can guess where he is.'

'I don't know. Is he dead?' Matilda guessed.

'Finn?' Sian asked.

'I'll say prison.'

'Finn wins,' Sian tossed him the mini bar of chocolate.

'What's he doing in prison?'

Sian flicked over a couple of pages in her notebook. 'In 2004, he was jailed for raping and murdering two nine-year-old boys in Doncaster. He's currently in Wakefield Prison.'

'Bloody hell,' Matilda said. 'I think we're going to have to pop along to Wakefield and have a chat with Mr Tate.'

'I'd rather not accompany you, if you don't mind,' Sian said. 'That's where Stuart is.'

'No worries. Finn, fancy getting out from behind the desk tomorrow?' Matilda asked.

'A trip to Wakefield? Wow, and there was me thinking I wouldn't be getting a holiday this year,' he said, rolling his eyes in sarcasm.

Matilda's mobile started ringing. She fished it out of her trouser pocket and looked at the display. The number was withheld. She swiped to answer.

'DCI Darke.' There was no reply, so she said her name again. Still no reply, though she was sure she could hear breathing. The call ended.

You're a survivor, aren't you, Matilda? She shook Jake's voice from her head.

'Finn, everything all right?' Sian asked, looking across at the DC and seeing a perplexed look on his face.

'I've been thinking,' he said.

'I know I should encourage independent thought, but

something tells me I'm not going to want to hear what's going on in your head,' Matilda said, tossing her phone onto a desk and wrapping her hands around the steaming mug.

It was probably a call centre. Don't read so much into a silent call. It was nothing. Forget about it.

'I've got a dark feeling about this,' Finn said, quietly, his furrowed brow heavy. 'When was the first boy adopted by Duncan Shivers?'

Matilda looked back at her laptop. 'October 1997.'

'And the little boy, Sean Evans, he was killed in January 1997?'

'That's right.'

'Could it be possible that Richard, or maybe one of his cronies, panicked at Sean's death and decided there needed to be a better way of getting hold of the kids? Maybe they invented this Duncan character, who was an abuser himself, to play the part of someone who worked for the council, and he simply took the boys away to order.'

Matilda felt a cold shiver run down her spine.

Sian's mouth fell open. 'That's very dark, Finn.'

'I know. I hate myself for even thinking it. It's just, if there is this massive cover-up to stop the abuse from being made public, then there is obviously some serious manipulation going on here. Richard, and whoever else was involved, wouldn't simply say, "Oh well, we've had a good run, but now we've killed one, we'll have to stop." They'd find another way to get hold of the boys without raising suspicion.'

'He's right,' Matilda admitted. 'Sian, I'm going to email you this list of twelve boys. I want you to contact Social Services and try and find out if they were adopted. If so, where?'

'Will do.'

'How do we trace this Duncan Shivers?' Finn asked.

'I'm not sure,' Matilda chewed her lip. 'I'll need to go back to Peter Ogilvy, ask him for a description, and we can go from there.' She turned to look back at the board and Ashton's evil smile. 'I hope to God those twelve didn't end up in the same place as Sean Evans.'

Chapter Ten

The HMCU suite was empty. Everyone had gone home for the day, leaving Matilda alone. The first day of a new investigation had gone as smoothly as hoped. The magnitude of the case, the expectation on her shoulders from Peter Ogilvy, the victims, herself, was intense. There were darker days to come, she could feel it. She was so pleased she had the right people around her.

Outside, it was dark, and the room was lit only by the light from Matilda's office. She sat at Sian's desk and looked up at the murder board. In the darkness, Richard Ashton looked even more sinister. What must those small boys at Magnolia House have thought when something so big and gross pawed over them? She felt sick just thinking about it.

She turned away. Through the window, out into the darkness, she could see the memorial to the fallen police officers, the small eternal blue flame flickering. She closed her eyes, and she was back to that cold day in January last year. She stood in the car park looking up at Jake Harrison as he aimed a gun at her from the roof of the building opposite. He squeezed the trigger. The first bullet went into her shoulder, she staggered backwards. He fired again. Everything went black as the second bullet entered her head.

'Matilda.'

She jumped, opened her eyes, and saw ACC Ridley standing in the doorway.

'I thought you'd gone home,' he said.

It was possible to tell the time of day by the state of Ridley's personal appearance. In the morning he was clean shaven, neat and pristine in his uniform. He smelled nice and his hair was in perfect place. As the day wore on, the tie was loosened, the jacket was removed and the shirt untucked. The hair had been ruffled and the five o'clock shadow gave him a rugged look. Right now, he looked like he'd been ridden hard and put away wet.

'I was just about to.'

Ridley followed Matilda's gaze to the photograph of Ashton. 'I'd heard Richard Ashton had been found dead.'

'Yes.'

'Castrated, I've been told.'

Matilda looked at him and frowned. *How did you know that?* 'That's right. Did you know him?'

'No. No,' he was quick to answer. 'Where are you with the investigation? Any suspects, theories?'

Matilda studied her boss. She couldn't read his face, and there was something about his rapid eye movement she found unsettling. 'Erm, nothing concrete at the moment. His neighbours rave about him, his employees only say good things. He doesn't seem to have an enemy in the world.'

A small smile appeared on Ridley's face. 'Oh,' was all he said.

'However, the manner of his death suggests otherwise,

doesn't it? Castration – that's a sexual motive. We're wondering along the lines of if he's ever been suspected of rape or abuse of some kind,' she said slowly, watching Ridley out of the corner of her eye for a reaction.

'Wouldn't there be something on the system if that were the case?'

'You'd have thought so, but there isn't. However, it doesn't mean to say something wasn't hushed up.Or perhaps Ashton paid the victims off.'

'Is that likely?' he asked, shuffling from foot to foot.

'Ashton wasn't without controversy in his business life. We've discovered backhanders with councils, buying land for less than it was worth, corruption. It's no great leap to suggest he used the same tactics with his personal life. None of his staff or neighbours ever saw him with a partner. He was never married, yet he gave very generously to several children's charities. We're opening a line of inquiry to see if he was mixed up in any child abuse.'

Ridley turned to Matilda. His eyes widened. 'Child abuse?'

'In Ashton's house he has framed photographs of himself with important people dotted about the place. The Prime Minister, other senior politicians, big businesspeople like Richard Branson and James Dyson. There was even one with him and Jimmy Savile.'

'Really?'

Matilda nodded. 'I mean, even if you were a friend of Jimmy Savile's and had no knowledge of the disgusting things he did, you wouldn't keep his photo on your wall, would you?'

'Huh. I suppose not,' Ridley said softly. 'Matilda, I don't want you spending too much time on this.'

'I'm sorry?'

'Ashton. You've said yourself he was a controversial business figure. It's obvious someone took exception to a deal he was working on and took the law into their own hands. I think that's where you, and your team, should concentrate your energies.'

'If someone didn't want Ashton building a housing development close to where they lived, or something, they would have stabbed him, shot him, cut the brakes on his car – they wouldn't cut his balls off,' she said, a smile in her voice.

'You know that for a fact?'

'No, but it's obvious sexually related.'

'Has anyone come forward to say they were sexually abused by Ashton?'

She thought for a moment, wondering if she should take the ACC into her confidence. 'No. Not yet. It's early days. His death hasn't even been widely reported in the press yet.'

'I need you to keep me in the loop on this one, Matilda. Whatever you're working on, I need to know about it before you take action. Is that understood?'

Matilda studied Ridley. He looked uncomfortable. 'What's going on?'

'Nothing is going on, Matilda,' he said, raising his voice. 'Just … don't do anything without running it by me first.'

He turned and left the suite before Matilda could say anything else.

She leaned back in her chair. Someone knew more about Ashton's life than was already in the public domain and they wanted to stop it from being revealed, and it was someone higher up the chain of command than ACC Ridley who could force him into putting pressure on her and her team.

She looked back at Ashton. 'You really were a vile, despicable man, weren't you?'

Matilda stood up and dragged her tired limbs into her office where she grabbed her coat and mobile phone. Scott had already left so she'd have to call for a taxi. She was about to make the call when her phone rang. The screen told her it was 'StrangeBob-Forensics' calling. She smiled as she swiped to answer.

'Good evening Bob, you're working late.'

'I've actually finished for the day and I'm currently on the hard shoulder of the dual carriageway waiting for the AA.'

'Oh. Car broken down?'

'No. Car set on fire.'

'Are you all right?'

'Yes. I managed to pull over before anything serious happened, like it exploded and I took a coachload of school kids out or something.' He laughed.

Matilda smiled and frowned at his bizarre sense of humour.

'I was going to email you once I got home but thought as I've got time on my hands now, I'll give you a call. Not interrupting anything, am I?'

'No. What can I do for you?' She pulled out a chair and sat down.

'We were delivered a laptop, two iPads and two mobile phones this morning in the case of Richard Ashton. The laptop and one of the iPads held all things work-related. His camera roll on the phone was incredibly dull with pictures of buildings in various states of erection. His other iPad, though, which I believe was found under his bed, is of more interest to your investigation, I'm assuming,' he said in his best business-like voice.

'Go on,' Matilda prompted.

'Four thousand seven hundred and nineteen images of children and six hundred and twelve videos of children engaged in various forms of sexual activity. We haven't been through them all yet, obviously, but if they're all like the ones I've seen so far, this man was an evil bastard.' He sighed. 'It's days like these when I fucking hate my job.'

Matilda blew out her cheeks. They'd got the evidence they needed to start an investigation into child abuse.

'Bob, I know it's horrific, and it makes me sick myself, but, hopefully, with these images we'll be able to put some perverted men away for a very long time.'

'I bloody hope so. I'm going to put a team together to go through them all, starting tomorrow. It's not going to be an easy task, but we'll keep you updated.'

'Bob, I shall take you and your team out for a meal as a thank-you.'

'You're only saying that because a pandemic is going to close all the restaurants.' He laughed.

'Oh. I'll think of something. Thanks again, Bob. I hope you manage to get your car sorted soon.'

She ended the call and felt the relief lift from her. It didn't matter what Ridley said to her now, there was no chance she was going to allow Ashton and his sick friends to get away with this.

As she passed the murder board, she punched Ashton's picture in the face. 'I've got you, you pervert,' she spat.

Chapter Eleven

Matilda's taxi driver kept trying to engage her in conversation, but she wasn't in the mood. She gave monosyllabic answers and he soon cottoned onto the fact that this particular passenger wasn't a talker.

Her mind was all over the place. She did not envy the forensic team the arduous task of looking through almost five thousand indecent images of children or having to watch those videos. She wondered if any of the twelve adopted by Duncan Shivers, or whoever he really was, were on there. She hoped she wouldn't have to take any of the images to Peter Ogilvy to identify. She liked him. He was a good man. He didn't need to see any of that. She certainly didn't need to see any of that.

Matilda could feel the memory stick Peter gave her burning a hole in her pocket. She hadn't been through everything yet buthad looked at some of the photographs and felt a great sadness sweep over her. These were young boys who had been dealt a poor hand in life. Peter had tried his best to give them some fun, something to look forward to, a realisation that life was what you made it, and that anything was possible with hard work and determination. Then someone like Richard Ashton came along and destroyed everything.

Matilda looked up and saw the taxi had stopped. She looked out of the window and saw her house in front of her.

'Sorry, I was miles away,' she said, digging around in her bag for her purse.

How many times have I said that today?

'You look like you've got the weight of the world on your shoulders.'

'It feels like it sometimes.' She handed him a twenty-pound note and told him to keep the change.

'Have a few glasses of wine, love. I always find the world looks rosier when I'm half-cut,' he said, grinning.

She smiled in return, but it felt pained. 'I couldn't agree with you more.'

The sky was empty of clouds and pinpricks of stars and a bright crescent moon provided the light casting long shadows from naked trees onto Matilda's driveway. A stiff breeze had picked up. Branches were swaying, as if waving, clanking together. She could hear no other noise once the taxi had driven away. Since being shot, her fear of people, the sense of danger in others, had mutated into paranoia, and she saw risk in everything, even her own comforting surroundings.

As she put her key in the lock, she paused, and glanced over her left shoulder. She could have sworn she heard something – someone – among the trees. She chastised herself. She lived on the edge of the Peak District countryside, so of course there was going to be something running among the undergrowth.

Stupid cow.

Her eyes adjusted to the light in the hallway, and the warmth from the central heating wrapped itself around her like a security blanket. She locked the door behind her and shrugged out of her coat. A box was in the corner. She'd ordered a case of twenty-four bottles of wine. Since Adele had moved in, they'd been drinking more, so Matilda had decided to order wholesale. If the country was going to enter a lockdown, wine was something she could not do without.

The relationship between Matilda and Adele had been a strong one until the shooting. They were more like sisters than friends. However, when Adele's son was killed, she hit rock bottom. The killer was after Matilda, yet he'd got her son instead. She couldn't get over that and she blamed Matilda. She wouldn't speak to her, wouldn't see her, and shut everyone out. At her lowest ebb, she took an overdose, trying to end her own life. Fortunately, she didn't succeed. It was only then that she sought help, and she turned to Matilda Darke.

Adele felt she couldn't live alone anymore, so sold the house and moved in with Matilda. Together, they would support each other. Up until then, Matilda's sister, Harriet, had been living with her since the breakdown of her marriage, but had since moved out, and was currently decorating a three-bedroom house in Greenhill, close to their mother.

Matilda's house, a former farmhouse on the outskirts of Sheffield, was far too big for just the two of them, but they had space for when they wanted to be on their own. It worked, and they were as happy as they could be, considering the horrors they'd both endured in the past couple of years.

'I've made a decision,' Adele said when Matilda entered the living room.

Matilda didn't say anything. She dropped herself onto the

opposite sofa. There was an open bottle of wine on the coffee table with a clean glass next to it. She poured herself a large measureand took a big swig. She could feel the cold alcohol as it ran down her body. It was bliss.

She looked at the clock on the mantel. It was a little after seven. She wondered how many people had raised a glass to Richard Ashton at six o'clock.

'I'm going to buy a Porsche 911.'

Matilda remained impassive.

'Did you hear what I said?'

'Sorry?'

'Is everything all right?'

Matilda shook her head as if to clear it of her dark thoughts. 'Yes. Sorry. Just … I'm fine. What did you say? You're buying a what?'

Adele's smile grew. 'A Porsche 911.'

'Have you been watching *The Bridge* again?' Matilda took another drink, finishing the glass in just two large gulps. She shouldn't really be drinking on the medication she was taking for the headaches and anxiety, but an occasional glass was fine, she told herself.

'Well, yes, but I got more for the house than I was expecting. My book is selling very well, and I've been lecturing at the university, too. I've got more money now than I've ever had. It was all going to go to Chris, but now he's not here, what am I going to do with it? Who am I going to leave it to? I may as well spend it, enjoy it, have some fun. That's what Chris would want me to do,' she said, her eyes filling with tears. 'Besides, how cool would it be turning up at a crime scene in a Porsche?' She smiled.

'You'd be like Inspector Morse and his Jag,' Matilda replied.

'Exactly. What do you think?'

'It's your money.'

'I wouldn't look like I was having a mid-life crisis, would I?'

'No. Besides, you're only forty—'

'Language!' Adele interrupted. 'We do not use the f-word in this house.'

Matilda gave a weak smile. 'I think women can pull off driving an amazing car when they get older. It's men who look ridiculous driving a convertible with a bald head and paunch. You should get one. Treat yourself.'

Adele thought for a moment before a smile spread across her face. 'I'm going to get one.'

'Are you going to get a coat like Saga Norén?'

'No. I'm going to develop my own style. Elegant, fashionable and understated.'

'Will you take me to Sainsbury's in it?' Matilda asked.

'I think we may have to upgrade to Waitrose,' Adele smiled.

Matilda sat and watched Adele. She returned to scrolling through her iPad and her lips were moving, so she was obviously talking about cars, but Matilda couldn't hear a single word. Her mind was elsewhere. ACC Ridley had blatantly warned her not to look into Richard Ashton's personal life. Why? She hadn't known Ridley long, but she thought he was a fair man, a good man. Was he involved in whatever Ashton had been doing over the years, or was he being controlled by those higher up the chain of command than him?

'Is everything all right?' Adele asked.

'Sorry?'

'You've spaced out.'

'It's been a strange day.'

'True. It's not every day you see a bloke chewing on his own balls, is it? What do you want for your tea?'

'I can't believe you've mentioned food and castration in the same sentence,' Matilda said with a forced smile.

'Sorry. I'm guessing you won't be wanting sausages or meat balls.' She grinned.

'I've changed my mind. I think you'll look like a sad, desperate cougar in a Porsche.' Matilda grinned as she stood up and left the living room.

For their evening meal, they warmed up the leftover curry from last night. They were in the lounge, bowls of curry on their laps, and watching a film. They were working their way through the Marvel films in chronological order. They enjoyed picking out the plot holes and were currently on *Thor: The Dark World*. Matilda wasn't watching it. She pushed her food around her bowl, her mind going over everything ACC Ridley had said and wondering how dangerous this was going to get.

'Sian officially handed her notice in today,' Matilda said, to get her thoughts away from the investigation.

'You couldn't change her mind, then?'

'No. I'm not giving up, though. She's here for another four weeks. I'll keep working on her. The thing is, I need her, Adele. Her and Christian are the two I rely on the most.' She sighed. 'Maybe that's the problem. Maybe I shouldn't.'

'Of course you should. You're a DCI. You build up the team around you with people you can rely on. I thought that was the point.'

'It is. It's just … I don't know,' she said, slumping further down into the sofa.

'If Sian goes you'll have to find someone else to trust just as much, and you don't think you can do that.'

'How did you know that's what I was thinking?'

'Because since the shooting you've changed. It's understandable, obviously. You can't expect to be shot twice and not change, but you've become more suspicious of people, more paranoid. It'll take years for you to get to where you are now with Sian, with another person.'

'I can't force her to stay, though.'

'No. You can't.'

'So, what do I do?'

'You learn to be more trusting.'

'How do I do that?'

'You know how.'

'Bloody hell, Adele, you sound like Diana Copper-bloody-sodding-Smith. She's always expecting me to answer my own questions.' She placed her half-eaten leftover curry on the coffee table. 'One hundred and ten pounds per session, and I have to ask the questions and answer them as well. It's a bloody racket.'

Adele smiled. 'Go on, then.'

'What?'

'Answer your own question. How do you learn to be more trusting?'

'Pass.'

'There are no passes in this game.'

'The buzzer's gone.'

'I've started, so I'll finish. Answer the question,' Adele said firmly.

Matilda sighed. 'I learn to be more trusting by opening myself up and letting more people in,' she said in a tired voice. She was fed up with going over this with Cooper-bloody-sodding-Smith, but it was true, and she knew it.

'Precisely.'

'Okay, now you answer the question as my friend rather than an armchair psychiatrist.'

Adele thought for a moment. 'You replace Sian with the best person for the job and be an ice-cold bitch, demanding respect, and if they don't like it, they can piss off,' she said, grinning.

'That's not the kind of person I am.'

'Go with your answer, then.'

'Everything's become more difficult since the shooting. I'm worried … I'm …'

'You're worried people are going to leave you. Or they're going to get hurt and move away, like Sian. Or they're going to get killed, like Valerie and Rory.' Adele stood up, went over to Matilda's sofa and sat beside her. She placed her arm around her shoulder and pulled her close. 'The job you're in is not an easy one. Unfortunately, detectives get injured and killed in the line of duty, but it's not an everyday occurrence. You can't blame yourself for Sian's husband turning out to be a killer, or for Zofia getting injured. All you can do is be there for the survivors, to help them through the dark times – just like people like me, Scott, Harriet and your mum help you when you're going through dark times.'

Matilda felt comforted. Not only by Adele's words, but by feeling her presence. It was soothing to feel someone so close again. There were tears in her eyes, but they didn't fall. She was so pleased Adele had moved in with her. She had no idea what she'd be like if completely alone.

'You see, I tell myself I can be strong again, but when it comes to it, I can't.'

'What holds you back?'

'I do.'

'Why?'

'Because I'm worried I'll screw up and someone will get hurt because I've done something wrong.'

'Why would you screw up?'

Matilda took a deep breath. 'Because I screwed up when I saw Sian's husband behind the wheel of that car. I froze and he ended up ploughing into Zofia and paralysing her.'

'You weren't fully recovered from the shooting then. You've come on in leaps and bounds since last autumn. Speaking of Zofia, did you do what you said you were going to do?'

'Yes.'

'Any response?'

'Not yet.'

'Okay, I'm going to go all tough love on you now, Mat. You need to stop the self-loathing and pity crap, and remember the Matilda Darke you were before the shooting. You were gutsy, you had balls, and you used them. You've had a setback, but you've survived. Others haven't. But we keep going, because that's what life is all about. You've still got your balls. Use them again.'

Matilda sniggered.

'What?'

'Peter Ogilvy said I had balls earlier this afternoon.'

'Who's he?'

'Someone who needs my help.'

'Are you going to help him?'

Matilda looked at Adele. 'Too fucking right, I am.'

'That's my girl.'

Chapter Twelve

The night Sian's husband was unmasked as a serial killer of sex workers, Sian left the house she had lived in with her family for more than twenty-five years and vowed never to return. The safety, warmth and security wereruined, and it could never be recaptured. While waiting for the house to be sold, she was renting a shitty three-bedroom terraced house with a shitty square patch of concrete passing itself off as a back garden in shitty Woodseats.

There were two double bedrooms and one minute box room. Danny and Gregory shared the main room, something they complained about on an almost hourly basis, and Belinda had the other. Sian was relegated to a single bed in the box room. Unfortunately, with universities closing due to the pandemic, Anthony had returned home. She relinquished her room for him and was now sleeping on the sofa-bed in the living room. It wasn't ideal. In fact, she hated it. The house hadn't had any serious offers and she was considering reducing the asking price for a third time, even though she needed every penny to set up home again.

She sat on the sofa, legs curled up beside her, glass of wine in hand, and watched what passed for entertainment on prime-time ITV.

The door to the living room opened and Belinda tentatively walked in, sitting beside her mother on the small sofa.

'How did it go at work today?' she asked.

'A man was castrated, and his testicles were rammed down his throat.'

'Oh, my God, really?' Belinda exclaimed. Sian nodded. 'Maybe you should have done that to Dad years ago.'

'Belinda!' Sian chastised.

'Sorry. Did you hand your notice in?'

'Yes,' Sian said, draining the last of the wine from her glass.

'Why?'

'I've told you why.'

'But work is the only thing you look forward to. You're going to be so miserable if you're not a detective.'

'I can't go on working there, Bel. Your father ruined it for me.'

'Has anyone said anything?'

'No.'

'If they were going to gossip or talk about you, they'd have done it by now. They all really love you there, Mum. You don't have to do this.'

Sian leaned forward and picked up the bottle of wine from the floor and poured another large measure into the glass.

'I'm worried about you, Mum. We all are.'

'There really is no need,' she said with a false smile. 'Once the house is sold and we move away, we'll be able to start afresh, and life can begin again. A new chapter.'

'Do you honestly think you'll be happier, just by moving?'

'Yes,' she lied.

Sian picked up the remote and began flicking through the channels. She could feel her only daughter's eyes burning into her.

'How would you feel about changing your name?' Sian asked.

'What?'

'I've been thinking of going back to my maiden name. I don't really fancy being reminded of what your father did every time I see the post arrive or I have to sign my name somewhere. What do you think? We could all change our names. You could even change your first name if you like. I know you've never really been a fan of Belinda.'

'Mum ...'

Sian grabbed her iPad from the coffee table. 'I've been looking up names. I like Selina. Olivia is very popular, too. Actually, when I was pregnant with you it was a toss-up between Belinda and Mary. Any ideas?' She turned to Belinda, her eyes wide and staring.

Belinda swallowed hard. Tears welled up in her eyes. 'I'll think about it, Mum.'

'Okay. Have a think. I've also been on RightMove this evening. I've seen a lovely four-bedroom home in Liverpool for sale.'

'Liverpool!'

'Yes.' She grinned. 'Fresh start. New home. New name. New city.'

Belinda reached out for the iPad, took it from her mother and placed it on the coffee table. She curled up on the sofa and pulled Sian's arm around her. She started crying.

'What's wrong?' Sian asked.

'You're so unhappy, Mum. I wish there was something I could do.'

'I'm fine,' she lied, her voice shaking. 'As long as I've got you four around me, I'm absolutely fine.'

'You're not, though. Are you?'

It was a long while before Sian replied. 'I will be,' she said, barely above a whisper.

Matilda was in her dining room. The printer on the sideboard was whirring away and spitting out photo after photo from Peter Ogilvy's memory stick. Matilda Blu-tacked them all to the far wall. It was almost covered. She stood back and inspected them, wine glass in hand. So many boys. So many lives lost and damaged. She felt emotion rise up inside her but didn't know whether that was the sadness emanating from the photographs or the effects of the wine.

The printer spat out the final picture. Matilda picked it up and looked at the smiling faces of three boys surrounding Peter Ogilvy. He was much younger in the photo, his thick hair a healthy brown. He stood tall and was the picture of happiness.

Matilda pulled out a chair and slumped into it. She could feel a tear roll down her face. She didn't wipe it away. She and James had never wanted children. They were perfectly happy to spend their lives, just the two of them. She often looked to Sian and what she had – a career, a happy marriage, four amazing kids – and wished she could have that, too. But Stuart had ruined that. His life, however idyllic from the outside, wasn't enough for him. Maybe Scott was right. People are selfish. If you have a child, they should become your sole focus. If you can't do that, you shouldn't have them.

'Okay, enough wine for one night,' Matilda said, pushing her glass away. It was empty anyway.

She looked at her watch. It was a little after one o'clock. She heaved herself up out of the chair and made to leave the room, when her mobile starting ringing. The number was withheld. She swiped to answer.

'Hello?' she asked, keeping her voice low so as not to wake Adele.

There was no reply, but, as before, she distinctly thought she could hear someone breathing.

'Hello?' she asked again.

'I need to talk to you.' The voice was quiet, soft, barely a whisper.

Matilda sat back down. 'Who is this?'

'I'd rather not tell you my name.'

Matilda braced herself. She hoped this wasn't someone taunting her. The last thing she needed was more things to worry about.

'Okay. What do you want to talk about?'

There was a long silence. Matilda looked at the phone to make sure they were still connected.

'Richard Ashton,' the reply eventually came.

'Did you know him?'

'You could say that. I've been told you're a fair woman. That you'll listen to me and understand me.'

'I will,' Matilda frowned as she tried to work out if she knew the voice. It was male, but that's all she could decipher.

'I killed him.'

Those three small words sent a shockwave straight through Matilda. She took a deep, silent breath.

'Why?' It was all she could think of to ask.

'He hurt me. He hurt others.'

'I can help you. I really can,' she tried to reassure him.

'I need to kill them all,' he said.

The call ended.

'Hello. Are you still there?' She looked at her phone. The screen was blank.

Matilda relaxed back into the chair and let out a heavy sigh. The police received many calls from cranks during murder investigations. People often claimed to know the killer, to have seen the killer in action, or sometimes professed to be the killer. But there was something about the tone of the voice, the pain and sadness etched into every word, that made Matilda believe everything he said. She'd just spoken to the person who'd castrated Richard Ashton, and there was no doubt in her mind he would kill again.

Chapter Thirteen

Thursday 19th March 2020

Christian was in his bedroom getting ready for work when his phone rang. It was Matilda. When the conversation was over, he slumped on the bed and remained there, staring into space, until his wife came in.

'I'm loving the socks-and-pants combo, but I think your colleagues would prefer it if you put trousers on,' Jennifer said from the doorway, a smile on her face. The new member of the Brady household, a Dalmatian puppy, followed Jennifer into the bedroom. Despite him being bought for Phoebe as a birthday present last autumn, he seemed to have latched onto Jennifer and followed her everywhere.

Christian snapped out of his reverie and looked down. He wondered why he'd gone cold. He jumped up and began getting dressed.

'Is everything all right? You looked miles away,' she said, going into the en suite and picking up the laundry basket.

'Fine. I've just had a call from Matilda. I need to get going,' he said, pulling on his trousers and looking around for his shirt.

'You haven't had breakfast yet.'

'I know. I'll pick something up from ... somewhere,' he said, distracted. 'Where's my ...? Found it.'

'Is everything all right?' she asked again.

'Yes. Fine.'

'I could feel you tossing and turning all night. Is it a new case?'

Christian looked up at his wife, at her expectant face. He couldn't lie to her. He nodded.

'Do you want to talk about it?'

'It's to do with Paul Chattle. We've finally uncovered the abuse.'

'That's good, isn't it?'

He shrugged.

Jennifer placed the laundry basket on the floor and went over to sit next to him on the bed. She took his cold hand in hers. 'Should you really be working on this case?'

'Of course I should,' he said, almost too loud.

'Have you spoken to Matilda?'

'No.'

'I thought you said you were going to.'

'I was ... I ... I haven't found the right time yet.'

'You really should, Christian. She'll not hold anything against you.'

'I know,' he looked at his watch. 'I really should get going.' He stood up and put on his shirt.

'Christian, I'm thinking of keeping the kids off,' Jennifer said. 'Phoebe said she had a bad dream last night. She was really upset, and it took the promise of Coco Pops on a weekday to convince her to tell me. She said she dreamt this virus killed me and you, and she was left on her own. I don't want them going to school.'

Christian stopped buttoning up his shirt. He thought of his children. Phoebe was only eight and she was worried about her parents dying. He had no brothers and sisters and neither did Jennifer. What *would* happen to her and Zachery if they died? They'd end up in care. Just like Sean Evans. Just like Paul Chattle and Guy Grayston.

'No. You're right. We should keep them off school. They'll not miss much at their age. You're not planning on going out, are you?'

'I was thinking of popping to the supermarket and buying a few extra things. What do you think?' Jennifer asked, looking worried.

'No. I'd rather you didn't. I'd prefer it if you stayed in with the kids. It's bad enough me having to go out. Look, go online, do a shop from there and we'll get it delivered.'

'I went online and none of the big supermarkets have any delivery slots left,' she said, fighting back the tears.

Christian sat back down on the bed next to her. He wrapped his arms around her, pulling her into a tight embrace.

'We've got plenty of food in the house for now. We're not going to starve or anything like that. Look, have a fun day with the kids, bake, watch DVDs, play that annoying game that splats cream in their faces, and keep away from the news. I'll pop into a shop on my way home and pick up whatever I can.' He squeezed her, took in her scent and wished he could stay like that for the whole day.

'Mum, Zach's showing me the food in his mouth again,' Phoebe called from downstairs.

That lightened the mood. Christian stepped back and wiped his wife's tears away.

'I really need to go,' he said.

He grabbed his jacket from the end of the bed, his car keys and warrant card from the bedside table.

'I love you so much,' he said, kissing her firmly on the lips.

Christian drove into town and parked as close to the Moor Market as he could. As he walked the rest of the way, he watched as people gave each other a wide berth on the pavements, and many had already taken to wearing masks. He had a box of disposable masks in his car and made a mental note to carry a few in his jacket pocket. Nobody knew anything about this Coronavirus. He wasn't scared, but seeing his children frightened had made him realise how serious this was getting. He'd take the necessary precautions in order to protect his kids.

Christian found Guy Grayston setting up his stall. He was wearing wireless headphones, nodding along to whatever he was listening to, mouthing along to the song. He seemed content, happy, almost. He turned and made eye contact with Christian. His face dropped. He pulled out his phone and stopped the music.

'I had a feeling you'd turn up,' Guy said. 'Before you even open your mouth, let me save your breath. That answer is still no.'

He emptied the last of the oranges from a cardboard box and began to break it up. His face looked hard.

Christian walked closer to the stall. 'Guy, Duncan Shivers didn't exist,' he said, his voice low.

'What?'

'The bloke who came to Magnolia House and took away

twelve boys for adoption. Duncan Shivers. Do you remember him?'

'Yes.'

'He didn't exist. He didn't work for the council. We think he was someone connected with Ashton who was trying to find an easier way to get access to the boys, without raising suspicion after Sean Evans was killed.'

Guy paled and held onto the edge of the stall to keep him upright. 'What happened to the twelve who were taken?' he asked, quietly.

'We don't know. That's what we need to find out. Guy, we've also found thousands of indecent images on one of Ashton's iPads. We can name him as being a prolific child abuser, but we need your help to identify other victims. Peter Ogilvy is helping us.'

Guy's mouth was turned down. He looked as if he was about to be sick. 'They're dead, aren't they?' he asked in a whisper. 'The twelve who were taken. They were abused, then disposed of, weren't they?'

'I really don't know. I don't even want to make any guesses at this stage. Guy, please help us.'

It was a while before he reacted, but he eventually nodded. 'All right. I'll help you. But I don't want you at my flat. I'm sorry, but that's my safe space. It's just me and my dog, and we're happy like that.'

'That's fine,' Christian said, a small smile on his face. 'Thank you.'

On the way into work, Matilda didn't tell Scott about the call from the killer last night, and explained her constant yawning by saying she'd been engrossed in a book she'd been unable to put down. He accepted her excuse and changed the subject to what they could do to make Sian retract her resignation. Matilda was happy to go with blackmail. She'd known Sian for about twenty years and had seen her get up to all kinds of behaviour on a drunken night out. She was sure she could get something on her. Scott preferred physical restraints and keeping her locked up in the HMCU suite during the night and bringing her out during working hours.

Matilda headed to the suite with a smile on her face. It was this kind of levity that was needed, especially when dealing with a dark and disturbing case. Her phone vibrated in her pocket. She took it out and saw it was 'StrangeBob-Forensics' calling.

'Good morning Bob, did you manage to get home in one piece?' she asked. She nodded a greeting to Sian and Finn and headed for her office.

'I did, yes – several hours later than expected, though. I'm afraid I've got some bad news for you.'

'Oh.' Matilda's smile dropped. She shimmied out of her coat and turned on her computer.

'We've had a break-in.'

Matilda stopped. She knew exactly what he was going to say next.

'Several items were either smashed or stolen. Among the stolen items was everything to do with the Richard Ashton case.'

Matilda flopped into her chair. 'I'm not at all surprised. I should have expected something like this would happen. Please tell me you backed everything up.'

'I didn't. I'm sorry, Mat. The iPad with the indecent images was placed in a strong room, though.'

'Then how did they get in?'

'They blew the lock.'

'Jesus Christ!'

'I really am sorry. We're dusting for prints and checking CCTV. Hopefully, we'll find something.'

'You won't find anything. This was a deliberate, targeted attack to stop us finding evidence against Richard Ashton. They knew exactly what they were doing.' She ended the call without saying goodbye and entered the suite, her limbs feeling heavy. She filled Sian, Scott and Finn in on the call with Strange Bob and then told them about Ridley's visit yesterday evening.

'Surely backing everything up would have been the first thing you do,' Finn said.

'You'd have thought so,' Matilda shook her head.

'I know they're short staffed,' Sian said. 'There used to be a team of six working there. Last time I went down, it was just Strange Bob.'

'They're trying to silence us,' Scott said.

'It would appear so.'

'What are we going to do?'

'I have no idea,' she said, pacing back and forth as she thought.

'I'm guessing me and Finn looking up Barbara Usher and Duncan Shivers was flagged and set off a few alarm bells,' Sian said.

'I think so. We're being watched. Okay, we may no longer have physical proof about Ashton, but we've got potential witnesses we can contact and get statements from, and we've still got people we can talk to,to try and track down this Duncan Shivers bloke. The problem is, we can't do it from here and we can't use the police computers.'

'What do you suggest?' Sian asked.

'We can't log anything on the system, as it ends up getting back to whoever, and they're putting the screws on Ridley to put the screws on us. I'm going to have to set up some kind of an incident room in my dining room.'

'But Ridley's going to notice if there's nobody here and we're all at your house,' Finn said.

'Maybe,' Matilda said, a deep frown on her forehead. 'Hang on. This pandemic could work in our favour. Ridley was saying that when the lockdown happens, he and all the other top brass will be working from home. Civilian staff will be furloughed, as will anyone physically vulnerable to the virus. It's not going to be impossible for one or two of us to be missing from the station for a few days at a time.'

Two uniformed officers passed each other in the corridor outside the suite, stopped, chatted in low voices for a few minutes, before heading off in opposite directions.

'The news said this morning that Benny Hill will be conferring with his cabinet over the weekend and possibly calling any lockdown on Monday. Until then we have to look like we're following Ridley's orders. So, we look into Ashton's business life. We talk to his staff and competitors. We look into any dodgy dealings and controversial building projects he had going on, and see where it takes us.'

'I don't like this,' Finn said, looking nervous. 'We're detectives. We're in an elite unit. We should be able to investigate any crime we need to and follow the evidence.'

'I know, Finn. I don't like it either. But there is someone who wants to cover up sexual-abuse allegations and they're willing to go to extreme lengths to do so. We have to play them at their own game. Ashton had nearly five thousand images on his iPad. Six hundred videos, too. I'm guessing others could be identified in those photos. We need to find them.'

Matilda's phone started ringing from her office. She went in to answer it.

'Christian, how are you?' she answered.

'I'm fine. I've managed to convince Guy to talk to us. I'm on my way in with him now.He's agreed to give a statement.'

'Are you talking hands-free?'

'Yes.'

'Break the law, just this once. I need to say something to you in private.'

There was a slight pause and Matilda heard Christian apologising to Guy.

'What's wrong?'

'Forensics was broken into last night. All the Richard Ashton stuff was stolen.'

'Fuck!' he exclaimed.

'I know. Someone is monitoring what we're doing. Listen, I don't want you bringing Guy to the station, in case he's seen.'

'Where am I supposed to go?'

Matilda thought for a moment. 'Go to the house on Manchester Road we use as a rape interview suite. I'll meet you there.'She ended the call.'Scott, go to Watery Street. Adele said she'd do the post mortem first thing.'

'Will do.'

Scott left the suite and Matilda returned to her office to get her jacket and have a few moments on her own, just to get her head in order.

'If this goes high up, and I'm talking chief constables and politicians here,' Finn said to Sian, 'do you think MI5 could get involved in trying to get the case shut down?'

'I don't know, Finn,' Sian said, looking worried.

'They could use all kinds of tactics to silence us. Look what happened to Barbara Usher. That was no random mugging, was it?'

'No. I don't think it was.'

'I don't blame you for resigning, Sian. I might have to consider it myself.'

Chapter Fourteen

Christian explained to Guy that it would be more comfortable for him to give his very sensitive and personal statement away from the clinical confines of a police station interview room, and that South Yorkshire Police had a house on Manchester Road that was designed for victims of rape and sexual abuse, and vulnerable children to give statements. He didn't tell him about the break-in and the evidence being stolen.

They remained silent on the journey. Christian kept looking over, stealing glances of Guy, trying to read his blank expression and wondering what was going through his mind, but he couldn't. He'd obviously spent years perfecting his poker face, showing the world that everything was fine, and life was good. He was like a male version of Matilda.

Christian managed to find a parking space outside the house. He pulled up and turned the engine off.

'Are you taking the piss?' Guy asked.

'What's wrong?' Christian asked, taking off his seatbelt.

'What the fuck have you brought me here for?' he asked through clenched teeth.

'I told you. This house is owned by South Yorkshire Police. We bring vulnerable witnesses here so they're in more comfortable surroundings. It's set up like an ordinary house,' he said.

'This one. This house here with the red door?'

'Yes.'

'You're fucking joking!'

'Guy, what's wrong?' Christian asked.

'This is where he brought me. This is where I was raped. There's no fucking way I'm going back in that house.' He tore off his seatbelt, opened the car door and charged out into the afternoon sun.

Christian sat, open mouthed, and stared at the space Guy had occupied. He looked back at the house. To him, and to the rest of South Yorkshire Police, it was an innocuous-looking building where victims and vulnerable witnesses could feel protected and safe enough to give statements. Now he knew it was also the scene of a vile crime.

Matilda was putting on her jacket. Finn was standing in the doorway, revelling in the fact he'd soon be driving his boss's amazing Range Rover. Reluctantly, she handed him the keys.

'I'll be keeping a very close eye on you, young man,' she warned. 'I want you to channel your inner elderly lady and drive like a ninety-year-old nun on the way to church.'

'Best behaviour. Honestly.' He smiled.

Matilda's phone vibrated in her pocket. Christian was calling. She swiped to answer. Her face dropped at the sound of his worried voice as he filled her in on everything that had just happened.

'Jesus Christ!' she exclaimed, running her fingers through her hair.

'It's supposed to be a safe house for vulnerable people to give their statements in. Only the police know about it,' Christian said, calming down slightly. 'That means a police officer, a serving police officer, was abusing—'

'I'm aware, Christian,' Matilda silenced him. 'How's Guy now?'

'I've managed to calm him down, but I don't know what to say to him. Where am I supposed to take him if I can't bring him to the police station?'

'Shit.' She thought for a moment. 'Take him to my house.'

'Are you sure? Aren't you going to Wakefield Prison?'

'Yes. Sian will meet you there. I'll give her a key.' She ended the call.

'What's going on?' Finn asked.

Matilda ignored him and went over to Sian's desk. She was bent over and rummaging around in her snack drawer.

'A moment on the lips, a lifetime on the hips,' Matilda said.

Sian sat up quickly with a start. 'I was just looking.'

'I'm sure you were. Here,' she said, handing her the keys to her house. 'Go to my house. Christian and Guy will be waiting for you. I want you to interview him with Christian. Don't let him go into the dining room; I've stuck all those photos from Peter's memory stick on the walls.'

'I thought you wanted to talk to him.'

'I do, but I'll just have to rely on your amazing and irreplaceable note-taking skills.'

'I'm still leaving in four weeks, you know.'

'Bugger. It was worth a shot.' Matilda grinned.

'I thought Christian was taking him to the house on Manchester Road?' Finn asked.

'He was. Guy recognised it. He was taken there as a child and abused.'

'By a police officer?'

'It would appear so.'

'Bloody hell!' Sian said, putting her coat on. 'You mean there are actually serving police officers abusing kids?'

'I don't know, Sian, but it would appear there were in the nineties.'

'Oh, my God, we could know them!'

'I'm aware. Look, go and talk to Guy, see what he tells you.'

'That poor man. I'll see you both later,' Sian said, leaving the room.

Matilda turned to Finn. 'Right, then, remember, you're an elderly nun driving to church.'

Finn followed Matilda out of the suite, loudly humming the theme tune to *Top Gear*.

Chapter Fifteen

Christian and Guy were waiting in the car when Sian pulled up next to them. Christian introduced her and Sian made a joke about being given the keys to the house and rifling Matilda's cupboards for the best biscuits. Guy smiled, but it didn't reach his eyes.

Sian led the way into the large kitchen, quickly pulling the door to the dining room closed as she passed. She set about filling the kettle and flicking it on, telling the others to make themselves at home. Neither of them did.

Drinks made, they all sat around the table, mugs in front of them, open box of Fox's biscuits untouched. The atmosphere was heavy. Christian and Sian had conducted many difficult interviews over the years, but in an official interview room with a solicitor present and the recording equipment buzzing away, it gave the detectives a feeling of superiority; they were leading proceedings, and they knew what to say. Now, it was just three people sitting around a kitchen table. There was a huge elephant in the room, and nobody wanted to be the first to acknowledge it.

'It was my birthday yesterday,' Guy eventually said. His voice was cracked and quiet. 'I was thirty-one. I didn't get any cards or presents. Nobody wished me happy birthday. You know, I didn't even remember it was my birthday until I looked at my phone, saw the date and thought it seemed familiar.' He gave a painful smile.

'I bought you a latte, what more do you want?' Christian said, a laugh in his voice to lighten the mood. It didn't work.

Guy's mouth twitched. There was a hint of a smile there, but it was too deeply hidden.

'Didn't Peter Ogilvy wish you a happy birthday?' Sian asked.

'He would have done. I told him years ago I didn't want to celebrate my birthday anymore. In the dark days it was a reminder that I was still alive when I didn't want to be. Now it's a reminder of the time I didn't want to be alive,' he sniggered.

'And you still want to be alive now?'

He didn't answer. 'Everyone deals with things in their own way, don't they? I've tried to live a normal life, but I couldn't. It was too much.'

'How do you mean, too much?' Sian asked.

'When you've had things happen to you, when you've witnessed things nobody should have to see, it sours how you see the world, and other people. My first girlfriend, Deborah, whenever she said she liked me, enjoyed being with me, even when she said she loved me, I didn't believe her. I kept wondering why she was saying these things, what was she trying to do to me.'

'You didn't trust her?'

'No. I didn't. I didn't trust anyone. I still don't.'

'What about Peter?' Christian asked.

'I like Peter. He's a good man, but he's suffering himself. He's tried so hard over the years and been silenced at every turn. Did he tell you what happened to him on the night he reported Sean Evans's murder?'

'No.'

'Get him to tell you. It'll chill you to the bone.'

Sian and Christian exchanged another withered glance. The temperature in the room seemed to plummet.

Sian cleared her throat. 'Are you with anyone at the moment?'

'No. I don't want to be, either. It hurts. It's too painful. I have a dog. There's just me and him, and that's fine,' he said, looking down into his mug. Sian knew his life was far from fine.

'Guy, tell me how you ended up at Magnolia House,' she said.

He looked up, sniffed hard and released a sharp breath. 'I was the product of a one-night stand. My mum was seventeen when she had me and gave me up for adoption more or less straight away, by all accounts. I was in care for a couple of years, then I was fostered, but it didn't work out. I was four when I arrived at Magnolia House, and I was there until it closed in 2001 when I was twelve.'

'What was it like there?'

'Oh, it was a paradise. Parties day and night,' he said with sarcasm etched in his voice.

'Sorry, I didn't mean … I meant …' Sian floundered.

He smiled, and this time it seemed genuine. 'It's okay. I know what you meant. Peter did his best. All the boys went to school as usual, we just had nowhere to call home. Peter tried to make our lives as normal as possible. It's just … well, it was the most abnormal childhood a person could have.'

'The abuse …' Christian struggled to turn the conversation to the topic he wanted to talk about. 'Was it all the boys, or …?' He left the question to hang in the air.

'It's strange. We all knew it was happening, but none of us talked about it. It was like the world's worst-kept secret. We could see in each other's eyes what we'd been forced to go through, how much pain we were in, how much more we'd died inside, but we never said anything to each other.'

'Why not? You could have supported each other,' Sian said.

'When you've been through something so traumatic, the last thing you want to do is talk about it.'

Guy couldn't make eye contact with either Christian or Sian. He was either staring down into his mug or his eyes were darting quickly from one to the other.

'What happened to you? The first time?' Sian asked quietly.

'Peter liked us to play team sports. He felt it would help us grow into better people if we learned to cooperate as a team. When the weather was nice, we'd be out on the grounds playing rounders and football. We had five-a-side matches. They really were fun.' He smiled at the memory. 'But we all took it so seriously. We all wanted to win. Peter saw that in us and created teams and a league. He even got kits for us. This one particular Saturday, I was tackled, and I fell wrong and twisted my ankle. I couldn't put my foot to the floor without screaming. I thought I'd broken it. I hobbled off and was told to sit in the lounge. I was in there on my own when Richard Ashton walked in.

'You've seen him. A big, fat, ugly, nasty bloke. He always wore a suit with a waistcoat, even in the summer when it was boiling hot. You could see he was baking. The sweat would be dripping down his face, but he'd never take his jacket off. He came in to see how I was. He sat next to me, lifted up my leg and looked at my ankle as if he knew how to treat it. It was swollen, but the pain was going. I think it was just a nasty twist.'

Guy took another drink of his coffee. His mouth had dried. He swallowed, which seemed to cause him pain. He licked his lips and continued.

'He said all the right things. He made me laugh. He made me feel better. I didn't realise he'd pressed my bare foot right up against his crotch and was rubbing it with my foot. He said I should get changed out of my dirty kit, that I'd feel better after a shower and putting on clean clothes. When you're a child, you do what the grown-ups tell you, don't you? So, I did. I took off my top and pulled down my shorts and pants. I stumbled. My ankle was aching, and he reached out to grab me and stop me from falling. He sat me on his knee. He … he'd unzipped himself.'

Guy's face was devoid of emotion, but Sian was willing herself not to cry.

'How old were you?' she asked, her voice cracking.

'I was six.'

'Oh, my God!' Sian slapped a hand to her mouth and looked away.

'Bastard!' Christian exclaimed through gritted teeth.

'Did you ever tell anyone?'

'No. Ashton told me not to. When he'd finished, I was in tears. I was in so much pain. He gave me a five-pound note. It was the most money I'd ever had.' He gave a hollow laugh. 'The next time he did it, I kept hoping I'd get another fiver.' A tear rolled down his face, the first display of emotion.

Sian wanted to hug him. She wanted to run around the table, hold him tight, and never let go.

'He started bringing other men round,' Christian said. It wasn't a question.

'Yes. That didn't start until later. I was eight when I was first gang raped, but I was so drunk that I hardly knew what was happening. Don't ask me to give you any details, because I don't know any. I just remember being given alcohol, hating the taste of it, but being told it was a party and that's what people had to drink at parties.'

'How do you know you were gang raped?' Sian asked.

'Because the next morning I had thirty pounds in my pocket. A fiver from each of them. That's all they had to pay to rape a child.'

Sian baulked. She squeezed her eyes shut at the horror of the story to stop the tears from falling. When she opened her eyes and looked at the man opposite her, devoid of all emotion, she felt even worse. He'd been hurt and abused so many times that the gravity of what he was saying no longer had an effect on him.

It was a while before anyone said anything. Sian didn't trust herself to speak without a torrent of emotions falling.

'Why didn't you tell Peter?' Sian asked.

'Because Sean Evans was killed, and that scared us all more than anything else.'

'Do you know what happened to Sean?'

Guy shook his head. 'I saw him. On the night it happened, nothing happened to me, if you know what I mean. I was in a room in the attic with this bloke. It was obviously his first time. I think he was more scared than I was. We just sat there. The next thing, all hell broke loose. There was shouting and panic and voices talking over each other. The door was flung open, and this bloke was told to get out. I was grabbed and practically thrown down the stairs. I looked back, though. I looked into one of the rooms. I saw Sean. He was lying on the bed. Face down. I didn't know he was dead at the time, but there was something about the position he was in that, when he didn't appear for breakfast the next morning, I knew – I knew he was dead.'

'Did nobody ask where he was?' Christian asked.

'Yes. I did. I liked Sean. He was a good lad. I asked Peter many times. He ignored my questions at first. Then told me he'd been adopted. I knew it was a lie. I asked him straight out. "He's dead, isn't he?"Peter couldn't even look at me. That's when we all realised that it could get so much worse.'

Sian felt drained. She felt sick and could perfectly well understand why someone had taken a pair of scissors to Richard Ashton's balls.

'What happened to you when you left Magnolia House?'

'I went to an emergency foster carer. It was only supposed to be temporary until a place could be found for me, but I was there for three years.'

'Then where did you go?'

'Back into Council care until I was eighteen and old enough to look after myself. The council gave me a shitty bedsit in Pitsmoor. I got a job at a fruit-and-veg stall in the Castle Market. Then when the bloke who ran it died, I took it over.'

'Have you ever told anyone what happened to you while you were at Magnolia House?'

He nodded. 'When I was in my late teens, I started drinking and doing drugs. I went to this flat on the Manor to get some MJ and there was police tape all around it. The dealer had been stabbed to death, some kind of drug war thing. Anyway, that was like a wake-up call to me. I went to the doctors and asked for help in coming off the drink and drugs, which they did. And I went to see a counsellor, too. I told him all about being abused and he said I should get some legal advice from a solicitor. He put me in touch with someone and I told him what happened, and the first question he asked me was if I had any proof. I said no. He asked if I had a criminal record. I said yes. Only petty stuff like drunk and disorderly and a bit of criminal damage, nothing huge, but he said my character would get torn apart in the witness stand. My record would be brought up and the defence team would say I was unreliable.And who would a jury believe – a teenager with no qualifications and a drug habit, or a businessman who donated to several children's charities? What could I do?'

'Unfortunately, he was right,' Sian said, looking despondent. 'Ashton would have been able to afford a top team of lawyers to defend him. They really would have convinced the jury you were simply out to get money.'

'I tried to move on. I met Deborah, but that ended pretty quickly, so I thought, "Fuck it, just keep your head down." I got the job with Ian – he's the fruit-and-veg bloke – and he and his wife looked out for me. They helped me move into my flat, gave me some of their old furniture. I had independence, money in the bank and Ian was a laugh.' Guy shrugged. 'That's been my life ever since. Well, Ian died and Margaret, his wife, moved away. I've got my dog. He's all I need.'

Sian smiled. She knew he was lying. He'd convinced himself all he needed was his dog, but he really wanted more. She could see it in his eyes. But she fully understood why he was living the way he was.

'Guy, did all the abuse take place in Magnolia House?'

'No. There were parties at this big house somewhere. Sometimes, after school, there'd be a car waiting at the school gates. He'd offer to take me for a McDonalds or something, but he took me to that house on Manchester Road you were taking me to.'

Sian and Christian looked at each other. Their eyes widened.Sian took out her phone and began scrolling through her emails.

'What was this man's name?' Christian asked.

'I've no idea.'

'What did he look like?'

'He was tall, brown hair, going grey at the temples, swept back, about mid-forties, I think. He wasn't fat, but solid. He had large hands.'

'Any distinguishing features? Scars or tattoos?'

'No.'

'Was he a policeman, do you think?'Sian asked.

'I honestly don't know.'

'Would you recognise him again if you saw him?'

'Absolutely.'

Sian nodded. 'I think he was a policeman. Only a detective would have had access to that house. I think we should be able to identify him,' she said, fully alert for the first time since the interview began, knowing she was getting somewhere.

'But it's my word against his.'

'It doesn't matter. The fact you were at that house in Manchester Road in the first place is enough evidence. Can you remember what car he picked you up in?'

'Yes. It was a white Volvo.'

'Always the same one?'

'Yes.'

'Okay. Not a police pool car, so obviously his own, or he'd borrowed it from a mate. We should be able to track it back to someone, with some digging. Guy, we're not going to let this drop. I'll get justice for you. And all the others,' Christian said firmly.

'You're saying all the right things, but please forgive me if I don't believe them.'

Sian showed Guy a photo on her phone. 'Guy, this house you went to for the parties, was it this one?'

He nodded straight away. 'How did you know?'

'This was Richard Ashton's house. He held the parties in his own home.'

Chapter Sixteen

I t took five people to lift Richard Ashton up onto the scanner bed. He landed with a thud and the scanner groaned under the weight.

'Will he fit in?' Adele Kean asked.

'I hope so,' Claire Alexander said. 'I've never known a body get stuck in one of these before.'

'It'll be like a paper jam in a printer,' Adele said, a twinkle in her eye.

Claire stifled a laugh and went into the small anteroom attached to the scanning suite. Claire was a radiographer who specialised in Digital Autopsies where a body, still in a sealed body bag, was placed into a scanner for a 3D image to be taken. From there, Claire was able to view the body on a computer in different forms: as an X-ray image, skeletonised, or as a clear image, to see where there were any wounds either on or in the body. On screen, she was able to turn the body over and look at it from all angles without the worry of destroying any trace evidence. It was a discreet post-mortem, and rather than replacing the traditional post-mortem, where

Adele would make a Y-incision on the body and take out all the organs to analyse, it was an aid to direct the pathologist about where to look for signs of death or any anomalies inside the body.

The small room was overheated due to the computer equipment and the number of people in the room gathered around the screens.

The results were as expected. There were no stab wounds, no gunshot wounds, but Claire could tell exactly where the cuts had been made to Richard Ashton's genitals.

'The femoral vessels have been completely severed,' Claire said, zooming in on the area.

'Which would account for the amount of blood,' Adele commented.

'He's a big bloke, though. I can't see how the killer would have been able to get in there to cut. He must have held the stomach up with one hand and used the other to cut, but then he's going to need a third hand to hold the genitals. Unless more than one person is involved.'

'Or he's unconscious. That would give the killer more time.'

'True,' Claire said, leaning forward to the screen. 'It's a clean cut. There are no errors or nicks, no false attempts. The killer knew exactly where to cut.'

'Someone with medical training?'

'Not necessarily. I'm sure you can look it up on Google. There's probably even a YouTube video showing you how to castrate your cheating husband,' she scoffed.

'Anything I should be looking at when I cut him open?' Adele asked.

'There's nothing suspicious lurking anywhere, apart from the testicles in the throat.'

They both stared at the images on the screen for a long moment.

'Have you considered writing a textbook? You could definitely use this as a case study,' Adele said.

'*Britain's Strangest Murders*,' Claire said. 'As told through the eyes of a digital pathologist. It's got a nice ring to it,' she said, smiling.

'There's this one, the one with the homeless bloke who had that packet of tissues stuffed in his throat, and remember the woman with the broom handle?' Adele almost winced at the memory.

'Don't! I had nightmares for weeks after that one.'

'It would make a great read.'

'Are you wanting to co-author?'

'We could do.'

'I thought you were writing one about body decomposition with Simon Browes?'

'I am, but my publishers really like me,' Adele said with a wide grin.

'I'll think about it. Now, give me a hand getting him off my scanner. I don't want him breaking it.'

Once Richard Ashton was in the post-mortem suite, Adele broke the seal on the body bag and set about finding out if he had been drugged. Sending a blood sample off to be tested was an expensive process, and there was no sense in wasting money. The Medico-Legal Centre in Sheffield was the first in the country to use Intelligent Fingerprinting to decipher if there were any drugs in the bloodstream.

Adele pressed all ten of the body's fingers in sequence onto a small plastic cartridge for five seconds each. That's all the time it took to collect fingertip sweat, absorbed into the cartridge. The sealed cartridge was placed into a small reader where, within ten minutes, Adele was told whether any illegal substances such as cocaine, cannabis, amphetamines or opiates had been found. In the case of Richard Ashton, the reader returned a non-negative result for opiates. Adele then instructed her technical assistant to take a blood sample and send it off for testing to find which opiate he had swimming around in his body. At least they now knew he had been drugged.

A knock came on the door, and she looked up as DS Scott Andrews hesitated to enter.

'It's all right. It's safe. You can come in.'

'You look like you're performing an alien autopsy,' he said, looking perplexed from the doorway. 'They look frightening.'

Since the outbreak of Coronavirus had been announced, personal protection equipment was being used more in the post-mortem suites. Adele and her team were doubling up gloves, and wearing visors and the newly created personal respirators – a large hood with a visor at the front and a pipe at the back connected to a belt-mounted fan pack that delivered clean air through a fine filter that removed any trace of the virus. It was cumbersome, but necessary.

'You get used to them.'

'How can you breathe properly?'

'That's what they're all about. These fans are blowing in clean air. I can breathe perfectly well.'

'Do you need me to wear one?'

'No. But I'd prefer it if you did mask up.'

'No worries.' He went over to the worktop, where he washed his hands with sanitiser before pulling on a pair of gloves and a face mask. 'It's strange. I still keep expecting to see Lucy.'

Lucy Dauman had been Adele's anatomical assistant before Donal was hired. Last December, Lucy was due to be married. It was all she'd been speaking about for the majority of the year. She was so in love and so happy. Twelve days before the wedding, Lucy disappeared on her way home from work. Two days later, her car was found abandoned in woodland. There had been no trace of her since.

'Yes,' Adele said, a sadness to her voice. 'It's not the same without her.'

'Have you heard from her fiancé?'

'Ben? Yes. I spoke to him at the weekend. He's struggling but functioning. Just about. I don't suppose there's any news.'

Scott shook his head. 'CID would have said. They're keeping the case open, but there's nothing to go on.'

'Something must have happened to her. She wouldn't have run away. I just wish ...' She stopped herself, as she felt tears rise up inside her.

'So,' Scott began, changing the subject, 'I'm guessing that's Richard Ashton on the trolley.'

'It is. Most considerate of him to die just as we've had wider fridges installed.'

'Well, people are getting bigger.'

'Tell me about it. I'm going to have to start wearing a weight-lifting belt to protect my back before too long,' she said, smiling nervously.

'So, what can you tell me about this particular mound?'

'I can tell you he was drugged with an opiate, but not which one. That'll come later. I can tell you something else very interesting, however.'

'Go on.'

'He was cleaned.'

'Sorry?' He frowned. 'How can he have been cleaned? He was drenched in blood.'

'His face was cleaned. As you've said, he was drenched in blood, which means the killer would have been, too. He stuffed the penis and testicles into his mouth and taped it shut, yet there was no sign of blood on his face at all. When the killer had finished, he wiped his face clean.'

Scott frowned. 'What does that mean?'

'You tell me.'

'Well, normally, I'd have said the killer had some kind of feelings towards the victim, some kind of sympathy, but he'd just castrated him. How can you show such levels of violence one moment, and the next you're washing his face?'

'I've no idea. I don't think I want to know, either. I do the science part. You can do the psychological reasoning behind it all.'

'You say he was drugged. What kind of thing could he have been injected with?'

'Scott, do you have any idea how many drugs there are on the market? I'm not even going to attempt a guess. It could be an anaesthetic or a relaxant or even a very strong painkiller. As soon as I know, you'll know,' she said, sounding stressed.

'Sorry.'

'That's okay. I know you need to ask these questions; I'm just preparing you for the long wait ahead, and it will be a long wait, too. This pandemic is causing all kinds of backlogs at the labs.'

'Understandable. Was he tied up at all?'

'No. There's no evidence of any ligatures around the wrists and ankles, no burn marks from ropes, no residue from tape.'

'So, if he wasn't incapacitated, he obviously knew his killer in order to let them get into his house and close enough to inject him with something.'

'Well, don't you usually say the victims know their killers?'

'Stranger murders are rare.'

'It almost makes you wonder if it's worth having a large circle of friends.'

'Bloody hell, Adele, what kind of friends do you have that might consider castrating someone if they have a falling out?'

She looked at him with a twinkle in her eye. 'Dangerous ones.'

'You scare me.'

'Would you like to come and watch while we cut him open? Maybe his stomach contents will give us some clue.'

'I can't wait.'

'I'll just go and change.'

Adele left and Scott wandered into her office to have a seat and think about their conversation. There was obviously a level of trust between the killer and victim, but the relationship between the two was viewed incredibly differently from each side. The victim thought they had an amicable relationship, as he was comfortable getting naked and going to bed with the killer. However, the killer felt such animosity towards the victim that he castrated him and force-fed him his own penis and testicles.

Something caught Scott's eye. He looked up and saw a young man enter the suite and walk towards the wall of fridges. He couldn't have been older than his mid-twenties. His hair was so black, it was almost blue. He was tall and slim, clean shaven with a firm jawline and sharp cheekbones. He should have been striding down a catwalk, not scrubbing up to stick his hands into a fat man's stomach.

'Hello, we weren't introduced at the crime scene. Donal

Youngblood,' he said in a smooth Irish accent, entering Adele's office with his hand outstretched for Scott to shake.

Scott had only seen Donal's eyes behind his forensic suit. He'd spent several sleepless hours in bed last night thinking about him, wondering what the rest of him looked like. Now he knew. And he was far from disappointed.

Scott wiped his sweaty palm on his trousers, jumped up, and took his hand in his. It was a firm handshake and Scott felt a frisson of electricity as Donal's long fingers wrapped themselves around his hand.

'Andrews, Scott – sorry,' he gabbled. He tried to swallow but his mouth had died. 'DS Scott Andrews,' he said. 'Nice to meet you.'

'You, too.' Donal flashed a smile. 'Are you staying for the autopsy?'

'I don't think Adele has given me an option to leave.'

'She's very persuasive, isn't she?'

'It's not the word I'd use.'

'I have to be polite. I've only been here a week.' He smiled again.

Scott could hear his heart beating loudly in his chest.

'Well, must get on. Nice to meet you.'

'Yes, it was. I mean … yes … nice … it was.' Scott blushed and turned away. He couldn't believe how ridiculous he was being. He felt like a schoolgirl experiencing her first crush.

Scott felt something he hadn't felt since he first set eyes on Chris all those years ago, and, suddenly, he felt guilty. Chris has been dead just over a year. He was Adele's son and the love of Scott's life, and now Scott found himself lusting after another man. He felt sick.

'Is everything all right?' Adele asked.

Scott jumped. He hadn't realised Adele had returned. He wiped his eyes and turned away. 'I'm fine.'

'No, you're not. Come on, if you can't tell me, who can you tell?'

'Who's the new guy?' he asked, quietly.

'Sorry? Oh …' Adele looked over her shoulder. 'That's Donal. He joined last week. He's come all the way from Ireland just to work for me. Apparently, I'm *that* well respected,' she said with a grin. The smile dropped when she realised why Scott's manner had changed so rapidly. 'Oh. I must admit, he *is* a very handsome young man.'

'I just felt …'

'He's the first person you've found attractive since Chris died?'

Scott nodded.

'And you feel guilty.'

He nodded again.

'Scott, come here.' She stepped towards him, her arms outstretched.

'You can't touch me, you've scrubbed up.'

'Then I'll scrub up again.' She put her arms around him, but as Scott, at six foot three, towered over her, it looked like he was comforting her. 'First of all, Chris wouldn't want you to be single forever. Secondly, you're a young man, you're not even thirty yet. You could live for another sixty or seventy years. You can't be single all that time.'

'Chris has only been gone for fifteen months.'

'We can't help who we're attracted to. Besides, all you've done is prove to yourself you're still alive and have feelings. You're not an emotionless robot. Look, sit down, let me tell you something.'

Scott sat on the chair and Adele perched herself on the edge of her desk.

'We go through life, and we experience good things and bad things, and that's what shapes who we are. We have different levels of happiness and sadness. You and Chris were deliriously happy and in love, and it's sad and painful that it ended when it did. But you'll adapt and you'll find happiness with someone else. It won't be the same kind of happiness you had with Chris, but it will still be happiness. It's called life, Scott.'

'That's very profound.'

'I read it on the back of a cereal box,' she said, smiling.

Scott laughed. 'Thank you.'

'You're welcome. You know, between you and Matilda, I'm thinking of setting myself up as some kind of agony aunt.'

'Adele, we're ready when you are,' Donal said from the doorway. He smiled a greeting at Scott then walked away.

'He is handsome, isn't he?' Scott said.

'He is. Let's see how handsome you find him when he's elbow deep in stomach contents.'

———————————

Scott didn't join Adele and her team on the main floor of the autopsy room. He acted as exhibits officer in an anteroom behind a plexiglass screen and watched with rapt attention. He'd been in this situation many times before and was no longer repulsed by what he saw. Occasionally, he had to remind himself that he was witnessing a once-living person being cut open, and that was generally when he needed a fresh-air break.

'I'm cutting the abdominal muscles along the sub-costal

margins,' Adele said into the microphone hanging down from the ceiling to record the process. 'I'm separating the stomach from the greater and lesser omentum and tying a double ligature at the cardiac and pyloric ends to prevent the soiling of the abdominal cavity. Donal, could you take this?'

Donal took the heavy stomach from Adele and placed it in a clean tray. He took it over to the bench at the back of the room and cut along the greater curvature, exposing the contents. He baulked at the smell.

'Jesus Christ,' he said in a harsh southern Irish accent. 'It's like he drank a whole brewery.'

As the rancid smell emanated around the room, several technicians reacted. Even Adele had to stand back momentarily.

'There lies your answer, DS Andrews, into how he was incapacitated. Apart from whatever he was injected with, he was also drunk. The blood sample will come back with a high alcohol content, but the smell alone is enough to tell you he was well and truly pissed.'

'Thank you,' Scott nodded.

'Hang on a minute,' Donal said, leaning forward to look at the stomach contents in the tray. 'Adele, can you come and take a look at something for me?'

Scott frowned as he tried to see what they were looking at. As much as he'd rather not study the contents of someone's stomach, his interest was piqued.

'Is that what I think it is?' Donal asked.

'It certainly is,' Adele replied.

'What have you found?' Scott asked.

Adele turned and made eye contact with Scott. 'One of his testicles appears to be among his stomach contents.'

Scott winced. 'Didn't you check there were two of them in his mouth?'

'We haven't analysed them yet. They're in a bag in the fridge. I did assume, as they were removed in a single, clean cut, *en bloc*, they would still be attached to the scrotum by the gubernaculum. Obviously not.'

'Hang on a minute, does this mean Richard Ashton was alive when he was force-fed his testicles?'

'In order to swallow one, yes, he was.'

Chapter Seventeen

It was starting to go dark by the time Sian and Christian had finished chatting with Guy. He'd told them as much as he could remember about the men who had abused him at Magnolia House and the house on Manchester Road, and he brought up the parties like they were simply something he thought he should mention.

'Ashton wasn't too keen on boys when they reached a certain age. By the time I was about eleven or twelve, I was too old for him. I was like something to be passed around. The younger boys, they were more carefully handled, if you know what I mean.'

'Richard liked them young?' Sian asked.

'He liked them tight. When you get fucked as often as I was, you tend to loosen up. I overheard a couple of the blokes once at one of the parties. They said ... they said someone was bringing a four-year-old round for Ashton's birthday.' Guy was becoming visibly upset as he recounted a memory he'd obviously hoped was long since buried. 'I just kept thinking about how small a four-year-old would be compared to Ashton.'

'Did you see this child?'

'No.'

'Do you know what happened to him or who he belonged to?'

'No.'

'Can you give us full descriptions of these men?'

'There's nothing to tell. They were in the shadows. The rooms were very badly lit so we couldn't see them. All I remember is the smell of aftershave and the sound of belt buckles being opened.'

'The man you were with on the night Sean Evans was killed, you said he was nervous, and you thought it was his first time. Can you remember anything about him?' Sian asked, pleadingly.

'He spoke to me. He asked me my name. I told him. I asked him his and he said he wasn't allowed to tell me.'

'Did you see what he looked like?'

Guy nodded. 'The window was small and there was no curtain up. It was a full moon. It lit the room up. He didn't look very old. Maybe in his twenties.'

'So, he'd only be in his mid-forties now,' Christian said.

'Can you remember anything about this man?'

'I think he had a lisp. It wasn't a very pronounced one, but he struggled on an S-word. He had black hair, cut short. He was slim. He blinked hard. His eyes screwed up when he blinked. That might have been nerves, I don't know.'

'That's okay,' Sian smiled reassuringly. 'Guy, Peter gave us a memory stick with photos of the boys from Magnolia House. Do you think you'd be able to go through them, identify them, so we can try and track them down?'

'I'll try.'

'Thank you. Do you want to leave it here, for now, maybe chat again over the weekend?'

'Yes. I should be getting back to my dog, anyway.'

'What breed is he?'

'He's a golden retriever,' he said, his face lighting up. 'Toby.'

Sian found herself smiling back at him.

'I'll drive you home,' Christian said.

'Will you drop me off at the market, first? I want to see what Darren's been up to while I've been away.'

'Sure.'

They headed for the door, then Sian called after Guy.

'I'm sorry, but I have to ask this, Guy. Where were you on Tuesday night after eight o'clock in the evening?'

Guy smiled. 'I was waiting for you to ask me that. The staple question of every crime drama. I close the stall at six every evening. Whatever fruit and veg can't be sold the next day, I box up and take to a food bank. I got home around seven, took Toby out for a walk and was back in my flat about a quarter to eight, and had my tea. That's my routine every night. I don't really have an alibi as such.'

'That's okay. Thank you.'

Guy headed for the car, leaving Sian and Christian in the doorway.

'I don't know what to say to all that,' Sian said. 'I'm exhausted.'

'Me, too.'

'Are you all right? You were very quiet towards the end.'

He nodded. 'Just processing it all.'

'It's a lot to take in.'

'Are you staying on here for Matilda?'

'I may as well. I doubt she'll be much longer.'

Christian nodded again. He lingered, as if he wanted to say something else, but simply gave a weak smile and headed for the car.

Sian watched as Christian drove Guy away. She waved and Guy smiled back at her. It wasn't a friendly smile. It looked painful. She closed the door behind her and leaned against it. She felt empty, yet heavy. She couldn't get her head around why someone would want to have sex with a child. What was wrong with these people? The depravities of men never failed to shock her. Sian was glad she was in the house on her own. Nobody could see her sink to the floor and bawl her eyes out.

Chapter Eighteen

Matilda and Finn were kept waiting in the interview room at Wakefield Prison. She had been in prisons many times in the past, but they still made her nervous. It was all those doors being locked behind her – the fact that she couldn't simply stand up and leave.She was trapped in there. She turned to Finn and saw he was almost white.

'Are you all right?'

'Yes. Fine,' he said, looking, wide-eyed, at his surroundings. 'I was just thinking, somewhere in this building, Stuart's here.'

'As is Steve Harrison.'

'Do you think anyone would notice if we just ran off?' he asked quietly.

Matilda smiled. 'I think, if that was possible, this would be an empty building.'

They both looked up at the sound of a door opening. Nigel Tate was shown into the interview room. He was non-descript: average height, weight, looks, and mousey hair. His eyes were big and wide, staring and piercing.Their gaze almost cut through the glass separating him from the detectives. He pulled out the chair and sat carefully, perched on the edge. His eyes never once left Matilda. He was yet to blink.

There was nothing that stood out about Nigel that made people uneasy around him, but everything about him was creepy, and it was difficult to pinpoint what that was. Knowing his background added to that sense of danger. He looked a mild-mannered man, but he'd lured two boys away from where they were playing in scrubland in the summer of 2003, tied them up and took turns in raping them, making the other one watch. He then spent several hours torturing them. The pathologist counted more than one hundred wounds on each of their bodies. Their deaths had been slow and agonising. Throughout his trial, he sat in the dock, expressionless. When a whole-life sentence was handed to him, he stood up and applauded the judge.

Matilda swallowed hard. She turned to Finn and gave him the nod to begin the proceedings.

Finn cleared his throat. 'Mr Tate, you've been told why we're here?'

Nigel broke eye contact with Matilda and turned to Finn. His eyes lit up and a smile appeared on his pale face. He licked his lips and hitched his chair further up to the glass.

'You're a very handsome young man, aren't you?' he said, his voice low, a hint of a Yorkshire accent. 'I have to say, my tastes have changed over the years. Being in here, I've had to adapt, but I still like them young. How old are you? Early twenties?'

Finn was struck dumb. He was frozen. He couldn't move.

'Mr Tate,' Matilda began, 'you worked at Magnolia House Children's Home as a casual gardener during the nineties. Can you tell me about your time there?'

It was a while before he spoke. He winked at Finn before

turning back to Matilda. 'I was more of an odd-job man really. I cut the grass, did a bit of weeding, and fixed anything that needed doing in the house.'

'How did you get the job?'

'Richard Ashton gave it to me,' he said, smiling.

'How did you know Richard?'

'I'd known him a long time.' The smile turned into a grin. 'We went a long way back.'

Matilda felt unsettled. Nigel's glare, the slow way he spoke and kept licking his lips and glancing at Finn, was perverse.

'I met Richard when I was seven years old. I was at St Jude's then.'

'St Jude's?'

'A kids' home. I'd been there since birth. He used to come and take some of us out on day trips to the beach or the countryside. He used to sit me on his knee, cuddle me, ask me to call him Daddy. And I did. That's what he was like. He was like my dad.'

'Did he abuse you?' Matilda asked.

'No,' he answered sharply. The smile dropped. 'It wasn't abuse. He loved me.'

'Oh, my God,' Matilda said quietly.

'Don't look like that. Don't judge me. So there was a big age gap. Big deal. We didn't care, why should anyone else?'

'Moving on to your time at Magnolia House …' Matilda was keen to wrap this interview up so they could leave. 'You were only there for a couple of years. Why was that?'

'Richard got me a job on one of his building sites.'

'Did you want to change jobs?'

'No. I liked it at Magnolia House.'

'What did you like about it?'

Nigel took a deep breath. He closed his eyes momentarily and a smile swept across his face again. 'The outdoors, the fresh air,' he looked at Finn. 'The boys.'

Finn looked down.

'Did you abuse any of the boys at Magnolia House?' Matilda asked.

'It wasn't abuse; stop using that word,' he snapped.

'What was it, then?'

'I was loving them.'

'Just as Richard had loved you?'

'Exactly.'

'Were you at Magnolia House on Saturday the fourth of January 1997 when Sean Evans was killed?'

'Most likely.'

'Who else was there?'

'Richard Ashton. Some of the boys.'

'Who else?' Matilda asked, getting agitated.

Nigel leaned further in and lowered his voice. 'If I tell you, do you think he'll unbutton his shirt for me?' he said, looking across at Finn and winking again.

'No. He won't,' Matilda replied.

'Then I'm not telling you,' he said, sitting back, folding his arms and pouting.

Matilda turned away. She looked at Finn and saw the horror etched on his face.

'We're wasting our time here.' She started to get up. Finn jumped out of his seat.

'Wait. Hold on a minute. You've come all this way; I'll give you one name.' He looked over at Finn's crotch and licked his lips again. Finn quickly sat back down.

'Go on,' Matilda prompted when Nigel didn't say anything.

'Clive Rowley.'

'Who's he?'

'Justice Clive Rowley,' he said with a smile.

'Your judge?'

'My judge.'

'Your judge was at Magnolia House on the night Sean Evans was murdered?'

He nodded.

'Do you have any proof?'

'Of course I don't have any proof, you stupid bitch. We hardly had a group photo.'

'I think we're done here,' Matilda said, standing up once again.

Finn shot to his feet and headed for the door.

'Matilda Darke,' Nigel said. Matilda stopped and turned back. He was out of his seat, his arms folded across his chest. 'Detective Chief Inspector Matilda Darke. Steve Harrison has told me a great deal about you.'

'Really?' she asked, flippantly.

'Yes. He's got your photo in his cell. You know, I'm not sure if he wants to kill you or fuck you.'

Matilda felt an icy chill run down her spine. Her mouth dried up. She couldn't speak.

'I know what I'd like to do to that young man.' Nigel quickly pulled down his baggy jogging bottoms, grabbed his penis and started masturbating. 'You want some of this?'

The door was opened, and two prison guards came in, took hold of Nigel by the arms and dragged him out of the room, his trousers around his ankles.

'I'll be thinking of you tonight, lad,' Nigel screamed. 'I'd fuck you so hard.'

Matilda and Finn didn't speak until they were out of the prison and in the car park.

'I feel sick,' Finn eventually said. 'I feel violated.'

'I'm sorry, Finn. I had no idea he was like that. If I had, I'd have brought Sian with me.'

'I have never met anyone so vile before in my life. He was evil. We've just looked evil in the face.'

'I know.' She leaned against her car.

'It's going to take more than a scalding shower and a bottle of wine to get that interview off me,' Finn said. He shuddered. 'I can't believe there are people like him in the world. He actually thought he and Richard Ashton were boyfriends. He abused him, for crying out loud! He ...' He stopped when he saw the distressed look on Matilda's face. 'Are you okay? Is it what he said about Steve Harrison?'

She nodded.

'To be honest, I think we should take everything he said with a pinch of salt. I bet he says a lot of things just to get a reaction out of others. He takes delight in making people feel as uncomfortable as possible.'

'Maybe.'

'He's in here for life. He's got nothing to lose. He's also got nothing to look forward to. So, he gets his kicks out of scaring others. He'll be laughing about this interview for weeks to come.'

'Maybe,' she said again.

'So, are we just going to stand in this car park getting cold or are we heading back to Sheffield?'

'Oh. Sorry.' She dug the car keys out of her pocket and tossed them to Finn over the roof of her car.

'We need to add Clive Rowley and St Jude's to our list.'

'I'll get onto it first thing in the morning,' Finn said.

He started the car and reversed out of the parking space. As they were leaving, he looked through the rear-view mirror at the dark Victorian monolith retreating in the distance. He dreaded to think what he would be dreaming about tonight.

Chapter Nineteen

Finn parked Matilda's car on her driveway next to Sian's. She asked if he wanted to come in for a drink, but he said he wanted to get home and try to end this day as quickly as possible. He ordered an Uber on his phone, and one would be at the top of the makeshift road leading to Matilda's house by the time he'd got there. He walked away, head down, dragging his feet.

Matilda unlocked her front door, stepped inside, closed it behind her and leaned against it. She released a heavy sigh.

'How did it go?' Sian asked from the doorway leading to the kitchen.

'Don't ask.'

'Shall I make you a coffee?'

'No. I'll have a very large glass of wine.'

'That bad.'

'Sian, the man was vile. He took a shine to Finn and he was being … actually, I'd rather not go over it again. How did it go with Guy?'

She pulled the fridge door open and smiled as she saw a row of three bottles of wine, perfectly chilled, waiting to be opened and savoured. She grabbed one. If Sian hadn't been there, she'd have hugged it.

'Let's just say I had a little cry when he left,' she said. It was a lie. She'd cried her eyes out and didn't stop for over an hour.

Sian filled Matilda in on the interview with Guy. In the intervening time, while waiting for Matilda to return home, she'd done a bit of digging and discovered the Chief Constable of South Yorkshire Police in 1997 was Tony Bates, now deceased. He'd have been the man Peter Ogilvy reported Sean Evans's murder to.

'Do you know anything about him?' Matilda asked.

'No. You?'

'No. But I think I might know someone who does.'

Sian turned down the offer of a glass of wine and opted for a cup of tea. She said she'd been drinking more than usual since Stuart was sent to prison and if she wanted to lose weight, wine, along with chocolate, was going to have to go. They chatted about nothing in particular, a banal conversation to take their minds off the heaviness of their recent interviews. When Matilda turned to the topic of Sian's resignation, that was Sian's queue to leave.

'Four more weeks. I'll not give in,' Matilda said.

'Three weeks and five days, actually,' Sian smiled.

Matilda waved Sian off and headed back into the kitchen. She refilled her wine glass, picked up her phone and made a call.

'Pat, it's Matilda. Are you busy?'

Pat Campbell was a retired detective who Matilda had asked to help in the search for the missing Carl Meagan over the years. They had never worked together while Pat was on the force, but had become good friends recently, more so since the shooting.

'I'm rushed off my feet, Matilda. I've been to the shop for milk. Then I came back and cried my way through daytime television, and this afternoon I held the ladder while Anton changed a lightbulb. The fun never stops.' Her voice oozed with sarcasm.

Matilda stifled a laugh. 'Wow. I can't wait for retirement if that's what I have to look forward to.'

'If I have to sit through one more episode of *Bargain Cunt*, I may commit murder,' she said through gritted teeth.

'What did you call it?'

'You heard. Please tell me you've called to say South Yorkshire Police are bringing all retired detectives back into the force.'

'You wish. I am wanting to pick your brain, though.'

'If there's anything left of it, you can have it.'

'Do you remember a Chief Constable from the nineties called Tony Bates?'

'I do. Not a bad-looking bloke when he was younger.'

'What was he like to work for?' Matilda asked as she drained half her glass in one mouthful.

'I can't say I had much to do with him. He was a good man, though. He was very supportive of women officers seeking high office.'

'Any rumours about him?'

'Rumours? What's going on?'

'What do you know about Magnolia House Children's Home?'

'Nothing. Why? What's happened?'

'We're hearing rumblings of historical child sexual abuse at the home. A child was killed, and it was reported to Tony Bates yet never followed through. It looks like he covered it up.'

'Ah.'

'I don't like the sound of that.'

'Tony was a good man, but he was a little too fond of the drink. His wife was killed in a road accident in the mid-nineties, and it hit him hard. He started drinking more and, if memory serves me correctly, he got involved with something that finished his career.'

'Finished his career? How?'

'I don't know. There were rumours that he owed money to people who get a little annoyed if you're late with your repayments.'

'Loan sharks?'

'Lower down the food chain than that, I think.'

'So, what happened to him?'

'He passed out drunk in an armchair one evening with a lit cigarette in his hand. He burned to death.'

'Oh, my God!' Matilda exclaimed.

'Yes. Not a great way to go.'

'Any evidence of foul play?'

'Not officially.'

Matilda paused. She dreaded what was to come. 'And unofficially?'

'I happen to know that six months before he died, Tony Bates quit smoking.'

'Was this mentioned at the inquest?'

'I don't know, Mat. I did mention it to the DI in charge and he said that Tony often spoke about quitting smoking, like a lot of people do. They put it down to him lapsing and it being a tragic accident.'

'And what do you think?'

'Matilda, what's going on?'

Matilda took a breath. 'I really don't know, Pat.'

'Hang on, I might know someone you could talk to,' Pat said, thinking as she spoke. 'What was his name? There was a DS who was quite close to Tony. He got a transfer not long after Tony left. Bloody hell, what was his name? Billy something.'

'Joel? Butcher? Idol?'

'Maitland. Billy Maitland. Yes. I remember now. He put in a transfer on the Friday, and we never saw him again. Next thing I heard, he was with Northumberland CID.'

'That was a quick transfer. I don't suppose you know where I'll find this Billy Maitland now, do you?'

'No. I can make a few calls for you, if you like?'

'That would be wonderful, Pat.'

They chatted for a few more minutes and Pat mentioned how she'd been to one of Sally Meagan's restaurants for lunch last week and had a chat with Sally about Carl's recovery. It was slow progress, but they were doing well as a family.

Matilda ended the call. Her mobile was still in her hand when it burst into life again. She looked at the screen and saw it was ACC Ridley calling. She swiped to answer.

'How are things with the Richard Ashton case progressing?' he asked. No greeting, straight down to business.

'Slowly,' she said. 'His neighbours say he was a very private man, and his staff describe him as a veritable Father Christmas.' She hadn't been expecting his call and was thrown by it. What could she say, without giving too much away?

'Any persons of interest?'

'Not so far.'

'I've been told you've been looking into Barbara Usher's death and made enquiries about a Duncan Shivers.'

Matilda winced. 'That's ... right.' She couldn't deny it.

'Why?'

'Their names came up.'

'In what context?' he asked, his questions coming thick and fast.

'To do with Richard's involvement in Magnolia House.' She bit her lip hard. She shouldn't have mentioned Magnolia House. It slipped out.

'Why are you investigating Magnolia House?'

'I'm not.'

'Matilda, I don't know what you're doing, but you need to stop it right now,' Ridley said with urgency in his voice.

She sighed. 'Sir, there are rumours of Richard Ashton being involved in child sexual abuse. The method of his murder strengthens those rumours and I believe his killer may be one of his victims. I also think there is evidence of a cover-up of abuse allegations going back to the nineties.'

'Do you have any solid evidence for that?'

'Not at present. However, we have indecent images found on Ashton's tablet, and the convenient break-in at the forensic unit. Someone doesn't want Ashton's activities being released, which is just making me want to dig further and further. I need to look into the claims in order ...'

'No, Matilda,' he interrupted. 'I told you, in no uncertain terms, that you were not to pursue this line of enquiry, and you have defied me. Now, consider this your final warning. Stop investigating Magnolia House. Stop asking questions about

Barbara Usher and Duncan Shivers, and stop visiting Peter Ogilvy.'

Matilda's eyes widened. How did he know she'd been to see Peter Ogilvy? Was she being watched or followed or tracked? She couldn't think of anything to say.

'Do you understand me, Matilda?'

Matilda didn't say anything.

'I asked you a question, DCI Darke,' Ridley stated firmly.

'I understand,' she said, trying to sound confident, but her shaking voice belied her feelings.

The call was ended. The room descended into silence and Matilda stood there, phone in hand, feeling more scared than she had done in a very long time.

The vibrating of her mobile phone on the bedside table woke Matilda up a little after one o'clock. She winced at the brightness from the lamp as she flicked it on and picked up her phone. The display was a mobile number, but not one stored in the phone's memory. She wondered if it was the killer again. She swiped to answer.

'Hello?'

'Matilda. It is Matilda, isn't it?'

Matilda frowned. 'Yes. Who's this?'

'It's Jennifer Brady. Christian's wife.'

Matilda visibly relaxed. 'Of course. Jennifer. How are you?'

'Erm, slightly worried. I'm so sorry for calling you but I didn't know what else to do.'

A feeling of dread swept over Matilda. She gripped the phone tighter. 'What's happened? Is it Christian?'

'I don't know. He hasn't come home.'

'What?' She looked at the time on the phone: 01:12.

'I spoke to him at five o'clock this afternoon. Well, yesterday afternoon, I suppose. He said he'd be home at the usual time. I've tried ringing him, but his phone keeps going to voicemail. I've left message after message. I don't know what to do.' Jennifer's voice was getting more emotional with every word she quickly spat out.

'Okay, Jennifer, calm down. If anything had happened to him, I'd have been told. Leave it with me, I'll make a few calls and—'

'Hang on,' Jennifer interrupted. 'There's a car just pulled up on the drive. Hang on one moment, Matilda. Yes, it's him. He's just got out of the car. Oh, my goodness, what a relief,' she said. 'I'm sorry to have woken you.'

'That's okay. Jennifer, ask him—'

'I'd better go. I don't want him thinking I'm a neurotic. Goodnight.'

Jennifer ended the call. Matilda sat up in bed with the phone still pressed against her ear. She hadn't seen Christian since she left for Wakefield Prison before lunch. Sian had mentioned he'd been quiet during the interview with Guy, but it was understandable, given what they'd both heard.

Before settling back down and attempting to sleep, Matilda had to remake her bed. The fitted sheet had come away at three corners. She often thrashed about during her sleep. Whatever dark dreams swam around her mind manifested themselves in physical forms. The state of her bed most mornings made her glad she couldn't remember her nightmares. She climbed back into bed, thumped the pillow a few times and slumped onto it, pulling the duvet up under her chin. She was wide awake.

There was something wrong with Christian. He was

holding back, and Matilda had no idea why. She turned over, pulled the duvet over her head, and hoped complete darkness would dull some of her senses so she'd fall asleep. It was a trick she'd tried many times and her mind was onto her. Sleep would not claim her now. There were too many dark thoughts racing around her head, and they all involved Christian.

Chapter Twenty

The door to the HMCU suite was closed and a chair had been strategically placed in front of it. Should someone try to enter, the door would bang into the chair and alert Matilda, Christian, Sian, Scott and Finn, who were crammed into Matilda's office, where she could speak to them without the worry of them being overheard by anyone passing in the corridor outside.

'Ridley called me again last night to warn me off investigating the child sex-abuse allegations,' she said. She was sitting at her desk, with Sian on the seat in front of it. Christian was by the window and Scott and Finn were on the floor like children in a school assembly.

'What are you going to do?' Sian asked, looking worried.

'Ignore him, obviously.'

'I couldn't sleep last night, thinking about what Guy told us,' Christian said, glaring out of the window. 'When I did, I had such bad dreams. We think we've been through a lot over the past couple of years with the shooting and everything, but Guy and the others have been living with this for more than twenty years.'

Matilda couldn't take her eyes off Christian. Where had he been last night until one o'clock in the morning? There was something different about him that she couldn't put her finger on.

'I didn't sleep too well, either,' Finn said, giving an exaggerated shudder. 'You know, I believe in redemption and prison reform, but there are some people who are simply beyond help, and I think Nigel Tate is one of them. Creepy bastard.'

'Just make sure you stay on the straight and narrow,' Scott said, putting a hand on his shoulder. 'The last thing you want is him cuddling up to you every night in your cell,' he said, grinning.

Finn shook off his hand. 'That's not even funny, Scott.'

'There are several tasks we need to do,' Matilda said, bringing the conversation back to point. 'We need to discover where Sean Evans is buried. I asked Adele if she has any unidentified bodies at Watery Street and she doesn't have any matching Sean's description. However, if they hid his body, they could have dumped it outside her boundary. She's going to make a few discreet calls. Now, Guy said he was taken to some parties. Sian showed him a photo of Ashton's house and he identified it as where they took place.'

'Ashton had sex parties in his own house. That's a bit risky, isn't it?' Scott asked.

'I thought that myself, but the more I thought about it, the more I realised not. We don't know who else was involved in all this. We know that Peter Ogilvy went to Chief Constable Tony Bates in 1997 to report Sean's murder and it was covered up. Was Bates himself involved in the abuse or did it go higher than him? Either way, I think it's safe to say there was someone within South Yorkshire Police who attended the parties. Ashton was basically saying, "Yes, you can use my house, but I know your names. If I get caught, I'm taking you down with me."'

'Looking at it like that, it makes sense,' Scott said.

'But door-to-door enquiries didn't mention anything about truck-loads of boys turning up at the house,' Finn said. 'There's an old woman who lives opposite who is practically a one-woman neighbourhood watch. She definitely would have noticed.'

'I know. So, Scott, you and Finn go back out to Ashton's house. Look for a back entrance through the garden, have a good look around the house for … I don't know, secret rooms or something. The bloke was a property developer. I'm guessing it wouldn't take much to put a false wall up or something.'

'Will do,' Scott nodded.

'Sian, I need you to trace those twelve boys Duncan Shivers supposedly adopted. However, try not to raise suspicion. We can't have any of this getting back to Ridley. He already knows you made calls about Barbara Usher to the council.'

'So, how do I do it, then, without contacting the council?'

'I don't know. You seem to know loads of people; don't you have someone in the council you can ask?'

'Surprisingly, no, I don't. Leave it with me, though. I'll see what I can do.'

'Thank you,' Matilda proffered a smile.

'We could do with tracking down the other boys of Magnolia House,' Scott said.

'Peter doesn't know where they are. Neither does Guy,' Matilda said.

'Can't we put out an appeal?' Finn asked. 'Not about the sex abuse, obviously, but we could use the cold case of Sean Evans's murder. Ask for anyone who was a resident of the home at the time to come forward with any information.'

'No. It's a fishing expedition. If this gets to court, and high-profile men are in the dock, it will look like we were witch-hunting. The victims have to come to us.'

Christian kicked the wall hard. '*Fuck!* They're going to get away with it, aren't they?' he asked, anger evident in his voice. 'Twenty-odd years of that fat bastard and his perverted mates having their disgusting fun with those poor lads, and everyone's turned a sodding blind eye.'

'Christian, that's not going to happen. We will not let this drop, I promise you, but there's nothing we can do without evidence. Look, go to Guy, ask him to identify the lads from the photos Peter gave me, and track them down. Bring me the evidence and I'll make sure the world knows about it.'

The atmosphere in the small room was heavy as the tension mounted between Matilda and Christian. Nobody said anything, for fear of adding fuel to the flames. The silence lingered. Matilda's phone ringing made them all jump. She looked at the display.

'That's all I bollocking need. Danny cocking Hanson.'

'We'll leave you to it,' Sian said, grabbing the opportunity to leave and ushering Finn and Scott out of the room. As soon as the door was open, Christian stormed out.

Danny Hanson was a journalist who started out his career on the *Sheffield Star*, the city's local newspaper. He managed to get a few good stories, thanks to tailing Matilda, and soon found himself in front of the camera as the North of England correspondent for BBC News. Following his footage from the shooting fifteen months ago, he was promoted to presenting the news in the afternoons as a freelance presenter. His sleazy career was on the rise, all thanks to his dogged pursuit of Matilda Darke.

She took a deep breath and swiped to answer.

'Good morning to you, Detective Chief Inspector,' he said in his most cheerful and annoying voice. 'How are you?'

'Fine,' she replied.

'Really? All back to normal? No nightmares or flashbacks?'

'What do you want, Danny?'

'What makes you think I want something?'

'Oh, you mean you've just called for a friendly chat? Okay. So, have you planted you sweet peas yet?'

'You're a funny woman, Matilda. I've read about Richard Ashton being found dead yesterday. His staff are remaining tight-lipped, but a couple of his neighbours were very forthcoming. They like having someone off the telly knocking on their door asking questions.'

'You're in Sheffield?'

'Of course. Love it here.'

'Job at the BBC didn't work out?' she said with a smirk.

'I was presenting over the weekend. Didn't you see me?'

'No, Danny, I didn't. If I want to see a massive cock on TV, I'll subscribe to the porn channels.'

Danny gave an exaggerated laugh. 'That's a good one. Speaking of cock, is it true Mr Ashton had his cut off?'

'Who told you that?'

'So it *is* true.'

'No. I'm just asking who told you and where they got such a ridiculous story from.'

'So, the fact that his bedroom was dripping in blood, and he had his mouth taped shut, is all false, then?'

'There was a fair amount of blood and Richard Ashton is dead, but that's all you're getting from me. Statements to the press are released in the usual way, Danny. No preferential treatment for tossers.'

'You do realise I record all my calls, Matilda?'

'Oh, you should have said. I'd have called you a wanker, had I known.'

She ended the call and slammed the phone down on her desk. She went out into the suite. Finn and Scott were just leaving.

'Danny Hanson has been speaking to someone who told him Ashton was castrated. I know it's none of you, so it might have been one of Ashton's neighbours. Hanson is in Sheffield, so look out for him. Don't talk to him and don't mention this case to anyone – not even your Stephanie, Finn.'

'Don't worry. All we seem to be talking about at the moment is house hunting and pandemics.'

'I talk to myself a lot,' Scott smiled. 'But I promise not to talk about my work.'

Finn was putting on his jacket, ready to leave. 'Oh, by the way, I've done some digging into what Nigel Tate told us yesterday,' he said to Matilda.

'Go on.'

'St Jude's Children's Home doesn't exist. I've also looked into his file, and he was raised by an aunt. He had a very disturbed childhood. More bad dreams for me tonight. I've emailed you the highlights, if you're interested.'

'What about the judge?'

Finn smiled. 'He's dead now, unfortunately, but his wife was very helpful when I called her first thing. She even emailed me a photo of his passport. Every Christmas and New Year, the Rowley family went to their villa in Portugal. In 1997, they didn't get back to Sheffield until January the seventh. There was no way he could have been at Magnolia House on the night of Sean's murder on the fourth.'

'So, Nigel Tate was a big liar, then?'

'It would appear so.'

'I'm not surprised. We'll cross him off our list of useful people.'

'Thank God for that.'

'Are you all right now?' Matilda asked.

'I will be once I've washed my brain in bleach.' He smiled, before turning and leaving the room with Scott.

Sian looked up from her computer. 'And, are you all right?' she asked Matilda.

'No. I don't think I am,' she replied, a wave of sadness drifting over her.

'Oh. Is there anything I can do?'

'You can retract your resignation.' She smiled.

'Oh, piss off,' Sian grinned, throwing a small packet of Minstrels at her.

Chapter Twenty-One

Scott and Finn let themselves into Richard Ashton's back garden via the side gate rather than going through the house. The large expanse of lawn had the wild look most gardens get after a winter of being left to the elements. Yet, an early spring, and a warmer one than usual, was already causing signs of life to return to this suburban garden. Dots of colour were trying to poke their way through the soil. Despite the uncertainty in the air because of the encroaching pandemic, nature was continuing to thrive, as it always did.

'It's a gorgeous house,' Finn said, looking back at the Victorian stone-built property.

'Until you realise the horror that could have gone on in there,' Scott added.

'Could you live in a place that had such a dark history?'

'Absolutely not,' Scott replied quickly.

'Why not?'

'I don't think I could relax in a bedroom, knowing this was a room where children were raped on a regular basis. Would you be able to have eight hours' sleep a night with that going through your head?'

Finn thought for a moment, stopping to look back at the house that suddenly no longer seemed beautiful in its design, but had changed before his very eyes into a dark monolith that contained the trapped screams of the innocent. He quickly turned away and broke into a trot to catch up with Scott.

'Stephanie likes new-builds, but I think they lack character.'

'Houses make their own character by the people who live in them.'

'That's very profound,' Finn said with a chuckle in his voice.

'I have my moments,' Scott grinned. 'Speaking of being profound, answer me this, as a student of psychology ...'

'I'm studying criminology,' Finn interrupted.

'It's an ology, it'll do me. Why does someone sexually abuse children?'

'Bloody hell, Scott, can't you start me with an easier question?'

Towards the back of the garden there was a pub-style wooden table and chairs. Scott swung his leg over the bench and sat down. He invited Finn to join him on the other side and glared at him, prompting an answer.

Finn sighed. 'The simple answer is that there is no simple answer to your question. Each person who sexually abuses a child will have a motive that is unique to them. For the most part, I'm not sure they even know the reasoning behind it.'

'Isn't that a cop-out?'

'No. Some abusers will know what they're doing is wrong but will continue to do it because it's a need they're fulfilling. Some will believe what they're doing is perfectly fine, and really they are showing love to the children.'

'Love?' Scott pulled a sour face of disgust.

'I know. It sounds dark to us, because that's what it is, but to the abuser, they're loving the child and showing it in the most powerful and intense way possible.'

'But you can't sexually love a child. Love is a two-way street. And a child cannot consent. It's *always* rape.'

'Yes, but an abuser won't see it like that. Remember what DCI Darke said about Ashton being a member of a paedophile liberation group in the eighties? They wanted to have the law of age consent removed so they could openly have relationships with children. They saw it as a perfectly acceptable way of life. And that's what Richard Ashton was doing to Nigel Tate.'

'But consent has to work both ways?'

'Yes, it does. But that's a greyer area, isn't it? That's why the defence of a rapist is nearly always that the victim gave their consent at the time, until things went too far, or they regretted the act later. It's one person's word against another's.'

Scott blew out his cheeks. 'What do you think Ashton's motive was?'

'I think it was power. He couldn't get the power he had in his business life in any personal relationships because women weren't attracted to him, due to his size, so he turned his attention on those who are vulnerable, who were unable to resist him. For him, it was the ultimate power trip.'

'Do you think?'

'I do,' he nodded. 'Obviously, we can't ask him, and that's only my best guess, but it's what all the signs point to.'

'Surely people realise what they're doing is wrong?'

'Oh, absolutely. Abusers can give all the defence they want, but the law is very clear, and they know that. Some abusers are unhappy about what they're doing and will hate themselves for doing it, but continue.'

'Why? Why do something that isn't making you happy?'

'I don't know, Scott. Maybe there's something missing from their life they're trying to fill. Maybe they were abused themselves as a child and are wanting to understand why it happened. There are no hard-and-fast answers to these questions.'

A stiff breeze blew, and Scott shivered. He stood up from the bench. 'Come on, there's obviously no back way into the house from here.'

'Where are we going now?'

'Into the house. I want to go up to the attic.'

'Why?'

'I'll know when I get there.'

Scott stormed through the house with his usual long strides, his heavy designer shoes loud on the wooden floors. He took the first set of stairs two at a time, opened the door to the attic and stopped. He looked up into the darkness. There was a fusty smell. People didn't come up here often and fresh air rarely got in. He swallowed hard and as he gripped the banister and slowly ascended, he felt as if he was stepping into the unknown. Finn followed close behind.

The layout of the attic rooms had changed since the house was built at the beginning of the twentieth century. What was once two rooms, possibly for staff who served the master and mistress of the house, was now divided up into four small rooms. Each of them was empty of furniture and there were no blinds or curtains up at the windows, no lampshades hanging from the ceiling, just a naked bulb. The carpet was once cream, but the colour had long since been bleached by the sunlight. There was a dark and heavy atmosphere in these rooms. The ceilings were low and Scott had to bow his head to get through the doors. He stood in the middle of one of the tiny rooms and looked around him.

'It doesn't take someone with a criminology degree to work out what went on up here, does it?' he asked, his voice echoing off the walls.

'I'm afraid not,' Finn answered, crestfallen.

Scott knocked on one of the walls. It was hollow. 'Why would you purposely make these rooms so small?'

'We both know the answer to that.'

'You couldn't get more than a double bed in here.'

'That's all that was needed.'

'Sick bastard,' Scott spat. 'He had his mates up here, didn't he? Go upstairs. There's a boy on each bed. Help yourselves.' He shook his head and went over to the window where he placed his hands on the sill and looked out into the sunlight.

Finn didn't say anything. He looked around him, disgust etched on his face. There was nothing to see, but his imagination filled in the blanks.

'You can actually feel the sadness from the room leaching into you, can't you?' Finn asked, hugging himself. 'Why didn't anyone stop this from happening? How long do you reckon all this was going on for?'

'I think I may be able to answer that question for you, Finn,' Scott said, turning from the window and smiling.

'What? How?'

'Take a look across the garden at the house opposite.' He moved back so Finn could get a clear view.

'What am I looking at?'

'I can see right into the opposite attic room. Whoever lives there has got a model railway set on a large table. And if I can see right in there, they can see right in here.' He grinned.

———————

Scott and Finn knocked on the green door of the detached house opposite Richard Ashton's and stood back. A dog barked from within. Finn looked up at the Victorian building and marvelled at the large windows and orange brickwork.

'They knew how to build houses in the old days, didn't they?'

'How's the house search going?' Scott asked.

'Not good,' Finn pulled a face. 'There isn't much available we like and can afford. A couple of weeks ago, we went to look around a new-build. It was one of Ashton's. I wasn't impressed.'

'Why not?'

'It was pokey. Tiny gardens. Overlooked by the neighbours. They're certainly not worth the asking price.'

Scott knocked again.

'Whereabouts are you looking?'

'Somewhere not as busy as Heeley. We'd like a decent-size garden, too, but we're not really bothered about where. I like Dore, but I don't like their prices.' He smiled.

The front door was eventually opened by a man in his late thirties. He wore blue jeans and a white shirt, open at the neck. He had dark-brown hair that was in need of a trim – it flopped down, almost covering his eyes – and matching designer stubble adorned his thin face.

'Good morning. I'm Detective Sergeant Scott Andrews. This is DC Finn Cotton from South Yorkshire Police. We're investigating the death of one of your neighbours. Would it be possible to ask you a few questions?' They both held up their warrant cards.

'Of course. Come on in.' He stepped back and let them enter.

'Can I take your name please, sir?' Finn asked.

'Yes. It's Anthony Rivers.'

'And do you live here on your own?'

'Yes. I'm recently divorced.'

He showed them into a large, neat and tidy living room with a bay window and high ceiling. Framed prints of trains were on the walls and built-in bookcases were crammed with books on train journeys, famous trains and model trains. The scent of furniture polish hung in the air.

'Who's died? Is it Mr St Clare?'

'No. It's not. Am I all right to sit?' Scott asked.

'Yes, of course. Sorry, I should have said. You've completely thrown me. You don't expect the police to turn up on your doorstep.'

A dog started barking again.

'Can you give me a few moments, I'll just let him out into the back garden,' he said, scurrying from the room.

'Nice room,' Finn said, looking around. 'Love these tall ceilings.'

'He certainly likes his trains,' Scott said, nodding to the bookshelves either side of the fireplace. The pictures on the walls were prints of the Orient-Express and the Flying Scotsman.

The man came back into the room. 'Sorry about that. He gets excited when people come round.'

'That's okay.'

'He's only one, so he's still in the learning stages. You

mentioned someone had died,' he said, sitting on the edge of the armchair by the hearth.

'That's right. The man in the house over your back garden. Richard Ashton. Do you know him?'

The friendly smile dropped. 'I know of him. He owns Ashton Developments.'

'You've never met him?'

'No. I can't say I have. I know what he looks like, obviously. You can't miss him, can you?I heard on the radio he'd been found dead at his home. I must have been out when you were going door to door. I had a card popped through my letterbox. I'm guessing you'll want to know if I saw anything suspicious.'

'That would help.'

'Not that I'm aware of. When did he die?'

'Wednesday evening.'

'Wednesday evening,' he mused. 'I finished early on Wednesday as I had a dental appointment. They kept me waiting in the surgery and I didn't get home until gone seven o'clock. I struggled to eat a bowl of rice pudding, then I watched a couple of documentaries on TV, a bit of news, and had an early night.'

'You didn't see or hear anything out of the ordinary?'

'No. I'm afraid not. Sorry.'

'How long have you lived here?'

He thought for a moment. 'Coming up to seven years, I think.'

'Mr Rivers,have you heard or seen anything strange coming from Richard Ashton's house, either recently or in the past seven years?'

Anthony frowned. 'Strange? In what way?'

'Loud noises, perhaps. Music. Parties, that kind of thing.'

'No, I don't think so,' he answered quickly. 'These walls are pretty thick. My back garden overlooks his back garden and they're quite long.'

'What about when you've looked out of an upstairs window? Have you seen anything in his house?'

'No. I'm not in the habit of prying on my neighbours,' he said with a crooked smile.

'You like trains, I see,' Finn said.

'Yes. It's a hobby of mine. I was planning on going on the Orient-Express later this year, but it's been cancelled because of this virus.'

'I'd love to go on the Orient-Express,' Finn grinned. 'It's a trip for the bucket list.'

'Absolutely. I'm currently painting a model of the Orient-Express. Beautiful train.' His face seemed to brighten when he spoke about trains.

'If we could get back to Mr Ashton,' Scott said, raising his voice slightly. 'Did you ever see anyone going into or out of his house?'

'No. I can't see his front door from here. I can only see the back of his house.'

'Is there a way to get onto his property from the back?'

'I'm not sure.'

'Is there a way to access your property from the back?'

'There was when I moved in, but I had it blocked off. How did Mr Ashton die? Was it a burglary or something? Should I be worried?' he asked, a hand to his chest.

'No. We believe it was an isolated incident.'

'Oh, good. Well, not good, obviously, but you know what I mean.'

'What's it like around here?' Finn asked. 'Quiet neighbourhood?'

'It's quiet enough. You hear car doors slamming of an

evening and some of the houses have young children in, you hear them playing out in the gardens, but it's quiet enough,' he said with a smile.

'My wife and I are house hunting at the moment,' Finn said by way of an explanation for his question.

'Oh. Well, this is a nice enough area. Not much parking though, especially when—' He stopped himself.

'Especially when what?' Scott asked.

Anthony looked sheepish. 'I was just going to say, especially when people have guests round. You know what people are like, parking wherever they like.' His smile grew, but his eyes looked nervous, darting rapidly around the room.

'Did Richard Ashton have a lot of guests?'

'I wouldn't know.'

'So, why have you gone all shamefaced when talking about parking?'

'I haven't.'

'You have.'

Anthony took a deep breath and calmed himself down. 'Look, I know what you're hinting at. I know what you want me to say, but I'm not saying anything. I refuse to get involved.'

The atmosphere in the room grew tense as all three remained stock still, like mannequins in the men's department at John Lewis.

'Get involved in what?' Scott asked, shattering the silence.

Anthony pressed his lips together and looked down. He suddenly looked very nervous.

'Is there something you want to tell us?' Finn asked.

'What do you know, Mr Rivers?' Scott asked.

He didn't say anything, but sank deeper into his armchair.

Scott dug around his inside jacket pocket and took out a

card. 'I'll leave you my contact details. If you think of anything, give me a call.'

'I haven't seen anything,' Anthony said, unconvincingly.

'Well, you never know, something might come to mind,' Scott said, dropping his card on the coffee table.

Anthony nodded. 'You could try Mrs Jackson next door. She's always out pottering in the garden. She might have seen or heard something.'

'Thank you. We will.'

'Lying bastard,' Scott said through gritted teeth as he and Finn made their way down Anthony's front path, back to the car.

'He definitely saw something going on in Richard's house, didn't he?'

'Of course he did. Good work, bringing up the house-hunting thing. That's what tripped him up.'

'I'd love to say it was a deliberate ploy, but I was just wondering about the neighbourhood.' Finn turned back to look at the house. He saw Anthony in the window. 'I suppose you can't blame him for not saying anything. Would you really want to get involved in a case of child abuse if you didn't have to?'

'No, but if you see something, you should report it.'

Finn opened the front passenger door and was about to lower himself into the car when he stole a final glance at Anthony's house. He was still standing in the window, looking at them. 'Maybe he did. Maybe he called the police, and it was ignored, hushed up. We're seeing that a lot in this case.'

'It's possible, I suppose.'

'Would you trust the police when they eventually started

asking questions? I don't think I would. In fact, the more we find out about this case, I'm trusting them even less.'

'But you are the police.'

'Don't remind me,' Finn said, folding his arms and turning away.

Chapter Twenty-Two

Matilda was heading for the car park when her name was called out. She turned and saw a tall man around the same age as her standing at the open double doors. He was wearing a fitted black suit, a white shirt and a pink tie. He looked smart and dapper with his dark-blond hair slicked back.

'It is DCI Darke, isn't it?'

'Yes.'

'I don't get a chance to meet detectives very often, I'm afraid to say. Kenneth Burr,' he introduced himself, holding out a hand for her to shake, 'Police and Crime Commissioner.'

'Of course. Nice to meet you.'

He smiled and immediately whipped his hand back. 'Sorry, we shouldn't be shaking hands, should we?' He clasped his hands together and bowed. '*Namaste.*'

Matilda smiled and copied his greeting.

'Are you busy?' he asked.

'I'm always busy.'

'I know the feeling. Would it be possible for us to have a private word?' he asked, lowering his voice.

'Of course.'

'I'm not sure if you smoke – I don't – but I have the sudden urge for a fag break. Shall we go outside?'

Matilda frowned. 'Fine.'

Burr headed for the car park and Matilda followed, her frown getting heavier, wondering what the PCC could possibly want with her. She had noticed she was deeply mistrustful of new people she met, lately. In her job, it was a good quality to have, but since the shooting, it was leaching over to her personal life. With Ridley's constant questioning and his verbal warnings, she didn't trust him, and she was wondering about Kenneth Burr, and she'd only known him for five seconds.

Officially, the role of the Police and Crime Commissioner is to oversee local policing. Unofficially, they are politically affiliated fall guys. Any success South Yorkshire Police achieves, the government can claim it as their own. Any failures, and the government will maintain a wide berth and the PCC will carry the can. Ask any detective, and they'll tell you the PCC is a complete waste of resources.

Kenneth Burr hadn't been in the role long, barely six months, and Matilda only knew his name. She'd never met him, never had any reason to, and assumed, like his predecessors, their paths would never cross. This one seemed to want to involve himself in policing slightly more. She didn't like that.

They stepped out into the car park and Kenneth immediately headed for the memorial of those officers killed in the shooting.

'I can't even begin to imagine what it must have been like that day,' he said, placing his hand on the glass casing where an eternal blue flame burned inside. 'How is your recovery going?' he asked, turning to Matilda.

'Well, I'm back at work, so I'd say it's going very well.' She smiled, slightly suspiciously.

He gave her a sympathetic wan smile. 'You've dealt with some difficult cases over the years.'

'It goes with the job.'

'The serial killer last year, reuniting Carl Meagan with his parents after four years. You have a remarkable record.'

'Thank you,' she eyed with him scepticism, wondering where this was heading.

'And now you're working on the murder of Richard Ashton.'

'Indeed.'

Kenneth cleared his throat, looked at the building and turned his back on it. 'I've heard that ...' he seemed to struggle with finding the correct words, 'you're being told to focus your investigation on a particular angle and to ignore others. Am I correct?'

Matilda nodded. 'We've uncovered links between Ashton and suspected child abuse at a children's home in the nineties. I've been told not to go down that road.'

'Who by?'

'ACC Ridley.'

'And you believe that's the right path to go down in searching for Richard's killer?'

'I do.'

'So do I, especially when you take in the manner of his death. Do you believe there is someone within South Yorkshire Police who wants to cover this up?'

'I don't have any evidence for that, but that's the impression I'm getting.'

'I thought so,' Kenneth said, looking decidedly uncomfortable. 'Matilda – do you mind if I call you Matilda?'

'Not at all.

'Matilda, I want you to dig. If you believe Richard Ashton is a child sex abuser, then you move heaven and earth to prove it. We've seen far too many examples of systematic abuse being covered up by various forces around the country. South Yorkshire Police will not be one of them. If you suspect any serving officer of being involved, come directly to me. I'm independent of the police, so I'm not constrained by the rules and regulations. I'll make sure you're heard.'

Matilda looked up at Kenneth Burr. His severe stare and pursed lips seemed to tell her he feared losing his job, should he be connected with any sign of a cover-up.

'Thank you,' she said.

From his inside jacket pocket, he took out a card which he handed to her. 'My mobile is on there. You can call me any time if you have anything you want to share or run by me. It's probably best to do so out of office hours. Just in case.'

'Just in case of what?'

'Walls have ears. Ears can contain listening devices.' He walked away, his head down and his hands in his pockets.

Maybe my first impression of him was wrong.

Matilda remained where she was and looked up at the building she had worked in for more than twenty years. It was her home away from home but suddenly, she didn't recognise it anymore. She was pretty sure she could see ACC Benjamin Ridley watching her through the vertical blinds in his top-floor office. Suddenly, Matilda could perfectly understand why Sian had handed in her notice.

Chapter Twenty-Three

G uy and Christian were in Christian's car. There was nowhere else for them to go. Guy was flicking through the photographs Matilda had printed off from the memory stick Peter Ogilvy had supplied her with, and Christian watched his reaction.

He smiled at some of the shots of the boys playing football or pulling faces at the camera. He chuckled when he saw pictures of himself looking much more young and carefree than he was now. On the backs, he wrote down as many names as he could remember.

'I hope the killer isn't one of the lads I knew,' Guy said, going through the photos one more time. 'I got on with them. We were like brothers. We …' he stopped talking.

'Guy, do you remember the gardener, Nigel Tate?'

He nodded. 'Creepy bastard.'

'Was he involved in the abuse?'

'Not directly.'

'What do you mean?'

'I never saw him actually do anything, but he'd be there, watching, his hand down his trousers. You know he's in prison now, I'm guessing.'

'Yes. He was interviewed yesterday.'

'He killed a couple of boys. It could have been us. I'm not sure if that makes us lucky or not.'

Christian looked at him, saw the sadness on his face, and wondered how deep it went.

'Is there nothing you can tell me that could identify the men involved in the abuse?'

'No. I'm sorry,' he answered quickly.

'Do you know who could have killed Richard Ashton? Who'd be capable of doing that?'

'I don't know about capable, but any one of these could have done it,' he said, handing the stack of photographs back to Christian. 'Don't you have any forensic evidence or anything from the crime scene?'

'No. There are no fingerprints, no trace evidence. The killer seems to have covered their tracks.'

'I blame programmes like *CSI* and *Silent Witness*. If you're going to set out to kill someone, they tell you exactly what to do to avoid being caught,' Guy said with a hint of a smile.

'I suppose.'

'Is there anything else you'd like to ask? I need to be getting back,' Guy said, looking at the Moor Market building in front of him.

'No. Thanks, though, Guy. I really appreciate all your help.'

'You're welcome,' he said, getting out of the car and slamming the door behind him.

He pulled out his e-cigarette and took a few puffs on it and waved to Christian as he joined the traffic and drove away. As he turned and headed for the building, he pulled a photo he'd stolen from Christian's pile out of his pocket and looked at the image of three boys, smiling into the camera. He tore it in half, then in half again, and again, and again, until they were just tiny unidentifiable, infinitesimal pieces of paper.

Chapter Twenty-Four

Matilda went into the library in her home. She used to love coming in here; it calmed her down just being in the presence of her vast collection of books. She had never been a huge reader, buying the odd paperback at an airport kiosk when she and James went on holiday, but since inheriting the collection, mostly crime fiction, she enjoyed losing herself in a world where complex crimes were solved and wrapped up in under four hundred pages, order and normality restored by the turning of the final page.

Since the shooting, she'd been unable to relax with a book. She'd fallen back on books that she'd read before, that were safe, where she knew what was coming. A table by the window held the books she had bought in recent months but had no inclination to pick up and read just yet. As much as she wanted to read the next John Rebus novel, her mind wouldn't settle for more than two pages before drifting off into her past. And what if Rebus investigated a mass shooting? That would cause all kinds of anxiety she was desperate to avoid.

'Matilda, I've been calling you,' Adele said from the

doorway.

'Sorry. I was … choosing a new book,' she lied, faking a smile.

Adele held out Matilda's mobile. 'It's Pat. She wants a word.'

'Oh. Thanks.'

'Listen, I'm not very hungry so thought I'd just whip up an omelette. Do you want one?'

'Please.' She unmuted the phone. 'Hi, Pat.'

'Hang on one second. Anton, there's another delivery bloke coming down the path. Have you been ordering again?' Pat called out to her husband in the background. Matilda couldn't make out his reply. 'You don't even like Marmite. Sorry about that, Mat. My husband is confusing a pandemic with the outbreak of the Second World War. I'm half expecting him to build an air-raid shelter in the back garden.'

Matilda smiled. 'Is he hoarding?'

'Hoarding? My living room looks like a Red Cross relief centre. I can sort of get my head around him ordering tinned food. We both have health issues so we don't want to risk the queues in shops, but can you explain why he's bought two sleeping bags?'

Matilda burst out laughing. 'I'm sorry, Pat, I can't.'

'No. Neither can I. Anyway, the reason I've called is that I've been doing some digging and while I haven't exactly got any answers for you, I've found out where you can get them from.'

'Go on.'

'First of all, Chief Constable Tony Bates was a Freemason, which probably accounts for why he may have covered up the abuse and murder of the young boy, especially if he was asked to do so by a fellow Mason. Billy Maitland, I told you about, was also a Freemason, but what I didn't know, was that the real reason Billy was removed from South Yorkshire Police was because he had sex with an underage female witness.'

'Really?' Matilda plonked herself down in her Eames chair, suddenly fascinated with where this conversation was heading.

'Guess where Maitland is now?'

'With a dodgy past, I'm guessing on the front benches of Parliament.'

'Stafford Prison.'

'What for?'

'Same reason he was kicked out of the force. Underage sex. He's been there since 2017 and he's due for parole later this year. My thinking is, if you interview him and ask him to spill all the details on Tony Bates and who told him to keep his mouth shut, in return, you can say you'll give a statement to the parole board saying how he cooperated in your investigation, and it might help in his release. Quid pro quo.'

'I do like a bit of quid pro quo,' Matilda smiled. 'Pat, you're a star.'

'I've often said so myself,' she said with a smile in her voice.

'Listen, Pat, I know your kids don't live in Sheffield, so, if we do go into a lockdown, which is looking likely, and you need anything, you'll let me know, won't you?'

'I will. Thanks, Matilda.'

'Take care.'

Matilda ended the call. She guessed Billy Maitland would no longer be a member of the Freemasons now he was in prison, but she wondered how she was going to officially interview him without alerting Ridley and whoever was pulling his strings.

Chapter Twenty-Five

Holt House Grove, Millhouses

George Barker, MP for Sheffield South, was ready for a night in front of the television and a couple of glasses of whisky. His day had not gone as planned. His phone had not stopped ringing with businesses, schools and colleges all wanting to know what was happening with the pandemic. Several appointments had been cancelled and none of his calls to Number 10 had been returned. He was on his third whisky when his mobile rang. His three o'clock appointment was ringing to apologise and explain why he'd had to cancel. George made a joke about the general stupidity of the public. The joke was met with a guffaw of laughter and George invited him around for a drink and to have their meeting informally. Less than half an hour later, there was a knock on the door.

George had taken off his tie and undone a couple of top buttons. He remained in his smart trousers but changed his shoes for carpet slippers. He answered the door with a glass in hand.

'You'll have to forgive me, Martin, I've completely forgotten your surname,' George said, slurring slightly.

'Freelander,' the man on the doorstep said.

'Like the Land Rover?'

'That's right.'

George held out his hand and shook his visitor's vigorously. 'Come on in. I must warn you, my home isn't exactly spotless. I'm not very domesticated,' he said, smiling.

'That's fine. Neither am I.'

He stepped in and closed the door behind him. He stood in the large hallway and looked around him. 'Lovely house.'

'It is, isn't it? I bought it off an old dear about twenty years ago. She was going into a nursing home. I got the surveyor to say it needed more work than it did, and got her to knock twenty grand off the asking price. Shall we go into the kitchen?' George said, heading in that direction.

'Do you live here on your own?'

'I do. I'm not married and don't have any children. Well, not that I'm aware of,' he said, laughing. 'Can I get you a drink?'

'Please. I'll have whatever you're drinking.'

'Good man. Take a seat.' He grabbed a glass from a cupboard and poured two large measures from a bottle of Teacher's. 'People expect their MPs to be married with kids – no idea why, but they do. Getting married has never interested me. I prefer my own company. There's no-one to stop you downing a bottle of whisky after a hard day at work.' He grinned and flopped down into the seat opposite.

The visitor held up the glass and they clinked 'cheers'. He

swigged his drink back in one mouthful and felt the golden liquid warm him as it went down.

'So, you're wanting to talk about dishing out laptops to the poorer kids, so they can have lessons remotely during this pandemic, is that right?'

'It is,' the visitor said, lifting up his briefcase onto the kitchen table and opening it.

'Do we have a means-test approach in place, to see who actually qualifies?' George asked. 'I'm all in favour in helping out poor kids, but we don't want scummy parents flogging the laptops down the pub to feed a habit, do we?'

Hidden from George's view by the open briefcase, the visitor set about loading the syringe.

'Would you mind if I helped myself to another?' The visitor raised his empty glass.

'Certainly not. Help yourself,' George slurred.

The visitor stood up and went round the back of George. 'Would you like a top-up?'

'I never refuse a drink,' George said, handing over his already empty glass.

The visitor leaned down and stabbed George's arm with the needle. He depressed the plunger, giving him a large dose of opiate.

'What the fuck?' George tried to stand up, but the visitor pushed him down by the shoulders. 'What are you doing?'

'You looked surprised, George. Surely you're not telling me you didn't expect this, especially when you heard about Richard Ashton being killed.'

His eyes widened in horror. 'Richard ... Who are you?'

'Well, I'm certainly not Martin Freelander,' he said with a wink. 'Cast your mind back, George, to 1997, and those glorious parties Richard used to throw.'

'I don't know what you're talking about,' he said, defiantly.

'Don't you? Let me jog your memory. The top floor of Magnolia House was Richard's playroom where he and his sick bastard mates would choose a boy you liked the look of, to spend time with. You'd take me by the hand, ask me my name, how old I was, what I wanted to be when I grew up, then you gave me a drink. To me it looked like orange juice and I pulled a face because I thought it tasted funny, and you laughed and said it was a party, so it was a special drink for special children. Is this ringing any bells, George?'

'Who ... are you?' George asked, quietly, his speech starting to slow down.

The visitor stood up, arms on the table, leaned forward so his face was mere millimetres away from George's. 'I'm an eight-year-old who you fucked and violated and passed around your perverted friends to have their fun with. When you'd finished, you all walked away laughing and joking, leaving me on the bed, dazed, confused, bleeding, in agony and in tears.'

'I ...' George tried to stand up but couldn't. He fell and landed with a heavy bang on the tiled floor.

'Wakey wakey, Georgie Porgie.'

George opened his eyes. He was staring at a ceiling. He turned his head to the left and recognised his bedside table, the paperback copy of *Bring Up the Bodies* by Hilary Mantel he was a third of the way through, with his reading glasses on top. He looked down and saw he was naked. He tried to get up, but he couldn't move. How much had he had to drink?

'Georgie Porgie, pudding and pie, fucked the boys and made them cry,' his visitor sang.

George looked to the right and saw the stranger standing in the doorway to his bedroom wearing a white all-in-one suit, the hood pulled up, and putting on latex gloves. He walked over to him and squatted to his knees. He leaned in close.

'You're much easier to help upstairs than Richard Ashton. Fuck me, he was heavy.'

'What do you want?'

'What do I want? Hmm, let me think,' he said, posing with his hand on his chin as if wondering what George could give him. 'Nothing. I don't want anything from you. You've gone through life thinking you can do anything you want, haven't you? Just listening to you downstairs for a few minutes, talking about what you think of the public, your voters, made me sick. You don't have a single redeeming feature, do you? Someone should be funding me to kill bastards like you.'

'You don't have to kill me,' he cried, tears rolling down his face.

'You're right, I don't have to. But I want to. That's the difference.'

'I'm sorry. I'm so sorry for what I put you through.'

'But you're not. You're only sorry because I've put you in a position where you think saying the right thing will save you. You're not in the least bit sorry for the lives you've ruined, the lives you've destroyed, the lives you took.' He produced a pair of heavy-duty scissors from behind his back at dropped them on George's naked chest.

'Oh, good God, no,' he whimpered.

'Some of the boys didn't make it out of Richard's house alive. I don't know which one of you killed them, but you were there. You didn't have to join in the abuse. You could have called the police, done something to protect us, to save us, but you didn't ...'

'You don't understand,' George interrupted. 'Richard. He had us over a barrel. He was blackmailing us.'

'You're spineless,' the visitor said as he wiped away a tear. 'You've no balls.'

He smiled at George, picked up the scissors and with a swift movement, he grabbed George's penis and testicles in one hand and cut them off with the scissors in the other. George opened his mouth to scream, and the man rammed the dissected organs into his mouth, stuffing them down his throat.

'Choke on that, you sick, twisted fuck.'

He slapped his blood-covered hand over George's mouth, clamping it shut, holding him in place. He looked down at his groin and watched as blood gushed out of him. George was trying to scream, to cry out, but he was muffled. He was choking.

'Breathe in slowly through your nose, nice and calm,' the man said in a soothing voice. 'You're in agony, aren't you? What does it feel like? How much pain are you actually in? Is it as bad as living for twenty years with the memory of being raped as a child affecting every single decision you make? Is it like trying to settle down and trust someone enough to open up to them, but never quite being able to go that far, and your fiancée leaving you because you're so cold? I fucking hate you,' he spat.

The blood stopped gushing out and was reduced to a trickle. His heart had stopped beating. The mattress was saturated, as was the carpet by the bed. The metallic smell hung in the air; he could almost taste it.

He stood up, removed his gloves and looked down at

George's pale, dead body. He felt empty. There was no gratification for enacting revenge on another of the men who had abused him. There was no feeling of elation and closure was a long way off.

There was a chair by the bed. He sat down and sighed.

'I know this isn't going to be any form of atonement,' he said as if talking to George. 'Even when I've tracked you all down and killed every single last one of you, I won't suddenly feel better. What you did is burned into my memory, and no amount of therapy and pills will make it go away. But for a few minutes, I can enjoy the suffering in your face, and I think back to when I was a little boy, when you had me bent over, and I can say this is for him.' Tears rolled down his face, and he didn't wipe them away.

Chapter Twenty-Six

He was at his kitchen table. In front of him sat several empty cans of lager. His head was heavy, and his mind was spinning. He felt tired and sick. He'd been home for more than an hour and had had two showers. His clothes were in the washer, spinning around on a high temperature. The only light in the room came from the full moon outside, shining between the slats of the Venetian blind. In the corner of the room, his dog was fast asleep in his bed, whimpering away, legs kicking.

Killing his abusers was supposed to be cathartic. He was supposed to feel better, feel closer to some kind of recovery. He didn't feel anything like that. He was still in agony. It was eating away at him like a cancer.

He picked up his mobile and scrolled through the contacts, selected Matilda's number and was about to call, his finger hovering over the green button, but he couldn't bring himself to press it. He wanted to speak to her. He wanted to tell her what he'd done, explain everything, hope she'd understand, but he knew she wouldn't. Nobody ever had done.

He knew what she would be thinking; that he was a

psychopath, a monster, an evil killer who delighted in castrating people for his own sick pleasure. She'd be wrong. She would be one hundred percent wrong. Or, maybe she was right. Maybe he was a monster. If he was, he was made into a monster by circumstances. He started out in life as a quiet boy, lacking in confidence, slow to make friends and trust people. Then he ended up at Magnolia House and Richard fucking Ashton got his hands on him and tore away the last vestiges of innocence within him and turned him into this self-loathing, hating, hateful figure he saw reflected back at him every morning in the mirror when he was shaving.

'I should be enjoying watching them suffer the way I've suffered,' he whimpered, staring intently at Matilda's name on his phone. 'But I'm not. Not at all. What do I have to do to make myself feel better?'

He put the phone down on the table, went over to the drawer next to the sink and from the very back, he pulled out a handgun, wrapped in an old tea towel.

He returned to his seat at the table, pressed the barrel of the gun hard against his forehead, and his cold hands wrapped around the grip, his finger on the trigger.

He was crying. He was audibly crying. Tears were streaming down his face. He wanted to pull the trigger. He wanted the pain to go away. He wanted to end this right now.

He looked up, and through tear-stained eyes, saw the golden retriever looking up at him, wide-eyed. The dog stood up, trotted over to him and placed his head on his lap.

'I'm so sorry,' he said, looking down at the dog.

Chapter Twenty-Seven

Saturday 21st March 2020

Matilda had a heavy night. Her mind refused to switch off and, as much as she willed sleep to claim her, it didn't.

At midnight, she turned over, pulled the duvet over her head and let the darkness cocoon her. She squeezed her eyes closed and hoped that, by blocking any signals to her senses, she'd fall asleep. It didn't work. What was keeping her awake was inside her head. She kept seeing how sad Peter Ogilvy looked when he told her about Magnolia House and how impotent he was to stop the abuse; the thought of a police officer using the house on Manchester Road – a place of refuge for the vulnerable – for his own sick, perverted ends; the sound of the bullets ...

'*Shut up!*' she called, sitting up in bed, flinging back the duvet.

Matilda ran her fingers through her short hair. They came away damp. She was sweating. She switched on the light on her bedside table and grabbed her mobile. It was a little after half past twelve. How much longer was this night going to go on for?

She sent a text to Christian, asking if he was free in the morning. Her phone vibrated almost immediately. It wasn't a reply. Christian was calling. She swiped to answer.

'Sorry, did I wake you?' she asked, her voice quiet, so as not to wake Adele.

'No. I wasn't asleep. I've been thinking about Guy and … my mind won't shut off.'

'I know that feeling,' she said, smiling.

'Why do you want to know if I'm free in the morning?'

'I want to go and talk to Peter Ogilvy. I may have got a lead on what happened back in the nineties, but I need him to give us more information.'

'Okay. Do you want me to drive you?'

'Please.'

'No worries.'

'Is everything all right with you, Christian?' Matilda asked, feeling the cool of the spring night and pulling the duvet up around her. 'I know this is personal for you, after Paul Chattle killed himself, but you seem … I don't know. I mean, it's not like you to be losing sleep, for one thing.'

'I can't stop thinking of those young boys, and how terrified they must have been,' he said, a catch in his throat. 'How can someone like Ashton do something like that? They know it's wrong. They know it's illegal and they're inflicting physical and mental pain on them that they'll still be feeling years down the line, yet they still do it. Why?' His voice was almost pleading.

'I don't know, Christian.'

'And those who helped cover it up. Detectives. We could

have worked with them, for crying out loud! Those who knew about it are just as guilty as those who committed the abuse.'

'You're right. But we need to focus, Christian. We need to be so discreet here, so as not to get Ridley's back up. It's going to take time, but we'll find the evidence to expose everyone involved. You can't take this so personally, Christian.'

'It's not easy.'

'I know. When you've got kids of your own, it must be incredibly difficult to not feel personally involved.'

'No. It's not that ... I ...'

'What is it?' Matilda prompted when Christian fell silent.

'Nothing. You're right. It's having small kids and seeing how innocent and vulnerable they are, and knowing there are bastards out there willing to take advantage. It makes me sick.'

'I know. Look, it's easy for me to say, but go back to bed, Christian. Hold your wife. You'll feel so much better.'

Christian didn't say anything. Matilda could hear that he was struggling to hold back the tears. She said goodnight and ended the call.

———

Matilda entered the kitchen to see Adele sitting at the table in her dressing gown. Her hair was a tangled mess, and she had a painful expression on her face as she read from her iPad.

'You're up early, considering it's your day off,' Matilda said.

'I couldn't sleep.'

'Oh? Something on your mind?'

'No. It was ... no, it doesn't matter.'

Matilda pulled out a chair and sat down. 'You can tell me, Adele – come on.'

Adele sighed, placed her iPad on the table and looked up. 'You were screaming out in your sleep last night.'

'Was I?'

'Yes. I came in, but you'd stopped by then. I just couldn't get back to sleep afterwards.'

'What was I saying?' Matilda asked.

'You weren't very coherent. You mentioned Steve's name a couple of times.'

'Oh, God. Adele, I'm so sorry.'

'It's okay. The gap between screaming sessions is getting longer, so that's a good sign.'

'Well, I'm off out in a bit. Christian's coming for me, so you'll have the house to yourself. It'll be nice and quiet for you to have a nap.'

'I wish I could. I started reading this chapter Simon Browes sent me for the book. I had no idea how good he was.'

'What do you mean?'

'The level of research he's already done into decomposition is amazing, and his prose is almost beautiful. He's going to really show me up,' she said, looking worried.

Matilda went around to her side of the table and placed a comforting arm around her. 'Don't be silly. You're a wonderful writer. The publisher was full of compliments for your first book, and I'm sure she'll love this one, too.'

'I'm going to have to up my game to match Simon's level, though. This is Booker Prize-winning stuff, here.'

'Well, I'm sure—' The doorbell rang. 'Oh. That'll be Christian. Enjoy your lazy day, part-timer,' she said with a smile as she headed for the door.

'I worked more than ninety hours this week, cheeky cow,' Adele shouted after her. The front door slammed closed. 'Give or take fifteen hours,' she said quietly to herself.

'Is that Sian's car?' Christian asked once Matilda was in the front passenger seat and they'd set off down the drive.

'Yes. She's gone hiking with Scott. She's been doing a lot of comfort eating since everything that happened with Stuart and wants to lose a bit of weight.'

'Oh.'

'She turned up first thing in brand-new gear. She looked like she'd burgled a branch of North Face,' she said with a smirk. 'I put on weight after James died. It took being shot and in an induced coma for three weeks to get back down to a size ten. Mind you, when you see the prices Jenny Craig charges, I think I chose the right weight-loss plan.' She grinned and turned to Christian in the driver's seat. His expression was nonplussed. 'Did you get much sleep last night, in the end?'

'Not much. A couple of hours, maybe.'

'What's Jennifer and the kids up to today?'

'Staying indoors, I hope. Thank goodness for Netflix.'

'Christian, I got the feeling you wanted to tell me something on the phone last night. Is there something on your mind?'

'No,' he answered quickly.

'Are you sure?'

'Positive.'

'You can tell me anything. I won't judge or be angry or anything.'

'I know,' he turned to her and gave her a weak smile before quickly turning back to concentrate on the road.

They continued driving and Matilda filled Christian in on Tony Bates and Billy Maitland being in prison for a sex crime.

'Do you think Billy Maitland could have been an abuser at Magnolia House?' he asked.

'I'm not sure. His victims were female. I'm going to have to arrange an interview, but I don't want it getting back to Ridley.'

'What's the worst Ridley can do to us if we don't follow the line of enquiry he wants us to?'

'He'll play it by the book. I'll get an official written warning. I've already had two verbal ones. I suppose after that it'll be suspension, possibly demotion,' she said, looking out of the window.

'You don't seem too bothered about that.'

'I'm not. Once this is over, depending on what's happened to me, I'll write a book exposing South Yorkshire Police as being corrupt from top to bottom. Adele's getting on famously with her publisher. I'm sure they'll snatch my hand off.'

'You'd do it as well, wouldn't you?' he asked.

'Absolutely. I can't allow people who knew about the abuse to get away with it. Guy, and all the others, need to get on with their lives, and they won't be able to do that with everything bottled up like it is.'

The car fell silent, apart from the sound of the engine, and they drove for several miles before Christian spoke.

'Do you think that's true?'

'What?'

'What you said, about Guy only being able to relax once everything is out in the open?'

'I'm not a therapist, but Guy is keeping everything locked away inside, isn't he? He's refusing to allow people to get close because he's afraid of being vulnerable and hurt. If everything's out in the open, then the healing process can begin.' She turned to look at him. 'It's a shame he doesn't have anyone close he can unburden himself on. I mean, if it were you, you've got Jennifer and close friends around you who'll help. Haven't you?'

Christian turned to her and looked straight back at the road. 'Hmm,' he replied.

Christian pulled up outside Peter's cottage and immediately recognised the small white van he'd parked behind.

'Guy's here,' he said.

'Well, Peter did say he helps him. He's probably done some shopping for him.' Matilda looked over to Christian. 'Is something wrong?'

'No.'

'You've gone pale.'

'I'm fine. Just tired.' He undid his seatbelt and climbed out of the car.

Matilda wasn't convinced. She knew the sound of that particular 'I'm fine.' She'd used it herself more than once. It meant she was the polar opposite of fine but didn't want to talk about it. She hoped there was nothing going on between him and Jennifer. They needed each other right now. The kids needed them both to be strong.

Matilda led the way to the back garden where she found Peter and Guy at the iron table enjoying a coffee. A golden retriever lay at their feet, panting. He saw the visitors first, jumped up and barked. He came charging towards them and sat at Christian's feet. He bent down and scratched his ear.

'Hello again, Toby.'

'DCI Darke, I wasn't expecting you,' Peter Ogilvy said, struggling to stand up.

Matilda held up a hand to tell him to sit back down. 'I know I should have phoned first, but I was hoping to ask you a few more questions.'

'Of course. Guy, run in and pop the kettle back on.'

'There's no need,' Matilda said.

'Nobody comes to my house without refreshments. We were just talking about another cup anyway, weren't we, Guy?'

'Yes.' Guy stood up, picked up the tray and headed for the house. Toby followed.

'Peter, I'd like to introduce you to DI Christian Brady. He's practically my left arm at the station.'

Christian held out a hand to shake until Peter held up his.

'Probably best not to shake. Prince Charles was using the Hindu *namaste* method of greeting at Westminster Cathedral. I saw it on the news.' He clasped his hands together and bowed his head. 'I think this should replace the traditionalhandshake, don't you? The number of times I've shaken hands over the years, only to find something sticky on my hand afterwards! Have a seat, you two.'

Matilda and Christian pulled back a couple of chairs, making sure they were a safe distance apart from Peter who remained in his seat, a blanket over his lap.

'So, you wanted to talk to me again.'

'Yes,' Matilda said. 'You said Richard Ashton was the principal backer of Magnolia House. That must mean there were others who provided funding. Do you know who they were?'

'There were no other investors. Richard Ashton *was* the principal backer, but other money came from various charities, the council and the Church.'

'I see.'

'Things were donated to us. Richard would turn up on

many occasions with items we could use. He said he got a friend of his to donate a big TV and video once. I set up weekly video clubs after that. The boys loved it.'

Guy returned to the garden, with his faithful dog following, carrying a heavy tray which he carefully set down on the table.

'I loved film nights,' Guy said. 'Every Saturday, we'd all jostle for the best position to be able to see the screen. I've loved films ever since. I'll watch anything. Well, within reason, obviously.' He poured out the tea and handed round the mugs.

'Did you ever find out the names of those who donated items?'

'No. I did say to Richard a few times that he should invite these people over so we could thank them, but he never did. I wanted to send them letters of thanks and cards at Christmas time. Richard just said to give them to him, and he'd pass them on. I don't think he ever did.'

'You said he brought men to the home. Do you remember them, what they looked like, anything that stood out about them?' Matilda asked.

Peter thought for a moment before shaking his head. 'They always stood in the shadows.'

'Why did he bring them round?'

'He said they were potential investors; that they wanted to see where their money would be going. It made sense, I suppose. It's just … the money never came.'

'Did the abuse take place during these men's visits?'

'I don't know.'

'Yes,' Guy answered quickly. 'Nothing overly sexual, but Ashton would have us sit on his knee and he'd hold us a bit too close. It was as if he was bragging to these blokes how easy it was. Looking back, it was almost as if he was grooming the men as well as us, showing them what they could be doing, opening up a new perverse world for them.'

'Does the name Billy Maitland mean anything to either of you?' Matilda asked.

They both shook their heads.

'Who is he?' Peter asked.

'Someone I'm investigating,' she replied. She fidgeted in her seat. The lack of positive progress was almost annoying.

'Guy, when did the abuse stop for you?' Matilda asked.

'Guy, that chicken should be done, shouldn't it?' Peter said quickly.

'Oh yes. I'll just go and check.' He stood up and headed back to the kitchen.

Peter watched and waited until he disappeared inside. 'Oh, no, it's time for my tablets,' he said, unconvincingly. 'DI Brady, you couldn't pop indoors and ask Guy to bring them out for me, could you?'

'Of course.'

Matilda waited until Christian was out of earshot. 'You're not going to win any BAFTAs with acting like that.' She smiled.

'I'm no Benedict Whatshisname, but I know Guy won't talk about the abuse in front of me. He's trying to protect me, which is very kind of him, but he's the one who needs protection.'

Matilda finished her tea and replaced the empty cup on the table. 'Peter, we need to locate the other boys of Magnolia House to build up a case against Ashton and the other abusers. I'm struggling to track them down.'

'Surely Duncan Shivers will be able to help you.'

Matilda turned away.

'What is it?' Peter asked.

Matilda took a deep breath. 'I'm very sorry to have to tell you this, Peter, but there was never anyone employed at the council called Duncan Shivers. We think he may have been working for Richard Ashton and posing as an adoption worker to take the boys away.'

Peter visibly paled. He began shaking. His eyes darted rapidly left and right and tears ran down his face, following the wrinkles.

'What? No. No. Oh my good God in heaven, what have I done?' He struggled to get a handkerchief out of his pocket and dabbed at his eyes. 'I handed them over. I willingly allowed that man to come into the home and I handed the boys over to him. I even waved them off. I stood on the drive and waved as he drove off with them. What did I do?'

Matilda dropped to her knees and placed a comforting arm around Peter's bony shoulders.

'You can't blame yourself. Ashton was a manipulator. He fooled everyone into thinking he was a caring, honest, charitable man.'

'Twelve. Duncan Shivers adopted twelve boys. What did he do with them?' He looked to Matilda with wet eyes.

'I don't know, Peter. But I will find out, I can assure you.'

'How?'

She thought for a moment. 'By making myself heard.'

'But I tried that,' he said, wiping his eyes with his soggy hanky. 'I went back to the station. I made a nuisance of myself, and look what happened to—' He stopped himself.

'Peter, what happened to you when you reported Sean's murder to Chief Constable Tony Bates?'

Peter took a deep breath and adjusted himself on his seat. He looked uncomfortable. 'Are you sure you want to hear this?'

'No. But I really do need to know.'

It seemed dark inside Peter's cottage after the brightness of sitting outside. The windows were small, the ceiling was low and the rooms were full of a lifetime's achievements and collections. There wasn't a surface that wasn't filled with something.

Christian followed Guy into the kitchen. He'd taken a full chicken out of the oven and placed it carefully on the worktop. He stuck a meat thermometer inside it.

'That smells good.'

Guy turned around and smiled. 'I don't bother cooking just for me. At home I open a can of whatever and have it on toast.' He grinned. 'I should cook more. I enjoy it. I think I cook more for Toby than I do for me,' he said, looking down at his dog.

'I'm guessing you don't want to talk about the abuse in front of Peter.'

'We've never actually spoken about it to each other, but we seem to be able to look at each other and know exactly what the other wants to say. It doesn't need physical words.'

'It does help to talk, though, to say these things out loud.'

'To a therapist?' Guy asked.

'To a friendly face,' Christian smiled.

Guy looked at him, studied him, before speaking. 'In answer to your colleague's question outside, the abuse stopped when I became too old. Once puberty hits and hair starts growing, you're of no use to bastards like Ashton. The thing is, you've become immune to the rape and the dark feelings of the aftermath. It's good to down a bottle of cheap vodka and fall into oblivion. You wake up, you feel numb, and for a few minutes there's nothing there but blankness. That's the best feeling in the world. Unfortunately, there are still some sick bastards out there who'll enjoying shagging a fourteen-year-old boy. I think this chicken needs another twenty minutes.' He opened the oven door, pushed the roasting tin inside and slammed it closed.

'What did you do?'

'I sold myself,' he said, almost matter of fact. 'It's weird, but even though they're paying, even though it's disgusting and it's wrong and it's illegal, there's something about feeling someone close for a few minutes that makes you feel wanted.'

'How long did that go on for?'

'Until this happened.' He pulled up the sleeve of his sweater and showed Christian the scar from a suicide attempt. 'Don't tell Peter, he doesn't know.'

Christian swallowed hard. He struggled to find something to say. He could feel the walls closing in.

'People assume that once you've left the home and you're out of reach of the abusers, it stops. It doesn't. My abuser just changed. I turned into my own abuser. That's the worst kind.'

'But you got help,' he said, his voice barely above a whisper.

'But I had to visit hell first. Nobody should ever go there.' He looked at Christian firmly with a dead-eyed stare. 'Now, where did I put those carrots?'

'You must have been petrified,' Matilda said once Peter had finished telling his story about how he was dragged to the shed, tied up and had petrol poured over him.

'I was.'

'You were there all night?'

He nodded. 'I don't know how I managed to free myself, but it took me several hours. By the time I got back into Magnolia House, I was shaking with cold. I sat in that shower until I heard the boys moving around. Everything changed after that.'

'What do you mean?'

'I was scared about what could happen to them. I think I became slightly overprotective.'

'It's understandable.'

Peter wiped away a tear. 'When Duncan Shivers came and introduced himself, I thought ... I thought it was the salvation they needed. I thought it would be their route out of there and to a better life. I had no idea ...' He cried.

'Peter, can you remember what Duncan Shivers looked like?'

It was a while before Peter composed himself. He blew his nose hard. 'He was tall, slim build. He had a young face, but when he smiled, there were wrinkles at the sides of his eyes, so I think he looked younger than he was. I'd say early thirties, maybe. He had light-brown hair and was always smartly dressed.'

'Did he have a local accent?'

'Yes.'

'Any moles or scars, any distinguishing features?'

He thought for a moment. 'None that I can — Oh, wait a minute, yes. He came to the home once in the summer. It was a boiling-hot day so he was only wearing a short-sleeved shirt. He had a scar down his left arm, like a burn. I asked him about it. He said it was a childhood accident.'

Matilda thought that was a useful piece of information. A

scar like that should be easy to spot on a potential suspect. 'Anything else?'

'No.'

'Did he say anything to you that you think might help us?'

'No. We didn't really speak about anything important. It was always about the boys and them going off to a new home, a better home.' His voice broke and he lifted up the soggy hanky to his mouth again. 'I can't believe I handed them over to him. May God forgive me.'

Matilda leaned forward and took one of his fragile hands in hers. 'I promise, I will not stop until I know who was involved and where those twelve boys are now. You have my word,' she said, looking him directly in the eye.

He smiled, but his lips shook with emotion. 'Thank you.'

———————

Matilda and Christian drove away from Peter's cottage in Edale in silence. Christian turned into a nearby pub car park and turned off the engine. He was about to get out when he remembered the pub was closed.

'It seems strange, all the pubs being closed.'

'We can't even go for a coffee either,' Matilda stated.

'I need a drink,' he said.

'The more we talk to Peter and Guy, the worse it gets. Imagine how scared Peter would have been, having petrol poured over him. Poor man.'

'It sounds like Tony Bates instigated it,' Christian added. 'Who did he contact that meant Peter needed to be warned off in such a violent way?'

Matilda shook her head. 'I really don't have a clue. Unless

Bates was in league with Richard Ashton. It would be just like Ashton to have a Chief Constable in his pocket.'

'It's not like we can ask him. Bates is dead.'

'And his death is looking mighty suspicious.'

'You think Ashton arranged to have him killed?'

'He died in a fire. Peter had petrol poured over him and was threatened with a fire. The two are similar.'

Christian turned to Matilda in his seat. 'But Ashton is dead. Bates is dead. There's nobody to stop us from throwing this case wide open. We've got Guy's statement. We've got Peter, who'll definitely go on record saying there was abuse on a massive scale at Magnolia House. We can launch an official enquiry now,' he said, almost elated.

'But someone is pressing Ridley to stop us investigating,' she said firmly. 'There is still someone out there who doesn't want this seeing the light of day.'

'Who?'

'I don't know, Christian,' Matilda said, almost frustrated. 'Finn and Scott are going through Ashton's background. Hopefully, that will throw open ...'

'That's not going to tell us anything,' he interrupted. 'The bloke knew everybody. He's probably got contacts in his diary going back decades. Are people listed under their real names? Are they deeply hidden under pseudonyms or in plain sight? I don't know how the bastard's mind worked.'

'Christian, you really need to calm down,' Matilda said. 'This is not going to be solved overnight. Let's just hope that whoever was at Magnolia House in the nineties has seen the news about Richard Ashton's death and will come forward with their statements of abuse.'

'And, if they don't?'

Matilda didn't answer that. She couldn't. She could feel the knot in her throat when she swallowed. There was a deeply rooted sense that this was not going to have a happy ending setting up home in her stomach and it was making her feel constantly sick. She couldn't eat. She was hardly sleeping, though that was nothing new, and her head felt heavy. She was enveloped by sickness and depravity and it was squeezing the life out of her.

Chapter Twenty-Eight

Monday 23rd March 2020

'*And therefore, I urge you at this moment of national emergency to stay at home, protect our NHS and save lives. Thank you.*'

Matilda and Adele watched in rapt silence as the Prime Minster of Great Britain and Northern Ireland announced a national lockdown in which everyone should stay at home; all non-essential shops and other premises including libraries, playgrounds, and places of worship would close; and all social events including weddings, christenings and other ceremonies, but excluding funerals, would no longer be allowed.

It was something they were both expecting. It was what the whole country was expecting, but hearing it was a shock, and even after the broadcast, Matilda and Adele sat in silence as they took in the grave language used in the statement.

'It's given me chills listening to that,' Adele said. She turned to Matilda and saw a tear run down her face. She rushed over to her sofa, sat beside her and put her arm around her. 'Matilda, what's wrong?'

'I don't know,' she said, reaching for a tissue from the coffee table. 'I don't know why I'm crying. It's just, all of a sudden, I felt so emotional. Like you said, it gave me the chills. Who'd have thought, when we saw in the new year, that in just three months, the whole country would be locked down? It's difficult to get your head around, isn't it?'

'It is.'

Matilda wiped her eyes. 'I'm so glad you're living with me,' she said with a smile.

'So am I. We'll be fine. Besides, nothing's going to change for us, is it? We still have to go to work.'

'True.'

'Are you sure you're okay?'

Matilda blew her nose and nodded. 'It's been a strange day. Something's going on with Christian that I can't get out of him. We've got this bloke living opposite the back of Richard Ashton'shouse who Scott thinks definitely knows something, but who's keeping his mouth shut.And I still can't get Sian to change her mind about leaving. On top of all that, a buffoon who refuses to comb his hair has just locked us all down.'

'It could be worse.'

'How?' Matilda looked to Adele.

She thought for a moment. 'There could be an asteroid hurtling towards Earth.'

Matilda laughed. 'I suppose that would be worse. I'd better ring my mum; see how she is.'

'I'll pop across and see Scott,' Adele smiled.

Matilda called her mum, but it was engaged. She was probably talking to her sister. Matilda leaned back on the sofa and watched the muted television as the news presenter analysed the speech. She thought of Peter Ogilvy and dialled his number.

'Peter, it's Matilda. Have you seen the news?'

'I have. Uncertain times ahead.'

'Yes. I know you have Guy looking out for you, but if there's anything you need, I'd be more than happy to get some shopping for you.'

'That's very kind of you, thank you. I could probably set up a roadside stall with all the fruit and veg Guy's brought me, and I've been stocking up with canned food over the past couple of weeks. I should be fine for a while.'

'That's good.'

'My treatment's been cancelled. I received a call this afternoon.'

'Oh. I'm so sorry. Have they said when it will be rescheduled for?'

'No, not yet. As soon as it's possible to do so, I've been told. The thing is, my immune system isn't that great. I've survived cancer twice and I've other things wrong with me, and age isn't on my side. I very much doubt I'll see another Christmas.'

Matilda could feel the tears coming on again and grabbed for another tissue. 'You can't think like that, Peter. You need to be positive. You need to tell yourself you're going to get better. Mental strength is vital in these things.'

Do the words pot, kettle, and black sound familiar to you?

'Matilda, even with treatment, it's highly unlikely I'd survive the year anyway. I'd like to have seen justice done for the boys at Magnolia House, but I can't see that happening. However, I have every faith in you, Matilda.'

She shook her head and was so pleased he couldn't see her. She wished he wasn't saying this.

'I know you'll take the baton and run further with it than I ever could,' he said, his voice filled with tears.

Matilda put her head in her hands. She tried to think of

something to say, anything that could encourage him, but she couldn't find the words.

'Matilda, are you still there?' Peter asked.

'Yes,' she sniffed. 'I'm still here. Don't worry, I will do everything in my power to make sure the abusers are identified and brought to justice.'

She quickly ended the call and berated herself for making a promise she had no idea how to keep. She was working within the parameters allowed for a DCI, but those above her were being underhand and breaking every single rule to keep their secret hidden. If she wanted Peter to see justice prevail before he died, she'd need to up her game and throw the rulebook out of the window.

Chapter Twenty-Nine

MURDER OF BUSINESSMAN REVEALS COVER-UP OF SEXUAL ABUSE

By Danny Hanson

Millionaire property developer Richard Ashton was found dead in his period home in an affluent part of Sheffield last week, and so began an investigation which has revealed historical child sex abuse and a police cover-up spanning almost thirty years.

The mogul, 61, a controversial figure in the business world, was found by his housekeeper lying in a pool of blood, having been castrated. The manner of his death is obviously linked to Ashton's personal life. However, investigating officers, led by Detective Chief Inspector Matilda Darke in the Homicide and Major Enquiry Unit at South Yorkshire Police, have been stymied at every turn as they try to unravel the complicated layers of Ashton's past.

A police source said: 'We're uncovering crimes committed by Ashton which were reported in the 1990s and never investigated. Witnesses were threatened and intimidated and evidence was conveniently lost. Richard Ashton was a man who used his power and influence to devastating effect, and the powers that be turned a blind eye and allowed him free rein.'

Richard Ashton, awarded an OBE in 2013 for services to industry and his charity work, was patron of many children's charities. He established the Fresh Start Foundation which awards apprenticeships in the building industry to young offenders as an alternative to penal punishment, and the Homes For Life Scheme which helps first-time buyers find their way onto the property ladder. However, it is his work at Magnolia House Children's Home in Sheffield which has come under police scrutiny.

Magnolia House was opened in 1991 by Reverend Peter Ogilvy and closed ten years later when Rev. Ogilvy took early retirement from the Church due to ill health.

Records show Richard Ashton was the principal financial backer and used his own money to purchase the building from Sheffield City Council and make it habitable for wayward boys. The question is, why?

Former residents of Magnolia House have gone on record stating Ashton sexually abused a number of boys at the home; that he brought his friends with him to choose for themselves which boys they wanted to rape. Even when Magnolia House was closed down in 2001, the abuse continued with Ashton holding sex parties in his own home.

While the evidence against Ashton is mounting, DCI Darke and her team are being ordered to ignore what is clearly a cover-up and look for Ashton's killer elsewhere. Yet even an armchair criminologist could tell you the murder bears all the hallmarks of a sexually motivated crime.

So, why the cover-up?

Richard Ashton was a Freemason. So is the Chief Constable of South Yorkshire Police, along with many other people of influence who knew about Ashton's crimes. Who else was involved? How many of the boys at Magnolia House were raped? There are many questions that need answering and nobody is willing to allow DCI Darke to ask them.

'We're uncovering sexual abuse on a massive scale,' the police source continued. 'We thought after the Rotherham sex scandal, the Rochdale abuse, and the unmasking of Jimmy Savile and Cyril Smith as perverted predators, we would be applauded for uncovering more abuse, but the cover-ups continue. Those who knew about it are just as guilty as those who committed the offences. They should all be exposed.'

Not all the victims of Magnolia House have been identified and it is hoped more will come forward. In order to seek justice for these boys, we all need to shout as loud as we can. The forgotten children of society need a voice. We already have one virus spreading across the country.Don't let the virus of silence be another.

Chapter Thirty

Wednesday 25th March 2020

Matilda was woken by the annoying buzz from her vibrating mobile dancing on the bedside table. She peeked her head out from beneath the duvet, saw it was still dark and turned over. Whoever was calling her could do so during daylight hours. If it was urgent, they could ring 999.

The vibrating stopped and immediately started again.

'Oh, for fu—' she said as she scrambled to free herself from the tangle of duvet she'd managed to wrap around herself during her fitful sleep.

She blinked hard as she tried to focus on the screen but couldn't make out the name of who was calling. She swiped to answer.

'Yes,' she said.

'Matilda. It's ACC Ridley.'

'Oh. Sorry. I was asleep. What …?'

'My office. Nine o'clock sharp.' He ended the call.

The bluntness of his tone was enough to wake Matilda up.

She stretched out a hand in the dark and turned on the lamp and pulled herself up. What was he talking about? Why the urgent call to announce a meeting in the middle of the night?

She looked at her phone. It was three minutes after seven. She had four missed calls, three of them from Ridley, the other from Christian, and an email from Danny Hanson which she deleted without reading.

She placed her phone on the bedside table and tried to organise her thoughts. Why had Ridley called so early and barked an order at her? Something must have happened. She grabbed for her phone again and went to the BBC News app. The national news was full of pandemic-related stories and the country struggling to get used to living in lockdown. She clicked on the regional news section, but there was nothing there that warranted such a command by her boss.

There was no chance of her trying to get back to sleep now. It had taken until two o'clock to nod off in the first place. She flung back the duvet, swung her legs out, found her slippers and stumbled downstairs to make her first industrial-strength coffee of the day.

'Jesus Christ, Matilda, what have you done?' Adele said as she entered the kitchen.

'What are you talking about?' Matilda was chewing on a slice of toast and had a second mug of coffee in front of her.

'I didn't think you talked to the press, especially to Danny Hanson.'

'I don't.'

'So, you didn't speak to him about Magnolia House and Richard Ashton.'

'No. Why? What's happened?'

Adele handed Matilda her phone. The browser was open at an article on the *Guardian*'s website. Matilda read through it quickly, her eyes widening with each line.

'Fu— Oh, my God!' she said.

'You didn't know about it?'

'Of course I bloody didn't. Jesus Christ! No wonder Ridley called so early. I cannot believe he did this,' she said, putting her head in her hands.

'Who?'

'Christian sodding Brady. There's no-one else who would be so reckless.'

Adele had poured herself a coffee and pulled out the chair opposite Matilda. She sat down. 'The article doesn't name him, though. He won't get into too much trouble, will he?'

'This is Danny Hanson we're talking about. He's a slippery bastard. He'll come back further down the line when he wants information, and he'll use this as a threat. Oh, Christian, you stupid, stupid man!'

'What do you think Ridley will say?'

'You mean after he's roasted me? I'm not entirely sure. I think I might ask my mum to phone in sick for me.'

———————

It was strange walking through the station and not seeing any civilian staff walking the corridors or cooped up in offices. It was quiet, and as Matilda made her way to ACC Ridley's office on the top floor, she noticed an eerie atmosphere. She didn't like it. His secretary wasn't there so she simply knocked on the door and waited to be called in. She smoothed down her best jacket and ran her fingers through her hair. She felt nervous. It was the first day of big school all over again. Matilda knew he'd be angry, and she had no idea what she was going to say. Hopefully, when she opened her mouth, the correct placatory words would come out.

She was summoned inside.

Matilda opened the door and knew straight away she was screwed. Sitting a safe distance apart from ACC Ridley was Chief Constable Alistair Maynard. He hadn't been in the job long. He took over from Martin Featherstone following his resignation after the shooting in January 2019, but Maynard arrived with a reputation as a high achiever who expected his officers to tow the line, get the job done, and listen intently to every word that came out of his mouth. What he said was gospel and any deviation from what he wanted was met with swift and severe reproach.

You are so dead.

Matilda tried to smile at them both but her face, frozen in fear, wouldn't allow it. She waited to be offered a seat and nodded to them as she did so. Their faces told her nothing, though Ridley looked like he was about to explode. Maynard was a slim man in his early sixties, with a smooth bald head, dark-brown eyes and an intense glare which Matilda could feel cutting into her. He looked commanding in his uniform, buttons highly polished, collar stiffly starched. It was frightening just to look at him.

'I know why you've called me in here this morning,' she said, her voice higher than she would have liked. 'The *Guardian* in the article. I mean … the article … in the *Guardian*,' she stuttered. Her palms were sweating, and she could feel a prickly sensation creeping up her back. 'I had no idea it was going to be printed. I will, naturally, launch an investigation to find out who spoke to the press.'

'That won't be necessary,' Maynard said. His voice was low and deep. She had only spoken to him on two occasions, but she was sure his voice wasn't as booming then. 'I'm dealing with this personally. After all, I am mentioned in the article.'

'Right.'

'You know this Danny Hanson, I believe,' Ridley said.

'Erm, unfortunately, yes.'

'He's done quite well out of you over the years.'

'I've tried to shake him off, but he's like a terrier with an ankle.'

'You haven't spoken to him recently?' Ridley asked.

'Yes. He called the other day and asked about Ashton. I politely told him to go away. Told him statements are released through the usual channels. That sort of thing.'

Matilda kept stealing glances at Maynard. He was stony-faced. If he hadn't already spoken, she would have sworn he was a cardboard cut-out.

'Matilda, this could only have come from your team.'

She nodded. 'I'm aware of how it looks. I haven't spoken to my team yet, but I will do.'

'You take full responsibility for your team.'

'I do,' she said, reluctantly.

'Therefore, the buck stops with you.'

'I … yes. I suppose it does.'

'DCI Darke,' Maynard began. 'As you are aware, we're currently living in a period of great uncertainty. This pandemic is going to have unknown consequences for a long time to come. The government is throwing money at the economy to keep it going through the lockdown. When it recovers, this money will need to be paid back, which means budgets will have to be tightened. Since the announcement of restrictions, we've already seen a decrease in violent crime, and we expect it to keep dropping in the coming weeks. I'm afraid, a dedicated unit for homicide and major crime is no longer feasible in the current climate.'

'What?' Matilda asked, looking perplexed.

'You have four weeks to wind up any ongoing cases you have and prepare to hand them over to CID.'

'You're closing us down?'

'We are.'

She turned to Ridley. 'Not ten days ago, I had a meeting in this very room with you, where we went through the applications for the two new DCs we were promised.'

'The world has changed a great deal in the past ten days,' Maynard said.

'This has got nothing to do with budgets or the pandemic. You just don't want me asking questions about Richard Ashton,' she said, feeling her hackles rising.

'The Richard Ashton investigation will continue with a team looking for his killer.'

'And what about my officers?'

'DI Brady, DS Andrews and DC Cotton will be moved over to CID,' Ridley said. 'DC Nowak will still be given support when she is ready to return. As DS Mills has already handed in her notice, we thought it prudent to place her on gardening leave with immediate effect.'

'And what about me?'

There was a beat of heavy silence.

'I'm afraid there is no position available for someone of your rank within CID,' Maynard said. 'We are, therefore, issuing you with four weeks' notice. In that time, you will take on no new cases, but concentrate on the hand-over of current cases to CID. After that, you will be made redundant. This will not have any effect on your pension.'

Matilda stood up. 'You can't do this,' she said. Her words were spoken calmly, but she was minutes away from exploding.

'DCI Darke, as Chief Constable of South Yorkshire Police, I can do anything I wish within my remit. My main goal is to maintain the safety of the people of South Yorkshire, and I can only do so when the budget is spent correctly. The money used to fund your unit will go to frontline officers to tackle issues raised by this pandemic, and beyond.'

Matilda couldn't find the words to speak. She stood, rooted to the spot, hoping the ground would open up and swallow her whole.

'You can leave now, DCI Darke,' Maynard said.

Matilda looked to Ridley. He turned away. She wanted to cry. She wanted to scream. She wanted to jump across the desk and punch Maynard in his bony face until it was just pulp. She nodded, turned, and left the office with her head held high.

Chapter Thirty-One

'I think as long as we keep the windows open for ventilation and have the desks further away from each other, we should be fine,' Sian said as she went round the suite opening the windows. 'I suppose we'll just have to make sure we only get up from our desks when it's necessary and mask up during briefings.'

'The canteen's closed. It was strange seeing that all locked up,' Finn said.

'I hated not going to the gym this morning,' Scott said. 'It sets me up for the day. I feel all sluggish and unsettled.'

Sian looked across at Christian. He hadn't said a word since arriving. He simply pulled out his chair, flopped into it and stared into space. They'd all seen the article on the *Guardian*'s website, and they were all in agreement it was Christian who'd spoken to Danny Hanson, but until he, or Matilda, mentioned it, they continued with work as usual.

'How are the kids, Christian?' Sian asked.

He looked up. 'Sorry?'

'The kids. How are they doing?'

'Oh. Fine. They're enjoying having a lie-in.' He gave a painful smile.

'Are they having lessons remotely?'

'Yes. The school's setting up something to start next Monday.'

'It's good they're not going to miss out on their education,' she said.

The conversation was stilted, and Sian kept glancing over at Finn and Scott, raising her eyebrows and nodding her head towards Christian, asking them to join in. They remained silent. Nobody wanted to be the one to bring up the article, even though they all wanted to talk about it.

The door was flung open and banged against the wall. Matilda grabbed it and slammed it closed. The whole room shook. Her face was red and looked as if she could power the whole station with the amount of angry energy she was emitting.

'What the hell have you done?' she growled at Christian.

'I am *so* sorry,' he said, looking up like a child who'd been found out after stealing a fiver from his mother's purse.

'Really? Are you?' She turned to the others. 'I'm guessing you've all seen the article in the *Guardian*.' They nodded. 'Did you guess it was him who leaked it, or did he tell you?'

'We kind of guessed,' Scott said, reluctantly.

'And Danny Hanson, of all people,' she said, screwing up her face as if she had a bad taste in her mouth. 'Why, Christian? Why?'

'The case wasn't going anywhere. You said yourself we need the boys of Magnolia House to come forward. This was the only way I could think of to do that.'

'Why didn't you come to me and tell me what you were thinking of doing?'

'I knew you'd say no.'

'Yes, I would, but we could have sat down and found an alternative plan together. I told you this was going to be a long and slow burner of an investigation, and you've just ruined it.'

'I haven't,' he said, looking guilty. 'Danny said ...'

'*Don't!*' she snapped, holding up her hand to silence him. 'Don't mention that man's name. I feel my blood pressure rising just thinking of him, and right now I'm ready to explode after what you've done.'

Matilda looked at Christian, took in his hangdog expression, the dark circles beneath his eyes and the aura of sadness emanating from him.

'What's going on with you, Christian? What are you up to?' she asked, her voice calmer.

'I don't know what you mean.'

'When we went to see Peter Ogilvy, and Guy was there with his dog, the dog came running up to you and you said, "Hello again, Toby." You've met Toby before. When?'

Christian blinked rapidly a few times. 'Erm, the other day.'

'Why?'

'I went to Guy's flat.'

'Why?'

'To ... talk.'

'And did you find anything out?'

'Yes ... No ... not really.'

'Well, which is it, Christian? Yes, no or not really?' Matilda asked, losing patience.

'I ... look, we just chatted.'

'And what about when Jennifer called me at one o'clock in the morning, wondering why you hadn't come home yet? Where were you then?'

'I'm trying to get Guy to open up to me. I'm drawing him into my confidence,' he said, unconvincingly.

'He's already told us a great deal about what happened at Magnolia House,' Sian said.

'I want him to … Look, don't judge me, any of you!' he snapped. 'Look, it'll be fine,' Christian said, his voice and facial expression belying his words. 'Someone will come forward; we'll get the evidence we need and once …' He stopped when he saw Matilda's face turn dejected and look to the floor. 'What?'

'Do you know what the consequences are of what you've done?' Matilda said. Her voice was low, but there was strong emotion behind her words. 'If it's revealed it was you who talked to the press, you'll lose your job, you'll lose your pension, and you could very well serve six months in prison.'

'What? It's that serious?' Finn asked, shocked.

'Absolutely.'

'Danny won't tell anyone,' Christian said.

'Maybe not now, he won't. But he'll come back for more information. And when you say no, he'll hold this over you. You've screwed up big time, Christian, and I won't be able to help you now.'

'What do you mean?' he asked, looking furtive.

Matilda took a deep breath and let out a heavy sigh. 'I was summoned into Ridley's office. Sitting next to him was the Chief Constable. It's safe to say neither of them were too happy with the article. In fact, I'd say they were fucking furious. So much so, they've decided South Yorkshire Police can no longer afford a dedicated Homicide and Major Crime Unit.'

'What?' Scott gasped. 'They're closing us down?'

Matilda nodded. 'We've got four weeks to prepare our ongoing cases and hand them over to CID.'

'What about us?' Finn asked.

'You and Scott, along with DI Brady, will be merged back into CID. As Sian's handed in her notice, she'll be going on gardening leave with immediate effect. Unfortunately, there's no place for me on CID, so I've been given four weeks' notice.'

'Oh, my God,' Sian said.

The room fell silent as they took in what Matilda had said.

Christian slumped down onto his desk, his head on his arms. When he looked up, the colour had drained from his face. 'I am *so* sorry,' he said to them all, genuinely meaning it.

'You knew how serious this was,' Matilda said to Christian. 'For crying out loud, when Peter Ogilvy persisted in reporting Sean Evans's murder, they had him tied up and poured petrol over him to scare him off. Did you honestly think there wouldn't be consequences for talking to the press?'

'I didn't think they'd close us down,' he said.

'No. You didn't think, full stop.'

'Is there nothing we can do?' Scott asked.

'No.' Matilda composed herself. She took a few deep breaths and walked over to the window. She immediately turned her back on the uninspiring view. 'Well, we've had a good run. This unit was set up in 2010 as the Murder Investigation Team. We've solved plenty of murders in that time. This isn't the ideal way I wanted it to end, but we can't pick our hand, can we? I'm going to pop out for a while. I don't fancy watching you all clearing your desks.'

Matilda headed for the door with longstrides. Her head was down, and she didn't make eye contact with anyone.

The room descended into a dark silence. Nobody moved.

It was a long, excruciating minute before anyone said anything.

'Well, I think it's safe to say I didn't see this coming. I suppose I might as well get off home now.' Sian leaned forward, picked up the framed photograph of her kids and put it carefully in her bag. She opened her top drawer, removed her mug and other personal items she had.

'You're going right now?' Scott asked.

'With immediate effect, Matilda said.' She stood up and grabbed her coat from the back of the chair. There were tears in her eyes.

'What are you going to do?' Finn asked.

'I'm not sure. Belinda mentioned about me setting up a dog-walking business. I'd be losing weight and making money at the same time. Belinda suggested calling it Donnie Barko. I prefer Lady Chihuahua's Lover,' she gave a forced laugh. 'Well, it's been a pleasure working with you all over the years. I'm going to miss you.'

'We'll miss you, too,' Finn said.

'If you … no,' she said, deciding against what she wanted to say.

She didn't seem to want to leave, all of a sudden. She smiled, but her bottom lip was wobbling. She turned and walked out of the suite. Before the door had managed to close behind her, she came waltzing back in, pulled open her bottom drawer and emptied out the contents – chocolate bars, packets of biscuits, bags of crisps and nuts – into a carrier bag she'd pulled out of her handbag.

'If those in CID think they're having my snack drawer, they can piss off,' she said, turning and leaving the room for the final time.

'What do we do now?' Finn asked.

Scott thought for a moment. 'We go back to attending burglaries, arresting druggies, and if we're lucky, we might pop along to a school to inform little kiddies about the dangers of online chatrooms.'

'Well, my Open University degree is going to come in very handy,' Finn sighed.

'Look, I'm really sorry,' Christian said. 'I honestly didn't think this would happen.'

'What *did* you think would happen, Christian?' Scott asked, sitting back and folding his arms. 'We're dealing with a conspiracy here. We're facing a barrier of silence longer than the Great Wall of China, and you just went and told the world what we're trying to do. Not only have you fucked up this investigation, but you've fucked up the careers of every single member of this unit. So, thank you very much for that!' he spat. 'I'll see you tomorrow, Finn,' he said before storming out of the unit.

'Don't expect me to say anything,' Finn said. 'I'm only a DC. I'm not paid to have an opinion. I think I'll come back later to clear my desk.' He grabbed his phone and was already calling his wife as he left the room.

Christian was alone in the HMCU suite. He looked around him and sighed. In just one phone call, he'd ruined everything.

Chapter Thirty-Two

Matilda was sitting in Adele's office. Even though half her face was hidden behind a disposable face mask, she looked glum. There was a Rubik's Cube as an ornament on a shelf. She picked it up and began moving the squares to get the colours to align.

Adele pushed open the door. She was fully scrubbed up and wearing a Jupiter ventilation mask.

'You shouldn't be here,' she said.

'Have you ever managed to complete one of these?' Matilda asked. 'Surely it's the most annoying thing ever invented.' She tossed it down onto the messy desk.

'I've got bodies coming in by the minute, Matilda. Why don't you go home?'

'What am I going to do, Adele? I've been fired.'

'No you haven't. You've been made redundant.'

'Same thing.'

'No, it isn't.'

'That job was my life.'

'I'm aware.'

'So, what am I supposed to do? Sit around in my pyjamas all day, watching daytime television and eating cereal for lunch?'

'I'd love to do that,' Adele smiled. 'Matilda, I know you're disappointed. I would be, too, but you're in a much better position than anyone else who's lost their job. Look at all those people who've been furloughed, or those who live from pay cheque to pay cheque each month and are going to struggle to pay their bills during the lockdown.'

'You know, telling someone about people worse off than them never helps, Adele. It makes them feel worse for feeling bad in the first place. Yes, I have money in the bank, so I'm not going to lose my house, but I've lost my identity. I've lost my career. I have sacrificed everything for my job, and they've taken it away from me.'

'Adele, Nutwells have delivered. We could use a hand to help fit up the portable storage units,' Donal shouted from somewhere out in the mortuary suite.

'I need to get on, Matilda,' she said. She watched her best friend looking pained and dejected, standing on a cliff edge. 'Would you like some advice?'

Matilda looked up. 'Yes, please.'

'Okay. Well, first of all, the toxicology result from Richard Ashton came back.' She picked up a file from a confused-looking system only she knew the key to. 'He was drugged with Fentanyl. It's a powerful analgesic which would have rendered him immobile while the castration took place.'

'So, he was awake and knew what was happening, but unable to do anything about it?'

'Absolutely. Even more so, given the amount of alcohol in his system. Now, here's my advice. You've been given four weeks' notice in which you've been told to prepare your ongoing cases to hand over.So, do as they ask. Spend the next four weeks investigating Richard Ashton. Find his killer. They'll give you a motive, and add that to the evidence you've already got from the fruit-and-veg seller and the retired vicar.You should then be able to present a decent case direct to the CPS, to have them open an independent inquiry into Magnolia House. On the back of that, you can either make the Chief Constable change his mind to keep the unit open, or get a job elsewhere. Either way, you're a hero for uncovering historical child sex abuse.'

Matilda's eyes widened in excitement. 'Why didn't you tell me this when I came in?'

'Because I shouldn't have had to,' Adele exclaimed. 'You're a DCI. You've been in the job long enough to know what you have to do in order to survive. Don't let something minor like redundancy stop you.'

'You're right. They're expecting me to go quietly. They're in for a bloody shock. I'm going to make so much noise, they'll hear me in … where's far away?'

'Australia?'

Matilda grinned. 'No. It's not ladylike to shout that loud.' She jumped up and grabbed Adele by the shoulders. 'Adele, you're a marvel. If we weren't masked up and in the midst of a pandemic, I'd kiss you.'

'Thank goodness for small mercies.'

Matilda made her way to leave the office, before Adele grabbed her. 'By the way, if you see Scott before I do, tell him Donal is on his team,' she said, winking.

'How do you know that?'

'I asked him.'

'You asked him? Are you allowed to question staff about their sexuality these days?'

'I didn't. He questioned me. He heard you and I were living together and asked me if we were a couple.'

'It's a good job I didn't kiss you then.' She smiled. 'Are you matchmaking between Scott and Donal?'

'I want Scott to be happy. He's so lonely in that flat on his own.'

'Love in the time of Covid. It has a nice ring to it.'

Matilda left the mortuary suite with a bounce in her step. She removed her mask and cleaned her hands with sanitiser by the door, and took out her phone to call for an Uber to take her home. She had some serious sneaky plotting to do. There was a cab three minutes away. No sooner had she booked it than her phone started ringing. It wasn't a number stored in her phone's memory and she didn't recognise the number.

'Hello?' she answered.

'DCI Darke? It's Kenneth Burr. The Police and Crime Commissioner?'

She smiled. 'I remember, yes. Sorry, I don't have your number stored.'

'That's quite all right. It's probably for the best. I've heard what happened this morning. Someone has spoken to the press and your unit is being closed down.'

Matilda hardly needed reminding. 'That's right.'

'I'm sorry to hear that. I'm not sure where that decision has come from. I'm guessing it was the Chief Constable himself. Personally, I'm in favour of dedicated units. Not only are they a focus for the detectives, but they're a comfort to the public at large. Matilda, what are your plans?'

Matilda looked up and down the street for her Uber. It wasn't in sight. It was so quiet, it was almost eerie.

'Right now, I have no idea,' she answered honestly.

'May I make a suggestion?'

'Of course.'

'Don't let this stop you. Yes, you're being silenced, but you know who by and you know how to stop it.'

Matilda frowned. 'I'm not sure I do know who's silencing me.'

'You do. If you give it some serious thought, you'll work it out. Don't let them win.'

The call ended.

Matilda looked at the blank screen of her phone. She tried to recall the conversation but couldn't. The Chief Constable had closed down her unit to put a stop to her looking into the historical sex abuse. The question was, why? The answer could only be that he was involved in it himself. If closing down the Homicide and Major Crime Unit didn't work, and Matilda continued digging, which she had every intention of doing, what would he try next to shut her up?

Chapter Thirty-Three

D anny Hanson was proud of his article appearing in the *Guardian* newspaper. It wasn't trending on Twitter, but he read a few comments people posted, nearly all of them mentioning the castration rather than what the article was hoping to achieve. He had been in two minds whether to mention Ashton having his balls cut off.Now he wished he'd left it out, but to quote the old journalism adage: if it bleeds, it leads, and Richard Ashton had certainly bled.

Danny's bubble was burst by an email from the head of BBC News telling him they wouldn't be requiring him to front any news bulletins for the foreseeable future. The reasoning was the pandemic and the BBC wanting their presenters to do as little travelling as possible to help stop the spread of the virus. He couldn't help thinking of Christian's warning of a cover-up and wondered if someone was trying to stop him writing more articles about child abuse by taking his freelance jobs away. He hoped the *Guardian* wouldn't scare as easily.

Danny couldn't afford to live in London. When he was presenting for the BBC, he called on his mates to lend him a spare bed or a sofa for a few nights. He'd kept his flat on in Sheffield and used it as a base for when he was wearing his investigative journalist hat. Sheffield was ideally located in the country, so he could often return home from wherever his stories took him at the end of the day, even if it did mean a long train journey and not getting home until the small hours.

Journalism wasn't a glamorous job. He'd applied for posts abroad and, despite acing the interviews and making a good impression, he was always sent a rejection email a few days later. Fingers crossed, a story of the magnitude of historical child sex abuse could open doors for him. He'd love to present a report from a war zone. That was the goal.

He checked his inbox for any emails from readers of his article. None. It was only lunchtime so there was still plenty of time. He closed his laptop and went into the kitchen to find something to eat. His cupboards weren't exactly bursting at the seams. He should have started hoarding food when the pandemic was first announced, but he honestly didn't think things would go as far as a national lockdown. He grabbed for a can of beans and wondered if he had any bread in the flat, when his mobile started ringing. He ran back into the bedroom, unplugged it from the charger and swiped to answer.

'Danny Hanson,' he said.

There was a long silence before the caller spoke. 'Hello. Erm, I'm ringing about the article you wrote in the newspaper about Richard Ashton. You are that Danny Hanson, aren't you?'

'I am,' he said with a smile.

'I … I was at Magnolia House in 1995. I read about Ashton being found dead. I've been thinking of nothing else since it happened. I didn't know whether I should go to the police or not.' The man's voice cracked. It was quiet, shaky almost, and there was a hint of fear.

'Do you have information about Richard Ashton's murder?'

'No. Nothing like that. I don't … I've no idea who killed him. I … I was abused … by Richard, and others, at the home. You said in the article about other people coming forward. I've spoken to my wife about it, she knows everything that happened to me. She thinks it would be good for me to speak officially, like.'

Danny had to bite his lip to stop himself cheering. He could interview him, in depth, get him to reveal everything that went on at Magnolia House. He could picture the double-page interview in the *Guardian*. Maybe if he filmed it, the BBC would show clips of the interview as he set out to expose the scandal. He hoped this bloke was good looking. It would help if he was photogenic.

'Are you still there?' the man asked.

'Yes. Sorry, I was just grabbing a pen. I'd be more than happy to sit with you, take a statement, have you put your side of the story across.'

'I'm not sure, with this pandemic and everything.'

'We've got everything in place to protect you from that. I can meet you wherever you like. We can conduct the interview outdoors and sit far enough apart so we're both protected.' Danny crossed his fingers and swore on the Pulitzer Prize for Public Service he hoped to win one day, that this man agreed to go on record and open his heart. He hoped the man was a crier.

'Okay,' he said, reluctantly.

Danny punched the air.

After half an hour, Danny had taken down the basic details from Owen Fothergill. He went to Magnolia House at the age of eight, following his mother's rapid death from stomach cancer. He'd never known his father. He lived at the home for two years until he was fostered and later adopted. He was now thirty-three years old and worked as a supermarket manager. He lived in Gleadless with his wife and two young children. He told Danny many times that he and his wife were happy, but Danny wondered who he was trying to convince. The sexual abuse had affected him in ways he couldn't decipher. He was over-protective of his children and rarely let them out of his sight. He didn't trust the teachers at the school to look after them and never allowed them to sleep over at a friend's house if he didn't know the parents. He hoped talking about his own childhood would help put his demons to rest.

Danny arranged to meet him on Friday. When he ended the call, he fired a quick email off to his contact at the *Guardian* to inform him the article was working, and was about to head back into the kitchen to prepare his lunch when his phone rang again. The number was withheld. He swiped to answer.

'Danny Hanson,' he said in his usually bright and confident manner.

'Hello. I … erm … I … I think I might have some information for you about Richard Ashton and the abuse at Magnolia House.'

Danny was struggling to hold onto his emotions. He could almost hear his own award acceptance speech.

Chapter Thirty-Four

Matilda's house was in silence. Adele had come home late and gone straight to bed, taking a rapidly put-together sandwich with her. She was shattered. The Coronavirus pandemic, added to her already hectic workload, was having a draining effect on Adele and all the mortuary staff.Matilda was, therefore, left alone with her thoughts, and they were not pleasant ones.

Sitting in the dining room, a notepad open in front of her, looking up at the wall of photographs of the boys from Magnolia House, she wondered what her next step would be. How could she get to those boys, now grown men, and convince them to talk to her,when they'd been ignored and forgotten for almost thirty years?

Her silent mobile vibrated on the table next to her. She looked down at the screen. The number was withheld. She had a dark feeling about this.

'Hello,' she answered hesitantly.

'I wasn't expecting to see a newspaper story about the abuse already.'

Matilda's heart sank. It was the killer. She knew it.

'That didn't come from me or my department. It was leaked. Somehow.'

'It's out in the open now,' he said. His voice was quiet and slurred.

'It is.'

'I'm in so much pain,' he said. He sounded it too, as if every word was an effort.

'How can I help?'

'I don't know. I don't think you can.'

'Ashton abused you, didn't he?'

'Hu-huh.'

'And there were others, too, I'm guessing.'

'Yeah. The thing is, I'm not the only one. It wasn't just me who was abused, but I feel so alone in all this. I've tried reaching out. I've tried talking to the others,but they don't want to know.'

'People deal with these things in so many different ways,' Matilda said. 'Some want to talk, some don't.'

'I want to talk,' he said softly. There was pain and fear in every word he uttered.

'Would you talk to me?'

It was a while before he replied. 'I don't know you.'

'Does that matter? Sometimes it helps talking to a stranger.'

He gave a hint of a chuckle. 'You sound like a therapist.'

Oh, God, I do, don't I?

'Have you been to see a therapist at some point?'

'I've seen them all,' he said, tired.

'Would you like me to tell you something personal about me? Would that help?'

'I dunno. It might.'

Matilda finished what was left in the wine glass next to her and wished there was another bottle to hand. She took a deep breath and blew it out. Regulating her breathing used to help in composing herself. It didn't this time. She could feel herself shaking.

'Last year, I was shot. I was in a bad way for a number of months, and when I came home, I felt guilty for doing so when so many of my friends and colleagues didn't.'

'I remember reading about that.'

'I went to see a therapist. I'm still seeing her now. She says I'm suffering with survivor's guilt, among other things. I couldn't understand why I'd survived when my colleagues, my friends, my father, hadn't. I wanted to swap places with any one of them so they could live. But I can't. It doesn't work like that. Even now, all this time later, I'm still in pain. I still have flashbacks and nightmares. It doesn't go away, does it?'

'No,' he said. It was evident he was crying.

Matilda wanted to say more but thought it best to remain silent and see if he would react.

'How ...' He started to ask something but suddenly stopped himself.

'Go on.'

'No.'

'Please. I'd like you to ask.'

Almost a minute went by before he spoke. 'How do you feel about the man who shot you?'

Matilda swallowed hard. 'He's dead and I didn't really know much about him, so I don't have many feelings towards him. But I know he didn't orchestrate the shooting. That was down to his brother. He's in prison, and he'll never be released, but ...'

'But what?'

Matilda didn't want to finish her sentence. She wiped away a tear just as it was about to fall.

'But you wish he was dead too?' the killer asked.

Now it was Matilda's turn to leave a long silence. 'Sometimes.'

'It's the same with me. The men who abused me, they're untouchable. I know they won't see the inside of a prison cell, even if I come forward and gave a statement. They'd be able to afford fancy lawyers and it would be their word against mine. And, I know for a fact I'd be a mess in the witness box.'

'I know it seems that way, but I'm on your side. I can help put them behind bars if you give me names of those involved.'

'It's too late.'

'No it's not,' she almost pleaded.

'I've already started killing them.'

'And a jury will perfectly understand why you felt you needed to do so, but you can stop any time.'

'I want to,' he cried. 'I don't like what I'm doing. This isn't me.'

'I know it's not. You're a good man.'

'I used to be. But they've turned me into someone I don't recognise, someone I don't like.'

'Let me help you.'

'It's too late.'

'It's not.'

'They say killing gets easier after the first one. It doesn't. But there's no other option open to me.'

'There is. I promise I will help you,' Matilda said, her voice rising slightly.

'Can I call you again?'

Matilda closed her eyes. The conversation was coming to an end, but she needed him to know he had an ally.

'Of course you can. Any time.'

'You're a good woman, Matilda Darke. Everybody says so.'

The line went dead.

Matilda let out the breath she'd been holding and slumped onto the table in front of her. She felt exhausted.

Chapter Thirty-Five

Thursday 26th March 2020

I t seemed strange for Matilda to be at home on a weekday. She had woken up to an empty house. Adele had left for work early and Matilda padded around the ground floor with heavy legs, wondering what had happened. She tried to think about the conversation she'd had with the killer last night. He was in agony. If only she could get him to trust her.

In the kitchen, she put two slices of brown bread into the toaster and flicked on the kettle. While she waited for it to boil, surrounded by silence, she wondered if this was what her life would be like in four weeks' time. She could do anything she wanted to with her day. There was a whole library of books waiting to be read and the sun was shining. There was nobody stopping her sitting in the garden with a hardback and a packet of Jaffa Cakes until the sun went down.

Toast buttered, tea made, she went into the dining room and sat at the large table, facing the wall of photographs of the boys from Magnolia House.

'I'm being silenced,' she said to them after swallowing a mouthful of slightly flavoured cardboard. 'Nobody wants to know about you. But you're all victims. You should be heard. Everyone should know your names and what happened to you, but when it comes to sexual abuse, people would rather turn a blind eye and pretend it didn't happen. I can't accept that,' she said, pushing the plate of toast away.

'You're all victims,' she said again. 'The problem is, I think one of you might also be the killer. Which one? Tell me. Please. For the love of God.'

At ten o'clock, the doorbell rang, and Matilda pulled open the door to find Sian on the doorstep. Punctual as ever.

'How weird does this feel?' Sian said, stepping into the house. 'Both of us out of work.'

'You were leaving anyway, you traitor,' Matilda smirked.

'I phoned Christian last night,' Sian began, taking off her coat. 'We had a good long chat. He's wrestling with something but wouldn't tell me what. He is very sorry for going to the press behind our backs like that, but felt there was no other way for the case to progress. In a way, he's right.'

'Yes, he is right. He just went the wrong way about it. We're in the dining room. I have something to show you.'

Matilda led Sian into the dining room. Sian stopped when she saw the photographs on the back wall. Her mouth fell open.

'Are these all the boys from Magnolia House?' Matilda nodded. 'They look so young.'

'Eight, nine, ten. Around those ages.'

Sian stepped closer to the wall and studied each picture. 'They don't look happy.'

'When I first saw the photos, I thought the opposite. I saw boys excited about a game of football, but the more I look at them, the more I see the pain and sadness in their eyes.'

'They all look incredibly sad. It's like … I don't know, it's like they've had their innocence ripped from them.'

'They have. I don't know if all of them were abused or just a percentage, but they were at Magnolia House for a reason. Something happened to them that took them away from their parents. They'd already been through one kind of hell and Richard Ashton was putting them through another.'

Sian turned to Matilda. 'You're right. We can't keep quiet over this. I don't know how the Chief Constable and ACC Ridley can even think of telling us to stop digging.'

'I don't think Ridley had much choice. None of the words he said yesterday were his. There's something else, too,' she took a deep breath. 'The killer called me last night.'

'He called you?'

'It wasn't the first time either.'

'What did he say?'

'He told me about how much pain he's in; how he's tried speaking to therapists to figure out what happened to him, but he's unable to find an answer. He really does sound tortured.'

'Jesus! What are you going to do?'

'I don't know. I suppose I should keep my fingers crossed and hope he'll phone again, and I'll give it another go, try and get him to give himself up, I suppose.'

'Poor bloke. I never thought I'd feel sorry for a killer,' Sian said.

'Me neither. That's the thing, though.He's not a killer

because he's enjoying taking a life or having power over someone. He's not like Steve Harrison or ...' she stopped herself.

'Or my Stuart?' Sian added.

'No,' Matilda said flatly.

'He's up here, isn't he? The killer?' she asked, looking at the wall of photographs.

'Almost definitely.'

'And we need to find out which one?'

'Yep.'

'So, what's the plan of action?' Sian said, pulling out a chair and sitting down.

'You want to help?'

'I've got just under four weeks before I can start Zero Bark Thirty. I've got to do something to keep my mind occupied.'

Matilda smiled. 'I have an appointment to interview Billy Maitland at Stafford Prison tomorrow. Would you like to come with me?'

'Well, I had planned to stare at my living-room wall and cry, but I can do that on Saturday.' She grinned. 'What do you think he can tell us?'

'I don't know. I'm hoping he'll be able to give us names as to who else within South Yorkshire Police knew about the cover-up with Sean Evans's murder. Hopefully, that will lead to discovering who Richard Ashton's pervert mates were.I've been having a look at the Chief Constable's timeline, and he's never done anything out of line. He's worked his way up from being a PC. He's the perfect example of a dedicated copper.'

'Did Maynard and Ashton know each other?' Sian asked.

'I don't know. I've found nothing that can connect the two.'

'If they were both involved in this, on such a massive scale, they will have avoided each other at all costs in their everyday lives, won't they? They'll have made sure they weren't at the same social functions.'

'True. But other people will be able to connect them. There will be mutual acquaintances.'

'Then, that's who we need to look for.'

Matilda pulled out a chair and sat down. 'We still need to be careful over the next four weeks. There's nothing stopping us contacting the adoption services and trying to track down the twelve missing boys, or finding out who were legitimately adopted from Magnolia House and talking to them. Also, we've got the PCC on our side. He's given me his mobile number in case we need him.'

Sian pulled a face. 'He's a politician, though.'

'He's independent of the police and his views carry some weight. I think we should use him if we have to.'

'Fair enough. Are you supplying refreshments here?'

'I can't run to a snack drawer, but I've plenty of coffee and a double pack of dark-chocolate digestives.'

'You're only offering one type of biscuit? Amateur.'

'I'm going to miss your banter.'

'I suppose if you don't get your job back, we could go into business together and open a private detective agency. Mills and Darke. Maybe not. It sounds too much like Mills and Boon.'

'Darke and Mills?'

'Actually, I've been thinking of going back to my maiden name. I've been talking about it with the kids, and they'd change theirs, too. I know Mills is a fairly common surname, but they're not keen on being linked with a serial killer.'

Matilda smiled. 'It's good you're thinking so positively.'

'Well, I've been down about it all. I've felt shocking and beaten myself up that I should have known, but the truth is, I didn't. I thought I had the best marriage in the world. I thought we were a strong couple. There's sod all I can do about what he did, but I can try and make the future for my kids, and me, as happy as possible.'

Matilda stood up and went to leave the room to make the coffee. She stopped in the doorway and turned back. 'I think you should change your name. New start, new you.'

'Absolutely. But first we have to solve the first case of the Bultitude and Darke Detective Agency.'

'That's never your maiden name,' Matilda said, wide-eyed.

Sian laughed. 'No, it's not. I'm joking. It's Robinson.'

'Thank God for that,' she said, relieved.

The doorbell rang.

'I'll just go and get that, then I'll make the coffee.'

Matilda headed for the front door with a smile on her face. She had known Sian for more than twenty years. They'd been through a great deal together in the past couple of years. Sian had been stabbed, shot at, and had her husband unmasked as a serial killer, yet she was still able to get up in the morning, smile, and make jokes.

Be more Sian.

Matilda opened the door. Her face dropped at the sight of Danny Hanson on her doorstep.

'What the hell are you doing here?' she spat.

'I've had a phone call. Well, I've had several phone calls, actually, about the article, but one of the calls stood out among the rest.'

'What are you talking about?'

'I think the killer called me.'

'What?'

Sian came out of the dining room. 'Matilda, let him in.'

Matilda turned to face Sian. 'I don't want that reptile in my house,' she hissed.

'Look at his face.'

She turned back. Danny looked petrified.

Chapter Thirty-Six

D anny Hanson was a very handsome man. His thick, dark, wavy hair was perfectly coiffed. It was messy, yet stylish. Matilda had seen him on the news many times reporting from an outdoor location, the wind whipping his hair up in a frenzy, but it always managed to settle into a neat position. Whenever he appeared on television, 'Danny Hanson' and 'Danny Hanson's hair' were always trending on Twitter. He could be reporting on the most banal subject imaginable, yet people would tune in simply to ogle the man with the smooth skin, the fine cheekbones, the deep, dark, soulful eyes and the gorgeous hair. Matilda wanted to slap him the second she set eyes on him.

He may have been popular with viewers, but Matilda knew the real Danny Hanson. He was a journalist, so she instantly disliked him, but she knew his bravado was all an act. He couldn't handle the gritty side of his job and baulked at the depravities of human nature he was supposed to report upon. She despised him, even more so when he posed as a doctor and took photographs of her while she was in an induced coma following the shooting. And now he was sitting in her living room, drinking her coffee, and invading her personal space once again with his lecherousness.

'Danny, have you had much response to your article?' Sian asked. She could see the sour look on Matilda's face and thought it better to take the lead and give Matilda time to settle down.

He placed his mug of coffee on the table in front of him and licked his lips. From his satchel, he took out his iPad and began to scroll through.

'Yes. I've had more than twenty calls and emails from men who said they were at Magnolia House in the nineties. I'm seeing one bloke tomorrow to interview him. The others are cagier about being interviewed. Some have said they'll email me a statement about what happened to them.'

'And you think one of the callers was the killer?'

'Yes. He's called me three times now.'

'What has he said?'

'He's frightening the bloody life out of me, I don't mind admitting,' he said, looking from Sian to Matilda, then back to Sian. 'It's not just what he says, it's how he says it. He's … I don't know, he sounds haunted, like he's in pain or something.'

'In pain?'

'Not physical, obviously, but more emotional pain. He's also … he's given me a name,' he said, looking scared.

Matilda and Sian exchanged glances.

'Go on,' Sian prompted.

'The thing is, this man is someone you both know. When I tell you, it could have major repercussions.'

'Danny, why do you think I'm at Matilda's house in the

middle of a weekday? Our unit has been closed down. Matilda has been made redundant.'

'What? Is this true?' He turned to Matilda.

'Of course it is,' Sian said. 'Whoever is pulling the strings does not want us asking questions about Richard Ashton and his child-abuse past. We're being silenced.'

'So, what are you going to do?'

Sian almost smiled. 'They want us silent, so we'll shout.'

'Whose name did the killer mention, Danny?' Matilda asked firmly.

Danny glanced back down at his iPad, then looked back up at Matilda. 'Alistair Maynard.'

Both Matilda and Sian's mouths fell open.

'The Chief Constable?' Matilda asked.

'I don't believe it,' Sian said.

'Neither did I. I asked him more than once if he was sure and he said he was one hundred percent positive.'

'What did he actually say?' Matilda sat further forward on the armchair.

'He said he was at Magnolia House in the nineties, that Richard Ashton abused him, and he brought some friends round to the home too. He didn't know their names at the time, but he's seen Alistair Maynard's photo in the papers since, and it's definitely him. He said he'd know his face anywhere.'

'Bloody hell!' Sian exclaimed.

'Did he say anything else that might give you a hint as to his identity?' Matilda asked.

'No. To be honest, I'm glad when the calls end. I'm not a psychiatrist. I don't know what to say to him.'

Matilda opened her mouth to say something, but stopped

when a thought popped into her head. She stood up and went over to the window.

'What is it?' Sian asked.

'He said something last night. I don't know why I've just remembered it. He said that people say killing gets easier after the first one, but it doesn't.'

'Wait, the killer's calling you, too?' Danny asked.

Matilda waved him into silence. 'He was talking in the present tense. Killing gets *easier* after the first one. It *doesn't*. He's already killed again.'

'He's killed another of his abusers?' Sian asked.

'I think so.'

'Do you have another victim?' Danny asked.

'Not that I'm aware of.' Matilda looked at Danny. She really loathed him and everything he stood for, but the fact that the killer was calling him, and other victims were contacting him following his article, meant he could be useful. Matilda chewed on the inside of her mouth. She could taste blood. She could also taste the words on her tongue that were about to come out of her mouth, and they tasted worse. The fact that she was even contemplating sharing information with a journalist was enough to make her want to slam her face through the window.

She returned to her armchair and sat on the edge. She leaned close to Danny. The urge to pick up the heavy Le Creuset coffee pot on the coffee table and insert it into him was too great to ignore. She sat on her hands.

'Danny, why are you here? Why didn't you phone me or go to the station?'

'I've tried calling you, your mobile's switched off.'

'Bugger. I must have forgotten to charge it last night.'

'I called your office, and it just rang out. I called CID and they said you were working from home today.'

'Did they?' She turned to Sian and raised her eyebrows. 'How considerate of them.'

'So, what's going on then? What are you going to do?'

'We have the names and photos of all the boys who were at Magnolia House throughout the nineties, but we have no way of contacting them. Despite your article leading to us being closed down, it's the best way to get in touch with them and find out just how prolific the abuse was and who else, apart from Ashton, was involved.' Matilda closed her eyes and took a breath. 'Now, as much as I'm hating myself for saying this, if you share what you've got, when all of this is over, I will give you all of what I've got. I'll even sit down with you and give an interview and help you write a book about this whole thing.'

Danny's eyes lit up.

'Weren't you writing a book about Carl Meagan?' Sian asked.

'Not now, Sian.'

'You'll not renege on your offer?'

'Sian is my witness. She's the most truthful person I know. She'll hold me to it, even though I'll try to wriggle out of it,' Matilda said, hating herself for making a deal with a hack.

'You're on,' he said, greedily.

With great reluctance, Matilda took Danny into her dining room and while he was studying the photographs, Matilda linked his iPad up to her wireless printer and began to print off the interviews and emails he'd received from callers in the wake of his article.

'So, how many of these boys were abused?' Danny asked Sian.

'We don't know,' she replied. 'Hopefully, we can match your interviews with some of these photos.'

'Are these phone calls accurate?' Matilda asked, flicking through the printed pages.

'As accurate as they can be. My shorthand has always been rusty, and I tend to lose track when someone is telling me how they were gang raped when they were nine years old.'

'Are you all right?' Sian asked, genuinely concerned.

Matilda looked up.

'Yes. I'm fine,' he shrugged. 'I just can't understand how people can do this. It makes me sick just thinking about it.'

'I hate to say it, but this is good work, Danny. All of the blokes you've talked to are on our list of boys who were at Magnolia House.'

'Are you working on the assumption that the killer is also one of the abused boys?'

'It certainly sounds like it,' Sian said.

'And he definitely castrated Ashton?'

'Yes. And he rammed his penis and testicles into his mouth,' Matilda revealed.

'Bloody hell,' Danny crossed his legs and winced. 'Please tell me Ashton was already dead when he did that.'

'Nope. Still very much alive.'

'I suppose I shouldn't show sympathy to Ashton, but what a horrific way to go. So, what do you want from me?'

Matilda looked up at him.

I want you out of my house.

'Well, interview this Owen Fothergill tomorrow, get his story, and ask him if he's willing to make a formal statement with the police. It's fine having people email you and call you up, but we need official statements taken by a police officer. If they're willing, we can do it here. We need names. That's the key. We need to know the names of the men Ashton brought to Magnolia House and who attended his parties.'

Danny nodded. 'But will they have given their real names?'

'Probably not. So ask for detailed descriptions. Did anything stand out about these men? Accents, height, weight, hair and eye colour, any tattoos, birthmarks, piercings, scars, distinguishing features. Did they have a lisp, a lazy eye, wear glasses, jewellery ...'

'It's like a game of Guess Who,' Danny said, laughing.

'I remember playing that as a child with my sister. I don't recall ever asking, "Is your person circumcised?"' Matilda said with an icy stare.

'You want me to ask that?' He paled.

'You need to ask everything that will identify the abusers. Look, if you don't feel comfortable asking these questions, tell them to come to me,' Matilda said. 'Don't mention my unit has been closed down, or that someone is trying to silence us, but tell them we're a dedicated team who are trying to put together enough evidence to make sure the abusers are in prison for a long time. That's the angle you need to drive home with the victims.'

'I will,' he said, looking nervous.

'Look, Danny, forget you're a journalist for now. Forget about writing a story. We need to get as many statements as possible, build up the evidence, then you can go public. I'll even arrange an appointment with Adele's publisher friend, if you want.'

'Okay.' He beamed. 'What do I do if the killer calls me back?'

'Nothing. Let him do the talking. Sympathise with him. Tell

him you understand how he's feeling and allow him to direct the conversation, but try to get him to open up to you. Become his friend.'

'But he's a killer,' Danny said, the shocked expression appearing back on his face.

'Yes. But he's also a victim,' Matilda pointed to the wall of photos. 'He's up there. He's been abused. He's frightened.'

Danny nodded. He looked at his expensive watch. 'I need to go. I'm supposed to be interviewing a GP about Covid at two.' He gathered up his things and put the iPad in his satchel. 'I really appreciate this, Matilda,' he said. 'I know we haven't seen eye to eye over the years, but I really do have a great deal of respect for you.'

Matilda raised her eyebrows. 'Really? You have a funny way of showing it.'

'I'll see you out,' Sian said. She led Danny out of the room, turning back and winking to Matilda.

Matilda gathered up the printed statements and tried to put them into some kind of order on the large table.

'Well?' Sian asked as she came back into the room. 'What do you think?'

'I think we might finally be starting to get somewhere.'

'All thanks to a scuzzy journalist.'

Matilda screwed up her face. 'I hate myself for including him.'

'He's dedicated. You can't fault him for that.'

'I don't have to like him, though.'

'I bet you one hundred pounds, when all this is over, you and he will be friends,' Sian smiled.

'There are times when I could really go off you,' Matilda said.

Chapter Thirty-Seven

Friday 27th March 2020

'I think you should go with The Whole Canine Yards,' Matilda said as Sian squeezed into a tight parking space outside Stafford Prison.

'Gregory suggested The Bark Knight Rises andAnthony said I should go risqué with Fifty Shades of Greyhound.'

Matilda laughed. 'That's a good one.'

She opened the front passenger door of her Range Rover and stepped out. There was a chill in the air, and she shivered. The comfort of the heated seats and scented air freshener was replaced by a sense of dread and apprehension when she looked up at the depressing redbrick monolith.

HMP Stafford had been operating as a prison since 1793. It was a Category C prison and in 2014 it became a sex offenders-only prison.

'I always feel nervous when I arrive at a prison,' Matilda said. 'It's not because of the people inside, it's the actual building. They scare me.'

'It may look archaic and primitive but it's Category C. They've got it cushy,' Sian said as she handed Matilda her car keys. 'You should see the cell Stuart's in. He's got his own TV, a Blu-ray player and an en suite bathroom. He's got more mod cons than our Anthony's got in his halls of residence at university.'

'You've been in touch with Stuart?' Matilda asked as they made their way to the entrance.

'No. Gregory was interested when he first went inside and did some research online, looking at all the cells and what happens inside a prison.'

'Does he want to go and visit him?'

'He did at first. I was willing to take him but then he changed his mind. I think Belinda might have talked him out of it.'

Matilda linked arms with Sian. 'It's not been easy, has it?'

'No. Still, we plod along, don't we?

'It's good you have people around you who'll support you and look after you.'

Sian looked at Matilda. 'I'm not retracting my resignation.'

'Damn.'

'Nice try,' she said with a smile. 'Besides, I've nothing to come back to. The unit's being closed down and I doubt they need another DS in CID.'

'If I managed to get the unit reinstated, would you come back?'

Sian thought momentarily. 'I don't think so. Besides, I'm looking forward to getting Jurassic Bark off the ground.'

'Now that one's good,' Matilda smiled.

Matilda and Sian had to wear face masks and keep their distance from the prison officer as they were led to an interview room.

'How are you coping with the lockdown?' Sian asked.

'We're a prison. We're used to lockdowns,' the officer said over his shoulder. 'I should be asking how you're coping.'

'It takes more than a pandemic to keep detectives off the streets. It's just assumed we carry on as normal. We've had to buy our own face masks,' Matilda said.

'Well, what do you expect when you put a cartoon character in charge of the country?'

Matilda stifled a laugh. 'So, what's Billy Maitland like?'

'Model prisoner. You don't hear a peep out of him. He should be out before the end of the year, Coronavirus permitting.'

They were shown into a room and the door was locked behind them.

Prison interview rooms were seemingly designed with a pandemic in mind. Matilda and Sian were on one side of a desk, the prisoner on the other, and in between, a thick sheet of glass separating them, ostensibly from harm should a prisoner become violent, but it helped in keeping germs away, too. Matilda hoped this wasn't going to be a repeat of the interview with Nigel Tate. She could still feel her flesh crawling.

From the opposite side of the glass, Billy Maitland was led into the room. He looked older than his forty-nine years. His hair was shaved to a buzz cut and greying at the temples. His face was craggy.Dark lines beneath his eyes and heavy eyelidswere evidence of a man struggling to sleep. Matilda wondered what was keeping him awake at night.

He pulled out a chair and sat down with a deep sigh. He looked defeated by life, drawn and grey.

'Good morning, Billy. How are you?' Matilda asked.

Billy looked up and his eyes widened. A hint of a smile appeared on his dry lips. Someone was asking how he was, probably for the first time in years.

'I'm doing okay – thank you for asking,' he said in a soft voice.

Matilda smiled. 'Is there anything you need?'

The smile spread. 'No. I'm fine. But thank you.'

'Have you been told why we're here?'

'You want to talk about Richard Ashton and Magnolia House,' he said, blinking hard.

'Yes. Billy, in 1997, a boy, Sean Evans, was murdered at Magnolia House. The crime was reported on three occasions and no actions were taken. The home was run by Reverend Peter Ogilvy. He reported the murder a fourth time and went straight to Chief Constable Tony Bates. Do you remember that?'

He nodded.

Sian was sitting with a pen poised, hovering over a pad on her lap.

'You were a DS at the time. What happened?'

'I remember Bates coming into CID to talk to the DI, but he wasn't there – I can't remember why – so he spoke to me about it. He asked what actions we'd been taking. I said none. I hadn't been given any orders to investigate.'

'So, CID weren't looking into Sean Evans's murder?'

'No.'

'Who was your DI?'

'Alistair Maynard.'

Matilda's mouth dropped open. Alistair Maynard was now her Chief Constable who had closed down her department to stop her looking into the sex abuse and had also been identified by the killer as an abuser. It was not looking good for Maynard. She looked over to Sian, who started writing.

'When Maynard came back into the office, I went to see him. I mentioned that Bates had been looking for him and told him about the Evans murder, and he told me to leave it, as he was dealing with it.'

'Did anything happen after that?'

'No. To be honest, I was that busy, I didn't give it much thought. You deal with what you're given, don't you?'

'You certainly do,' Sian said.

'You knew Richard Ashton, didn't you?' Matilda asked.

Billy looked down at his hands. He was scraping at the loose skin around the tip of his thumb. His fingernails were bitten down to the quick; they looked sore. He nodded.

'How?'

He shook his head, and it was a while before he answered. 'I'm not a paedophile,' he said, a lump in his throat. 'I like women who are younger than me, that's all. The reason why I'm in here – Rachel Price – she told me she was seventeen. I swear on my mother's life. I had no idea she was really fifteen.'

Matilda looked uncomfortable. 'No offence, Billy, but you were forty-six at the time. Even if she was seventeen, she was still too young for you.'

'Who's to say?' he asked, animatedly. 'If she'd been twenty-nine years older than me, nobody would have batted an eyelid, would they?'

'I suppose not.'

'She lied. She was rebelling against her strict father. It all came out in court. She saw me on Tinder, and thought she'd use me to stick two fingers up to her father, and I get put in prison for it. I'll hold my hand up to sleeping with an underage girl, but I wouldn't have done it if I'd known her real age, and that's the truth. She lied.'

'Okay, Billy,' Matilda put her hands up to get him to calm down. 'I believe you. Look, if you help me, I'll let the parole board know, and that should help with your release.'

Billy looked Matilda in the eye again and gave her a slight smile. He seemed to have warmed to her. 'Thank you,' he said in his low, soft voice again.

'How did you know Richard Ashton, Billy?'

He shrugged. 'I don't know. He came to me. He said he'd heard I liked young women and asked if I wanted to attend a party.'

'Did he say young women?'

'Yes, he did. Look, I was twenty-six. I was a newly promoted DS. Looking back, I was a cocky wanker, and I was told about a party where there would be young women. I was single. Who was I hurting?'

'What happened at this party?'

'I'd been lied to, that's what happened. I was told to go to Magnolia House. I knew it was a children's home, but Ashton said he owned it and the top floor was practically his playroom. I got there and there were other blokes there having a drink and looking sheepish. I'm shown upstairs and sent into this room, and there's a fucking lad sitting on a bed. I turned to Richard, I asked him what the fuck was going on. Do you know what he said to me? He had this grin on his face that chills me even to this day, and he told me to do whatever I wanted to him.'

'What did you do?' Matilda asked when Billy fell silent and showed no sign of continuing.

'Nothing. I was scared to death. I was way out of my depth and didn't have a fucking clue what was going on. What was I supposed to do? I wanted to leave but didn't know if Ashton would be waiting for me outside. In the end, I just sat there. I tried talking to the boy, but I didn't know what to say. He looked just as scared as I was. Then all hell broke loose.'

'What do you mean?'

'I don't know how long I'd been in that room, it felt like years, but suddenly the door burst open and the lad's dragged out. There's pandemonium. Young lads are being pulled out of rooms half-dressed and hurried downstairs, and I'm stood there like a spare part wondering what's going on.'

'Were there any other men there? Did you see them?'

'I saw them. They were doing up their trousers or putting their shirts back on. I didn't want to look at them.'

'What happened?'

'Some were saying how they couldn't be seen to be there, whatever that meant, and ran down the stairs. I followed but Ashton grabbed me. He asked me to go into one of the rooms.There was a bloke on the bed who was pissed, and Ashton wanted me to help him out, take him home.'

'How did Richard seem?'

'He was calm, smiling, acting like nothing had happened.'

'What had happened?'

'The boy, Sean Evans, he was dead.'

'Did you see him?'

Billy nodded. 'I didn't know it was him, obviously, but I saw a young boy, face down on a bed. I could tell he was dead.'

'Could you see how he'd died?'

'No.'

'Didn't you try to do anything?'

'I told DI Maynard the next day.'

'What did he say?'

'He told me he'd take care of it.'

'And did he?'

'Was Sean Evans ever found? Was anyone ever prosecuted for his murder? What do you think?'

'Did you recognise any of the men at Magnolia House with you?' Sian asked, speaking for the first time.

Billy took a deep breath and nodded. 'I recognised three blokes. Not at the time, but I recognised them later. I only knew the name of one man on that night.'

'Go on,' Matilda prompted.

'George Barker was there.'

'Who's he?' Matilda asked.

'Shit!' Sian said. 'He's the Labour MP for Sheffield South. He's also the Shadow Education Secretary.'

'Bloody hell,' Matilda said. 'Who else?'

'Donald Eddington.'

'Who?' Sian asked.

'Name sounds familiar,' Matilda said.

Billy nodded. 'He was on the council back in '97. He ended up being leader for a few years. I'm pretty sure he's dead now.'

'Who else?' Matilda asked.

'Miles Ogilvy.'

Matilda's eyes widened. 'Ogilvy?'

'That's right. The Reverend Peter Ogilvy's younger brother. He was the man who was pissed on the bed, who I had to take home.'

'Wait ...' Matilda stopped and tried to settle her thoughts. 'You're telling me Peter Ogilvy, who ran Magnolia House, had a brother who attended the sex party there?'

'Yes,' Billy replied.

'Did you talk to him? Did he say anything?' Matilda asked.

'He was practically comatose. I had to get his address off

his driver's licence.'

'Did you see him before you were taken upstairs?'

'No.'

Matilda looked to Sian. Both were wide-eyed in shock.

'Why didn't Peter tell you any of this?' Sian asked.

'I've absolutely no idea,' she said. 'Billy, were you ever asked back to these parties?'

'No.'

'Did Ashton ever approach you again?'

'No. I never saw him again.'

Matilda fell silent. It was a while before she spoke. 'Billy, thank you so much for talking to us,' she said, standing up. 'I'll definitely make sure the parole board know of your cooperation.'

'Thank you,' he said with a genuine smile.

———

'What's going on?' Sian asked when they were outside of the prison walls and heading back to the car. 'Why did you end the interview so abruptly?'

'I think it was a set-up,' Matilda said.

'What was?'

'All this time I've just assumed Sean Evans's murder was a tragic accident, a sex game gone wrong, but I think it was planned.'

'Who by?'

'Richard Ashton, obviously.'

'But why?'

Matilda rummaged around in her bag for her keys and tossed them to Sian. 'Billy Maitland, who has never shown the slightest interest in having sex with boys, is approached by

Richard Ashton and invited to a party. And on the night of that party, a child just happens to die. Why?'

'I don't know.'

'So that if Ashton is questioned by police he can turn around and say a member of the police was also at the party. If he's going down, he'll take Maitland with him, and who knows what will happen to the top brass at South Yorkshire Police? I wouldn't be surprised if that's the reason why Peter Ogilvy's brother was there, too,' she said, climbing into the car.

'Go on,' Sian prompted.

'Peter's already questioning Ashton about the abuse. He's alerted Barbara Usher, who's also started asking questions, but she's soon got rid of in a convenient mugging gone wrong. So, to silence Peter, he arranges for Miles to be at the party so he can use his brother against him.'

'But if Miles is a paedophile, Peter isn't going to stick up for him, is he? Brother or no brother.'

'Billy didn't see Miles with the other men before they went up to the top floor. He was already there and pissed out of his mind. When Billy was shown into that room, it was Guy Grayston who was there on the bed. Guy said it was only a matter of minutes before the door was opened and he was dragged out. It felt longer to Billy, as he was scared to death. Guy was used to it by then. It's just possible Miles was drunk and planted in Magnolia House as a set-up. I need to talk to Peter Ogilvy again. Head back to Derbyshire.'

'What about this Donald ... whatshisname ... Eddington?' Sian asked.

'We need to find him, too.'

Sian started the car and pulled out into the quiet road. 'So, Richard Ashton invited Eddington and Barker so he could blackmail them, too?'

'Yes. I'm not sure if Barker was an MP back then, but he's bound to have had some kind of a job on the council or in local government. The same for Eddington too. I bet Ashton invited everyone who'd be able to help in some way, if he ever needed to call in a favour.'

'Sick bastard,' Sian uttered.

'Exactly.'

'And what about Maynard?'

'I'm going to need to tread carefully with him,' Matilda said while she thought. 'Jesus! I knew Ashton was sick, but I had no idea how bloody depraved and evil he really was. Thank God he's dead, because if he was still alive, I'd be taking a pair of scissors to his balls myself.'

'So, what do we do now?'

Matilda blew out a heavy breath and relaxed. 'If Ashton set up that night so he could blackmail people, he's going to use every opportunity. Look into Ashton Developments' history. Find out what they were doing before and after 1997. If I'm right, I bet his turnover more than quadrupled overnight after '97. Bugger,' Matilda said, looking down at her phone.

'What is it?'

'Donald Eddington is in a nursing home. He's got Alzheimer's, according to this article here from a couple of years ago.'

'He won't be much use, then.'

'No. However, we still have George Barker. We'll go and pay him a visit. An MP caught up in a sex scandal. He'll crumble like a gingerbread house.'Matilda turned to look at Sian who had a smile on her face. 'What?'

'Nothing. It's seeing you like this, with fire in your belly – it's nice to see it again.'

'I'm on a mission,' she rubbed her hands together.

Chapter Thirty-Eight

Matilda and Sian pulled up outside Peter Ogilvy's cottage in Edale.

'Do you want me to come in with you?' Sian asked.

'No. I'll chat to him on my own. You look up Ashton Developments' history and get an address for George Barker. We'll go and see him after I've finished with Peter.'

'You've got your determined face on,' Sian said as Matilda climbed out of the car.

'I don't like being lied to.'

Matilda had called Peter on the way over and asked if she could call. He said he'd meet her in the back garden, and that's where he was when Matilda went around the back of the cottage and through the gate. He was sitting at the table and wearing more layers than last time, a look of foreboding on his face. The sun was hidden behind thick clouds and the temperature was hovering around ten degrees.

He smiled when he saw her. She smiled back, but she could feel it hadn't reached her eyes. She pulled out a chair and sat down.

'How are you?' Peter asked. 'How's the investigation going?'

'That's what I wanted to talk to you about. I've just been to Stafford Prison to interview a former detective. Billy Maitland. Do you know him?'

Peter inhaled. His face remained unchanged as he thought. 'I can't say as I do, no.'

'Never mind. It's not important. Tell me about your brother.'

Peter deflated in his seat. 'I'm sorry. I shouldn't have kept it from you. I knew you'd find out.' He leaned forward and picked up his glass of orange juice with a shaking hand. He took a small sip and placed it back on the table. 'Would you like a drink?'

'No. I'm fine, thank you.'

A plethora of emotions seemed to pass over Peter's face. He opened and closed his mouth a few times as if he was trying to find the right words to use, but nothing coherent would come. It was a long moment before he spoke.

'The day after I had the petrol poured over me in the shed, Richard Ashton came to see me. I told him what had happened. I told him it wouldn't silence me. Then he showed me some photographs from the night Sean Evans was killed. They were disgusting. I was sick. I was physically sick.'

Matilda frowned. 'What were the pictures of?'

'My brother, Miles. He was in one of the rooms in Magnolia House. He was on a bed, naked, and one of the boys was performing a sex act on him. It was obvious from the photos that Miles was unconscious, but it was a compromising photo.'

'Did you ask Miles about it?'

Peter nodded. 'He had no recollection of that night whatsoever. We sat down and talked about it at length and deduced that Miles had had his drink spiked with something. One of the boys was told to … well, you can guess what, and Richard took the photographs. It was all done to stop me asking questions. If I persisted in getting Sean's murder investigated, Richard would reveal the photographs to the media and the police,and say I was allowing the abuse to take place and even letting my own brother take part.'

Matilda softened. She'd felt angry and betrayed on the drive over, but hearing Peter's side of the story, hearing how completely helpless he was, made her realise he was a victim, just like the boys he was trying to protect.

'What did you do?'

'Miles wanted to murder Richard. He was serious about it, too. There was a very dark time when I wanted to join him. I've met some disturbed people over the years, but Richard Ashton is the closest I've got to meeting someone who was pure evil.'

'Where is Miles now? Can I talk to him?'

'You can talk to him, but he won't answer you. He's in an urn on a shelf in my bedroom.'

'Oh. I'm sorry.'

'He took his own life in 2000. He couldn't live with the shame of what happened. Richard held it over him, over both of us, ever since it happened.'

'That's the real reason you closed Magnolia House down?'

He nodded. His bottom lip quivered with emotion.

'That's when you lost your faith in humanity?'

He nodded again.

'Is there anything else you haven't told me?'

Peter blinked and tears ran down his face.

Once again, Matilda knelt beside him and placed her arm around his shoulders. She pulled him close, resting his head against her chest. He was so slight; she could feel his bony arms through his layers of clothing.

'I can understand you not telling me about Miles. He's family. It was private. I will not judge you for anything you think you've done wrong, Peter.'

He broke himself free from Matilda's embrace and fished in his pocket for a handkerchief and wiped his eyes and nose. The tears didn't stop.

'How do you think I could afford a cottage in Edale on a retired reverend's pension?'

'Richard Ashton bought it for you?'

'Blood money,' he spat. 'I told the Church I was retiring because I was ill. It wasn't a lie, I was ill, but I'd planned to retire long before then. Cancer just gave me a legitimate excuse. I'd lost all faith, all hope. There was no way I could afford a decent place to live. I went to Richard, and I said I deserved something for keeping my mouth shut all these years. A couple of months later he gave me the keys to this place. I hate myself for being bought like this, but my hands were tied, Matilda. I tried, so many times, to expose Richard, and nobody would listen.'

Matilda was on the verge of tears as she watched this fragile man in front of her crumble as he spilled out the horrors he'd endured for the past twenty years.

'I wanted to do good. That's all I ever wanted.'

'You did do good, Peter.'

'I let the devil in. I wish I'd let Miles kill Richard all those years ago – maybe he would still have been alive now. I'm so lonely, Matilda,' he said through the tears. 'Do you have any idea what that's like?'

'I do,' she said, resting her head on his shoulder. 'I really do.'

He took a breath.'I wish I'd had the guts to kill Richard myself.'

'Peter, we're building a case against Richard, and others – witnesses – are coming forward. Your boys are speaking out,' she said with a hopeful smile. 'I will make sure you're free from the burden you've been holding onto all these years,' she said, gripping his hands hard.

'Will you do a dying man a favour?' Peter asked.

'Of course.'

'The man who murdered Richard Ashton is one of my boys, isn't he?'

'It's more than likely, yes.'

'When you find out which one, when you catch him, let him go. For my sake. Will you do that for me?'

Matilda looked into his eyes and answered as truthfully as she could.

'I've had a text from Danny Hanson,' Sian said as Matilda climbed back into the car. 'He's recorded the interview with Owen Fothergill. He said it went very well, though he couldn't name any names, unfortunately. Also … what's wrong?' she asked when she looked up and saw the tears streaming down Matilda's face.

'I've just lied to a dying vicar,' she said.

'Well, it's not like you were getting into heaven anyway, is it?' Sian grinned.

Matilda turned to her and started laughing. She wiped her eyes. She filled Sian in on everything Peter had told her.

'So, Richard Ashton knew he was facing some serious questions, so he decided to kill a boy and make sure there were people at the scene of the crime, like a detective sergeant and a reverend's brother, so it would be covered up,' Sian said.

'It looks like it.'

'We need to talk to the people who were at Magnolia House on that night.'

'Well, Billy's told us everything he knows, as has Guy Grayston. Miles killed himself. Donald Eddington has Alzheimer's. That just leaves George Barker.'

'While you were talking to Peter, I called Finn and he's found me George Barker's address. He lives at Millhouses, so we can pop along there now if you like.'

'Now is as good a time as any.'

Sian started the engine. 'I've also spoken to Christian and he's going to show Guy a photo of Billy, just to double check he was the man who was with him on the night of the murder.'

'Good thinking.'

'Here,' Sian handed Matilda her notepad. 'I was scouring the Ashton Developments website as well and wrote down a few items of interest. It seems that before 1997, Ashton Developments mostly bought run-down houses at auction, gave them a makeover and sold them on for profit. He was quite successful as well. However, in the summer of 1997, he bought a strip of scrubland from Sheffield City Council and built eighteen homes and two small apartment blocks on it. The following year he won a contract to build St Thomas's Secondary School at Tapton and the parade of twelve shops at the Manor. In three short years, he made more than sixty million pounds.'

'Bloody hell,' Matilda said as she flicked through the pad.

'Ashton was greedy, power hungry and immoral,' Sian said. 'No wonder Peter's in such a state. He's had to sit back and watch his successes. Can you imagine how he felt when he discovered Ashton was being awarded an OBE? Poor bloke.'

As they headed back to Sheffield, Matilda sat back in her seat and looked out of the passenger window. She wasn't looking at the view, she was looking through it, as her mind ran through a thousand thoughts. What had happened to Richard Ashton to make him so evil that he had no qualms over murdering a seven-year-old boy, simply for the purpose of furthering his empire and satisfying his own perverted tastes?

When investigating a murder, Matilda felt it important to have sympathy for the victims. The number-one priority was to find the killer and seek justice for those who had died. But in this case, the murder victim richly deserved to die, and the more she learned about Richard and his nefarious deeds, the more she wanted to keep her promise to Peter Ogilvy.

Chapter Thirty-Nine

M atilda was reading from her mobile as Sian drove through the quiet streets of Sheffield towards Millhouses where George Barker, MP for Sheffield South, lived.

'George was elected an MP in 2010,' Matilda said. 'In 2012, he was on the Labour front benches and has held various posts, including Shadow Foreign Secretary and Shadow Environment Minister. He was even the Shadow Brexit Minister during negotiations with the EU.'

'I'm liking him less and less with every sentence,' Sian said.

'He's currently the Shadow Education Secretary and has caused controversy in recent weeks by saying that during any subsequent lockdown, children should still be going to school. Teachers have said he isn't considering their safety or the parents of younger children who take their kids to school.'

'That's true,' Sian agreed.

'According to *Wikipedia*, he's single, lives alone and has never owned a car. He's quoted in the *Daily Mail* as saying he prefers to cycle where possible and use public transport at all other times. He dislikes cars and thinks there should be an extra tax on four-wheel drives for city use. Bastard.'

'Should I park this around the back?' Sian asked.

'I live on the edge of the countryside, I need a four by four,' Matilda stated.

'When was the last time you went off-roading?' Sian scoffed. 'You use this to come to work and pop to the supermarket.'

'Did I tell you Adele's buying a Porsche 911?'

'Wow. Really?' Sian looked at her with wide-eyed excitement.

'You've no issue with a sports car for city-centre use, then?'

They arrived at Holt House Grove and managed to find a parking space opposite George's house. They both looked over to the house. The windows were closed and the curtains in the living room were pulled slightly open.

'It doesn't look as if he's home,' Sian said.

'We're in a lockdown. Surely there's only doctors and nurses and us pillocks in the police who are allowed out. Unless MPs are classed as key workers as well.'

'Well, they're mostly pillocks, so very probably,' Sian smiled.

It was eerie walking along a deserted street in the middle of the afternoon. There was little background traffic noise, no people on the street going about their everyday life, and the only sounds seemed to be coming from the birds in the trees. Strangely, despite the worry of a high death toll from the pandemic, Matilda quite liked this new quiescent Sheffield. She could get used to it.

She rang George Barker's doorbell and banged the knocker. The sounds echoed around the neighbourhood. She listened intently for any kind of movement inside the house but couldn't hear anything.

She rang again and bent down to look through the letterbox.

'Anything?' Sian asked.

'There are smart shoes in the hallway and a bicycle helmet on a hook. The doors to the ground-floor rooms are all closed. Did you get a number for him?'

'No. Round the back?'

'Sure.'

Sian led the way through an unlocked side gate. Matilda cupped her hands around her eyes and looked through the kitchen window. It was neat and tidy, nothing out of place, and no used dishes in the sink.

'Mat, I think you'd better come and look at this.'

Matilda looked over to Sian who was standing in the middle of the back garden looking up at the house, shielding her eyes from the sun.

'What?'

She followed Sian's gaze and looked at the large bay window on the first floor above the kitchen. The curtains were closed but a swarm of flies was buzzing around the window.

'Call Christian,' Matilda said.

While Sian made the call, Matilda looked around her for something to use to gain entry. She found a rock which fitted in the palm of her hand and hurled it at the window in the double-glazed back door. It bounced straight off the glass, and she had to jump out of the way to stop it from landing on her foot. She picked it up and rather than throw it this time, she banged it hard on the glass until it smashed.

'I don't think you should be doing that,' Sian said.

'I'm still a serving police officer, and there's a concern to life of the occupant of this house.'

'Tell that to the curtain twitcher next door who's on the phone to the police, by the look of it.'

There was a key in the lock on the inside of the kitchen door. Matilda took out a pair of latex gloves from her back pocket and put them on. She reached in and unlocked it. She pushed it open and carefully entered the house, striding over the shattered glass.

The room smelled stale, as if fresh air hadn't circulated for a few days. There was a bowl of fruit on the worktop that contained a few wrinkled apples and a bunch of brown bananas. Matilda walked slowly through the ground floor of the house, taking careful footsteps as if the floor was unstable and she could fall through at any moment. When she reached the bottom of the stairs in the hallway, she looked up. She looked at Sian, who nodded. They'd come this far; they may as well go all the way.

Neither of them held onto the banister as they ascended the stairs, in case fingerprints had been left. The landing was a good size with four closed doors leading off. They didn't need telling which was the bedroom they were interested in, as a couple of flies had escaped from the gap at the bottom of the door and seemed to be trying to get back in. Matilda placed her gloved right hand on the handle and turned to Sian.

'Are you ready?' she asked quietly.

Sian's face was grave. 'No.'

'Right then,' she said, swallowing hard.

She pushed the door open.

The sound of the swarm of insects was deafening and the smell hit them like a juggernaut. They both recoiled. Despite having attended gruesome crime scenes many times over the years and recognising the smell of decomposition, it wasn't a smell you became used to. They covered their mouths and noses with their sleeves, and carefully stepped into the room.

The double bed had been stripped of its duvet, which was lying in a heap by the fitted wardrobe. The mattress was drenched in blood, as was the surrounding carpet. Lying in the centre was a naked man – George Barker, Matilda presumed. His eyes were wide open in a death stare and a strip of electrical tape covered his mouth. She stepped closer. Compared to Richard Ashton, George Barker was a much thinner man, and it was easier to see the gaping hole in him where his penis and testicles used to be.

The wound was infested with maggots and flies, feeding on the rotting fleshthat had taken on a green hue imparted by bacteria adding sulphur to the blood. The smell was rancid.

Christian's arrival was announced by the sound of tyres squealing on the tarmac as he turned into the road at speed and slammed on the brakes, as if he was Lewis Hamilton pulling into a pit-stop.

'Sian? Matilda?' he called out from downstairs.

'We're up here. Don't touch anything,' Sian called.

His heavy feet pounded the stairs. 'I'm a DI. I think I know by now not to … fuck me!' he said as he entered the master bedroom and saw the horrific sight that greeted him.

Sian was looking around the room, trying to focus on anything other than the shocking sight on the bed. Matilda's gaze was fixed on the body.

'Hasn't anybody missed him?' Christian asked. 'He's an MP, isn't he?'

Matilda nodded. 'That's something you'll need to find out. I'm not allowed to take on any new cases.'

In the background, the sound of approaching sirens grew louder.

'That'll be thanks to the nosy neighbour,' Sian said.

Matilda dug her mobile out of her back pocket. She opened the camera and began taking photos of George Barker and the surrounding scene.

'What are you doing?' Sian asked.

'I don't trust this not to be covered up. We've lost a great deal of information thanks to the break-in at the forensic store and Ashton's tablet being stolen. I want to make sure I have this on record.'

'Are you any closer to finding out who's doing this?' Christian asked.

'Not really,' Sian answered for Matilda who was busy zooming in on Barker's crotch.

'Hello! Police!' a deep voice shouted from downstairs.

'I'll deal with this,' Christian said. He couldn't leave the room fast enough.

'Matilda, uniform are here. We'd better make a move. The fewer people who know we're here, the better.'

'True. I've got enough here.' She put the phone away and gave the room a quick glance. Her eyes went back to the body. 'How long do you reckon he's been dead for?'

'I've no idea. You'd need to ask Adele that. Come on,' Sian urged from the doorway.

'I'm just trying to work out if he's victim number two or three, and how many more we're going to find like this.'

—————

Matilda and Sian were sitting on a wooden bench in the middle of George Barker's back garden as Adele Kean and her new assistant Donal Youngblood suited up and entered the house, followed by a team of white-suited forensics.

Christian approached them. He looked grim.

'ACC Ridley's on his way. He's discovered it was you who found him.'

'I thought he might be.'

Matilda took her car keys from her pocket and handed them to Sian. 'Go home. There's no point both of us losing our pensions.'

'No. We both found him. I'm staying.'

'Sian, you're supposed to be on gardening leave. I'm not. I can just about get away with an excuse for being here. You can't.'

Reluctantly, Sian took the keys. 'You'll keep me informed.'

'Of course.'

Christian took Sian's vacated seat. 'So, what are you thinking?'

'Well, he's been dead for some time. A good few days, maybe even longer. Like I said to Sian, is he victim two or three? There's no denying now that this all stems from the night of Sean Evans's murder. Richard Ashton planned to kill one of the kids, it didn't matter which, and he made sure the men there for the party were ones he could use for his own gain. He made sure there was a policeman there, Billy Maitland, and he took compromising photos of Miles Ogilvy, Peter's brother. We need to know who else was at Magnolia House on that night. Maitland said George Barker was there, as was Donald Eddington, former leader of Sheffield City Council, but who else? And where the hell does Maynard fit into this?'

'Mat,' Sian called out as she re-entered the garden.

'What's wrong? If you've dented my car, there'll be hell to pay,' she said with a slight smile.

'I've done nothing to your car. But your back two tyres have been slashed.'

Matilda squatted down to her haunches and inspected the left rear tyre. She stuck her finger through the hole in the tyre wall.

'Carving knife, do you reckon?' she asked Christian who was at the other rear tyre.

'Something like that. Uniform are doing door to door; I'll get them to ask if they've seen anyone in the past half hour or so.'

'Thanks, Christian.'

'This is a warning, isn't it?' Sian asked.

'I've known I've been followed since Ridley told me to stop visiting Peter Ogilvy. I didn't listen, so they've upped their game and taken out my transport.'

'We can use my car,' Sian said.

'I mean, this is childish. Do they honestly think slashing my tyres is going to stop me asking questions? It's desperation on their part. They're panicking.'

A car pulled up behind Matilda's and ACC Ridley stepped out from behind the wheel. He was in full uniform and put his hat on. He did not look happy. Matilda could see the vein throbbing in his neck from fifty paces.

'DS Mills, shouldn't you be tending your garden?' He flicked his head sharply, indicting she should leave.

Sian made to go but Matilda grabbed her sleeve. 'She's with me.'

'She's also in danger of losing her pension.'

'It's all right,' Sian said. 'I'll give my Anthony a ring, get him to pick me up. I'll see you later.'

As she walked away, she made the universal sign for *wanker* behind Ridley's back. Matilda stifled a smile.

Ridley returned to his car and opened the front passenger door. 'Get in,' he ordered Matilda.

'Should we be sharing a confined space during a pandemic?' Matilda asked, her voice laced with sarcasm.

'In,' he barked.

Once inside, Ridley slammed the door and went around to the driver's side. She was about to speak but Ridley held up a hand to silence her. Her reached over to the glove box, took out an envelope and handed it to her. Written on the front in neat capitals, it said: 'DON'T SAY ANYTHING INCRIMINATING. OPEN THIS WHEN YOU GET HOME. CAR MAY BE BUGGED.'

She looked at him with alarm. He nodded.

'So, care to explain why you defied my orders?' he asked. He looked sharply at the envelope, back at Matilda, then to the envelope again, willing her to play along.

'I'm investigating a murder, sir,' she said.

'You've been removed from active duties pending your redundancy and told to wrap up any ongoing cases.'

'In the course of my ...'

'I don't want to hear any more of your excuses,' Ridley interrupted, raising his voice. 'I've given you several warnings and made you aware of the consequences, should you continue to defy my instructions. You didn't listen, so I have no option but to suspend you with immediate effect.'

Matilda glared at him.

Ridley mouthed, 'Play along.' He looked frightened, almost.

'Do you know what?Fine, suspend me. I'm in a union and I can afford a decent lawyer. If you think I'll go quietly, you've another think coming.' She was no Judi Dench, but she hoped she'd given a convincing performance on the spur of the moment. She placed the envelope in her jacket pocket, climbed out of the car and slammed the door behind her. As she walked away, she turned and looked back. Ridley nodded and gave her an encouraging smile, but she couldn't take her eyes away from his. He was nervous. No, it was more than that – he was terrified.

Chapter Forty

Matilda

I'm sorry for the cloak and dagger and the hastily put-together note, but upon hearing of you finding George Barker's body, I felt I had to warn you of how grave this situation is going to get. CC Maynard is worried and decidedly cagey about the Richard Ashton case. He knows more than he's telling me and I've a feeling he's being pressured from elsewhere to stop this sex abuse angle from being made public. Danny Hanson's article has ruffled more than a few feathers and I'm worried myself about how much further this is going to go. I've been told to suspend you, but I want you to continue digging. At the heart of this, there is a dead boy who needs finding and laying to rest. I'll try and help you as much as I can. Talk to Maynard. Ask him about his wife.

'It's not signed,' Adele said after she finished reading the note Ridley had given to Matilda.

'He's hardly going to put love and kisses on the bottom, is he? He doesn't want it getting back to him.'

'How high up is this thing going if the Assistant Chief Constable of South Yorkshire Police is scared?'

Matilda shook her head. 'I've no idea.'

'Are you scared?'

'Surprisingly, I'm not,' she said, sitting back on the sofa and folding her arms. 'I'm more pissed off that someone's slashed my tyres.'

It was getting dark outside. Matilda went over to the curtains and pulled them together. There was no doubt in her mind that if she was still living here alone, she would be a bag of nerves. Fortunately, Adele was with her, and Scott was only a scream away from coming to her aid.

'What did you make of George Barker?' Matilda asked, turning her back on the window.

'He's dead,' she said, dead pan.

'Thank you for confirming that for me. I was in two minds.' She smirked and sat back down. 'Were his testicles found in his mouth?'

'They were.'

'Had he been drugged?'

'Intelligent fingerprinting tested non-negative for an opiate. I've sent a blood sample for a full toxicology report. What do you think this means, here?' Adele asked, looking back at the note. 'Ask about Maynard's wife?'

'I don't know. I don't know much about Maynard, let alone his family. I'm going to pop along to his house tomorrow after I've been to the cemetery.'

'On your own?' Adele asked, looking worried.

'Probably. Look, if Ridley says Maynard is scared, then this is obviously coming from higher up. We could be talking senior politicians here, members of the Cabinet. Maynard is more likely to tell me if I approach him at his house, informally, onetoone.'

'But if he was involved in the abuse himself, then he's more likely to be involved in the cover-up. If this does go higher than a Chief Constable, they'll use him as a fall guy.'

'All the more reason for him to reveal names.'

'What about whatshisname, the PCC bloke? Won't he know?'

'Kenneth Burr? I'm not sure. He's not really been in the job long enough to know anyone.'

'Maybe that's a good thing,' Adele said. 'He hasn't made friendships so won't mind asking awkward questions.'

'It could ruin his career if he speaks to the wrong people.'

'But, like you said, there's a dead little boy out there, somewhere. That's all that matters.'

'It should be, but there are many who only think of themselves. I'll ask him, though.'

'Just be very careful, Mat. What if you have an accident like Barbara Usher did?' she asked, putting quotation marks around 'accident'.

'I'm not going to have an accident. It would look too obvious if I did.'

'It doesn't matter if it does look obvious. You'll be dead and out of the way, unable to ask any more questions.'

Matilda frowned as she considered Adele's words. She quickly shrugged them off. 'Nothing is going to happen to me. They wouldn't risk it. Besides, there is a killer – one of the boys from Magnolia House, most likely – going around trying to kill them. They're more likely to be scared than I am. Whoever *they* actually are.'

'You still don't know?' Adele leaned forward and refilled

her wine glass. She proffered the bottle to Matilda, but she waved it away. She needed a clear head for tomorrow.

'Billy Maitland gave me three names – George Barker, Miles Ogilvy and Donald Eddington – who were at Magnolia House on the night of the murder. Barker's dead. Ogilvy killed himself and Maitland is tucked away safely in prison. Donald Eddington is in a nursing home with advanced Alzheimer's. It is possible the killer will go after him, but what's the point if he's not going to know why he's being killed? There were more men there on that night, and they have two options: they either come to me and admit to being involved in child abuse, or they wait for the killer to knock on their door and cut their balls off.'

There was a knock on the front door. Matilda and Adele froze in terror.

'Well, it can't be the killer,' Adele said. 'Neither of us have any balls, to start with.' She went over to the window and gingerly peeled back the curtain to take a peek at who the late-night caller was. 'It's Christian.'

Matilda sighed. 'I was thinking it might have been Danny Hanson,' she said, standing up and heading for the door.

'You're becoming quite pally with Danny Hanson, aren't you?' Adele grinned as she followed her into the hallway.

'He wanted to come over earlier. I managed to put him off until tomorrow. Clingy sod.'

Matilda pulled the door open and shivered as a gust of wind let itself in.

'Christian, you're out and about late.'

'I had a call from uniform about half an hour ago. Your car's been burnt out.'

In normal times, having two tyres changed would have been simple. In a national lockdown, it was no easy task. Garages were closed and it took a lot of phoning around simply to find a low loader to pick up Matilda's car from Millhouses and take it to her house where she could try and find someone to replace her tyres.

The hazard of living in the countryside was the narrow, meandering lane leading to Matilda's house, and the driver of the low loader didn't even attempt it. So, the Range Rover was left at the side of Ringinglow Road. It couldn't be stolen as the back wheels were flat, but she was worried someone might try and break in – not that there was anything left in there to steal. What she hadn't expected and what she, Adele, Christian and Scott discovered as they approached on foot, was the burnt-out shell of a £120,000 car.

The fire had been put out, yet smoke was still rising from the charred remains and the acrid smell hung in the cool spring air.

It didn't look like her car. If it wasn't for the number plate, Matilda wouldn't have believed it was hers.

'Oh, my God!' Adele exclaimed.

'I feel like I want to cry,' Scott said. 'I loved driving this car.'

Matilda stood back from the others as they walked around it, observing the damage. This was no random act of vandalism, the same way Barbara Usher's death wasn't a random mugging. This was a deliberate, targeted attack by someone who was scared she was getting to the truth of who else was involved in the historical child abuse.

A stiff breeze blew, and Matilda wrapped her arms around herself. She couldn't take her eyes from the wreck of her car. She felt numb. If it had been mindless violence, she would have been angry, but she knew this was an attempt to silence her, and it wasn't working. She turned and walked away, heading back to the warmth of her house. She couldn't help but think what they would be willing to try next to get her to stop.

Chapter Forty-One

Saturday 28th March 2020 – Rotherham Road, Catcliffe. 01:00

Heavy clouds filled the sky, blocking out the light from the moon. The road was as quiet as the grave and he walked, stealthily like a cat, keeping to the shadows, and headed for number 184, an innocuous semi-detached house with two cars in the driveway, bins neatly lined up, still wind chimes hanging from the roof of the porch, and empty milk bottles on the doorstep. A picture of domestic bliss. A cover for the evil that lived inside.

He slid through a gap in the gate and headed for the back of the house. Weeks of watching the property at various times of the day had given him everything he needed to know about their security system. There was an alarm, but it was never activated, and a spare key was placed under a white painted rock if someone was coming when both occupiers were going to be out. It was so easy to snatch the key and have a duplicate made. People were so wrapped up in their own little lives, they didn't realise how lax they were, how much they opened themselves up to be invaded.

He unlocked the back door and stepped into the warmth of the utility room. He closed it behind him, but left it unlocked for a quick getaway.

This was his most daring one yet. Richard Ashton and George Barker had lived alone, but Adam Ingells was married.

He'd been watching Adam and Paula Ingells for a while, and they seemed to live separate lives. They went to work at different times to each other and although Adam arrived home at 4:30 every weekday evening, Paula sometimes turned up at five, sometimes seven, sometimes later. She seemed to be living her own life. Even at the weekends, they never went out in the car together.

He tip-toed through the house, taking in the scent of last night's meal. He looked at framed photographs on the wall of the stairs showing the couple in happier times on holiday or at a family wedding. He wondered what had happened to them that meant they were living together, but apart.

The landing was small. He stood and looked at the closed doors, wondering which one was the master bedroom. The door to the bathroom was slightly ajar. He tried the room next to it, depressed the handle and pushed it slowly open. The door brushed against the thickness of the carpet. It sounded loud against the eerie silence of night.

There was a double bed in the centre of the room, but only one person sleeping in it. From this angle, he couldn't tell if it was a man or woman. He moved further into the room, took out his phone from his back pocket and turned the torch on. He covered the light with the palm of his hand and let only a chink of light through a gap in his fingers. He saw an untidy mound of blonde hair splayed out on the pillow. This was definitely Paula Ingells, as Adam had dark hair. He prayed Paula was a heavy sleeper, and left the room, closing the door behind him.

In the room next door, Adam Ingells lay on his back, mouth open slightly, a gentle snore as he inhaled.

He shook off his backpack and took out the roll of electrical tape, cut off a strip, and placed it over Adam's mouth. He woke within seconds.

He grabbed his wrists and tied them together with the tape and did the same with the ankles. While Adam was thrashing around on the bed, wondering what was going on, the intruder was filling a syringe with Fentanyl. After he'd been injected, Adam soon began to calm down. The intruder hadn't given him as much as he'd given Richard Ashton and George Barker. He couldn't risk hanging around and Paula waking up. He wanted Adam conscious, but still.

'Do you know who I am?' he whispered as he dropped to his knees, mere centimetres from Adam's head.

Adam frowned, then shook his head.

'No. I don't suppose you remember me. My name wasn't important. It was my arse you were interested in, wasn't it?'

Adam's frowned deepened.

'Oh, please, don't look so shocked. You must have known your time was nigh when Richard Ashton was found dead. I'll be honest, I thought they would have found George Barker before now. I suppose it shows MPs aren't as important as they like to think they are. As for you, well, you'll be found straight away, won't you?'

Adam mumbled behind the tape.

'I doubt she'll hear you. She looked pretty out of it when I looked in on her. Still, better not linger, had I?'

Using the scissors, he cut open the boxer shorts to reveal Adam's flaccid penis.

'It's been twenty-three years since that night in Magnolia House. You've obviously been able to put it all behind you, get married and have a life, such as it is. Me? Well, I've tried, but it's not been possible. You see, when you're raped, repeatedly – when you're abused, passed around, and had disgusting, filthy perverts use you for their own fun – it tends to stay in here,' he said, tapping the side of his head hard with the scissors. 'To everyone else, I seem like a normal bloke. I've got a job. I have a place to live. But you and your sick fucking friends have set up home in my head and I can't get you out,' he spat. 'Why, Adam? Why did you do it?'

Tears were running down Adam's face. He shook his head, unable to answer.

'You can't give me an answer, can you?' Adam shook his head again. 'But I need an answer. I need one of you to tell me why you did what you did.'

He stared at Adam's petrified face, waiting for a flicker of something that would lead to an understanding of why he was abused, but there was nothing there, just the fear he had for his own life. The intruder sighed. Disappointed. Another opportunity for closure lost.

'It'll only hurt for a while, then you'll be at peace,' he said, flatly. 'If only the same could be said for me.'

Adam tried to move, but the drug wouldn't let him.

He took Adam's penis and testicles in one hand and removed them from his body with a clean, concise cut. Adam's cries were muffled by the tape.

He sat back on his haunches and watched as Adam bled to death. It took less than two minutes for his eyes to close for the final time. Despite the initial pain from the cut, the release of death was a warm, gently comforting one.

The intruder looked down at the genitals dripping blood in his hand. It was a shame they didn't have a dog or a cat he could feed them to.

The release and satisfaction of taking the life of one of his abusers didn't last long. Almost immediately, the pain and suffering returned. What was he doing? This wasn't how it was supposed to be. He lobbed the genitals onto the bedside table, took off the latex gloves and reached for his mobile in his back pocket.

He could feel himself sweating. His entire body was rigid. Panic had taken over. Maybe he should take the scissors to his own genitals, put himself out of the misery and torment he was feeling. He dialled the number from memory and willed for it to be answered.

———————

In the next room, Paula Ingells woke up and yawned. She looked at the time on her phone. It was a little after half past one. She gave a little smile. There was another seven hours until her alarm would sound, and the working day would begin. She turned over, pulled the duvet up around her and fell back to sleep. Bliss.

Chapter Forty-Two

The vibration of the phone against the wood of the bedside table woke Matilda. The room was already lit, and she had an Ian Rankin open on her lap. She must have nodded off halfway through a chapter. She blinked hard a few times, reached for the phone and looked at the screen. The number was withheld but she knew exactly who would be calling at this hour.

'Hello.'

'Can I ask you a question, Matilda?'

'Of course you can,' she said, closing the book and sitting up to be more comfortable.

'Why do men abuse children?'

'I don't know. I honestly do not know. I've been asking myself the same question recently.'

'Can you try and find out for me?' he asked, whimpering.

'I will.'

'I've asked three people now, and neither could give me a straight answer.'

Matilda's eyes widened. 'Three? Have you … have you killed another one?'

'I just want to know why,' he cried, his voice barely above a whisper. 'Why me? Why us?'

'Who have you killed?'

'He's called Adam. Adam Ingells. I'm just waiting for the blood to finish draining out of him, then I'll go.'

'You're there now? You're still at the scene?'

'He wouldn't answer my question.'

'Are you on your own?'

'His wife is in the next room.'

Oh, my God!

'Okay. Look, why don't I come over to meet you? We can discuss this and try to find an answer between us.'

The killer didn't reply.

'Where are you?'

'I'm in Catcliffe. Rotherham Road.'

'Okay.' Matilda threw back the duvet and swung her legs out of bed. 'Stay where you are. I'll come to you. I promise. Okay?' She waited for the killer to say something, but he didn't. She ended the call and screamed for Adele.

———————

Adele drove at speed through the dark, empty streets of Sheffield. The window was down, and the cold air was blasting in, but it was keeping her awake.

'We'd be so much faster in a Porsche,' she said.

'We'll get there. Just drive,' Matilda seethed.

'I can't believe I'm doing this,' she said. 'I'm not even sure where I'm going.'

Matilda had her own mobile in her left hand and Adele's in

her right. She was using Adele's to type *Rotherham Road* into the satnav while dialling the station with her left hand.

'Here you go. Follow the blue line. This is DCI Matilda Darke,' she said into her phone. 'I need you to get me an address for Adam Ingells. He lives on Rotherham Road in Catcliffe. I need the house number and a unit despatched to the address, but to stay back for my instructions.'

'Stand by, DCI Darke,' the controller said.

'We could do with a third phone. Do you know where you're going now?' she asked Adele.

'I think so.'

'Good.' Matilda snatched the phone and searched through the contacts list. 'Bloody hell, Adele, how many people do you know?' She found Christian's name and called him.

'DCI Darke,' the controller was back on the line. 'Adam and PaulaIngells live at number one-eight-four. A unit has been despatched and will await your instructions. Would you like me to contact the DI on call?'

'Not necessary. Can you send the landline number through to my phone as well, please?' She ended the call and realised she could hear Christian in her right ear. 'Shit. Sorry, Christian, I'm doing several things at once. The killer's called me again.'

'Again? What do you mean,*again*?'

'It doesn't matter. Look, he's committed another murder and is still in the house. Adam Ingells. 184 Rotherham Road, Catcliffe.'

'I'm on my way,' he said and ended the call without adding anything else.

'Adele, put your foot down. You're driving slower than my nan, and she's been dead for more than ten years.'

'I've lost where I am again,' she said, looking all around her.

'Fuck!'

Paula Ingells opened her eyes. She was comfortable, wrapped up in the thick duvet, but she needed a pee. She knew she'd never get back to sleep with a full bladder, so trotted into the en suite on tiptoe and let out a little gasp as she sat on the cold toilet seat. Less than a minute later she was back in bed, punching the pillows into a comfortable mound and pulling the duvet up over her head.

'There's nowhere for me to park,' Adele said as she turned into Rotherham Road.

'Just pull up anywhere.'

Matilda jumped out of the car, mobile in hand, and looked up at the row of houses in darkness. She turned to see a uniformed car turning into the road. She went over to the driver's side and showed him her warrant card. 'DCI Darke. I need you to stay back until we know the situation in there. I don't think he's dangerous, but we may need to restrain him.'

The PC nodded. Matilda looked up to see Christian Brady brake hard behind the marked police car, almost bumper to bumper.

'Matilda,' he said. 'What's happening?'

'His wife is asleep in the next room. We need to get her out of the house without her going into her husband's room.'

'Jesus. Is there a door open?'

'I don't know.' She turned to the uniformed officers. 'Go around the back, see if there's evidence of a break-in.'

Matilda stepped back and looked up at the house. The people in the neighbouring houses had no idea of the nightmare unfolding inches away from their beds.

'He sounded really distressed,' Matilda said. 'More than last time.'

'I can't believe the killer's been calling you and you haven't said anything. How many times is this now?'

'Three.'

'Three?'

The two PCs came back from the rear of the house. 'No sign of forced entry, but there's blood on the door handle and frame.'

'Which means he's gone. Shit. I'm going to call Paula and try to talk her out of there. Hopefully, there's no blood to cause her alarm.' She made the call and stepped closer to the house.

Five rings. Ten rings. Twenty. No answer.

'Come on, Paula, answer, for fuck's sake,' she seethed.

'Yes?' the tired voice said.

'Paula Ingells?'

'Yes.'

'My name is DCI Matilda Darke. I'm with South Yorkshire Police. I'd like to have a word. Could you come down and let me in, please?'

'Let you in? Where are you?' she asked, sounding more awake.

'I'm outside your front door. If you come to the window, you'll see me on your driveway.'

'What do you want?'

'If you could just come downstairs and let me in,' Matilda said, trying to keep panic out of her voice.

'How do I know you're really police?'

'Open your curtains, Mrs Ingells.' Matilda held up her ID for Paula to see.

Paula looked from Matilda to the uniformed officers behind her, a shocked expression on her face. 'What's going on? Has something happened?'

'Paula, I need you to come downstairs and open the door.'

'Hang on. I'll go and wake Adam.'

'*No!*' Matilda shouted. 'Paula, please, listen to me. Something has happened. It's important you come straight downstairs and open the front door to allow me and my officers into the house. Please, don't do anything else.'

The look of fear on Paula's face was heart-breaking. Her bottom lip was quivering and a tear running down her face caught the light of the streetlamp outside her house.

'Paula, I know you're scared, but please, trust me. Look at me. I'll stay with you on the phone while you come down the stairs. Okay?'

Paula nodded.

'Okay. Good. I'll wait by your front door.'

'I'm in my nightie.'

'Paula, don't worry. I've got my pyjamas on under my jeans.'

'I'll be right down,' she said quietly.

Matilda turned to Christian. He was standing by with the two uniformed officers. His expression was grave.

'What am I going to see when I open my bedroom door?' Paula asked.

'I don't know,' Matilda said. She squatted and lifted the letterbox flap. She couldn't see anything in the darkness. 'Hopefully, nothing. But stay calm, breathe, and I'm right here waiting for you, Paula.'

'Why won't you let me wake Adam up?' she asked, tears in her voice.

'I really need you to open this front door right now, Paula. I'll explain everything, I promise.'

'Okay.'

Matilda listened intently, but she couldn't hear a sound, not even Paula breathing.

'Oh my God. There's blood,' Paula panicked. 'There's blood on Adam's door. There's blood all over it. Oh, my God, what the hell's happening?'

'Paula, come down the stairs right now!' Matilda screamed. 'Do not open your husband's bedroom door.'

'Get the ram,' Christian said to one of the uniformed officers.

'I don't understand. What's going on? Adam? Adam? Are you in there?'

'Paula, don't go in that room! I'm begging you.'

'*Adam!*' Paula screamed.

'Break it down,' Matilda said to the uniformed officers.

It took two swings of the ram before the white uPVC door began to split. Two more whacks and the door was swung open. Matilda barged past the uniformed officers, climbed over the broken door and ran inside. She took the stairs two at a time and found Paula standing in the doorway of one of the bedrooms. Her face was white, and she was screaming.

Matilda grabbed her by the shoulders, turned her around, and pulled her into a tight embrace. They fell against the wall and slid down to the carpet. Over Paula's shoulder she could see the dead body of Adam Ingells in the centre of the double bed. His mouth was wide open, his severed genitals sticking out.

Chapter Forty-Three

'I'm still in my nightie,' Paula Ingells said as Matilda Darke handed her a mug of tea.

'I can have an officer collect something from the house for you.'

They were in the family room at South Yorkshire Police HQ. It was decorated for comfort to help distressed witnesses feel at home, but it was difficult to feel comfortable when you looked through the windows and saw uniformed officers walking up and down the corridor and the walls were plastered with posters about terrorism and sexual abuse.

'Why do you and your husband have separate bedrooms?'

Paula had both hands wrapped around the mug. She looked cold, despite the blanket over her shoulders. She blew on the hot drink and took a sip.

'We don't get along as much as we used to do,' she said quietly. 'We lead separate lives but neither of us can afford to buy each other out just yet.'

'You weren't together then?'

'No. We decided to go our separate ways about three years

ago. It was amicable. There were no affairs or screaming matches. We'd just, I don't know, reached the end of the road.' She half-laughed. 'It's strange, though. I mean, since we decided to split up, we were actually getting on better.'

'How long have you been married?'

'Twelve years. We met in 2006, got engaged in 2007 and married in 2008.' She smiled.

'What did you know about your husband?'

'Very little, it seems,' she said, her face hardening. 'I read the article about Richard Ashton. I know he was castrated and that he was a child abuser. Are you telling me I was married to a paedophile?'

Matilda leaned forward. 'Paula, we're working on the assumption that the killer is targeting men who abused him as a child when he was living at Magnolia House Children's Home in Oughtibridge. Did Adam have any connection with Magnolia House?'

'I've never even heard of it.' She wiped a tear away. 'Look, he was a science teacher, for crying out loud! Has he been abusing kids all this time, all through our marriage?'

'I really don't know, Paula. That's something we're going to have to investigate. Did he know Richard Ashton or ever mention him?'

'No.'

'We're going to need a list of his friends so we can contact them.'

She nodded. Then more tears came. 'This can't be happening. We had a pizza last night. We shared a bottle of wine and watched a comedy together to take our minds off this pandemic. We said goodnight, went to bed and everything was normal. Now you're telling me my entire marriage has been a lie.' She placed the mug on the coffee table and snatched a few tissues out of the box to wipe her eyes.

'Paula, we don't know anything yet. Don't make any assumptions until we have the facts. But I promise, I will keep you informed on everything we find out.'

Paula looked up and gave Matilda a weak smile. 'Thank you.'

'Have you noticed anyone hanging around lately, any strange phone calls or people coming to the house?'

'No. It's a quiet area.'

'Have your neighbours mentioned anything about strange people coming around asking about you or Adam?'

'To be honest, I don't speak to any of the neighbours. I don't have time to gossip over the garden fence. Nearly all the Christmas cards are signed by house numbers rather than names.'

There was a soft knock at the door. It opened a crack, and a PC stuck her head through the gap. 'Mrs Ingells's sister has arrived in reception.'

'Thanks,' Matilda said. 'Your sister is going to take you back to her house. As soon as we've finished in your home, we'll let you know.'

'I don't think I want to go back into that house ever again,' Paula shuddered.

'I can understand that.'

Matilda entered the now defunct HMCU suite to find Christian sitting at his desk having a coffee, a perplexed expression on his face. It was still dark outside. Matilda didn't have a clue what time it was.

'How is she?' Christian asked.

'I've no idea. She didn't know if Adam had any connection with Richard Ashton and had never heard of Magnolia House. Is there a coffee going begging?'

'I'll make you one,' Christian said, going over to the kettle. 'Matilda,' he began as the kettle boiled. 'How did you know about all this tonight?'

Matilda dropped into what used to be Sian's chair. She was shattered. 'The killer called me. He told me where he was.'

'Why would he do that?'

'He … I don't know, Christian. He's conflicted. He's going through something I can't even begin to understand.' She took the proffered coffee from Christian and breathed in the strong aroma. She smiled.

'And you said he's called you three times now. What's he saying?'

Matilda shook her head. 'To be honest with you, Christian, he's scaring the living daylights out of me. He's in so much pain. I can hear it in his voice. He's a tortured soul and carrying so much horror around with him. He's killing those who abused him, but he doesn't want to. He's doing it because it's the only way he can think of to silence whatever's screaming inside him.'

'You feel sorry for him?'

'Of course I do. Despite the fact he's killed three men, I just want to hug him and make everything better for him, but I don't know how.'

Christian pulled up a chair and sat down. 'Do you have any idea who it might be who's calling you?' Matilda shook her head as she sipped her coffee. 'Any accent or tell-tale signs?'

'None at all. If only we knew who was at that party on the night Sean Evans was murdered. I'm sure that's where this all comes from. I thought I might have been getting somewhere after talking to Billy Maitland, but he didn't mention anything about Adam Ingells. That's come completely out of left field. The thing is, who else is out there we don't know about?'

'So, where do we go from here?'

'If this does stem from that night in January 1997, then we need to know the names of all the men and boys who were there. The only person who can help us here is Guy Grayston.'

Christian stood up and went over to the window. It was pitch dark outside so he couldn't see beyond what was reflected at him from the bright light in the room. From where Matilda was sitting, she could also see his reflection. It was pained. He seemed to have aged so much in the past few days.

'Guy's helping, but it's not easy trying to remember something you've been forcing yourself to forget for the past twenty-odd years.'

Matilda studied Christian for a while. She looked around her at the empty room. Now was the perfect opportunity for him to open up and tell her what had been preying on his mind recently.

'Christian, come and sit down.' She leaned down and opened Sian's snack drawer. It was empty. *Cheeky cow.*

Christian slowly walked back to the desk and sat. 'I'll go and visit Guy later this morning. I'll tell him of the new developments.'

'Why does this case mean so much to you?'

He looked up at her with wet eyes.

'I've never known you take something so personally before,' she said. 'I know Paul Chattle killing himself in front of you last year affected you. It's only natural. Nobody should ever have to witness something like that. But you've been doing so well, lately. Now, all of a sudden, you've … I don't know, there's a heaviness about you. A sadness. Is everything all right at home?'

He gave her a weak smile. 'Pandemic aside, yes.'

'Then what's wrong?'

Christian's face was devoid of emotions as he stared somewhere into the distance. Yet, despite the blank expression, he was clearly in conflict with something deeply buried.

'Christian, you can tell me absolutely anything. I won't think any differently of you. I won't judge you.'

He opened his mouth to say something and closed it without uttering a word.

'This case is very personal to you, isn't it?'

He gave a slight, almost unnoticeable, nod.

'It's opened a door to a memory you thought was long since buried and forgotten.'

He nodded again and bit down hard on his bottom lip to stave off revealing whatever emotion he was struggling with.

'You were …'

'Do you mind if we don't talk about it?' he interrupted. 'You're an intelligent woman, you've worked it out. We don't need to say the words.'

Matilda swallowed hard. 'That's fine. But I'm always here for you, Christian. Always.'

They made eye contact. Christian smiled, and it was genuine and heartfelt. The killer wasn't the only person Matilda wanted to hug and make everything better for.

'Would you like a lift home?' he asked.

'That would be great, thank you.' She drained what was left of her coffee and stood up. Her legs felt heavy as she headed for the door.

'Matilda, I really am sorry for getting the unit closed down.'

She looked back and saw the genuine sorrow on his face.

She shrugged. 'You did what you thought was right. And it's turned out for the best. We're getting victims of abuse coming forward. That's the main thing.'

'But you're out of a job.'

'True. I might join Sian in her dog-walking business. We could walk dogs by day and solve crimes by night. I might pitch that idea to ITV. It could be just what they're seeking for their Sunday-night schedule.' She smiled.

'Don't you want to scream at me, hit me or something?'

'No. I was angry with you at first, but, well, like I said, it's turned out for the best. If my job means justice for all these lads, then it's a small price to pay.'

'Why are you being so positive about this?'

'I don't know. All I do know is that I'm tired of all the negativity in my life. Sian's talked about starting a new chapter and if she can still smile after everything she's been through, then so can I,' she said, then smiled at him.

'I wish I had your strength.'

Matilda could see he was wrestling with wanting to tell her something he'd kept hidden for decades but was unsure of. He clearly wasn't ready. Rather than make the situation any more confused, Matilda decided to go for levity to lighten the mood.

'There's something you need to know about women, Christian, and that is we've had to fight for everything. You had your freedom and the right to vote. Women had to scream and shout in order for change to happen. Through evolution, we've learned to be tough, and I'm sorry to say this to you, but we're tougher than you now,' she winked.

'I'm not going to argue with that.'

'Look at the Marvel films. Iron Man, Captain America, Hawkeye and Thor. They've all got something that gives them strength – a suit of armour, a shield, a bow and arrow, and a hammer. But Black Widow, she doesn't need anything. She's got fighting strength and mental power.'

'You really need to stop watching those films.'

'I know. But they're good, mindless fun, and I've got a huge crush on Bucky. Come on, drive me home, then you can get back to Jessica and the kids.'

Christian placed his half-drunk coffee on Sian's old desk and grabbed his coat.

At the door, Matilda stopped, turned around, and took one last look at the office. Despite everything she was doing, she doubted it would be enough to see her team reinstated. If CID wanted her ongoing cases, they could sort them out for themselves. She wouldn't be coming back into this room again.

Chapter Forty-Four

I t was still dark when Christian dropped Matilda off. The house was empty, with Adele following the body of Adam Ingells to the mortuary on Watery Street. Matilda locked the door behind her and looked up at the stairs. She didn't have the energy to pull herself up them so went into the living room, where she flopped onto one of the sofas. The room was still warm from the log fire burning out, but she grabbed a blanket from the back of the sofa, pulled it over herself and fell asleep within minutes.

When she opened her eyes, daylight was beaming through the window. She tried to block out the sun with her hand as she sat up. She stretched and winced as her body ached. Chesterfield sofas may be comfortable for sitting in to watch a film and eat a pizza on your lap, but they're not designed for sleeping on. Her back was agony.

She dragged herself into the kitchen in search of food. She was famished. She opened the fridge door and saw three sausage links on a plate. Usually, she loved a sausage sandwich with lashings of tomato ketchup, but then she remembered Adam Ingells dead in his bed, his severed genitals dangling out of his mouth.

'Oh, grow up,' she told herself, grabbing the plate.

She gently fried the sausages and put them between two thick slices of white bread. She sat at the table in the kitchen and enjoyed her breakfast, washed down with a mug of tea. She felt so much better having eaten and given herself energy for the day ahead. She had a lot to do. It was the 28th of March. Today marked the fifth anniversary of James's death. Lockdown be damned, she wanted to pay a visit to her husband.

James and Matilda were sickeningly happy. Everyone said so. They simply enjoyed being in each other's company, had the same warped sense of humour and similar interests. They were a perfect partnership and they both saw themselves growing old disgracefully together. Fate, obviously, had other ideas. James's cancer diagnosis came out of the blue. Before they had time to come to terms with it, it was already too late to halt its growth. It was progressive and the headaches increased in their intensity. It wasn't long before James's sight began to fail, his motor functions were impaired, and the strong drugs that eased the pain were making him vomit. Within weeks, all that could be offered was palliative care. The end was coming.

It was a bright, sunny day, and Matilda wore sunglasses as she made her way to James's grave. She hated not being able to bring any flowers, but the florists were closed and all she had growing in her garden were weeds. James wasn't a fan of flowers, anyway. He never understood how people would lean into them, sniff up and marvel at their fragrance. Every time he sniffed one, he said it smelled of cat piss. Maybe she could plant a tree in the garden in his memory, a mighty oak tree. He'd like that.

Matilda squatted down to her knees and began to pull away at the long grass and weeds that had grown around the grave. She always came ill-prepared. She found a tissue in her pocket, spat on it and rubbed at the dried bird crap on the stone. She wondered if there was a product one could buy to buff up gravestones. Amazon was bound to sell something along those lines.

JAMES MATHEW DARKE
6 OCTOBER 1970 – 28 MARCH 2015
LOVING HUSBAND, SON, BROTHER & UNCLE

'Lately, whenever I've thought about you, it's been with fondness,' she said. 'I've remembered the good times we shared, and I've smiled. Before, I've been in tears because I miss you so much, and I still miss you, and I'm incredibly sad you're not with me, but the tears aren't there. I don't know what that means.'

She thought for a long moment. A stiff breeze blew around and chilled her. 'I think it means I'm used to you not being here and I'm moving on. Part of me doesn't like that. If I'm moving on, I want you by my side, but I know that's not going to happen. I should be moving on, enjoying myself, having fun. Life is fragile, we know that more than most, and this pandemic is testament to how uncertain things are. Maybe being made redundant isn't such a bad thing after all. We'll see.

'I remember us saying that when we reached a certain age, we'd sell up and move to somewhere sunny and warm.' She smiled at the memory. 'I could never imagine you settling for the slower pace of life. I wish ...' She stopped herself. There was no point in wishing. They never came true. She remained on her knees, and stared at the gravestone, unblinking, until her vision blurred. Her mind was blank, but she felt comforted by being so close to James again. She'd stay here all day if she could.

She struggled to get up off the ground and her knees clicked.

'When the shops open up again, I'll buy something to polish this stone up, and I'll bring something to sort these weeds out, too. I'm sorry I've been neglecting you. You're always up here though,' she said, tapping her head. 'And you're always in here,' she tapped her heart. 'I love you so much, James Darke.'

As she turned and walked away, she saw a figure sitting on a bench up ahead with two dogs she instantly recognised. She went overand fussed over the dogs.

'What are you doing here?'

'I came to see you. I had a feeling you'd come here today.'

The penny dropped. Five years ago today for Matilda also meant five years ago for Carl Meagan. On the day of James's death, Matilda was investigating the kidnapping of seven-year-old Carl; 28 March was the day of the ransom drop. She should have handed over the case. She was in no fit state to continue as the lead investigator, but she went on as normal, as if nothing had happened, and went to the wrong car park to drop off the money. The kidnappers fled, taking Carl with them. It was another four years before he was found and brought back home.

She sat down next to him. 'How are you feeling?'

'Strange. It doesn't seem to be getting any better,' he said.

'Recovery is a long process. My husband has been dead for five years and I think I'm only just about coming to terms with it,' she said, stealing a glance to the gravestone.

Carl stared straight ahead. He opened his mouth to speak but seemed to change his mind.

'How is everything at home?'

'Horrible.'

'In what way?'

'I don't like living there anymore. It's different. Mum and Dad put walls up around the house. I can't get used to them. It's like a prison. I keep seeing Gran, dead, in the living room. I can't get the image out of my head,' he said, close to tears.

'Last time I spoke to your mum, she mentioned about you moving away.'

'Yes. Dad's found a restaurant in the Lake District he'd like to buy, but with the lockdown and everything, we can't do much at the moment. I just don't want to stay there anymore,' he said, a catch in his throat.

Matilda didn't know what to say. She leaned down to stroke both Labradors who seemed to be enjoying the rest after walking all the way from Dore.

'How's therapy going?'

'That's going okay, actually,' he said with a smile. 'I wasn't bothered at first, but he's all right.'

'That's good.'

'You don't come and see us as much as you used to,' Carl said, turning to Matilda. 'I enjoyed your visits.'

'I know. I felt I should give you all some space. You need to get on with your own lives, as a family, without me butting in.'

'I didn't think that.'

'Didn't you?'

'No.'

'Well, I'll start coming round more, then. Screw the lockdown,' she said, smiling.

Carl laughed. 'I'd better be getting back. Mum starts to worry if she hasn't seen me for five minutes.'

'Go easy on her, Carl. She's worried about losing you again.'

'I'm not going anywhere,' he said. 'I'm not bloody allowed, am I?'

He stood up. The dogs copied him and he sloped off towards the exit of the cemetery. His head was down, and he was dragging his feet. Everyone assumed once he'd been found and brought back home, everything would get back to normal, but normal no longer existed for the Meagan family.

It was difficult to see Carl Meagan as an eleven-year-old boy. He seemed much more grown-up than his years. He'd been through a great deal during his four years away and that had made him tougher, stronger, but he was still a child. It must be so confusing for him.

She was about to shout after him but stopped herself. She didn't know what to say to make him feel any better. She hoped he'd find peace soon. Maybe once he left Sheffield it would be a fresh start for the whole family, and they could begin their lives again.

Chapter Forty-Five

Christian had phoned Guy four times, and each time it had rung out until the voicemail kicked in. He called Peter Ogilvy who told him that occasionally, Guy liked to take some time out, reflect, and revisit the scene where life went wrong for him.

Christian pulled up behind Guy's van at the gates to the driveway of Magnolia House. They were locked with a heavy, rusted padlock, but a gap at the side of the gates next to the trees, big enough for a slim adult to squeeze through, rendered the security obsolete. He wondered how many children had sneaked through with ease to play among the dangers of a dilapidated building.

The gravel drive was lost to weeds. The grounds were overgrown, and the building looked beyond salvage. Surely it should be pulled down, to put the minds of those who were abused here to rest, and someone should do something constructive with the land – give it back to nature, or build a new housing development.

The closer Christian got to the redbrick building, the more

he could feel the sadness and pain emanating from it. All the windows on the ground floor had steel-mesh sheeting over them, all graffitied and mottled with age. Upstairs windows had been smashed, and the front door had been replaced with heavy-duty fire doors, a shiny steel padlock holding them in place.

Sitting on the steps was Guy with his dog at his feet. He looked up at the sound of approaching footsteps and smiled when he saw Christian.

'I'm guessing Peter told you I was here.' Christian nodded. 'I don't know why I keep coming back. I get depressed a lot. Maudlin. I think of what I've been through, and it gets me down. I don't know why, but when I come here, it seems to take the weight from my shoulders. I sit here, look out at the grounds, and I remember the football matches, the rounders games, the endless summers just running around in the sun, getting high on orange juice and laughing. I don't think of what happened in the building behind me, even though it's so scarily close.'

Christian sat down next to him. He stroked Toby. 'There's been another murder.'

Guy turned to him. 'Who?'

'Adam Ingells.' Guy shrugged his shoulders. 'He was a science teacher at Catcliffe High School.'

'Never heard of him.'

'We think whoever is doing this is someone who was at Magnolia House on the night of Sean Evans's murder back in 1997. We think it's one of the boys going around killing the men who killed Sean. The only way we can find him is by identifying all the boys who were there on that night.'

Guy nodded. 'There was seven of us. Sean. Me and Paul Chattle. Keith Smith, Johnny Black,' he bit his bottom lip while he thought of the other two names. 'Robert Chalk and ... oh, what was he called? Jason Cobb. No, Jamie Cobb.'

'And you were all on the top floor, here, on the night Sean was killed in 1997?'

'Yes. I'm positive.'

'No-one else?'

'No. You think one of them is the killer?'

'I think it's likely. Guy, you know all their names.Have you considered looking them up over the years?'

It was a while before he replied. He nodded. 'I looked Robert Chalk up on Facebook years ago. He lives in Selby now. I messaged him but it was a long time before he messaged back. When he did ... well, he didn't say anything nice. He basically said he'd worked hard to put it all behind him and didn't want the past raking up. Then he blocked me. The thing is, me and Robert were quite close when we were here. We had a lot in common. I suppose I was reaching out for someone to be my friend, someone who had been through the same things as me, who could understand the dark days. Under normal circumstances, we might have met up, had a pint and a few laughs and become buddies again. I don't blame him, though. Why would you want to be reminded of what happened?'

'You can't forget though, can you?' Christian asked.

'No. I haven't forgotten. Robert hasn't either. He's obviously fine with bottling it up, whereas I'm not. I'm trying to live a normal life, but ... I've no idea what "normal" means.' He wrapped his arms tighter around Toby and snuggled into him.

'Tell me about Paul Chattle.'

Guy turned to him. 'Why?'

'I'd like to know what he was like.'

'He's dead. Does it matter?'

'It does to me.'

'Why?'

'I only saw Paul when he was at his lowest point. His girlfriend had been murdered and he was all alone in the world. He was dealing with emotions and experiences that I can't even begin to understand, and in front of me, the same distance apart as you and I are now, he put a gun in his mouth and pulled the trigger. What I saw in his eyes was hopelessness, despair, horror, torment. I saw death. I actually saw the moment death claimed him. I've never seen that before. I don't want to see it again. But I often see Paul Chattle in my mind, and I'd like to know something of him other than whatever pain was eating away at him.'

Guy leaned back against the wall of Magnolia House. 'Paul was one of the funniest lads I ever met,' he said with a smile. 'He always had something to say, a comeback or a put-down. He wasn't nasty with it, but he had a quick wit. He was a terrible footballer, but he loved having a go and would throw himself about the pitch like he had the ball, and it was one all in the final minutes of the World Cup. He gave it his all, and he'd mess it up, but he'd just laugh. He was a cheeky sod, though. We'd go into the paper shop round the corner. It's not there now. And he'd snatch a couple of chocolate bars while having a chat to the woman behind the counter like it was the most normal thing in the world. Then he'd buy a Mars, walk out and divvy up his loot. We all made ourselves sick scoffing it all before we got back, so Peter wouldn't find out.'

Christian found himself smiling. He could picture a young Paul Chattle being the cocky ringleader of a gang of young boys.

'I'm kind of glad Robert Chalk blocked me on Facebook,' Guy said.

'Why?'

'If we'd got talking again and we'd swapped horror stories, I would have probably tried to contact the others. I'd have heard more horror stories and before you know it, my head would be full of them. At least now, I can sit here and remember Paul and Sean and Robert as young lads having fun in the sun; nicking chocolate, giving wedgies to the new boys and daring each other to go down to the kitchen in the middle of the night and steal a few biscuits. It's better to remember people how they were, isn't it?'

Christian nodded.

'Can I ask you a question?' Guy asked Christian after a long silence had developed.

'Of course.' Christian turned to Guy. Their eyes met and locked.

'Who abused you?'

'What?' Christian asked, incredulous.

'Whenever you talk about Paul or Sean or the abuse, you get this look in your eye. There's a sadness inside you and you think you're keeping it at bay, but you're not. You've become a master at putting on a brave face, and the only people who can see it are others who've mastered the same look.'

Christian looked away. He swallowed hard and his shoulders drooped. It was a while before he spoke.

'My uncle,' he began, quietly. 'He ran a hardware shop. During the school holidays Mum and Dad worked and I used to spend my days in the back room of the shop. My uncle lived above it with my auntie. She died when I was seven and my uncle took it hard. Sometimes, I'd stay over so he wouldn't be on his own as much. It was only a two-bedroom flat and the second bedroom was mostly used as storage, so I had to share a bed with him. I didn't mind at first. He was sad and he often cried himself to sleep. He cuddled up to me and I was there to comfort him, but, as time went on … shit …' Christian stood up and moved away from the step of Magnolia House.

Guy followed, with Toby at his heels.

At the bottom of the steps was a wall, made unstable by the ravages of the elements over the years. Christian sat precariously on the edge, his feet dangling in mid-air. Guy sat next to him. He didn't prompt Christian to continue. His presence was enough to get Christian talking again.

'He used to hold me tight. He'd be pressed up against me and I'd feel …' It was difficult for Christian to say it out loud. 'I'd feel him against me. He was …'

'Hard,' Guy finished his sentence. Christian nodded.

'He'd rub himself up against me. He wasn't crying anymore, and he seemed like he was enjoying himself. I thought that at least he was no longer sad. Mum and Dad always said that me going over there to stay with him was helping him not be sad, that I was company for him.'

'Did you ever tell your parents what he did?'

'No.'

'How long did it go on for?'

'A few years. I tried to stop going but, well, Mum and Dad worked loads, so it was like free childcare, me going there all the time.'

'Why did it stop?'

'He died. He went fishing with a friend for a weekend. They got into difficulty out on the North Sea and they both drowned.'

'How did that make you feel?'

Christian turned to Guy. There were tears in his eyes. 'I was sad. I loved my uncle.'

'But relieved?'

He nodded.

'And you've never told anyone about this?'

'My wife knows.'

'I think there's a difference when it comes to being able to move on. Your abuser died. Mine didn't. You knew who your abuser was. I didn't. I could bump into them at any time. That's the frightening part. That's why it never goes away. That chapter of your life is closed. For me, and for whoever is killing these men, it isn't. It's always there. Constantly.'

'You understand why the killer is doing this?' Christian asked.

'Of course I do. I actually wish I had the guts to do it myself. These men, they need destroying.'

The atmosphere between the two grew heavy.

'Surely *you* understand that,' Guy said. 'What if your uncle hadn't died? The abuse would have continued, and it wouldn't have been long before him rubbing up against you wasn't enough. He would have gone further. He would have raped you, Christian. Would you have felt sad then when he died? What if he was still alive now? The secret between you both would have weighed so heavily on you that it could have destroyed your relationship with your wife even before you got married. Your children may not have been born, simply because you couldn't cope with the enormity of the abuse you suffered. Imagine what that feels like. That's what it's like for me, it's what it was like for Paul Chattle, and it's exactly what the killer is feeling. So, yes, I'm pleased he's capable of killing them. I hope he finds them all and fucking annihilates them.'

They both fell silent. Against the backdrop of a city in lockdown, the silence was palpable.

'You're a police officer, so you believe in the justice system. You're also a victim of abuse, and a part of you wants revenge.

Do you honestly think these men are going to answer for their crimes and go to prison?'

'Yes. I do,' Christian replied firmly.

'I don't.'

'I have to believe that, otherwise what's the point in my job?'

Guy shrugged.

'I can't stand back and allow someone to kill these men. We don't know how many of them there are, for crying out loud.' He dug into his inside pocket and took out his phone. 'That's actually why I wanted to see you. I want you to take a look at some of these photos.'

'I'd rather not, but go on.'

Christian selected the photos app and showed him the phone. 'Do you recognise this man?'

Guy nodded. 'Who is he?'

'George Barker. He was found dead yesterday. We think he'd been dead about a week. He was a Labour MP. Was he at the party on the night Sean was killed?'

'Yes.'

'This man?' he asked, showing another picture.

Guy nodded again. 'He was the one who was in the room with me. He was more scared than I was.'

'He was planted there by Richard Ashton so he could blackmail the police into not investigating Sean's death. He's called Billy Maitland. He's a former detective. This one?' He showed him a third photo.

Guy frowned as he tried to remember. 'He looks familiar. I can't say for sure if he was there that night or not.'

'That's Adam Ingells. We found him dead earlier this morning. Last one.'

'Oh my God,' Guy turned away.

'You recognise him?'

'He's the one who took me to that house on Manchester Road.'

'Are you sure?'

'Of course I'm sure,' Guy snapped. 'I'm not likely to forget, am I?Who is he?'

'Jesus! I need to make a phone call,' Christian said. 'I'll be in touch.' He headed for his car at speed, scrolling through his contacts with one hand and fishing for his car keys with the other.

'Wait!' Guy called after Christian. 'He's not … Christian!' He stopped when he saw Christian couldn't hear him over the sound of his heavy footfalls on the gravel driveway. He rummaged in his jacket pocket for his mobile, unlocked it and made a call.

Chapter Forty-Six

M atilda's phone started ringing as she climbed out of the taxi. She whipped off her face mask, took in a lungful of fresh air and swiped to answer Christian's call.

'Matilda, where are you?' He sounded panicked.

'I'm at Endcliffe,' she said. 'I've just got out of the worst-smelling Uber. I wouldn't be surprised if there was a dead body in the boot.'

'What are you doing at Endcliffe?'

'It's where Chief Constable Maynard lives.'

'Are you on your own?'

'Yes. Christian, what's wrong? You sound like a blood vessel's about to explode.'

He blew out a sharp breath. 'I've just been chatting with Guy. I showed him a few photos and he ID'd the man who took him to the house on Manchester Road as Alistair Maynard.'

Matilda froze. 'Maynard abused Guy?'

'Yes.'

'Bloody hell! Will Guy give an official statement?'

'Shit. I didn't ask. Probably.'

'But we've looked back over his timeline. There's no evidence of him knowing Ashton.'

'There doesn't need to be, does there? He covered up the Sean Evans murder investigation back in '97 and I wouldn't be surprised if he hadn't told Ashton about Billy Maitland's sexual interests to lure him to Magnolia House.'

'Shit.'

'Do you want me to come with you to see Maynard?' Christian asked. 'I can be there in less than twenty minutes.'

'No. I shouldn't even be investigating this. I don't mind if I end up getting fired, but I don't want to drag you down with me.'

'I don't mind. I put you in this position in the first place.'

'No. It's fine,' she said, though her voice shook slightly with nerves.

'Okay. Promise me you'll call the second you leave his house. And if you don't call within the next hour, I'm sending back-up.'

Matilda smiled. 'You're on.'

She ended the call and made her way to Maynard's house. When Matilda was with other people, when she had someone to talk to, she was fine. When she was on her own, like now, the doubt, the fear, the nerves, and the despondency set in. She started questioning her own ability as a detective and whether she'd see the end of the case without having a nervous breakdown. Where had this paranoia come from? She could hear Diana Cooper-bloody-sodding-Smith in her head telling her to answer her own question. Matilda blamed the shooting. But how much longer was she going to blame Steve Harrison and his brother for her hang-ups?

She didn't get a chance to answer that one, as she spotted

Maynard in the front garden, digging away at the soil with a fork. Dressed in light-coloured baggy trousers and a beige cardigan, he didn't look the severe Chief Constable with a face of granite, an aura of malevolence and an exaggerated booming voice as if he gargled every morning with a mugful of gravel. He looked like a kindly old grandad, tending his beloved roses.

Matilda stood and watched him. His face was soft and there seemed to be a hint of a smile on his face. He looked blissfully content in his garden. She cleared her throat. He looked up, and as soon as he recognised her, the smile fell from his lips and the colour drained from his face. She'd ruined his weekend just by turning up at his house.

'DCI Darke,' he said, his voice was soft and quiet. 'I didn't expect to see you here.'

'I need to ask you some questions. About Magnolia House.'

'No,' he said firmly, throwing down the fork. 'No. I have told you about taking on that line of investigation. You shouldn't be investigating anything. You've been told to prepare your cases for hand-over.'

'I'm aware, but three men are dead. Richard Ashton, George Barker and Adam Ingells. They were all killed in the same way. This is linked to Magnolia House and the murder of Sean Evans in 1997. Now, you can do what you like with me. You can fire me, take my pension away, slander me in the press, but I will not stop until I discover who was at that home on the night Sean was killed and an investigation is launched into the historical sex abuse at Magnolia House.'

Go for the jugular. You've got the upper hand here.

'Keep your voice down,' Maynard hissed, looking around to see if he was being overheard by the neighbours.

'No. I'm sorry, but I won't keep my voice down,' Matilda

said, getting louder. 'I'm done taking orders from corrupt officials. I already have evidence of boys being sexually abused at Magnolia House, enough to go to the press and have them slap it all over the front pages.'

'Al, is everything all right?' a grey-haired woman called out from the open doorway of the house. She was tiny, not even close to five feet tall, but looked a comfortable grandmother figure in her pastel-coloured clothing and flowery apron. She was the perfect match for Maynard.

'Shit,' Maynard said under his breath. He turned to his wife. 'Everything's fine, Claire. Just a colleague from work come to see how we're both doing.'

'Oh...' She smiled, but it looked painful. 'That's nice. We'd invite you in but, of course, we're not allowed.'

'That's fine. Lovely to meet you, Mrs Maynard,' Matilda said. 'You have a lovely garden.'

'That's Al's department. I'm not at all green-fingered, but I do like to sit in it with a glass of wine and a good book.'

'I'm with you there.' She smiled. 'Any chance I can borrow your husband to tend to my overgrown plot?' She gave an exaggerated laugh.

'He'd be in his element, wouldn't you, Al?'

'Claire, do you think you could leave us for a bit? We need a private talk.'

'Oh,' her face dropped. 'Okay. Sorry. I didn't mean to ... It was so nice to meet you, dear.' She turned and headed back into the house, holding onto the door frame for stability.

'Your wife seems lovely,' Matilda said.

'She is. She isn't well, though.'

'Oh. I'm sorry. Nothing serious, I hope.'

'Nothing physical. She suffers with ... look, what do you want from me?' He folded his arms in defiance. He tried to look the mean Chief Constable with a heavy brow and white pursed lips, but it didn't work without the uniform.

'One of my questions is to do with your wife. I'm told she has a connection to all this.'

'Leave my wife out of this,' he leaned forward and threatened.

'Look, I'm not going anywhere until you give me some answers. I've got nothing to lose, so I'm more than prepared to make a spectacle of myself by setting up camp on the pavement outside your home.'

'You have no idea what you're getting involved with here.'

'Yes, I do,' she said softly. 'I've lost my unit, my team and my job. I've had my tyres slashed. I've had my car burnt out, and I'm pretty sure I'm being followed. I know this is all connected with a massive cover-up, but I don't know exactly who is involved. I do, however, have a witness who has named you as someone of particular interest. Now, you either talk to me now or I go to the press. And before you say anything, I'm aware it's blackmail, but I'm getting desperate here.'

Maynard thought for a moment. He looked around him and settled his gaze on Matilda. He relented.

'Go round the back of these houses. There's an overgrown gennel, but you're slim enough to squeeze down it. I don't want this conversation in front of prying eyes.'

Matilda felt herself relax at the prospect of finally getting answers. 'Thank you.'

When Matilda stepped into the Maynards' back garden, she had to dust herself down. The overgrown gennel was more like a wilderness. She was lucky it was still only spring, and the trees and bushes weren't teeming with life yet.

The garden was long and narrow. Perfectly manicured evergreens acted as a border with the garden next door. The grass was neatly trimmed and lusciously green. It would put Centre Court at Wimbledon to shame. There was a square of decking towards the house and a pristine set of garden furniture sat in the middle of it. Alistair Maynard stepped out of the conservatory doors and closed them behind him, leaving his wife to look through the glass, a perplexed expression on her face. He pulled one of the cast-iron chairs away from the table and sat down, inviting Matilda to do the same. He made sure they were more than the required two metres apart.

'Let me tell you what I need to say first before you start with your questions,' he said. His legs were together, his hands sandwiched between them. There were so many conflicting emotions on his lined face. He looked confused and frightened, appalled and sad.

'Okay,' Matilda said, trying to get as comfortable as it was possible to get on cast iron.

'I'll start with Richard Ashton, and I'll tell you how my wife fits into this, and it starts much earlier than 1997. God, I need a drink.'

It was a while before he began. He looked as if he was marshalling his thoughts, trying to get his story into some kind of order.

'My wife was an accountant. She worked for Thornton Wright. I don't know if you know them. They're a big local firm.'

'My husband used them.' She smiled.

'Ah ... Anyway, one day they got a call from Ashton Developments who were looking for new accountants and, apparently, a mutual acquaintance had given Richard Ashton my wife's name. Thornton Wright sent Claire round and she began working on their behalf for Richard Ashton. That was in 1995, and things were going relatively smoothly.

'I was a Detective Inspector in 1997 and when I was told about a child being murdered at Magnolia House, of course, I investigated. On the first night, I had a visit to my office by Richard Ashton. I'd only vaguely heard of him from Claire. I didn't know anything about him. Jesus, I really do need a drink. Can I get you one?' he asked, standing up.

'No. I'm fine.'

Alistair went into the house and returned less than a minute later with a large measure of whisky. He sat down before he took his first swig.

'I don't usually drink until six o'clock, but ... anyway, where was I?'

'Richard Ashton came to see you at work.'

'Oh, yes. Like I said, I didn't know him and had no idea what he was going to say. Well, you've seen him, a great big barrel of a man. He was a frightening figure. He waltzed into my office, slammed a heavy ledger down on my desk and said for the past two years my wife had been helping herself to his money and squirrelling it away into a private bank account. I didn't believe him, obviously. I know my Claire; she wouldn't do that. But he had all the information, all the evidence. There was indeed a private bank account in Claire's name with over half a million pounds in it, deposits going back two years. It was as if she'd started embezzling from her first day in the job.'

'What did you say to Ashton?'

'I didn't, at first. I was so stunned. I knew, hand on my heart, that Claire was not this type of person. She didn't need to be. We were both earning good money. We didn't have any real debt and we had a good holiday every year. There was no reasoning behind it. I told that to him as well, but he was all for getting an official investigation going and having Claire charged with fraud. She'd have gone to prison. I couldn't allow that. It was lies. It was all lies,' he said, getting more and more frustrated and upset.

'It was a set-up?' Matilda asked.

'Of course it was. Ashton had arranged it all so he could ask me not to investigate the Sean Evans murder, in return for him dropping the charges against my wife.'

'Which you did?'

'I had no choice. Claire, she ...' he bowed his head. 'She fell apart. She was never the most confident sort of person, and when Ashton came round to the house one night to threaten her with prison if I didn't comply, well, she lost it completely. She ran upstairs screaming. By the time I'd got Ashton out of the house and went to her, she was in the bathroom looking for pills to take. I had to protect my wife.'

Matilda nodded. She fully understood.

'Years later, I realised the whole of that night was a set-up. Ashton had arranged for Billy Maitland to be there so it would disgrace the Force if it came out, and for Miles Ogilvy to be there to keep Peter quiet. I heard that Donald Eddington was there. He was leader for Sheffield Council at the time, which explains why Ashton Developments suddenly started winning contracts for housing estates.'

'Did you ever find out what happened to Sean Evans?'

'No,' he shook his head. 'I don't think anyone knows how he died or where he is now.'

'Does the name Duncan Shivers mean anything to you?'

'No. I've had this conversation with Ridley. You think

Ashton created this Shivers character to act as an adoption liaison to get the boys away from Magnolia House?'

'Yes.'

'I think you're right. Ashton was a psychopath. That's the only word for it. He was a manipulator. He was a narcissist and a sadist. He delighted in seeing others squirm, especially if they were in a position of power and he could lord it over them.'

'Who told you to close down the Homicide and Major Enquiry Unit?'

'It came through as an official email from the Home Office. To be perfectly honest, we can't afford a dedicated unit in the current climate, but I wanted to keep it in operation. You and your team do amazing work.' He gave her a faint smile.

She ignored it. 'Do you know a man by the name of Guy Grayston?'

'No.'

'He was only a child when you saw him. DI Brady showed your photograph to him this morning and he named you as the man who sexually abused him at the house on Manchester Road that we use to interview vulnerable witnesses.'

'What? That's a lie,' he fumed, his face reddening. 'I've never abused anyone in my life. I wouldn't. I'm not like that.'

'He's going to give an official statement. He will go to court, stand up, and tell everyone that you picked him up from school in your white Volvo, drove him to Manchester Road and raped him on more than one occasion.'

'Oh my God. No. You've got it all wrong, Matilda,' he said before downing the rest of his drink. 'I'd get a call from Ashton. They'd come completely out of the blue. He'd tell me to go to a school and a boy would get in the car and I was to drive him to Manchester Road. I never got out of the car. The boy did. He went into the house. There was someone there waiting for him.'

'Who?'

'I don't know. I never knew.'

'How did Ashton know about the house in the first place?'

'He had Tony Bates in his pocket. I assume Bates told him.'

'Did Tony Bates abuse any of the boys?'

'No. When his wife died, he fell apart, turned to drink and gambling. He was in serious debt. Ashton gave him money.'

'Did Ashton kill Tony Bates?'

'I don't know,' Maynard shook his head. He looked defeated. 'By the end he was a heavy drinker and smoker. It's possible he could have nodded off in his chair with a lit cigarette. Ashton could have seen him as a loose cannon. I really don't know, Matilda.'

'There is someone else out there who was at Magnolia House in 1997, on the night Sean Evans was murdered, who is pulling a lot of strings to silence me. I don't think my unit being closed down is simply bad timing. Someone arranged for the forensic store to be broken into and vital evidence stolen. Someone arranged for my car to be destroyed. Who is doing this?' she asked, almost through gritted teeth.

'I don't know,' he replied, warily. 'The only way to save your department, I suppose, it by appealing to the PCC. That might work.'

'I don't care about my department,' Matilda exclaimed, standing up. 'Well, I do, obviously, but my main priority is these boys, these men, who are still living in torment twenty-three years later.'

'I can't help you. I never knew who else was involved. I only knew of Richard Ashton. Matilda, the article in the newspaper, has it had any effect?'

She nodded. 'We're getting calls through all the time from men saying they were at Magnolia House and abused there.'

'Are they naming their abusers?'

'Some are. Ashton has been named. As has George Barker, and Peter Ogilvy has given me another dead MP, Lionel Barlow.'

'So, that's three men you can name.'

'Yes.'

'Do it.'

'What?'

'Name them. Get another article printed. Arrest them. Interview them under caution and charge them if necessary. I'll hand in my resignation. I'll have no say in how this case goes then, and I'll be out of reach of whoever else was in league with Richard Ashton.'

Matilda sat back down. She studied him. 'You know, don't you?'

'What?'

'You know who else is involved?'

'I have my suspicions.'

'You're not going to tell me?' He shook his head. 'Why not?'

'The evidence needs to lead you there, not rumour.'

She nodded. She knew he was right.

'I'm so sorry for everything you and your wife have been through.'

'So am I.'

'This is going to destroy South Yorkshire Police. Isn't it?'

'I think so.'

Chapter Forty-Seven

Matilda felt buoyed up in the taxi back to her house. She sent a raft of texts to Christian, Sian, Finn and Scott, asking them to be at her house for seven o'clock. She then sent a text to Danny asking him to come for eight. Despite learning to appreciate his journalistic skills over the past few days, she didn't want him listening in on sensitive police information.

She closed the front door behind her, shook off her jacket, and went into the living room where Adele and Scott were watching the news.

'Should you be in my living room?' Matilda asked Scott.

'I think we're in a bubble,' he said.

'Are we?'

'I have eggs and toilet rolls,' he said with a cheeky smile.

'You're welcome any time,' she said, sitting on the sofa next to him. 'What's Baldrick saying now?' she asked, nodding to the television as the Prime Minister was in the middle of a press conference.

'I've no idea,' Adele said. 'He waffles too much for my liking.'

'Say what you want about Theresa May, but she never scratched her arse at a press conference,' Scott added.

Adele leaned forward, picked up the remote and turned the TV off. 'So, Scott said you've been doing some sleuthing.'

'Yes. I think I'm turning into Jessica Fletcher.'

'Have you uncovered anything?'

She sat on the arm of the sofa and sighed. 'To be honest, I'm not entirely sure.'

'Oh. Jessica Fletcher would be more confident.' Adele smiled.

'Jessica Fletcher was the world's most prolific serial killer. Nobody stumbles across that many murders without having something to do with it. Now, I'm hungry. I haven't eaten since breakfast. Have you had anything?' she asked Adele.

'I had a sandwich at work.'

'Have we got anything to cook a meal with?'

'I think there's some pasta.'

'I've got some meatballs in the freezer,' Scott said.

'I'd rather not eat anything in the shape of balls at the moment,' Matilda made a face.

'Quorn mince? I could make you both a spag bol.'

'I didn't know you were vegetarian, Scott,' Adele said.

'I'm not, but it's better for you than meat. Full of protein.'

'I don't think we should have a healthy eater in our bubble,' Matilda said.

'But if he's willing to cook for us …' Adele grinned.

'Swings and roundabouts. Go on then. I'm going to grab a quick shower.'

Matilda said she'd fill them both in on what she'd uncovered when everyone was there so she wouldn't have to repeat herself, and the topic of the Coronavirus was off the menu. All three sat around the table in the kitchen eating Scott's delicious spaghetti bolognese and chatted about trivial topics. It was light and fun, and they all relaxed and laughed as they sipped red wine (water for Scott) and forgot about the pandemic and the dark deeds some people were capable of.

'Can I say something?' Scott asked. He placed his knife and fork neatly together on his empty plate and sat back. 'Well, I'd like your advice, really.'

Matilda and Adele looked at each other. Scott looked worried.

'Is everything all right?' Matilda asked.

'The other day, I had a text from Donal, and we've been chatting, and things have been ... you know ... progressing.'

Adele smiled. She placed a hand on Scott's. 'Scott, I've said this to you many times. I don't know how else to say it before it'll sink in. Chris would not expect you to live the life of a monk.'

Scott's eyes filled with tears at the mention of Chris's name. 'I know. It's just ... it's only been fifteen months.'

'You can't put a time limit on these things. If you want to go out with Donal, see where things lead, then do so. I want you to be happy. Chris would want you to be happy.'

'I miss him so much,' Scott choked.

'So do I,' Adele said. 'But we can't live in the past, can we?' she added, looking at Matilda.

'No,' Matilda agreed. 'Scott, do you really want to end up like me? It's five years today since James died and I'm still pining for him. Don't wake up in five, ten, twenty years' time and realise you've missed out on so much because you couldn't let go.'

'Besides,' Adele said, 'there's no harm in going on a couple of dates with Donal. Test the water. See where it goes. Enjoy yourself.'

Scott smiled. He looked at Adele and Matilda in turn. 'Thank you.'

'One word of advice,' Adele said. 'If you do end up getting married, don't take his surname. I don't think I could call you Scott Youngblood.'

'He's got the perfect name for a pathologist, hasn't he?' Matilda laughed.

The doorbell rang.

'It's never seven o'clock already, is it?' Matilda asked, looking at her watch.

'Should we be having all these people in the house?' Adele asked.

'Well, no, but we'd be all together at work in the briefing room anyway, we're just bringing it into the house. The government don't give a tiny rat's arse about the police, Adele. Shop workers, restaurant staff, office workers and teachers can all stay at home. Police officers and those in the NHS have to suck it up and fend for themselves. It's as simple as that.'

———————

It was a little after seven o'clock when the last to arrive, Finn, entered the dining room. He elected to keep on a face covering. Matilda was standing at the wall with the photographs of the boys from Magnolia House while Christian, Sian, Scott and Finn were sitting, dotted around the room as far apart as was comfortable. Adele had decided not to join them and was in the living room watching TV. The theme tune from *Murder, She Wrote* could be heard through the walls.

'Did we all clap for carers on Thursday night?' Sian asked. There were nods of agreement from around the room.

'Do you think there'll be a clap for police officers?' Finn asked. 'I'm guessing you've all heard what happened to Debbie Fielding at Darnall.'

'What?' Matilda asked.

'Uniform were out breaking up a party of about fifty people crammed into a tiny flat. This bloke grabs hold of Debbie and starts spitting in her face. It took three officers to get him off her. She's having to self-isolate now.'

'People aren't taking this seriously, are they?' Sian asked.

'They would do if they listened to the science and not what their neighbour's aunt posts on Facebook,' Finn replied. 'I bloody hate social media.'

They fell silent as they reflected on all this. Then Matilda filled them all in on what she'd learned in talking to the Chief Constable. 'Despite Richard Ashton being a member of the Paedophile Liberation Front in the eighties, saying he believed what he was doing was right, he didn't believe his own words.'

'How do you know that?' Scott asked.

'A person with strong beliefs will stick by them, no matter what. Ashton didn't. He knew he was a paedophile and used every trick in the book to cover up his crimes and avoid punishment. He murdered Sean Evans deliberately in order to blackmail the men he chose to be there on that night. Unfortunately, we don't know how many men were there. Ashton, Barker and Ingells were and are now dead. Billy Maitland is safely in prison and Miles Ogilvy killed himself. That's five.Donald Eddington, former leader of the council, was also there. Six. We can assume he's on the killer's hit list, but as he has advanced Alzheimer's, is it worth the risk to kill him? We need to find out who else was there that night before the killer gets to them. I think we need to concentrate on finding the killer, and leave the exposing of child abusers to Danny Hanson. What do you think?'

'I agree,' Sian said.

There were nods around the room.

'The forensic report from the Ingellses' house found no sign of a forced entry,' Scott said. 'However, Paula Ingells has said she often left a key under a rock if they ever had anyone coming to the house to do any work. If the killer has been following these men for a while to learn their routine, it's possible he could have seen Paula leave a key and had a duplicate made. Also, there's a chair in Adam Ingells's bedroom and two dog hairs were found on the seat. The Ingellses don't have a dog.'

'A dog hair has been found at the scene of all three murders,' Finn said. 'Ashton's cleaner allowed her to take her dog occasionally, but what if the killer has a dog and it's come from him? Is there any way we can find out the breed from the hair?'

'I'm not sure. Finn, go and ask Adele to come in,' said Scott.

He nodded and left the room.

'Several people on Richard Ashton's road had dogs,' Scott continued. 'Anthony Rivers had one, too.'

'Who's he?' Matilda asked.

'Lives over the back of Ashton's house.'

'Oh, yes, the train enthusiast who saw something but doesn't want to get involved. Let's hope he has a change of heart when this all comes out, and he can give us the final missing pieces.'

'Guy Grayston has a dog,' Christian said hesitantly.

Adele stood in the doorway and Matilda asked her the question.

'To be honest, without a DNA sample, it's not easy to differentiate a hair sample as being from a dog or cat,' she replied. 'Structurally, they're the same. The forensic report says dog hair as it's the most obvious. It could be cat, rabbit, or mouse.'

'You're not helping, Adele,' Matilda said with a smile.

'I'm not here to help. I'm here to provide facts.'

'So, an animal hair found at the scene of a crime isn't helpful?'

'Not without extracting DNA, and that's going to be a lengthy and costly process. There was a study done in America where the cars of pet owners and non-pet owners were checked for hairs. Animal hair was found in the cars of the non-pet owners just as much as in the pet owners' cars. It all depends on who we come into contact with in our daily lives, and we all know about Locard's exchange principle, don't we? Hairs are transmitted so easily.'

'Is there a way to find out if all the hairs came from the same animal?' Finn asked.

'Yes, if you can extract DNA from the hairs. But then you'll need to match the hairs with a particular animal. It's not going to be cheap.'

The room fell silent.

'May I go now?' Adele asked.

'Yes. Thank you, Adele. Round of applause for Dr Kean,' Matilda said sarcastically and began clapping.

Everyone joined in and Adele bowed as she left.

'I've been chatting with Guy,' Christian said. 'And he said there were five other boys, besides him and Sean Evans, who were at Magnolia House on the night of Sean's murder. Paul Chattle is one, also dead, which leaves four others: Keith Smith, Johnny Black, Robert Chalk and Jamie Cobb,' he said, reading from his notebook.

'Is one of those four the killer?' Scott asked.

'More than likely,' Matilda said. She looked to the photographs on the wall and felt a great sadness wash over her. Usually, she felt contempt for a killer, taking the law into their own hands, but these boys had been abused and ignored for years. It was perfectly understandable for one of them to snap.

'Guy also said that Sean was good friends with Jamie Cobb. We could start with him.'

'Have you tried to track them down?' Matilda asked.

'Not yet. I've looked on social media and I can't seem to find a match with any of the names.'

'Well, we have their names and roughly know when they were born. Phone the tax office up and go from there. They'll have their National Insurance numbers and addresses,' Sian said. 'Although, the tax office will only speak to an accredited financial investigator, and I'm no longer a part of the Force. You'll have to go to the Financial Intelligence Unitand speak to someone and keep your fingers crossed that it won't get back to anyone.'

'Let me look at the electoral register first,' Christian said. 'I might get lucky. If not, I'll risk FIU.'

'Sian, did you read through all that stuff I sent you?' Matilda asked.

'Unfortunately, yes, I did.' Sian leaned down and pulled an iPad out of the bag she'd placed under her chair.

Before Matilda went to speak to Chief Constable Maynard, she emailed all the statements Danny Hanson had sent her, along with the phone calls he'd recorded with the killer, and asked Sian to go through them.

'There are statements from more than sixty men here, and more than forty of those went to Magnolia House,' Sian said, scrolling down her report. 'Some have named names. Adam Ingells and Donald Eddington are named. A couple of the boys have mentioned a man with a scar that, to me, sounds like a burn mark, on his left arm. That should definitely identify one of the blokes.'

'Peter Ogilvy said Duncan Shivers had scars from a burn down his left arm,' Matilda said.

'So, Duncan Shivers, whoever he is, didn't only steal the boys away, he took part in the abuse, too?' Finn asked, adjusting his face mask slightly.

'Also, about these phone calls Danny is having with the killer. There's something about them that's troubling me,' Sian said, sitting back in her chair, a deep worry line on her forehead.

'In what way?'

'He's recorded a few of them and, well, they don't sound like how you describe the calls you're getting.'

'You're getting calls as well?' Finn asked.

Matilda waved him to be silent and told Sian to carry on.

'You've said he sounds in pain, tormented by what he's been through, that he's conflicted about being a killer, but the person calling Danny sounds stronger, more determined. There's no – what's the word I'm looking for? – fear to his voice.'

'Do you think it could be two different people making the calls?' Matilda asked.

'Hang on,' Sian said, searching on her iPad for a particular file.

'Are you thinking there are two killers?' Finn asked.

'No. I was thinking of one killer and a prank caller.'

'But which one is the prank caller?' Scott asked.

'If it's the person calling me, then he deserves an Oscar,' said Matilda.

'Here we go,' Sian said.

The room fell silent, and she played the recording.

'*I'm in pain, Danny.*'

'*I know. I can help. I really can.*'

'*There is no help for me.*'

'*There is. I know you've been through a lot in your life, but there's more help available for you now than there was years ago when you were a child. You can still turn your life around.*'

'*It's too late.*'

'*It's not.*'

'*I've gone too far.*'

'*I can understand why you think that, but you're a victim here. You're not going to go to prison.*'

'*They shouldn't be allowed to get away with what they've done.*'

'*They won't. Look, I know the people in charge of the investigation. They're good people. They'll make sure your abusers are caught.*'

'*I need to finish what I've started. I can't stop now. I can't.*'

'*Let me help you.*'

'*How can you help?*'

'*Tell me who abused you. I can get them prosecuted.*'

'*He's untouchable.*'

'*Nobody's untouchable.*'

'*He really is.*'

'*Who?*'

'*Ma—*'

The call ended.

'That's not the person who's calling me,' Matilda said.

'That's definitely a fake,' Finn said.

'How do you know?' Scott asked.

'It's subtle, but he's disguised his voice. Can we listen to it again?'

Sian replayed it and they all leaned in and listened intently.

'He says the word "help" twice,' Finn said. 'Each time he pronounces it differently. Once he drops the aitch, and the second time he doesn't. He's trying to disguise his accent.'

'Why do people do this? Make fake claims about crimes? I don't understand it,' Scott said.

'It's attention seeking. There's something lacking in their lives, and they need to feel important,' Finn said.

'Be quiet a moment, you two,' Matilda said. She had a pensive look on her face. She chewed her bottom lip as she thought. 'Finn, what was it you just said about his accent?'

'I said he was disguising it.'

'Yes. And why would someone do that?'

'To avoid us knowing who he is.'

'And why would someone do *that*?'

Sian cottoned on to what Matilda was getting at. 'Because the caller knows that we'd recognise his voice. Because we already know who he is.'

'Precisely.' Matilda smiled. 'Give that woman a promotion and a twenty-grand pay increase.'

'I'm not coming back.'

'So, let me get this straight,' Christian began. 'The caller is ringing Danny Hanson pretending to be the killer, and disguising his voice because he knows journalists usually record their conversations and is worried about being recognised?'

'Yes,' Scott answered.

'But if he has information, why not just tell Danny rather than pretend to be the killer?'

'Maybe the information he has will give away his real identity and he doesn't want to get involved, like that train bloke me and Finn spoke to.'

'No. I don't think that's it at all,' Matilda said. 'I think the person calling Danny is someone on a par with Richard Ashton who abused the boys. He's panicking now they're all being killed off, and there's a risk of exposure, so he's making these calls, drip feeding us misinformation, to lead us in a different direction from where we should be looking. This is pure misdirection and manipulation. The real killer is calling me, not Danny Hanson. Trust me, I know torment when I hear it.'

'So, we just ignore him, then?' Sian asked.

'No. We listen to him and collect the information to try and ID the caller.'

Matilda looked to Christian. Their eyes met and he quickly looked away.

'Christian,' she began.

'I know what you're going to say,' he interrupted. 'I saw it in your eyes when Adele was talking about dog hairs.'

'I have to. What is Guy's alibi for all three murders?'

'It's not him.'

'You don't know that.'

'I do. It's not. He's not the killer. I'd know if he was.'

'Christian, he has the motive. He turned up at Paul Chattle's funeral even though nobody else did. It was obviously on his mind. He's still in contact with Peter Ogilvy. He can't let go of the past.'

'It's not him,' he said, quietly and unconvincingly.

'We need his alibi,' she said firmly.

'And if he doesn't have one?'

'We have to consider him as a serious suspect.'

Christian shook his head. 'Guy is not the killer. He's been helping us, for crying out loud.'

'I hope you're right.'

'So, what happens next? Where do we go from here?' Finn asked.

'Well, we need to wrap this up quickly. As soon as Maynard hands in his resignation, whoever is pulling his strings will realise he's got very little time left with someone in his pocket, so he'll want this to go away. We have enough information for this to be made public. Danny Hanson is due here any minute, so I'm going to ask him to write an article and name names.'

'That's risky,' Sian said. 'Do you think he will?'

'We have the statements from the men who were abused at Magnolia House. He'll just be reporting the facts as told to him, the same as with every other story he's worked on. As soon as it's printed, Christian, I want you and your team to go and question everyone connected with Donald Eddington, George Barker, Lionel Barlow and Richard Ashton. We need to know who knew what they were up to, who their closest friends were, who else might have been involved and any connections between them all. It's what we'd do under any other circumstances.'

'Will do.'

'We're reaching the endgame, now,' Matilda said to the room as a whole. 'If everything goes as planned, we'll be able to expose a paedophile ring and stop a killer before he strikes again. But we need to work together and coordinate. As soon as I've spoken to Danny, I'll let you all know what's going to happen.'

'Do you think we'll be able to get the unit reopened?' Finn asked.

'I bloody hope so,' Scott said. 'I'm being threatened with sodding Covid patrols.'

'Will I have to come back and work my notice?' Sian asked.

'I've told you, you're not going anywhere,' Matilda reminded her.

'I've already set up a Facebook page for Mission Impawsible.'

'Oh, God, that's terrible,' Finn said.

'Come on, all of you, out of my house. If we're going to start with painful puns, you can all leave.'

Everyone stood up and started to leave.

'I'll message you all later once I've spoken to Danny. Remember, talk to no-one about all this. Act like everything's normal.'

'Apart from a deadly pandemic and the entire country being locked down?' Scott asked.

'Well, yes, apart from that.'

Chapter Forty-Eight

Matilda decided not to tell Danny she thought the calls he was receiving were fake. If he believed them to be genuine, it would help when he spoke to the supposed killer and, hopefully, get him to reveal more about himself. Knowing the truth might belie that. She knew journalists were good at lying and cheating and deceiving, but she had no idea how good an actor Danny Hanson was.Could he pull off such a con to a man whom she assumed was a master manipulator.

'Are you adding more photographs to that wall?' Danny asked as he entered the dining room. He placed his satchel on the table with a thud and sat down comfortably without being offered a seat.

He was getting too pally with Matilda, and she didn't like it.

'No. There's the same amount there as before. Any more calls from the killer?' she asked.

'No. Thank God. I mean, I know I should be sympathetic towards him after everything he's been through, but, bloody hell, he's cutting their balls off, for crying out loud. What kind of a diseased mind comes up with that idea in the first place?'

Matilda knew the real answer to that question. The person capable of such an unheard-of act was someone who had been drugged and raped from a young age, never sought help for their problems, and never found justice. But now wasn't the time or the place to go into that, and she didn't think Danny would understand.

'Danny, I need you to do something for me,' she said, hesitantly. She hated having to be at the mercy of a reporter, especially Danny-cocking-Hanson, of all people. She would never forgive him for sneaking into her hospital room while she was in a coma, taking photos of her and plastering them all over the Internet. The bastard.

'Sure.' He smiled at her, and she felt her flesh crawl as she mentally signed a contract with the devil using her own blood as ink.

She smiled back. She wondered if he could tell it was fake.

'I want you to write another feature.' She could feel the sweat running down her back. 'You've got more than fifty statements from men saying they were abused at Magnolia House, yes?'

'Over sixty now,' he said, grinning.

'And they mentioned Richard Ashton by name?'

Danny reached into his satchel and pulled out his iPad. He scrolled through various folders before selecting the one he was looking for. 'Fifty-six men mention Ashton by name. Four mentioned Donald Eddington and one mentioned George Barker.'

Matilda took a deep breath. 'I need you to write the story and get it published. Talk about the systematic abuse at

Magnolia House, everything Ashton was up to, and name names.'

'Really?'

'We need to get an official inquiry opened into Magnolia House and a reason to officially investigate Donald Eddington and the others, and, hopefully, find out about anyone else who's still alive and involved.'

'But you're not on the Force anymore. You can't make sure this happens.'

'I know, but Christian can. We need this in the public domain so people know about it, and it won't get swept under the carpet. This isn't based on rumour, this is fact. We have actual evidence of abuse and names have been given. Four men mention Donald Eddington. He was the leader of the council, for crying out loud. Who knows what other lines of corruption he was involved with? Only you can start this process.'

Danny blew out his cheeks. 'I suddenly feel very sick.'

Matilda stood up and pushed her chair back. 'Oh, come on, Danny. This is a journalist's dream come true. You get to expose a massive paedophile ring and bring down some top people. We're talking MPs, leaders of councils, people high up within the police force. This is a massive scoop for you.'

He stood up and went over to the window, looking out into the darkness, but seeing only his reflection looking back at him.

'I don't want to get sued or anything,' he said, quietly.

'Why would you get sued? You have evidence. The onus will be on Donald Eddington to prove the allegations aren't true, and he won't be able to do that. As soon as the abusers' namesare mentioned, you're going to get more victims contacting you, naming them. I know it. Look at those boys,

Danny,' Matilda said. She went over to the wall of photographs. 'They're children. They're eight, nine and ten years old. They'd all had tragedies befall them. They're separated from their parents through no fault of their own. They were scared. They were vulnerable. And Richard Ashton and Donald Eddington and George Barker took advantage of that and used them for their own sick, perverted pleasure. Twelve of them are missing, presumed dead. Sean Evans was murdered,' she said, pointing him out. 'And one of them is calling you in absolute torment because he can't get over what happened to him more than twenty years ago. You can't allow this to continue any longer. You need to expose these men. Then let the law do the rest,' she said, hoping she'd won him over to her side.

It was a while before Danny reacted. When he did, it was with a simple nod.

'Give me a couple of days. This needs to be written sensitively.'

Matilda sighed with relief. *Thank God for that.* She needed to throw him a bone, or he might end up vomiting on her carpet. 'If I didn't despise you so much, I'd kiss you,' she said with a smile.

Danny laughed. 'You're a good woman, DCI Darke.'

Matilda waited a few long seconds before she spoke. 'I'm supposed to say something nice about you now, aren't I?'

'It would help.'

Matilda chewed her bottom lip. It was causing her considerable pain to think of something pleasant to say about a journalist.

'I like your hair. What conditioner do you use?'

Chapter Forty-Nine

Matilda stepped out of the shower, dried her hair with a towel, threw it in the laundry basket and reached for her big thick dressing gown, which she wrapped around her and tied at the waist. There was fresh bedding on the bed, and she loved getting under the duvet, fresh from the shower. Ian Rankin waited for her on the bedside table, and she was keen to immerse herself into a fictional world and leave the horrors of reality behind for a few hours. She was about to pop downstairs to make a cup of tea when her mobile rang. The caller had withheld their number. She guessed it was the killer calling and sat down on the edge of the bed before swiping to answer.

'Hello,' she said softly.

The was a lengthy silence before the caller said anything. 'Have you found out why people abuse children yet?'

A wave of sadness swept over Matilda. The killer was going through hell right now. If only he'd tell her who he was and allow her to help him.

'I wish I did. I really do wish I could answer your question.

I think there are many different factors, and each abuser will give you a different answer. There's obviously something seriously lacking in their lives that's made them that way. Maybe they were abused themselves and …'

'You see, that's what I don't understand,' he interrupted. He suddenly sounded animated. 'Why would someone who has been abused become an abuser? When you've visited hell, you know the horrors that are there. Why would you put someone else through that?'

'I'm not sure. I think, maybe, they're trying to make sense of what happened to them by putting themselves in the abuser's position. You'd need to speak to an expert about this.'

'Maybe they're incredibly lonely and need someone to know the same pain they went through, so they'll have a connection, another person to talk to about the darkness,' he said, a heavy sadness in his voice.

'Don't you have anyone to talk to?' Matilda asked.

Adele appeared in the doorway. She mouthed, asking if Matilda was talking to the killer. Matilda nodded. She came and sat beside her on the bed and Matilda turned the phone to loudspeaker.

'No. Talking to a therapist isn't easy. They just tell you textbook information. They speak words but there's no emotion behind them.'

'I understand that.'

'Does it help you, talking to a therapist about being shot?'

She looked to Adele. 'Sort of,' she struggled to say. She didn't want to lie to him.

'In what way didn't it help?'

'It's like you said. I cried my eyes out talking to my therapist. I opened up and spilled my emotions, and all I got back was jargon.'

'Exactly. It's like talking to C3PO.'

Matilda smiled. 'It helps to talk to someone who's been through what you've been through, so they fully understand what you're saying.'

'Yes. Yes. You're right.'

Matilda looked to Adele again, who smiled and gave her the thumbs-up sign.

'Only ...' he began, then stopped himself.

'Go on.'

'Over the years, I've spoken to many people who've been abused. They've told me their stories, but none have been similar to what I went through. None have had the same impact. I've still not been able to understand why it happened to me.' He sounded on the verge of tears.

'It wasn't just you, though. There were others there. You weren't singled out. Ashton and his friends took advantage. They abused their position. There was nothing you could have done differently to stop it happening. I don't think you should dwell on *why* it happened to you.'

'But that's what I need to know. I asked Ashton. I asked Barker and Ingells and they couldn't tell me. Why couldn't they tell me, Matilda?'

She wanted, desperately, to give him an answer, but she couldn't. 'I don't know. I wish I did.'

'I have a gun,' he stated. 'I bought it from a bloke in a pub down Pitsmoor. Can you believe how easy it is to buy a gun these days? I spend hours, sometimes, at my kitchen table, with it pressed against my head, my finger on the trigger. It's the easiest thing in the world to push it, but I can't. I can't. I want to, but I can't. It's ... I ... I don't want to die until I'm ready.'

Matilda wiped away a tear. 'I will meet you anywhere you

want. We can sit down and talk for as long as you want. Just
me and you.'

'I wish I'd been killed instead of Sean Evans.'

'I'm so sorry you feel like this.'

The line went dead.

Adele put her arm around Matilda's shoulders and pulled
her into an embrace.

'Oh, that poor man,' Adele said.

'There's nothing I can do for him, is there?' Matilda asked.

'I really don't think there is.'

Chapter Fifty

'I don't know why I thought Matilda might be able to help. I was led to believe she was an intelligent, determined woman. I thought she'd understand, but she doesn't. She just wants to catch a killer.'

It was two o'clock in the morning and the conversation with DCI Darke had left him shattered and unable to sleep. He sat on the floor in the living room by his dog's bed and snuggled up to him. It was nice to feel the closeness of a faithful companion.

The dog was asleep, his head on the killer's lap, breathing heavily and making sweet whimpering noises. He stroked him gently, feeling his soft, warm fur. It was comforting. It was what he needed in his life. It had come far too late.

'I'm so sorry,' he said, tears building in his eyes, emotion lodged in his throat. 'I thought we'd go on a journey together – trips to the countryside and the coast – but I've gone too far down the rabbit hole.'

He looked down at the dog, who had woken at the change

in tone in his voice. The dog looked back at him with big sad eyes.

'I love you,' he said.

The tears came and rolled from his face onto his dog.

'That's the first time I've ever said those words. I never knew what they meant before. I do now.'

Chapter Fifty-One

Monday 30th March 2020

Matilda Darke wasn't suited to having time on her hands. Yesterday, Adele was home, so she had someone to talk to, someone to moan to, someone to complain to, but today, she was alone in the vast farmhouse. Just her, and her thoughts. Unfortunately, her thoughts were not great companions. She wondered how Danny was doing, compiling his feature. How much of it had he written? Had he contacted a newspaper and told them what was coming?

She was standing by the kettle in the kitchen, waiting for it to boil, mobile phone in hand, and kept looking at the screen, checking to see if a text or email had come through. How was Christian doing, trying to track down those four remaining boys? It couldn't be that difficult, surely.

The kettle boiled and she made a mug of tea. She didn't really want it. She wasn't especially thirsty, but she was tired of this inaction.

She unlocked her phone and rang Sian, hoping she was just as bored.

'Good morning. The Hound That Rocks The Cradle – may I help you?' Sian answered.

Matilda laughed. 'Oh, I do like that one. What happened to Mission Impawsible?'

'Can you believe there already is a Mission Impawsible?'

'That's impawsible, surely?' she said, laughing.

'Oh dear. I thought I was the one with the terrible puns. How are you, anyway?'

'Bored out of my mind. Now I see why Pat Campbell complains all the time about having nothing to do. I hate not having a job. At least when I was off sick I had my recovery to concentrate on. This is torture. Have you seen daytime television? I could feel my brain cells dying by the second.'

Sian laughed. 'What are you going to do if the unit doesn't get reinstated?'

'I suppose I could try another force. Don't you know people in Manchester?'

'I do. Do you really want to move out of Sheffield, though?'

'A couple of years ago I would have said yes.Now, not really. Adele's here, which is great. My mum and sister are close by. Then there's you and Scott and Christian.'

'You could always become my business partner, walking dogs.'

'As great as that sounds, I need a job that stimulates my brain. I'm going bonkers already.'

'Well, unless … Sorry, Mat, I'm going to have to go. Gregory's started his Zoom lessons and apparently I'm being too loud.' She lowered her voice. 'I hate how small this bloody house is.'

'I'll call you later.'

'Okay. Keep me up to date if there's any news on the case.'

Matilda ended the call and remained standing in the kitchen, looking around. The silence shrouded her. She hated it. She picked up her mug of tea and headed for the living room.

On the doormat in the hallway was an envelope. She hadn't heard the postman's van on the gravel driveway, and when she bent to pick it up, she saw it was hand delivered. It was addressed to her, her name written in black block capitals. She took it into the living room, placed her mug of tea on the coffee table and ran her finger under the flap. Inside was a card. The picture on the front was of the local countryside. She recognised it as not being far from where she lived. She smiled. When she opened the card and read the message inside, she almost dropped to the floor:

You're a survivor, aren't you, Matilda? But what's the point of surviving when everyone around you is dead?

Those were the exact words Jake Harrison said to her over the phone right before he opened fire, killing many of her colleagues, killing her father, killing Adele's son and putting Matilda in an induced coma.

Matilda flopped onto the sofa and stared at the innocuous card. She didn't need a reminder of that day in January fifteen months ago, as it was something she constantly lived with. Her dreams were full of the devastation. She suffered flashbacks and was still struggling with survivor's guilt, but when something like this happened, someone taunting her, it reminded her of just how fragile she still was.

As much as she wanted to believe the card was delivered by the same person who set her car on fire, and this was a warning to stop the hunt for Richard Ashton's fellow abusers, she knew it was connected to Jake and Steve. This wasn't the first card she'd received. And she knew it wouldn't be the last.

Matilda needed to get out of the house. She had images of someone watching from a distance, using high-powered binoculars to look through the windows, follow her from room to room, getting a kick out of seeing her scared and frightened in her own home. She could feel the walls closing in around her. It was oppressive. It was at times like this she wished she had a dog she could take for long walks.

'Screw it,' she said to herself.

She put on a pair of walking shoes from the cupboard under the stairs, pulled on a padded jacket and left the house, setting the alarm and securing all the locks behind her. With her hands plunged deep into the pockets of her coat, and her head down, she set off walking with determined strides. She needed to clear her mind and didn't care where she ended up.

She had no idea how long she'd been walking. The phone in her pocket was purposely switched off and she wasn't wearing a watch. She was thirsty and wished she'd thought more about this impromptu trek. A bottle of water and a bar of something chocolatey would taste amazing right now. There were no shops open, no cafés or coffee shops. She'd have to wait until she was home. She looked up at her surroundings. The Summer House restaurant was locked up and sat in darkness in the corner close to Dore Railway Station. To her right, the long, steep, winding Dore Road led to the village where more shops and cafés would be closed. This felt so strange. It was like living in the days of the end of the world.

There was a hint of salvation as she remembered that Dore Road led, eventually, to the home of Sally and Philip Meagan. They owned restaurants. They'd have food in their house. She knew she shouldn't visit – it was against the law, after all – but so was covering up child sex abuse, and someone high up in South Yorkshire Police didn't care about that, so why should she care about visiting a friend in a pandemic?

The Meagan family had been through a great deal over the years, and Matilda had been with them on (almost) every step of the terrifying journey. When Carl was seven years old in 2015, he was kidnapped from their home one night while Philip and Sally were attending a business award ceremony in Leeds. Sally's mother was babysitting, and she was killed in the event. Their world stopped turning. It was four long, gruelling years before Carl was brought home and life could begin again. Carl had been back for six months and although he was physically well, she knew the psychological recovery was going to be an arduous one, as was her own after the shooting.

It was another half an hour of walking before Matilda reached their house, and she was out of breath. Dore Road was steeper than she thought. She pressed the buzzer on the intercom and Sally sounded pleased a friendly face had come to visit. As Matilda made her way down the gravel driveway, she looked at the high walls the Meagans had built not long after Carl's disappearance, to make it a safer and more secure home for when he returned. It was oppressive and she could fully understand how Carl felt like a prisoner in his own home, even more so thanks to the lockdown. The walls would never have been built had he not been kidnapped, and the sprawling view of the Derbyshire countryside in the distance would still be there, a symbol of freedom. Now, all he saw from his bedroom window was a constant reminder of what had happened. No wonder he was so keen to move.

As she waited for the front door to be opened, she couldn't take her eyes from the walls. She could remember them not being there, when she was first summoned to the house when Carl was taken.Now she knew what they signified, she wanted to take a sledgehammer to them herself.

'Hello, Matilda, it's lovely to see you,' Sally welcomed her with a warm smile. She was barged to one side by two excitable Labradors who wanted to greet their guest.

Matilda squatted and made a fuss over the dogs. 'I know I'm not supposed to visit. If you don't want me here, I'll go. I just … I needed to get out of the house.'

'You're welcome here any time. It's a lovely day – why don't you go round to the back garden with the dogs, and I'll meet you round there with a coffee and some cake. We'll have a catch-up.'

'I'd like that,' Matilda said. She'd felt emotional, momentarily, and had no idea why. She stood up and trotted around the side of the house, clapping her hands at the golden Labradors, getting them excited to follow her.

By the time Sally came out with a heavy tray, Matilda was already sitting on a garden chair. One of the dogs had brought

her a soggy tennis ball, dropped it at her feet for her to lob, and
stood back, tail wagging, tongue lolling.

'He'll have you doing that all day,' Sally said as she placed
the tray on the table.

Matilda wondered what the power of dogs was, that they
instantly made you feel better about yourself, about life, just by
being with you. It was as if a warm energy had washed over
her. She was smiling as she squatted to pick up the tennis ball,
soaked in drool, then threw it as hard as she could for them to
chase. Maybe Sian had the right idea about going into the dog-
walking business. Maybe she should join her after all. There
was no doubt in her mind that her mental health would
improve almost instantly.

'Where's Carl?' It was unusual for him to be separated from
his dogs.

'He's in his room having a Zoom therapy session. He'll be
down soon.'

'How's he taking the lockdown?'

A sadness crept over Sally's face. She let out a heavy sigh.
'Not well. Fortunately, he has the dogs to take out several
times a day. He hates being tied to the house. This has come at
the wrong time for him. It's reminding him of … well, when he
was trapped in that house in Sweden, unable to go out when
he wanted to.'

'Is he talking to you about it?' Matilda asked, pouring milk
into her mug and wrapping her hands around it. The sun had
disappeared behind a dark cloud and a chill had descended.

Sally wrinkled her nose. 'Not so much. I have to really
press him if I want to know anything, and I don't want to push
him away.'

'Is there anything I can do?'

Emotion got the better of Sally and she clamped a hand to

her mouth to stave off her crying. Tears ran down her face. Matilda placed her mug on the table and went over to her, wrapping an arm around her shoulders.

'Sally, what's the matter?'

'I don't know what to do. I'm at my wits' end, Matilda. He's my boy, my son, but I don't know how to talk to him. It's painful. I don't know him anymore.'

Matilda squeezed her tightly. 'Oh, Sally, why didn't you say something? I thought you were all settled.'

Sally sniffled hard and wiped her eyes with her sleeves. 'It's so awkward. He was fine, but lately, he's become withdrawn again. I've spoken to his therapist myself and he's put it down to the pandemic and the uncertainty.'

'Maybe he's right.'

'He probably is but we were taking little baby steps forward and now we've taken one giant leap backwards.'

The dogs started barking excitedly. They both looked around to see Carl coming out of the house.

'Shit,' Sally said, wiping her eyes harder, making them even more red than the tears did. 'I don't want him to see I'm upset.'

Matilda covered Sally by standing up and turning to Carl. 'Hello Carl. I've come for an illegal visit.'

Carl's face brightened. 'I could call the police on you.'

'Will you accept a bribe?'

'Is it edible?'

Matilda frowned. 'Hmm, everywhere decent is closed and I'm not so good at baking. How about I bribe your mum into making that layered chocolate cake she's so good at?'

Carl's face turned into one big smile. 'That would be amazing.'

Sally stood up from the chair. She'd managed to compose

herself. 'Do you have any idea how many calories are in each slice?'

Matilda winked at Carl. 'These are desperate times, Sally. We need cake for comfort and support.'

A light rain started to fall. Sally picked up the tray of tea things and headed for the house. 'I'd better check my ingredients store.'

Matilda and Carl followed, as did the dogs. Carl headed for the living room. He slumped down onto the white sofa. Matilda sat in the armchair opposite. She studied the eleven-year-old. He was smiling as he stroked one of the Labradors who'd jumped up onto the sofa next to him, but his eyes were telling. They were sad. He was struggling with something he was keeping to himself.He reminded her of the photos of the boys on her dining-room wall.

'Is everything all right?'

'Yes. Fine,' he said, without looking up.

'You need to get better at lying, Carl. I've been saying I'm fine for years and can spot a fib at fifty paces.'

He looked up and gave a hint of a smile. 'Have you ever had therapy?'

'I'm still having it.'

'What do you think of your therapist?'

Diana Cooper-sodding-bloody-Smith. 'I like her,' she lied. 'It took me a while to warm to her. She was too quiet in the earlier sessions. I sometimes felt like I was talking to a cardboard cut-out. But she's helping.' *LIAR!* 'What do you think of yours?'

'He's ... okay,' he said, struggling for something to say.

'Only okay?'

He smiled. 'He's actually a nice bloke. We don't always talk about me being kidnapped. We talk about things going on in our lives and he sneakily says things that make me feel a bit better.'

'That's good. So, it's helping?'

'Yes. He's told me a lot about himself, too, about his own life. He said I should get a hobby as well, something to distract myself, especially during the lockdown.'

'That's a good idea.'

'He's given me a few magazines about model trains. Dad's ordered me one from Amazon to build.'

Matilda frowned. Something seemed familiar. 'Model trains?'

'Yes. Dad's found a model of the Orient-Express. I think he's looking forward to putting it together more than me,' Carl laughed. 'We watched the film the other night with the foreign detective and the dodgy moustache. I'd love to go on that train. Can you imagine …'

Matilda leaned forward in her seat. 'Carl, what's your therapist called?'she interrupted.

'Why?'

'Just wondered.'

'Dr Rivers. I call him Anthony, though.'

Matilda tried not to show that the name sounded familiar. She could feel the blood pound through her brain as her mind went into overdrive.

'Carl, could you ask your mum to make me another coffee? I think I got rain in this one.'

'Sure.'

Matilda waited until Carl was out of the room before she dug her mobile out of her inside pocket and began scrolling through her emails. She found what she was looking for and, if she hadn't been sitting, she would have fallen to the floor in a dead faint. She selected Sian's number and called her.

'Sian, I need you to come and pick me up from Sally Meagan's house,' she said, her voice stern, but quiet.

'Why? What's happened? Is Carl all right?'

'I'll explain everything when you've picked me up.'

Matilda ended the call, looked to the doorway to make sure Carl was nowhere near the living room, then called Christian.

'Christian, it's me. I …'

'I was just about to call you,' he interrupted. 'I'm with Guy. Peter Ogilvy's been rushed to hospital. He's caught Covid.'

'Oh, my God! Is he okay?'

'I'm not sure. He's in intensive care.'

'Bloody hell,' she looked over her shoulder. Still no sign of Carl. 'Listen, Christian. Scott and Finn went to interview a man named Anthony Rivers who lives in the house at the back of Richard Ashton's house. They said they thought he'd seen something dodgy about Ashton but didn't want to get involved.'

'So?'

'Anthony Rivers is Carl Meagan's therapist.'

'Again. So?'

'He's a child therapist. I was only talking to Danny on Saturday about how I think the killer is someone who is trying to work out how and why someone would want to abuse a child. The killer even told me that he's been searching for that answer for years. He's spoken to others, but never come close. We know the killer was at Magnolia House. What if he became a child therapist in order to meet other children who were abused, to try to understand why he was abused?'

'You think Anthony Rivers is the killer?'

'I don't know, but it's possible. Can you go round and interview him?'

'Erm … sure. What are you going to do?'

'Try and get Carl to tell me more about his therapist.'

She ended the call and turned around to see Sally in the doorway with a mug in her hand. Her face was white, her mouth open.

'What's going on?' Sally asked.

'Nothing. Sally, where's Carl?'

'One of the dogs needed a pee, so he's gone out the back with him. I heard you mention Anthony Rivers. What's wrong?'

'I don't know. It's this case I'm working on. I'm wondering who best to talk to about historical child sex abuse, and a child therapist would be the best person, wouldn't he?'

'I suppose,' she shrugged.

'Look, I'm going to have to go, something's come up. Erm, out of interest, how often does Carl see his therapist?'

'Once a week usually, but since the lockdown they've been having Zoom calls most days. Why?' Sally frowned.

'And they've had one today?'

'Yes.'

'Do they communicate any other way?'

'I'm not sure. I wouldn't have thought so. What's with all the questions?' Sally asked, her frown deepening.

'Nothing. Look, Sally, do me a favour ...' She stopped, not knowing what to say that wouldn't make her even more frightened than she already was.

'What?' Sally prompted.

'Nothing. Forget it. I'll be in touch. I promise.' She headed for the door.

'Matilda, has something happened? Is there something I should know about?' Sally called after her.

Matilda stopped at the front door. She turned and looked

back at Sally. 'I don't want to alarm you or anything, but can you look at Carl's texts and emails?'

'What for?'

'I need to know what his therapist has been saying to him.'

'But that's private, surely.'

'Please, Sally, will you do that for me?'

'What am I going to find out?'

'Hopefully, nothing.'

'But possibly, something?'

'Maybe.'

Sally bit her bottom lip hard to stave off the approaching tears. 'Has he been grooming my son?'

Matilda could feel her own tears rising. 'I really hope not.'

Chapter Fifty-Two

'Is everything all right?' Guy Grayston asked Christian when the DI ended the call. He remained still, a heavy frown etched on his face.

'Yes. Fine. Guy, does the name Anthony Rivers mean anything to you?'

'No. Why?' he answered quickly.

'It's a name that's come up in our investigation. I just wondered if you'd heard of him. Was he at Magnolia House at all?'

'No. I don't know anyone by that name.'

They were outside Guy's flat in Meersbrook. Christian had popped round again on the off-chance of catching him at home. Guy was returning from taking Toby for a walk in the park when Christian pulled up. Guy filled him in on where he'd been all morning: at the hospital, trying to get access to Peter, but due to the restrictions, he wasn't allowed any further than reception.

Peter had displayed symptoms of Covid the previous afternoon but wouldn't allow Guy to phone for an ambulance, putting it down to a seasonal cold, the many things he had wrong with him, and old age. Eventually, he relented when he was unable to breathe properly, and an ambulance arrived at the cottage within minutes. Peter was given oxygen on the way to the hospital, stabilised, and sent straight to intensive care, given the current state of his health. The last Guy saw of Peter was him being wheeled through double doors, a mask strapped to his pale face, flanked by serious-looking medical staff wearing face masks and visors. He hoped he would get a chance to see him again, but something told him his only friend was slipping away.

'I need to look into something,' Christian said, fishing his car keys out of his pocket. 'Will you keep me informed about Peter?'

'Sure. Erm, would you like me to come with you?'

'Sorry?'

'I mean, if this man was at Magnolia House, I might be able to help.'

'I thought you said you didn't recognise his name.'

'I don't, but I don't know everyone who was there. If there is something dodgy about him, it might be helpful if he sees someone who's been through the same kind of thing as him.'

Christian thought for a moment. 'I suppose it can't hurt. Get in,' he nodded to the car.

'I'll just get Toby settled and I'll be right with you.'

————

Sian was at the Meagans' house in less than ten minutes. Matilda was waiting at the bottom of the drive.

'What's going on?' Sian asked as soon as Matilda climbed into the car.

Matilda filled her in on Anthony Rivers being Carl's therapist.

'I don't get where you're going with this,' Sian said as she drove at speed towards Nether Edge.

'I just think that if Anthony saw something in Ashton's house, and Scott and Finn think he did, then, being a child therapist, he should have done something about it. He should have informed the authorities. But what if he remained silent for a reason?'

'What reason?'

Matilda took out her mobile and began tapping frantically into a search engine. 'I don't know. He could have been a child at Magnolia House himself. Maybe he's counselled people who went there and he's taking the law into his own hands. I don't know,' she said again, frustrated. 'I just get the feeling I really need to talk to him.'

Matilda found a photograph which she believed was of Anthony Rivers. She sent it to Sally, asking if this was Carl's therapist, and sent it to Christian, asking him to show Guy to see if he recognised him.

Sally messaged back straight away confirming it was Carl's therapist. Christian took a little while longer. Guy wasn't sure, but he looked vaguely familiar.

'Well, he checks out and he's got the correct letters after his name,' Matilda said, reading from her phone. 'Anthony Rivers is a genuine child therapist and has been working in the field for more than ten years. He's self-employed and rents rooms in various GP surgeries throughout the city, tending to both private and NHS patients.'

'Was there an Anthony Rivers on the list of names Peter Ogilvy gave you?' asked Sian.

Matilda looked up as she thought. 'No. I'm pretty sure I'd have remembered.'

'Maybe he changed his name.'

'Maybe.'

'Or maybe he is simply a regular child therapist.'

'Let's hope so.'

They pulled up outside Richard Ashton's house. It was locked up and shrouded in darkness. In a street where every house was lit up, it looked abandoned in the shadows, as if it was hiding from itself. Whatever dark deeds had taken place in this house would remain a secret forever, locked in behind the imposing front door, unless someone was brave enough to expose the truth of Ashton's deplorable parties.

Matilda climbed out of the car. She felt a chill, as the evening temperatures had plunged to single figures. She zipped up her jacket and looked around her. She had no idea which house Anthony Rivers lived in. Sian was on the phone to Finn, getting the information from him.

'It's round the back,' she said. 'Number eighty-three.'

Matilda ran around the corner with Sian on her heels. They reached the path just as Christian pulled up. He got out and told Guy to stay where he was.

'What have you brought him for?' Matilda asked, quietly.

'I was with him when you called. He was telling me about Peter. He heard me mention Anthony Rivers and thought he might be able to help, if Rivers was a child from Magnolia House.'

'Does he recognise the name?'

'No. He could have changed it, though.'

'Sian said the same. Come on.'

All three headed up the path and Matilda rapped hard on the front door. It echoed around the quiet neighbourhood. She stood back and looked up at the house. There were no lights on in any of the rooms and the curtains weren't drawn either, despite it growing darker by the minute.

Christian went to the living-room window, taking care he didn't stand on any of the budding daffodils in the flower bed. He cupped his hands around his eyes and glanced in. He turned to Matilda and shook his head.

'It looks empty.'

She knocked again, louder. And rang the doorbell.

'Are you looking for Mr Rivers?'

An elderly woman from the house next door popped her head out of an upstairs window.

Matilda looked up. 'Yes. DCI Darke from South Yorkshire Police. Mr Rivers is helping us with one of our enquiries. You don't know where he is, do you?'

'No. He came around earlier and asked if I'd look after his dog for him.'

'Has he done that before?'

'No. He said he might have to stay overnight.'

'Did he say where he was going?'

'No. I asked, but then, I'm a nosy bugger. He just said it was business. I assume it's because of this pandemic. He's medically trained, you know. Is everything all right?'

'Everything's fine,' Matilda said in her best placatory tone.

'Would you like me to give him a message when he comes back?'

'No. Thank you. I'm sure we'll catch up with him.'

She turned back to Christian and Sian.

'Where the hell is he?'

'Maybe he's off killing one of the other men,' Sian suggested.

'Or maybe he has just gone away for the evening,' Christian

said. 'He's never left his dog with his neighbour overnight before.'

'I don't like this. If he's seen something in Ashton's house, why not report it? Why keep it to himself?' Matilda asked.

She walked away a few paces. She was frustrated. She couldn't put her finger on what was niggling at the back of her brain. She took her phone from her jacket pocket and pulled open the front passenger door of Christian's car. Guy jumped and dropped his phone, which he was texting on. She showed Guy the photograph of Anthony Rivers.

'Guy, do you recognise this man?' she asked firmly.

'I don't know,' he said.

'Think. I need you to concentrate. It's important.'

'Why?'

Matilda's eyes fell on the lit screen of Guy's phone in the footwell. It vibrated with an incoming message from someone called Jamie. She picked it up. 'Who's Jamie?'

Guy swallowed hard. 'A friend,' he said, not looking at her.

'Unlock this phone. I need to read the message.'

'What? You can't do that.'

'Matilda, what's going on?' Christian asked from behind.

'Unlock the phone, Guy,' Matilda stated.

'No. You need a warrant, surely.'

'If you weren't hiding something, you'd open this phone to show me. Jamie. I'm guessing this is Jamie Cobb, one of the other boys who were at Magnolia House on the night of Sean's death in 1997. You know we're looking for him. Why haven't you told us you have his number?'

'Is this true?' Christian asked Guy. 'You've known Jamie all along?'

'No. I ...' he blustered. He removed his seat belt and climbed out of the car, barging past Matilda and Christian.

'Why didn't you tell us you were in contact with Jamie?' Christian asked.

'Do you know Anthony Rivers as well?' Sian asked.

Matilda held up a hand to stop them both asking questions. 'Guy, did Jamie Cobb change his name to Anthony Rivers?'

Guy refused to turn back to look at them.

Christian stepped forward, grabbed Guy by the shoulders and spun him around. 'After everything we've talked about,' he said, quietly, almost under his breath. 'After everything I've told you. And you've been holding back all this time.'

Matilda and Sian exchanged worried glances.

'I haven't lied to you,' Guy said.

'You haven't been truthful, either. You've known right from the beginning who the killer is. You've known where we are in the investigation and you've been feeding back information to him, haven't you?' Christian asked, shaking him hard.

'Christian!' Matilda called out. She pushed him out of the way. 'Guy, is this true?'

Guy didn't say anything.

Matilda continued: 'Anthony's been trying to understand what happened for the past twenty years, hasn't he? You've managed to have a life, a job, and get through the day without thinking of the abuse all the time, but he hasn't. He's been searching for answers for twenty years. That's why he became a child therapist, isn't it? He's thought that if he could help other children through their trauma, he'll be able to understand his own. I'm right. Aren't I?'

'Yes,' Guy said quietly.

'But it hasn't worked out that way, has it? He's spoken to children, listened to their stories of abuse, and hasn't quite managed to translate it to his own life. Paul killing himself made him realise how screwed up everyone was who was at Magnolia House, and he's seeking revenge for you all.'

Guy nodded.

'Do you know where he is?'

He looked away. 'No.'

'I don't believe you.'

'That's not my problem.'

'It bloody is. Where is he? What's his plan?'

'I honestly don't know,' Guy looked at Christian for the first time. Tears were running down his face.

'Anthony is Jamie Cobb, isn't he? I'm right, aren't I?' Matilda asked.

'Yes.'

'I should have known,' Matilda exclaimed. 'He was Sean Evans's best mate. They were like brothers. You said so yourself. You've known all along who is responsible, and you've kept it from us. Why?'

Guy wiped his eyes with his sleeves and took a deep breath. 'They all need to die. For what they've done, a prison sentence isn't enough. They need to die,' he said with conviction.

'We don't do that in this country,' Matilda said. 'We have courts and laws to enact justice.'

'The law isn't working,' Guy screamed. 'Look at Jimmy Savile. Look at Cyril Smith. They went to their graves as free men. Richard Ashton and all his perverted mates, they're people in power, they're politicians, they have money. Corruption oozes out of their pores. As soon as we realised Ke —' He stopped himself.

Matilda, Christian and Sian all froze. All six eyes were on Guy.

'Go on,' Matilda prompted.

Guy didn't say anything.

'You were going to name someone then, weren't you? You know exactly where Anthony is right now, and you know who's with him. Tell me.'

'They need to die,' Guy said softly.

'Why?' Sian asked.

'Because they'll never see the inside of a prison cell. It'll be covered up.'

'What do you think we've been trying to do here?' Matilda asked. 'I'm losing my job over this. My unit has been closed down, yet I'm still digging. I will not allow them to escape justice.'

'This goes way above you,' Guy said. 'Richard Ashton, Tony Bates, Alistair Maynard, what do they all have in common? They're all Freemasons. They'll call upon their mates – judges and MPs –and this will all be swept away. There is nothing you can do, Matilda. The only way to get justice for Sean, for Paul, for all the others and ourselves, was to take the law into our own hands. Those bastards deserve to die.'

'That's not your decision to make,' Matilda said.

'Let me ask you a question. Have you ever been raped? Have you ever been drugged, stripped naked, violated, had men more than five times your age pass you around to fuck, to beat, to hurt, to maim, to put their cigarettes out on? Have you ever been tied to a bed, gagged, blindfolded, and had men come into the room one by one to fuck you, then leave you in the cold for hours on end? Have you ever sat in a bath with a razor blade to your wrists, willing yourself to cut open a vein because it's the only way you can think of to stop the pain from hurting? Have you?'

Matilda didn't answer. The transformation in Guy was stark and frightening.

'I thought not. Well, until all of that's happened to you, don't you dare judge me.' Guy walked a few paces then turned back. 'I was with Jamie when Richard Ashton was killed. We did it together. We pretended to be journalists wanting to interview him about his great empire. We had to sit there for over an hour while he lorded it over us, telling us how he'd made his millions. Jamie injected him and we carried the fat fucker upstairs. We hadn't discussed how we were going to do it. I wanted to smother him, but then Jamie got out a pair of scissors he'd bought from Amazon. Big industrial things. He told me to help strip him and hold up his fat gut. He had it all planned out. He cut off his balls and rammed them down his throat. And do you know something? I didn't stop him.'

'What about the others?' Sian asked.

Guy looked down at the ground. 'I couldn't … I couldn't stop thinking about what we'd done. I knew it was wrong. It was keeping me awake at night. Jamie wanted to hunt down the others and kill them all. For me, it was just Ashton I wanted dead. Jamie's done all the others on his own.'

'But you've been feeding him information on how close we are to him,' Sian said.

Guy nodded. 'I had to. Jamie needs to do this. He's tried everything to silence what's going on in his head – believe me, he really has – but the fact they're still out there, living a normal life, it's killing him. He has to do this.'

'But he's not thinking about the consequences, about the future,' Sian stated.

'He doesn't have a future.'

Standing in the middle of a suburban street in the dark in early spring wasn't the ideal place for a confession. Matilda watched the emotions flutter across Guy's face as he told her about what he and Jamie had planned, how they'd executed it.

'I do understand,' Matilda said. 'The man who orchestrated the shooting last year, who killed my colleagues, my father, my friends, and left me with PTSD, flashbacks and nightmares – well, he's in prison and he's never coming out, but that's not good enough for me. I keep phoning the prison up to check he's still there.' Matilda bit her bottom lip hard. She was shaking with emotion. She could feel Christian and Sian's eyes burning into her. They'd never heard her say any of this before. 'I don't want him in a prison cell. I want him six feet under. I want him dead. I want him in hundreds of little pieces. And I want to be the one swinging the axe.But that's not how we deal with things.'

Guy looked up at her. 'Tell me – if you could, if someone brought him here right now and gave you an axe, would you do it?'

Their eyes locked.

Matilda could hear her heart beating loudly in her chest. She tried to picture the scenario: Steve Harrison, standing right where Guy was now, and an axe in her hand. She knew Steve would have a smirk on his lips, a glint in his eye, willing her to do it. He'd want her to do it.

'Guy, where is Jamie now?' Christian asked, stepping forward and blocking Matilda's view of Guy.

'I imagine he's at Magnolia House.'

'Is he on his own?'

Guy remained tight-lipped.

'Guy, answer me!' Christian shouted.

Sian went up to a silent and frozen Matilda, placed an arm around her shoulders and tried to beckon her to the car.

'He's got kids,' Guy said. 'Jamie said he wouldn't feel comfortable breaking into a house when there's kids there, so he'd have to get him away somehow.'

'Who?'

'Kenneth Burr.'

Matilda snapped out of her dark reverie. She looked over at Guy. 'Kenneth Burr? The Police and Crime Commissioner? He was at Magnolia House on the night Sean Evans was murdered?'

Guy nodded.

'The bastard. He's been practically telling me it's Maynard behind all this. Jesus-fucking-Christ,' she said, heading for the car.

'Where are we going?'

'Magnolia House,' she snapped. 'And if Anthony hasn't cut his balls off by the time we get there, I might just do it myself.'

Chapter Fifty-Three

Matilda played with the phone in her hand while Sian drove. In the car behind, Christian and Guy followed.

She couldn't stop thinking about Guy's question. She liked to imagine she was a sane and rational person who knew Steve Harrison'sincarceration was enough to satisfy her, but at the end of the day, the man was a stone-cold sadist. He'd murdered so many people. Those Matilda knew and loved, the survivors, were hurting, and would be for years to come, thanks to his actions, and he wasn't suffering. Yes, he was in a Supermax wing, but he had his meals brought to him every day. He didn't have to worry about paying bills or shopping or shielding against a pandemic. He was well looked after. He was better off than most elderly people in nursing homes.

The silence between Matilda and Sian was palpable. Sian kept stealing side glances at Matilda.

'I know what you're thinking,' Matilda said.

'What am I thinking?'

'You're thinking about what my answer would have been to Guy's question, had Christian not intervened.'

'I'm not thinking that at all,' she said.

'Liar.'

'No. I'm not. I know exactly what you'd have said.'

Matilda turned to look at her. 'You do?'

'Yes. You'd have told him you'd have killed Steve Harrison, chopping him down like a dead tree until he was nothing but pulp, because that's what he wanted to hear. You wouldn't have meant it, though.'

'Wouldn't I?'

'No. Because you and I both know you're not a killer. You and I know that Steve is in the best place, to rot and suffer in isolation for twenty-three hours a day, every day, for the rest of his natural life. All on his own with just his warped mind for company. People like Steve, and my husband, deserve to be locked away for decades and decades to come and die lonely, alone and forgotten. That is the best punishment for degenerates like them.'

Matilda swallowed hard. She knew Sian was right. The fact Steve Harrison was on the never-never list was enough for her to relax and try to rebuild her life and recover from the trauma of what she'd lost. The law was there for a reason, to stop society descending into anarchy and people seeking their own revenge. Guy Grayston, Anthony Rivers, or Jamie Cobb as he was originally known, Paul Chattle, Sean Evans and all the other boys from Magnolia House had been failed by the law, but killing the abusers wasn't the answer. That's why Anthony was phoning Matilda, why he was in agony and conflicted. He wasn't getting the satisfaction from killing that he thought he would. His abusers needed to be locked up and left to rot, like Steve Harrison, like Sian's husband. Death was too good for them.

Sian swung the car to the left and smashed through the gates of the overgrown driveway of Magnolia House.

'I've always wanted to do that,' she said with a smile.

'You've buggered up the front of your car,' Matilda said.

'It was worth it.'

A red Vauxhall was parked outside the main entrance.

'What's the betting that's Anthony's car?' Matilda asked.

'Do you want me to call Finn, get him to run the number plate?'

'No. Who else could it be?'

They both climbed out of the car and looked up at the imposing, dull, redbrick building. Behind them, Christian pulled up. He said something to Guy before getting out and locking the car behind him, keeping Guy secure inside.

In darkness, with a full moon behind Magnolia House casting long shadows over the broken tarmac, the abandoned building looked like something from a horror film. The brickwork was tired, uncared for, and crumbling in places. Windows were boarded up along the ground floor, glass smashed in the rooms above. The grounds were overgrown; weeds sprouted up and drooped under the their own weight. Dracula could have used Magnolia House as a weekend getaway. Frankenstein could have used the basement to create his monster. Stephen King could have set his next chiller there. It was a real house of horrors.

'What's the plan?' Christian asked.

'I've no idea,' Matilda said. 'Someone like Jamie, he's fragile, unpredictable. If he's already killed Burr, then we can arrest him, but if Burr is still alive, who knows what we're going to be walking into?'

'Do you want me to call for back-up?'

'No. Not yet,' Matilda replied, walking slowly to what used to be the main entrance.

The interior of Magnolia House was heavy with dust. During daylight hours, very little natural light made its way into the building, through the cracks and gaps in the boards covering the windows, or the sides of the window frames where the brickwork had crumbled away due to twenty years of harsh weather and neglect.

The hallway was long and wide. A staircase to the left looked rickety. Spindles in the banister had either rotted away or been broken by vandals. The wooden floor was covered with a fine layer of dust, dried leaves, and the remnants of what squatters and the homeless had left behind before they were moved on.

There was a smell that hung in the air. It caught the back of the throat and left a nasty taste of decay in the mouth. Matilda stood and looked around her. This building held decades of torment and she could feel it leaching out of the walls, wrapping itself around her. She fully understood why Jamie had taken the law into his own hands, hunted down his abusers and made them suffer for their crimes. As Sian said, incarceration was the best place for these kinds of people, but sometimes, justice delivered by your own hand was the best kind.

Matilda reached into her inside pocket for her mobile, turned on the torch and held the phone up. There were several doors leading off the meandering hallway and she had no idea where Jamie Cobb would be hiding.

'Shall we split up?' Christian whispered, though his quiet voice echoed around the vast emptiness.

'Not bloody likely,' Sian said. 'I've seen more than enough horror films to know you don't split up when you enter an abandoned building.'

Matilda gave her a smile. 'We stay together.'

———————

Outside, locked in Christian's car, Guy looked up at the former children's home. It was shrouded in darkness. It was a place of evil and it caused him physical pain just to look at it. Why he kept coming back here and putting himself through such torture, he had no idea. In daylight, it didn't seem so menacing. In darkness, he could almost hear his younger self crying, biting his bottom lip so hard he could taste blood, to stop himself from screaming at the pain caused by Richard Ashton's weight on him as he forced himself inside him.

Guy swallowed hard. He didn't cry. There were no more tears left. He tried the handle on the door one more time, but it was no use. Christian had locked him in. He dug out his phone, selected Jamie's number and dialled.

Chapter Fifty-Four

Anthony Rivers, formerly known as Jamie Cobb, had tried to visit Donald Eddington, but the nursing home staff wouldn't allow him in, due to the pandemic. Even when he lied and said he was a relative, they refused to admit him. He turned his attention to Kenneth Burr. His observations revealed a livelier household than that of Adam and Paulalngells. Firstly, there were three teenagers living at home and Kenneth and his wife shared a bed. There was also a great deal more security. There was no way he was going to be able to sneak his way into the house one night. The only way to get to Burr was by kidnapping him. It wouldn't be easy, but he'd find a way, and, thankfully, the pandemic came to his aid.

Burr wasn't a man to be kept indoors. He liked to get out for regular exercise and fresh air. He left his home in Ranmoor at ten o'clock every morning to go for a long walk around the park. Fortunately, most people were heeding the advice from the government and staying at home. The streets were quiet, and the park was empty. All Jamie had to do was go up to Burr, stick the gun in his back, whisper into his ear what he had planned and walk him to his car. Kidnapping made simple.

As soon as he pulled up outside Magnolia House, and dragged Kenneth Burr out of the boot, the PCC looked up at the familiar building, and the look on his face revealed his complicity in the horror that had taken place there. He knew what lay in store for him.

'Who are you?' he asked Jamie. His voice was shaking with fear.

Jamie grinned. 'Allow me to take you back in time to January 1997. Your friend, Richard Ashton, held a party on the top floor of this building where you were each presented with a child to fuck,' he spat with venom.

'No. Wait. You've got it all wrong,' Burr suddenly waffled.

With a swift movement, Jamie elbowed Burr in the face, knocking him unconscious. He was tired of listening to excuses and denials. The time for talking was over. Actions would now speak louder than words ever could.

Jamie dragged him up the steps to Magnolia House, through the dusty hallway and into the main lounge. The comfortable sofas and paintings on the walls had long since gone. The carpet was faded, its original colour a mystery. Wallpaper was peeling from the walls, and paint from the ceiling had cracked and dropped off like giant snowflakes. A few broken items of cheap furniture dotted the room. He found a stable enough wooden chair, stripped Burr to his boxer shorts and sat him in it, tying him to it; ankles together, wrists around his back. Then, he waited until he regained consciousness. It was a long wait.

'Good evening, Mr Burr,' Jamie said once Kenneth was awake.

Confused, Kenneth blinked hard several times and looked around him, wondering where he was and how he'd managed to get here. When his eyes fell on Jamie, the penny dropped.

'Welcome back to Magnolia House. I'm guessing the last time you were here was twenty-three years ago. You won't remember me, so let me refresh your memory. I was sitting on a single bed in a small room, and you sat beside me, placed your hand on my lap, gave me a cruel smile and asked if I'd call you Daddy. Then you began taking off my clothes. I was eight years old.'

Kenneth was shivering. Was it due to the cold wind blowing through the gaps in the window frames, or was he scared for the first time in his life? Tears pricked at Kenneth's eyes, and they began to fall.

'Don't you fucking dare cry!' Jamie exploded. He jumped up, stormed over to Kenneth and slapped him hard across the face with the back of his hand. 'You have no right to cry. You called me Jonathan while you were fucking me. I've looked you up. Jonathan's your son. Did you fuck him as well or did you just want to, but were too afraid you'd get caught?'

'Don't. Please …' Kenneth pleaded.

Jamie smiled. 'I said that to you when you put your disgusting dick inside me. I begged you not to, but you ignored me. You stroked my hair and whispered that it would only hurt for a minute and that Daddy loves his little boy.'

Kenneth turned his head away. The tears ran down his face.

'My, how the tables have turned,' Jamie said. 'You showed me no mercy at all. I cried into that pillow. I begged you to stop and you just continued. So, tell me, Kenneth, why should I stop now? Why should I let you go?'

Kenneth fought against his emotions for the words. 'I know

… I know it won't make any difference if I say sorry, but I really am. I'm genuinely sorry for the pain I caused you.'

'No, you're not. You're only sorry because I've put you in this position. If you were really sorry, if you really felt remorse all these years, you'd have tracked me down and apologised. You're an abuser, Kenneth. You're vile. You're evil. You don't have a single remorseful bone in your body.'

'That's not true. Okay. Okay. What I did was wrong. I admit that. I know there's something inside me that's not right, but Richard Ashton saw that in me and used it against me. I had no choice.'

'Don't!' Jamie screamed. 'Don't pass the blame onto someone else. He didn't force you into that room. He didn't force you to get an erection and rape me. That was all you. You wanted to be there. You wanted to violate me for your own sick pleasure, so don't even think about looking for an excuse, you bastard.'

Reluctantly, Kenneth nodded. 'You're right. But the thing is, I've sought help over the years. I've had treatment. I've had therapy. I take medication to stop the urges. I'm sorry for the pain I put you through, but I've learned from it, and I've got help.'

'Is that supposed to make me feel better?'

Jamie walked away. He went over to one of the large windows, but it was covered on the outside by a sheet of corrugated metal. He saw nothing. He turned back.

'Can I ask you a question, Kenneth?' he asked, softly.

'Of course.'

'It's a question I've wanted answering for years. It doesn't matter who I talk to, I've never been able to find a true answer.'

'Ask me anything. I promise, I'll tell you the truth.'

'Why?'

'Sorry?'

'Why did you abuse me? Why me? Why us? What is it about young boys that makes you want to destroy their lives, their innocence?'

Kenneth looked down; the tears came once again. Eventually, he looked up. 'I've been asking myself that same question, too. I don't know.'

Jamie's face hardened. 'Wrong answer.' He clenched his fist and punched Burr hard in the face, knocking him off balance and sending him crashing to the floor.

Jamie went over to the fireplace and picked up the rucksack he had left leaning against it. From inside, he pulled out his gun, checked it was loaded, and went back over to Kenneth Burr.

———————

'What was that?' Matilda asked as she came out of the old dining room, back into the hallway.

'It sounded like something falling,' Sian whispered from behind.

'We could do with a floor plan of this place,' Christian said.

'I think it came from up here,' Matilda said, heading for the old lounge.

———————

Jamie's phone rang. It was loud and echoed around the room. He pulled it out of his back pocket and answered before it could ring a second time.

'Jamie, it's me,' Guy said in a hurry. 'The police are here. They know everything.'

The door to the living room was pushed slowly open. Matilda entered first, with Christian and Sian following behind. It took a while for their eyes to adjust to the darkness and by the time they had, Jamie had lifted Kenneth up from the floor and had the gun pointed to his head.

'Jamie. It is Jamie Cobb, isn't it?' Matilda asked, her hands spread out wide to show she wasn't armed.

'You know it is,' he answered. His voice was deep and tired.

'I'm DCI Matilda Darke. I'm ...'

'I know who you are. I've enjoyed our chats over the phone.' He gave a hint of a smile.

'Matilda, thank God you're here. Arrest this man,' Kenneth mumbled as he spat blood.

'Shut your mouth,' Jamie hit him in the face with the gun. Burr cried out in pain.

Sian and Christian both winced at the sound of teeth breaking.

'Jamie,' Matilda stepped forward. 'I know why you're here. I know what's happened to you. You don't need to do this. Trust me, Kenneth is not worth spending the rest of your life in prison for.'

'I've killed three men. I'm already going to spend the rest of my life in prison. Do you think one more is going to make any difference?'

'You won't go to prison,' Matilda said. 'I'll make sure you get the help you need.'

'I don't want help!' Jamie screamed. 'I'm tired of people trying to help and understand. I'm fed up of talking. This man needs to be destroyed.' He aimed the gun at Kenneth's head, who recoiled in fear.

Outside, Guy kicked at the front passenger-seat window with his left foot. He banged his walking shoes hard into the glass, but it wouldn't budge. He rained down blow after blow, but all he was doing was sending a shot of intense pain running up his leg. He almost gave up. He gave it one final kick and the glass shattered into thousands of tiny squares.

Guy smiled to himself. He scrambled through the hole, fell onto the gravel below, and ran into Magnolia House.

'Jamie, listen to me,' Matilda said. 'It's all out in the open. I've got a journalist who's spoken to all the boys who went to Magnolia House. They've given statements about the abuse that took place here. I'm going to get an inquiry open. Kenneth Burr will stand trial for what he did to you. If you kill him, there won't be a trial. He needs to be alive to suffer the consequences, to see his name tarnished and his family disown him. Killing him is not the answer. Trust me, I know.'

'He'll try to cover it up,' Jamie said, a sob in his throat.

'No, he won't. I won't let him.'

'I want to kill him,' he seethed, tightening his grip on the gun.

'I know you do, Jamie, and in your position, I'd feel exactly the same. But you've spoken to Guy – he's told you who I am, hasn't he?' Jamie nodded. 'I can help. I will make sure everyone in this country knows Kenneth Burr's name and what he's done.'

'The pain won't go away,' Jamie said, choking on his tears. 'It won't stop just because he's in prison.'

'It will ease. I promise you,' Matilda said, stepping forward slowly.

'Sometimes, the best form of justice is what you dish out with your own hand,' he said.

'And if you do that, you'll be the one who ends up in prison. He isn't worth doing time for, Jamie.'

Matilda looked down at the gun and tried not to think of that moment fifteen months ago when she saw Jake Harrison on the roof of the building overlooking the police station car park as he aimed it at her head. 'Please, Jamie, give me the gun, and I will make sure you get exactly what you need to feel better about things.'

They made eye contact. Matilda gave a sympathetic smile. Jamie's face softened. She reached out a hand for the gun and, reluctantly, Jamie handed it over.

Christian stepped forward and put his arm around Jamie. Matilda handed the gun to Christian, then she and Sian went over to Kenneth to untie him.

'Well said, Matilda,' Kenneth said, his broken jaw muffling the words. 'I don't know where he got all of that crap from.' Matilda shook her head in disgust. 'He's delusional. He's obviously mistaking me for someone else. He says I need destroying. That's rich! He's the one who should be ...'

'You've lied to me,' Matilda said. She was on her knees untying the rope around his ankles. 'All this time you've acted like you were on my side, but you were looking for a scapegoat. You were covering your own arse.'

'That's not true,' he almost laughed. 'The man is delusional. He's got the whole thing completely wrong.'

'Matilda,' Sian said.

Matilda looked up. Sian was standing behind Kenneth, untying the ropes behind his back. She signalled to Matilda where she was looking. As Matilda followed Sian's gaze, her eyes fell on his left arm and saw the rippling skin of an old burn injury.

Matilda looked at Kenneth, but he refused to look at her.

'You're Duncan Shivers, aren't you?' she asked.

'What? Of course I'm not,' he said, his face reddening. 'What?' he asked as Matilda's glare intensified.

'Anyone else would have asked me who Duncan Shivers was. You said straight away that you weren't him, but not who he was.'

'Okay. So, who was he?' he asked, almost flippantly. He still wouldn't look Matilda in the eye.

'My God, it is you, isn't it? You were working with Richard Ashton to get the boys away from Magnolia House. You posed as an adoption agent. You brazenly walked in here and took the boys from Peter Ogilvy and handed them over to Ashton.'

'You really are talking absolute rubbish,' he said with a hint of a smile.

'No. I'm not. Whose idea was it – yours or Richard's?'

'I don't know what you're talking about.'

'What happened to the boys? You took twelve boys from here. Where are they now?'

'How should I know?' He shrugged. 'Are you untying me or not?'

'Not until you tell me the truth. Look at me.' Reluctantly, he turned and looked down at Matilda who was still squatting on the floor beside him, untying his ankles from the chair. 'You're Duncan Shivers.'

The door to the lounge opened with a squeak and Guy Grayston entered. He stood beside Christian and Jamie and watched the drama unfold.

Kenneth didn't answer, but his face paled. He swallowed hard and a bead of sweat ran down the side of his face.

'We have men who can put you at the scene of Sean Evans's murder in 1997 and at Richard Ashton's Friday night parties. They'll identify you as a serial child abuser, a rapist,' Matilda said slowly. 'The burn scar on your arm is a dead giveaway.'

Kenneth was visibly shaking. 'It was all Richard Ashton.'

'Bullshit,' Matilda said.

'No. It was. Okay, I was weak. He knew … he knew I liked …'

'Fucking boys!' Christian spat.

'He took advantage of that. He blackmailed me. He did.'

'No,' Matilda shook her head. 'I think you were in it together. You could have reported him at any time, but you came here as Duncan Shivers on twelve separate occasions and took the boys away. What did you do with them? Where are they now?'

'I'm not answering any of your questions. You've got it all wrong.'

'You're lying.'

'I'm telling you the truth!' he yelled.

'I doubt you've spoken a word of truth in your life. You've been telling me to keep digging, that you'll help keep my department open, so I'll think you're a good guy. I have to admit, it worked. I didn't suspect you at all, but that was your plan all along, wasn't it? You were making sure it all fell on Alistair Maynard. He was your fall guy.'

'No.'

'Have you been calling Danny Hanson as well?' Sian asked. 'Have you been pretending to be the killer, giving him information to make sure the finger of suspicion points nowhere near you?'

'No. Of course not.'

'Another lie,' Matilda said.'Where are the twelve boys you took from here? Where's Sean Evans buried?'

'I don't know anything about any boys.'

'I will leave you tied to this chair all night long, if I have to,' Matilda seethed through gritted teeth.

Matilda looked up. Her gaze locked with Burr's. She saw deep into him and saw nothing but blackness.

'Where are they?' she asked, her voice barely above a whisper.

A small smile spread across Kenneth's face.

A gunshot rang out, throwing Kenneth to the ground. Matilda and Sian dived for safety. They were splattered with blood and their ears were ringing at the sound of the explosion.

You're a survivor, aren't you, Matilda?

'Sian?' Matilda called out.

'I'm all right. I'm okay. You?'

'Fine. I think.'

Matilda looked over to the chair and saw a large hole where Kenneth's left eye should have been. The whole side of his face was a mess of broken bone and torn muscle. The smell of cordite and burning flesh was in the air.

Matilda turned and looked over to Christian, Jamie and Guy. They all had exactly the same expression on their faces. She had no idea which one of them had fired the gun.

Chapter Fifty-Five

Friday 3rd April 2020. Four days later.

'South Yorkshire Police has been placed in special measures following the murder of the Police and Crime Commissioner and his link with the cover-up of child sexual abuse spanning more than twenty years.

'Chief Constable Alistair Maynard has tendered his resignation with immediate effect, stating that the level of abuse recently discovered should never have happened, and the fact that he is in charge of the police force that allowed it to be ignored has made his position untenable. In a statement, Mr Maynard says he hopes his replacement will go through the entire force with a fine-tooth comb and rid it of the vermin of corruption.'

Matilda turned off the television and threw the remote on the sofa next to her. She had no idea what a police force under special measures meant for her or the HMCU team, but she doubted she'd be returning to work any time soon, if at all.

She sat in silence and contemplated everything that had happened over the last few days and the fallout from the murders. Danny Hanson's article was due to be published in the coming days. She'd read an early copy and was surprised by the level of professionalism and sensitivity. He'd written a thought-provoking piece. Once it was published, Matilda was in no doubt there would be more damage to South Yorkshire Police, but she didn't care. The boys of Magnolia House, every boy who was abused by Richard Ashton and his sick friends, needed a voice to reveal their story.

Matilda dragged herself with heavy legs into the dining room where the photographs of the boys were still stuck to the wall. She began taking them down and studied each of them in turn. She wondered which were the ones Kenneth Burr had taken away in the guise of Duncan Shivers, what had happened to them, and if they'd ever be found. She hoped so. Not that there was anyone to mourn them.

She pulled out a chair and sat down. Warm tears pricked her eyes. She would mourn them.

The doorbell rang. She wasn't in the mood for visitors and when it rang again two more times, she realised whoever it was wasn't going to go away. When she opened the front door, she saw the last person she wanted to see standing on the doorstep.

'Hello. Mind if I come in?' Christian Brady asked. He seemed to have aged in the last four days. The bags under his eyes looked bigger. He looked gaunt, almost grey.

Matilda stepped to one side and let him in, closing the door firmly behind him and returning to the dining room to continue taking down the photographs. The silence between them was heavy.

Christian cleared his throat. 'Any news on Peter Ogilvy?'

'He died in the early hours of this morning.'

'Oh … I'm so sorry.'

'The nurse I spoke to said he never regained consciousness from when he was brought in. He never knew about the inquiry into Magnolia House.' She had her back to Christian. She didn't want him to see how sad she was about Peter's death. It had hit her hard.

'He handed you the baton. He knew you'd be able to get an inquiry open. He was happy to leave it in your hands.'

'I suppose,' she sighed. She took the last photo from the wall and turned around. 'Why have you come?'

'I wanted to keep you updated. I'm afraid we've received some bad news.'

'Oh?' Matilda pulled out a dining chair and sat down. She flicked through the photos, not wanting to look up at Christian.

'We're ripping apart Richard Ashton's house. We found a false wall in the basement that we've taken down and a forensic team are taking up the concrete floor. Human remains have been found.'

Matilda closed her eyes tightly shut. 'How many?'

'We don't know yet. Adele is with the team, trying to get them into some kind of an order. The bones aren't … well, they're not adult.'

Matilda nodded. She looked down at the photos in her hand. The one facing her was of three boys sitting on a wall. It was a sunny day, and they were laughing, enjoying themselves. On the back, three names had been written: Wesley Connor, Andrew Fletcher, Ian McMillan. She wondered if any of those three were in Ashton's basement.

'A single skeleton has also been found in the cellar at Magnolia House,' Christian continued. 'We're assuming it belongs to Sean Evans. Unfortunately, we don't have any DNA to make a match. It's just an educated guess.'

'Oh, my God,' Matilda crumbled. She dropped the photographs onto the floor. 'The bastard buried him at Magnolia House, right under Peter Ogilvy's nose.'

Christian went around to Matilda and tried to comfort her, but she shrugged him off. She stood up, went over to the window and looked out into her unkempt garden.

Christian cleared his throat again. 'Jamie Cobb has taken his own life. He hanged himself in his cell at the remand centre he was in. When we searched his house, we found a very detailed account.' From his coat pocket, he took out an A5 notebook which he placed on the dining table.

Matilda turned to look at it, then up at Christian.

'Have you read it?' she asked. He nodded. 'And?'

Christian swallowed hard. 'He admits everything he's done. He describes everything that happened to him. You were right when you said he seemed to be in pain when you spoke on the phone. He really was. You can feel the pain in every word.'

A silence grew between them.

Christian continued: 'He talks about becoming a child therapist to help other children who'd suffered abuse and trauma, so he could, hopefully, try to understand his own. He was Carl Meagan's therapist. He didn't ... he didn't do anything to Carl.'

'I know. I've been to see them. Carl showed me the emails and text messages they'd exchanged. There's certainly evidence of grooming going on, but I don't think Jamie would have done anything to Carl. He was in too much pain for that.'

'Matilda, is something ...'

'I need to know what happened to you, Christian,' she said, quickly turning to look at her DI. 'I need to understand your role in all of this.'

He pulled out a chair and slumped into it. It was a long while before he spoke. 'I'm sure you've guessed. I was abused myself, as a child, by an uncle. When Paul Chattle killed himself in front of me last year, when he told me what had happened to him, it brought it all back. I couldn't let it go, for some reason. My uncle died before I could get justice. I wanted to make sure Paul and whoever else received justice.'

'Why didn't you tell me?'she asked. The anger she felt towards him fell away completely.

'I ... couldn't. I ... I don't know why. I just ... couldn't.'

'Does Jennifer know?'

He nodded.

'That's why you were spending so much time with Guy. You wanted to help him where you couldn't help Paul.'

He nodded again.

'You should have told me, Christian.'

'I know. I was worried you'd say I was too involved and take me off the case.'

She thought about that for a moment. 'You're right. I probably would have done.' She watched him as the frustration and pain was played out on his face. She had no idea what he was working on, but assumed he was heavily involved in investigating the abuse cover-up. Finding human remains in Ashton's house and at the children's home would have been hard for him. If his uncle hadn't died, would he have killed Christian to hide his crimes?

'Christian, about what happened at Magnolia House ...'

Christian's mobile started ringing. He fished for it in his jacket pocket and looked at the screen. 'It's Adele. I need to take this.' He dashed out of the dining room before Matilda could say anything.

She leaned over the table and picked up the notebook. It

felt heavy. She opened it and saw the neat, slanted handwriting. She could feel the tears building up behind her eyes, just reading the first line. She couldn't even begin to understand the pain Jamie Cobb had been in.

'Sorry Mat, I've got to get back to Ashton's house. I'll keep you updated,' Christian called out from the hallway.

'Wait, Christian.'

The front door slammed closed.

Epilogue

Monday 6th July 2020

The taxi dropped Matilda off at the bottom of the drive. She looked up at the 'For Sale' sign with a massive 'SOLD' emblazoned diagonally across it. She felt sad. She was going to miss them.

The gates were unlocked, and Matilda walked slowly towards the house, her shoes crunching on the gravel. The front door opened and Carl Meagan, and two Labradors, came bounding out of the house to greet her. It was the first time Matilda had seen Carl with a genuine smile on his face.

'Today's the day,' she said with a lump in her throat.

'Yes. You'll come and visit us, won't you?'

'Of course I will. I've already chosen which room I plan on sleeping in. There's one at the back of the house overlooking the lake ...'

'That's my room,' he said, aghast.

'Is it?' Matilda asked, knowing full well. 'I suppose you'll have to sleep with the dogs when I come to visit, then.'

He laughed. It was natural and warm. Matilda wanted to scoop him up and not let go.

'I'm so glad to be going, but I'm really going to miss you,' Carl said.

'I'm going to miss you, too. All of you. But you need this. You need to start your life again.'

'Carl, the lorry will be here any minute, and there are still some boxes in your room that need bringing down,' Sally shouted from inside the house. She saw Matilda and came out to greet her.

Matilda couldn't hide her grin at the look of warmth and pure contentment on Sally's face. This was a family who were finally happy after so many years of torturous heartache.

Carl headed back in the house and Sally ruffled his hair as he passed.

'How's he doing?' Matilda asked.

'He's a new boy. Since that sold sign went up, the change in him is amazing.'

'I'm so happy for you all.'

Sally slapped a hand to her chest. 'I keep wanting to cry.'

'Tears of joy.'

'Absolutely. It's so overwhelming.'

'Where's Philip?'

'He's in the attic wrestling with a chest of drawers. It's actually quite funny,' she beamed.

'What are you going to do about the restaurants?' Matilda asked.

'They're all being sold individually. We're keeping the business and the name, so the new restaurant in the Lake District will be called Nature's Diner, but we're only going to have one. I think we got too big, took our minds off what really mattered. With all the extra money, we're just going to relax and enjoy it, and spend time together as a family, and go on a few amazing holidays.'

Matilda felt her smile begin to wobble. Sally stepped forward, grabbed her by her shoulders and pulled her into a tight embrace.

'Thank you,' Sally said into her ear. 'For everything you've done for us. Thank you for giving me my family back.'

Matilda held on tight. She didn't want to let go.

Tuesday 7th July 2020

Matilda and Sian were sitting on a park bench in Millhouses Park, a safe distance apart. The lockdown was over. Non-essential retailers had been allowed to re-open and the two-metre rule had been replaced with a one-metre-plus rule. Face masks were mandatory on public transport and in all shops and supermarkets, and there were plans to return to normality by Christmas, providing there wasn't a second wave of Coronavirus cases.

It was a beautiful sunny day, perfect summer weather. The park was full of kids running around, dogs off leads, adults chatting and having a picnic with their children. Everyone seemed to be acting like there hadn't been a recent threat to life and humanity, and the pandemic already seemed like a distant memory.

'It's strange how restrictions are eased because case numbers are down, and people are acting like there wasn't a virus in the first place. It's obvious case numbers are going to shoot back up again. The virus hasn't gone away,' Matilda said, sipping her black coffee.

'I know. And what about when winter comes with flus and colds?' Sian added.

They looked at each other.

'Are we being too pessimistic?' Sian asked.

'No. Just realistic.'

'How did it go with the Meagans? Did you wave them off?'

'I left them loading the van. I was in the way, so I gave them all a hug and left them to it. I sent them a gift to be waiting for them in Windermere. Sally rang me last night to say thank you. She sounds ... I don't know. She sounds like a completely different person.'

'She's happy.'

'She is,' Matilda smiled.

Sian studied Matilda. 'You're sad to see them go?'

'I am, but they need a fresh start. I just ...'

'Go on,' Sian prompted.

Matilda quickly changed the subject. 'So, I'm not to call you DS Sian Mills anymore.'

'You're not to call me DS anything.'

'I haven't given up on you yet, Sian Robinson.'

'Have you heard about the unit?'

'No. You've heard that Ridley has been made Chief Constable?'

'Yes. Good for him.'

'He was all in favour of HMCU, so we'll have to see how things go. The Force is still under special measures for now. The fallout from Danny Hanson's article continues.'

'Anymore arrests been made?'

'More than one hundred victims of abuse have come forward. Richard Ashton and Kenneth Burr have been named as well as Donald Eddington and Adam Ingells. Also, there's a bloke who used to read the news on *Calendar* in the eighties who's been named a few times. He's being questioned.'

'It's a shame Peter Ogilvy couldn't see all this happening.'

'I know.'

'I meant to ask,' Sian said, taking another sip of her latte. 'What happened to Guy?'

'Nothing. He should have been charged with aiding and abetting and perverting the course of justice, but Christian managed to keep his name out of it. He's just a witness now.'

'Good. I'm glad.'

Matilda turned to Sian and studied her. There was something she'd been wrestling with for some time.

'Sian, at Magnolia House, when we were untying Kenneth. I was on my knees untying his ankles. I had my back to Christian and Jamie and Guy, but you were round the back of Kenneth, untying the rope behind him. You could see all three perfectly well. Who pulled the trigger?'

Sian turned to Matilda. 'Jamie. Obviously,' she answered quickly.

'But Jamie wasn't holding the gun. I handed it to Christian.'

'Well, Jamie obviously took it from Christian.'

'You see, at the first opportunity, Jamie took his own life. He killed himself in his cell at the remand prison on his first night there. If he had the gun in his hand when he shot Kenneth, he'd have turned it on himself there and then. He didn't.'

'Maybe … I don't know, maybe he wanted to make sure he put his side of the story to the police in his statement before he killed himself,' Sian said, looking straight ahead.

'Unless he wasn't holding the gun in the first place,' Matilda said.

Sian turned to look at her. 'You don't think ... Christian? Surely not.'

Matilda didn't reply. She didn't know what to believe anymore.

Matilda stayed in the park. Adele said she would pick her up in her Porsche on her way home from work.

Matilda walked lazily around the park, avoiding people as much as she could, feeling the warm sun on her face. Her future lay before her, and for the first time in her life, it was empty. She had no idea what to do with the coming days, weeks, months and years. While the sun was shining, she was going to enjoy her freedom. She'd already transformed her garden and was working her way through the pile of books she had stacked up, waiting to be read. Surprisingly, she was enjoying the nothingness. She wondered how long it would last.

Her phone started to ring. She fished it out of the back of her jeans, expecting to see Adele's face smiling at her. It wasn't Adele. It was a number she didn't recognise. She swiped to answer.

'Matilda Darke?'

'Yes. Who's this?'

'Just a friend. I wanted to see how you are.'

Matilda frowned. 'I'm fine. Thank you. Who is this?'

'I've read about the recent case you've been involved in, the abuse scandal and the fact you've had your department closed down as a result.'

'Who is this?' Matilda asked again.

'The knife through the tyres of your car, then the car getting burnt out. I'm guessing you assumed that was the work of whoever was trying to keep you quiet. It wasn't. It was me. And I'm the one who's been sending you the cards, too.'

Matilda froze. She tried to concentrate on the voice to see if she recognised it. She didn't. All she knew was that it was female.

'Why are you doing this?' Matilda asked.

'I have my reasons. The thing is, Matilda, I've been taking advice, from a mutual friend of ours, and he's told me how to play the long game, and that's exactly what I'm doing. When I'm ready, I'll reveal my hand, and when I'm done with you, you're going to be begging for the hangman's noose.'

Matilda visibly baulked. Her mouth fell open.

'You look scared.'

Matilda looked around her in all directions. The park was full of people, and a great number of them were on their phones.

'Where are you?' Matilda asked.

'I'm right here.'

Matilda looked all around her. She saw families enjoying the sunny weather, couples walking arm in arm, grandparents playing with their grandkids. She heard the sound of loud conversation and ripples of laughter.

'Where?' she said, trying to keep her voice calm.

'Keep looking, Matilda. I'm right here. I'm almost within touching distance.'

'*Where?*' she screamed. The people closest to her stopped what they were doing and looked at her with perplexed expressions. She was drawing attention to herself.

'I'm right behind you.'

Matilda trembled with fear.

Slowly, she turned around.

Acknowledgments

There are many people I'd like to thank who helped in creating *The Lost Children*, the ninth in the DCI Matilda Darke series. Firstly, my esteemed editor, Bethan Morgan, and all the team of One More Chapter at HarperCollins. My agent, Jamie Cowen at The Ampersand Agency, for being an excellent sounding board.

I enjoy researching my novels and there are a few people I'd like to thank for helping me. However, this is a work of fiction, so, occasionally, I bend the truth to fit my narrative. Don't blame the experts, blame me if there are any errors.

Simon Browes is a good friend and a champion within the NHS. He answers all of my gruesome questions about knife entry wounds and the best way to inflict injuries without batting an eyelid. Philip Lumb, pathologist extraordinaire, who, despite the very long hours he works, always finds time to answer my questions about post mortem procedure and the daily workings of a pathologist. (Hello Carolyn and Elizabeth).

This book is dedicated to my police advisor, Mr Tidd (not his real name for obvious reasons). I'm sure my questions about police procedure all sound dumb and tame to him, but he never tires of answering them, so thank you, and thank you for all your hard work within the police service.

For forensic help, I turn to fellow crime writer Andy Barrett, who is also an eminent CSI. Not only does he provide me with chilling details on my crime scenes, but he gives me many ideas for future crimes I'm planning (fictional ones, of course).

Finally, thank you to Rebecca Hartley at Intelligent Fingerprinting for the information regarding the latest technology in what can be discovered from a single fingerprint.

Technical details aside, writing is a very lonely job, and it helps to have a smattering of people around to give you a boost when things get a little tough. The first person to thank is my mum, who listens when I have a plot hole to talk through over a coffee. She also supplies excellent home-made cake and cookies which are fuel for keeping me writing. My good friends, Christopher Human, The Beagle, Maxwell Dog for … I'll think of something to thank you for at some point. Chris Simmons, who I enjoy chatting all things books (and other things) with and Jonas Alexander for simply being there at the end of the phone. Now, go and win that BAFTA.

Lastly, but most importantly, my readers. Thank you for purchasing this book. Thank you for reading, enjoying, reviewing, spreading the word, loving Matilda and her team as much as I do, and for your messages of support via social media, just thank you, thank you, thank you.

Read on for an exclusive excerpt from the next nail-biting instalment in the DCI Matilda Darke Thriller series...

Chapter One

Tuesday 15th December 2020 – Brincliffe Edge Road, Sheffield

The van doors slammed shut, plunging Tilly Hall into darkness once again.

She was in pain.

She'd never known this much pain in her whole life. Her brain was struggling to comprehend what had just happened. It seemed like merely minutes ago she had been walking along the street listening to the Radio 1 podcast, laughing along to Greg James, when ... she had no understanding of what occurred next.

She tried to pull her skirt down below her knees, but it was torn. Her shirt had been torn open too. She'd heard the sound of the plastic buttons clanging off the sides of the metal bodywork of the van.

She was so cold.

She crawled into the furthermost corner of the van and pulled her knees up to her chest. She wanted to cry, but the tears wouldn't come. This was horror, pure and simple. She was living in a horror film, there was no other explanation for it.

The van began to move. Tilly tried to work out where she was, how many times they'd turned left and right, how long they'd been travelling for, but she had no idea. Were they even still in Sheffield? Was she being taken out of the country, sold into a paedophile ring or something?

She remembered her bag, her rucksack with all her books and folders in, and her mobile phone. She was alone in the van. Surely, she had time to make a quick call to her mum, tell her what had happened before the van came to a stop?

She fumbled around in the darkness, one hand running over the roughness of the floor in search of the rucksack while the other held her shirt and blazer in place across her exposed chest.

She found it. She almost laughed when she felt the familiar bag. Once her mother knew what had happened, she'd find her. Their phones were linked so that her mum could always locate her in an emergency. Tilly had always scoffed at that. What kind of emergency could there possibly be that her mother needed to track her down? Suddenly, it wasn't so funny.

She scrambled around in the bag, grabbed the phone and pulled it out. She unlocked the screen. The brightness lit up the whole van, and made her squint. The screen was cracked. It had probably broken when she'd been tossed inside. She was scrolling through the contacts when she heard the sound of the van doors being unlocked. They'd stopped. When had that happened? She quickly put the phone in the inside pocket of her blazer.

It was dark outside. The only light inside the van was from a nearby lamppost. Whoever had kidnapped her, slammed her head down on the floor of the van, torn her clothes open and raped her, was hidden in the shadows. She tried to make out his features. She knew it would be important when she was interviewed by police to tell them as much about the man as possible, but all she saw was a silhouette.

He climbed inside. Was he going to rape her again? She hoped not. She didn't think she could take so much pain again.

He grabbed her. His meaty hands gripped the front of her blazer and dragged her towards him. She tried to resist, but it was no use.

'Please. No,' she cried. She fumbled around for something to hold onto, to keep her in the relative safety of the van, but there was nothing there.

She fell onto the cold concrete of the ground. She shivered. A strong wind was blowing, and it was sleeting. She was pulled up off the pavement and swung around. The man had his left arm around her chest. She could feel his heart beating rapidly beside her. She saw what he was holding in his raised right hand and her legs buckled beneath her. If he hadn't been holding her so tightly, she would have fallen.

It was a knife. The sodium yellow from the streetlamps glistened against the sharp stainless steel. It wasn't an ordinary knife. It was a horror film knife. She'd seen the whole of the *Scream* series; she knew the damage something like that could do.

Tilly thought of her mum, and this time, the tears began to flow. There was only a week until Christmas. Her mother was so happy. They always had a wonderful time, just the two of them. Her mum tried to come across as a strong woman, but with the amount of grief she'd had to cope with over the years, she was close to losing it completely. Her daughter being raped and murdered would surely tip her over the edge.

'Mum,' Tilly cried out loud. The word barely left her lips. 'Please, no, don't do this. Please. I'll do anything,' she pleaded through the tears.

She felt the knife slice across her neck. Strangely, it didn't feel as painful as when she was raped. Her body began to relax, as if it had already died, yet she could see what was going on around her. She felt the warmth of the blood flow from her neck down her exposed chest. It was the warmest she'd felt in hours.

She tried to speak, but when she opened her mouth, nothing came out. If this was what death was like, it wasn't as bad as she'd expected it to be.

She was lifted up, but Tilly had no idea who by or what was happening. Was this God lifting her up to heaven? No, that was ridiculous. She felt light, and the pain seemed to be drifting away.

Suddenly, the pain was back with a thud, and she was rolling. She shut her eyes tightly as rocks and branches hit her face and pulled at her skin. She hit something heavy and stopped.

Tilly didn't dare open her eyes. She didn't want to see where she'd ended up. Her breathing was ragged and short and she tried to calm herself. There was a sound. It was the engine of the van starting up. She braved herself to open her eyes, looked up and saw the bright lights of the van fade away. It was going. She'd been dumped. And she was still alive. Wasn't she?

She looked around in the darkness and could make out bare trees and an uneven ground. She was in woods somewhere. How close was she to home? Could she walk it?

She put her hand to her throat. She could feel blood flowing. Jesus Christ, she was losing so much blood.

Tilly wasn't proficient in first aid, but she'd seen enough episodes of *Casualty* to know that you had to stem the flow of blood until help arrived. She struggled out of her blazer, balled it up, and pressed it firmly against her throat.

Her phone had fallen out of the pocket and landed beside her. She picked it up, unlocked it and cried at the smiling face of her boyfriend looking back at her.

She could feel herself weakening as death came for her. She was in a race against time.

With blood-soaked shaking fingers, she held down the side button and one of the volume buttons on the iPhone. A countdown came up on the screen. Within ten seconds, an emergency SOS message would be sent to the police, and her mother.

She just hoped they'd get here in time.

Don't forget to order the next book in the DCI Matilda Darke Thriller series to find out what happens next!

YOUR NUMBER ONE STOP

ONE MORE CHAPTER

FOR PAGETURNING BOOKS

One More Chapter is an
award-winning global
division of HarperCollins.

Sign up to our newsletter to get our
latest eBook deals and stay up to date
with our weekly Book Club!
<u>Subscribe here.</u>

Meet the team at
<u>www.onemorechapter.com</u>

Follow us!
🐦 <u>@OneMoreChapter_</u>
📘 <u>@0neMoreChapter</u>
📷 <u>@onemorechapterhc</u>

Do you write unputdownable fiction?
We love to hear from new voices.
Find out how to submit your novel at
<u>www.onemorechapter.com/submissions</u>